HEARTBREAK INCORPORATED

HEARTBREAK
INCORPORATED

ALEX DE CAMPI

SOLARIS
NOVA

This edition published 2024 by Solaris Nova
an imprint of Rebellion Publishing Ltd,
Riverside House, Osney Mead,
Oxford, OX2 0ES, UK

First published 2021 by Solaris

www.solarisbooks.com

ISBN: 978-1-83786-317-4

10 9 8 7 6 5 4 3 2 1

A CIP catalogue record for this book is available
from the British Library.

Designed & typeset by Rebellion Publishing

Cover design by Rebellion

CHAPTER ONE

EVIE STANDS ON the corner of Eighth Avenue, surrounded by the skitter and hustle of a Midtown New York morning, uncomfortably aware that she is looking at her last best chance. She's wearing a thousand-dollar dress she got for seventy-five bucks, only slightly shopworn, and her shoes and bra both pinch but she could conceivably belong among the neatly attired office workers flowing into the glass tower over the street from her. The little voice that tells her that she's a fake, she'll never belong, keeps her teetering on the curb until it is drowned out—first by the scream of a passing ambulance, then by the grumble of her own stomach. Breakfast is for people who can pay rent, and Evie is not one of those people.

The tourists milling behind her stare at their phones and quarrel over reviews of local diners, on a mission to find the most authentic New York bagel experience (good luck); they're shocked into silence as she flings herself into the street. Real New Yorkers don't wait for the light, and this is still, tenuously, her city. She jaywalks around a taxi and dodges the messengers in the bike lane and then she's across, feet on the curb and heart in her throat. She slips, an impostor, into the flow of the fully employed, spinning through the rotating golden doors of One Worldwide Plaza.

She's young, smart, on time, and vastly overqualified, and she manages to maintain her sense of optimism all the way up to the seventeenth floor, and Meserov & Co's small office suite. But there's another candidate already waiting, perched on a white sofa under a big, abstract black and white painting that could almost be a Franz Kline. While Evie understood that this wasn't her usual temp gig, that she'd have to interview, it didn't hit home until the competition was sitting right there in front of her. The girl glances up at Evie, brief and disinterested, before returning to scroll through her phone. She's got blonde highlights and fake eyelashes and a perfect manicure, and looks like she weighs 120 pounds soaking wet. Evie looks down at her own messy drugstore nail polish and feels her hopes founder in the storm of the other girl's perfection.

The HR woman, Abi, is wearing headphones and making quiet *mmhmm* sounds at a laptop balanced on the arm of her chair, presumably in the middle of a video call. She catches Evie's eye, smiles, and mouths *we're running late, have a seat* before returning to her meeting. Her braids are lavender this week.

Evie was used to temping. The agency calls you up, sends you out, you work one day to six months, rinse, repeat. It was an ideal gig for a girl who just needed to meet expenses while working on her freelance career. Or it was, until Evie blew it by walking out of a more than usually terrible assignment, and the agency stopped calling her all spring in retaliation. They probably wouldn't even have called her for this if Abi hadn't been handling the selection on the client side. The job was listed through Meyer, Luchins & Black, the big law firm that took up about five floors in the tower. Evie had temped there for three whole months over the winter, covering someone on maternity leave. She had hit it off with Abi, the law firm's bubbly HR person whose shoulder-length hair was an ever-changing rainbow of yarn braids. Part of Evie—the part that had student loans and rent and a maxed-out credit card— had hoped that the gig would be located on one of the law firm's floors. They always had leftover sandwiches from catered lunch meetings, and free sodas in the fridges. If a girl was careful at a job like that, she didn't have to buy food for the whole time she was temping.

But the consultancy is on a much lower floor, one comprised of hallways lined with the closed doors of mysterious small office suites. The Meserov office is tiny, just an outer foyer with a reception desk covered in paperwork that had clearly been dropped there on the way past never to be touched again, and closed double doors to the principal investigator's office. Which, presumably, had a window, unlike the outer office. There is a leather sofa and an armchair, but the blonde has the sofa, and Abi has the armchair. Evie is left to perch against the reception desk, trying not to dislodge the Matterhorn of folders and expense reports tossed haphazardly on it. Her stomach grumbles loudly. She'd been told to arrive at 10:30, and it's now 11 with no sign of a start in sight.

She touches her hair to make sure it's behaving, and tries to ignore the rapid spiral of her anxiety. The ad specified executive assistants with a track record of confidential work. The pay is good, enough to survive (and wasn't it pathetic that it had come down to that, *anything to survive in New York*, so different from five years ago when she'd arrived fresh out of college, planning to set the city on fire with her dreams). But the business had called itself a "small investigative consultancy" associated with Meyer, Luchins & Black, a description that would usually be anathema to career executive assistants like the blonde on the sofa. Those women wanted name-brand firms with cachet and fabulous benefits and biannual paid retreats where they could bat Sephora's best eyelashes at newly divorced managing directors. What was left for jobs like this was usually girls fresh off the plane from somewhere else; moms and misfits and back-to-workers with a hint of desperation in their eyes; and folks like Evie, who were still telling themselves this was the day job.

Still, she'd temped for enough law offices and venture capital firms that she qualified under the confidentiality angle. Hell, back when she first arrived, her journalism degree still shiny and new, she'd run back office at a strip club, and not a classy one, because it was colorful and maybe she'd get a book or a column out of it. But all she'd got was exhaustion migraines and a ferocious hatred of loud pop music. And investigative work? She was *beyond* qualified for that. And god, wouldn't that be better than booking flights and running expense reports and making PowerPoints and collecting dry-cleaning? It was still a day job, of course, but maybe it wouldn't be an *incredibly shit* day job.

Out of the corner of her eye, Evie sees Abi take off her headphones and close her laptop. "Sorry about that," Abi sighs, shaking her head. "This week's been a disaster. Thank god it's almost over." She leans back to peer at the closed wooden doors, as if she could see through them. "He's finishing up with the previous candidate, and then it's you, Gemma, and Evie, and that's it. So not too much longer, I hope."

Gemma, the blonde, looks up. "I'm happy to go last. I took the whole day off." She smiles at Evie. It doesn't reach her eyes. "You look like you've got places to be."

Evie doesn't have anywhere to be. She doesn't even have anything to take the day off from, and she knows exactly what Gemma is doing: angling for the last interview slot so she's the one who's freshest in memory when it comes to the hiring decision. But Evie smiles back, nonetheless, and tells Gemma that she'd prefer to keep their existing interview order. Then she turns to Abi and says, "So, can you tell us anything about"— she sweeps her hand around to encompass posh sofas, painting, paperwork—"this?"

"Well." Abigail clears her throat. "Meserov is an investigative agency frequently used by Meyer, Luchins & Black, mostly by the Family Law division. As you can see," she continues, indicating the messy reception desk covered in badly stacked paperwork, "its principal, Misha, needs—"

She is cut off by the sound of the inner doors opening, and the click of heels on thin carpet. An Asian-American woman in a sharp black cardigan and wide-legged trousers strides out, jaw clenched. She doesn't meet anyone's eye as she stomps out of the office suite and into the hall leading to the elevators.

"I guess that's a no, then," Abi says to the woman's retreating back.

"Next," sighs a low, husky male voice from the doorway, the sort of voice that sounds like it should be whispering lazy secrets across linen sheets. There is the smallest hint of another, older accent behind the cool, received-pronunciation British vowels; something from considerably further east.

Evie doesn't know what she's been expecting the principal of a *small investigative consultancy* to look like. Maybe a nervous, tired-eyed woman who washed out of Kroll for something quietly scandalous, and is still a little paranoid people will find out. Or a character out of an old film noir: middle-aged white guy with a shirt that smells like bourbon and a face like an unmade bed. Or, more realistically, an ex-FBI lifer trading up to private-sector pay to afford a house in a good school district on Long Island.

She is in no way prepared for the tall figure who slopes out of the inner office like a bored, hung-over panther.

Evie has been temping for a few years now, and the bosses never look like Misha Meserov.

He's about thirty, give or take, and over six feet tall, with the sort of aggressively v-shaped body that is only achieved from spending every spare moment at the gym, and his expensively understated charcoal-grey suit is tailored to show off every one of those angles. The suit looks bespoke; Evie would bet it cost more than her first car. Despite that, Misha looks like he's been partying for the past week: golden-tinted skin faded to sallow, and dark circles under the most arrestingly blue eyes Evie has ever seen. The areas around his pupils are ice-pale but the outer edges of the irises are ringed darker. The effect is startling, almost predatory.

His hair is dark brown, nearly black, and surprisingly long for someone who works with one of the snobbiest white-shoe law firms in Manhattan. It is caught in a low twist at the back of his neck, but a few strands have fallen loose and Evie watches as he reflexively tucks one lock back behind his ear. It lasts there for approximately three seconds before slipping forwards again across his high, aristocratic cheekbones.

She would have preferred the Walter Matthau jowls and the Jim Beam in the bottom desk drawer. Or the ex-Fed who'd eventually spill stories to her about Brighton Beach mobsters and jurisdictional fights with the NYPD. Not this pretty-boy Eurotrash who probably reeks of cologne and wouldn't know a real problem if it bit him in his unfairly perfect ass.

It's a job, Evie tells herself. *It's a job.* It wasn't as good as interning at the magazine, but unlike the magazine it would pay, and it would use some of her actual skills. She thinks back to her all-time worst temp gigs: the Canadian venture capitalist with an untreated short-term memory disorder that everyone in her firm had chosen to ignore because her name was on the door. She would give Evie three contradicting instructions in the same morning, and once called her at 4am on a Sunday to scream at her for not being in the office. Or the one she walked out of: a bond trader with hair plugs and a habit of sneaking so much vodka in his morning orange juice that it became almost translucent. Every morning he'd leave his sweat- and vomit-stained shirts from the previous night's client entertaining on her desk for her to dry-clean. She bore with it for three weeks and finally bailed when he dumped a pair of his chinos on her chair, and she picked them up to discover he'd shat in them. She takes a deep breath, and tells herself that everything is up from here.

Evie watches Misha Meserov watching them, those strange pale eyes raking slowly over the three women in the room as he takes into account how they're sitting, what they're doing. She forgets to smile when he gets to her, too lost in staring back at him, trying to figure him out.

He raises an eyebrow at her. She quickly plasters on her happy face.

The corners of his eyes crinkle and he makes a little huff of amusement. He doesn't look very thrilled to be here either.

Abigail thwacks Meserov in the chest with a manila folder. He flashes Abi a surprisingly wry smirk, then the mask of boredom descends again. "Who wants to be first?" he drawls, opening the folder and perusing its contents, before glancing up through lashes so dark that Evie briefly wonders if he's wearing mascara.

"You're seeing Gemma, then—" Abi begins.

"It's fine, I'll go now," says Evie, sliding off her perch on the reception desk. She feels odd; Meserov makes her anxious somehow, his very presence knocking her off balance. Sitting around waiting will only make it worse.

Gemma's eyes widen momentarily in surprise, and when she says, "Okay, good luck," she almost sounds sincere.

Abigail smiles gratefully to her, then says, "I have an 11:30 upstairs. I'll pop back once I'm done to see who you've decided on," and closes her laptop.

"If I decide," Meserov says, arch.

Abigail puts her hands on her hips and steps forwards. She's almost a foot shorter than him, soft and round, her dark skin set off by a pretty wrap dress in an ivory and green print, and she is giving zero quarter. "Misha, you're picking one and that's *final*. Look at this mess. I am not dealing with Don and Dee bitching to me about where your files are, or how they can't get anything out of you before 11am. It is not my job."

Misha glares at Abi, and Abi glares right back, until the sound of a stack of files cascading off the reception desk and scattering onto the ground distracts them.

Abigail looks pointedly at the jumbled mess of papers on the floor, folds her arms, and looks back at Misha. She raises an eyebrow.

"Fine," he growls.

"Good," Abigail counters, just as steely. She tucks her laptop under her arm. "I'll be back later." In the doorway, she points at Meserov. "Play nice," she says, her voice a mix of fond and scolding, as if he were a reckless nephew.

Meserov tilts his head and pouts, the brat. "I always do, Abi."

Abigail snorts in derision and shakes her lavender braids as she strides out the door.

Evie walks the few steps across the outer office to where Meserov waits, and lifts her head up to look him in the eye. Nope, no mascara, she thinks. Just lashes that girls like Gemma would maim for. She sticks her hand out. "Evie Cross. Hello."

Evie is close enough as Meserov takes her hand to realize he doesn't reek of loud cologne at all. What she can smell is very quiet, limes and old leather. Rather than shaking her hand, Meserov just holds it, pressing gently with his thumb on the back of her knuckles as he inclines his head. His hands aren't as soft as she expects, and for a moment Evie has the weird feeling he's going to raise her hand to his lips. But then he lets go, and turns towards the office. "Miss Cross," he says, indicating for her to follow with the file in his other hand.

The interior office gives surprisingly little away about the man. There's a window overlooking Madison Avenue that takes up an entire wall. The rest of the walls are painted the blooming, faded silver of an old mirror, which augments the daylight coming in and makes the entire room feel shimmery and bright. There's more modern art on the walls: something splattery and Pollock-esque over Meserov's desk, a steel-grey and rust Anselm Kiefer (or near as dammit) above a worn tobacco-leather chaise longue that reminds her uncomfortably of a psychiatrist's couch and looks about a hundred years old. Further down is a tall, narrow white canvas stenciled with a stack of huge black letters: *RUN DOG RUN*. The desk and bookcases are all mid-century modern, and the whole office would look quite sleek if it weren't for the fact that Misha Meserov is an unrepentant slob.

His desk is littered with papers and 8x10 photographs, all turned face down, and even the chaise longue where he motions for Evie to sit has a few files dumped on it. He doesn't need a secretary, he needs a containment crew.

Evie gingerly moves the files and stacks them crossways at one end of the chaise longue, then sits down, smoothing the skirt of her secondhand designer dress. She folds her hands and tries to look keen and professional and able to be trusted with secrets, and not at all like a girl who won't be able to make rent next week if she doesn't land a job by the end of this one.

New York is a cruel mistress. Evie and her roommate Claudia live in a tiny apartment in Bed-Stuy. It's all they can afford, and even so, they can't really afford it.

Meserov leans against his desk and sighs, glancing down at her résumé in the file. "So. Call me Misha." He seems tired.

"Are you Russian?" she asks.

"No. Georgian. Caviar and horses Georgia, not peaches and hip-hop Georgia." He smiles wearily, clearly accustomed to having to explain. "A small and fiercely independent country which has spent most of its history wedged between two large empires. Three, if you count Persia."

"I'm sorry," she says.

"It's okay," he murmurs, paging through her résumé. "Americans never know where anything is." He looks at her over the folder. "You're overqualified. Journalism degree from a top school; internships at a big magazine. What are you doing here?"

Evie sighs and glances out at the towers of Manhattan, arrayed outside the window, glittering in May's midday sun. "You know how many ads were in the print edition of the *New York Times* main section today?" she asks, with a sadness she can't keep out of her voice. "Three. Three ads. The news is free now, and even the papers lucky enough to still exist are employing half the people they did when I started my journalism degree. The newspapers are dying. Magazines are, too. Even the big digital sites can't make money; they've been shuttering for years."

She pinches the bridge of her nose, suddenly feeling entirely too emotional for a job interview. "Hundreds of journalists more experienced and better connected than me can't find work. The only way I can compete is working for free. And I do. I write my pieces on Medium and Vox and hope somebody notices. I took that internship, which didn't pay a dime, hoping it would pave my way. That I'd impress them enough they'd hire me. But they didn't." She tries to smile, but it still hurts, more than a year later. "They just got a new intern."

She realizes she's been staring down at her hands, which have curled into white-knuckled fists where they rest on her thighs. She forces herself to relax, and looks up to meet her fate.

Misha hasn't moved. He just watches her, his posture neither tense nor relaxed, letting her fill the quiet of the office with words. Somewhere in the back of Evie's mind she notes it down as something she wants to try later, the way he uses silence as a trap for the unwary.

For now, she shifts on the chaise longue, its horsehair stuffing creaking, and hopes she's not blushing too hard. "But yeah. That's what I'm doing here. I'm super organized and a great executive assistant, and I'm a trained investigative journalist. So whatever you investigate, I can, uh... help."

"Miss Cross." Misha smiles at her, wry and melancholy at the same time.

"Evie," she says, sitting up straighter. She will get through this interview and, dammit, she will do so with honor. Evie Cross is not a quitter.

"Evie," he repeats, inclining his head slightly in acknowledgement. "Most people think of the law as a shield, but it can also be a sword. It shouldn't be, but then many things in this world aren't as they should be. Sometimes the law can even be wielded like a stiletto, thin and sharp and hardly felt at all until it causes irreparable damage." Misha reaches back onto the surface of the desk he's leaning against and picks up a photo, seemingly at random. He shows it to Evie, his hand mostly covering the image. She doesn't catch much context, enough to see that it's of two mostly naked people in a compromising position.

Misha tosses the photo back on the desk, face down. "The work I do is... not for everyone. Most people will loathe it. A few people will enjoy it immensely. Neither of those groups do I wish to hire. So I'm going to ask you a couple of questions to give myself a feel for where you fit. They are not standard interview questions. It's okay if you don't want to answer some of them." He looks at her, face sincere and his wide, feminine lips slightly parted. "It's okay if you don't answer any of them."

Evie can't help but smile a little. "Though silence is an answer in itself."

A brief expression flickers across Misha's face, too fast for her to catch whether it's approval or annoyance, but bitter experience tells her it's the latter. Being too smart too soon never wins you anything as a woman, and Evie thinks it's one of the great flaws in the world. She'd always assumed if she were really good at something, if she worked hard to be the best, it would impress the boys, and then they'd like her as much as they liked the other girls. Maybe even more. But finally, at twenty-five, she'd realized that boys didn't want the best girls. They wanted girls like Gemma: decorative little blondes who were always a complement, never a challenge. She isn't surprised that Misha is so typical, but her shoulders slump a little further, and the weight of the world settles a little heavier upon them. She's blowing this, and she can't afford to blow this. Not if she wants to stay in New York.

Misha crosses his arms, which only serves to accentuate the thickness of his shoulders and upper arms over his narrow waist. "You're walking down the street and two men start kissing right in front of you. What do you do?" he asks.

"I look away and keep walking," Evie says. "Not because it's two guys, but because this is New York and I mind my own business. Plus, PDA is gross, no matter who's doing it." Then, before she can stop herself, she throws the question back. "Are you gay? Or is this because of" — she gestures towards the surface of the desk — "all the compromising photos?"

Evie internally cringes as she realizes what she's done. She's upset the implicit power balance of the interview and let her mouth run away with her because Misha is *interesting*, unexpectedly so, and she wants to find out what his deal is. By interviewing him. Good one. But still, she reasons, if he's going to ask invasive questions, he should be willing to answer them, too.

She is brought back into the room by a snort of amusement from Misha. "Yes," he answers, unhelpfully. "And I'm bi, actually. Next: are you religious?"

Play dumb, says Evie's internal voice. *Tone it down, or he'll never hire you.* "No. My grandparents are big-time Catholic. My mom and dad less so, me not at all. I can still recite a ton of scripture, though it's mostly from comp-lit courses in college."

"Are you superstitious? Ghosts and things like that?"

Evie rolls her eyes. "I mean, I have a lucky poker chip, and I read my horoscope, but I don't believe any of it. Well... I don't rationally think ghosts and things like that exist, but I'd be lying if I said I wasn't afraid of the dark."

Misha's expression never changes. "Hm," is all he says, and Evie can't tell if she's making a good impression, or talking herself out of a job.

"Last question, Evie. What's the strangest thing that ever happened to you?" Misha asks.

Evie thinks. Misha is still watching her. She begins to stutter a half-dozen things, then stops herself, as every story she's about to tell either involves bad-mouthing previous employers or making herself look dangerously irresponsible. She shakes her head. "I can't think of anything," she mumbles. "I guess I'm very dull."

The silence stretches across the room like a heavy snow, cold and suffocating.

"I very much doubt that," Misha says, soft and low. "But even so, I don't recommend seeking strange things out. You're right to be afraid of the dark."

Evie immediately, furiously rejects Misha's casual world-weariness, which only serves to rub in her face how much her own life hasn't even gotten off its launch pad yet. She stands up and stalks over to the window, looking down to the cars and pedestrians hurrying about like hot ants under the midday sunshine far below. The window is heavily polarized, dimming the intensity of the light and leaving New York a soundless pantomime at her feet.

Behind her, she can hear Misha drag his desk chair out and sit down in it. She turns around to see him stifling a yawn. She wants so badly to say *sorry I'm keeping you up, pal*, but on the very slim chance she hasn't blown this interview to smithereens already, she holds fast to her discretion.

"Do you have any questions for me?" he says, slumping back in his chair.

"Yes," Evie says. "What do you investigate?" Still-simmering anger gives her the courage to meet his pale eyes with her plain brown ones.

"Relationships. Marriages, affairs, things like that," Misha says, waving one hand vaguely in the air as he stretches his legs out beneath the desk. "There are tons of agencies and apps and services to bring people together. I do the opposite." He smiles, predatory. "I tear them apart."

"Is that... legal?" Evie frowns.

"Yes," Misha says. "In an obeying the letter, but not the spirit, way."

"Is it moral?"

Misha shrugs. "Not often. But the cases I take mainly involve the super-rich." He tips his head back and lifts one hand to point lazily up to the ceiling, to the lawyers' offices several floors above them. A wry smirk begins to pull at the edges of his lips. "No-one else can afford *them*." He looks at Evie, his expression oddly sincere. "And I don't harm anyone who doesn't deserve it."

"Oh, and you get to decide?" The words are, as usual, out of Evie's mouth before she can stop them. So much for playing dumb.

"Yes, I do," Misha replies, soft and final as he rises, no doubt to dismiss her. "Just as a journalist chooses who to write about." He gestures to the door. "Now, if you don't have any more questions?"

Evie knows she's blown it; flunked whatever test he was giving her. So she asks her last question, because there's nothing left to win. It's the oldest question in the world: "Why?"

Misha arches an eyebrow.

Evie continues. "People like you don't normally turn against their own kind."

"Excuse me?" Misha says, an edge of command creeping into his tone.

"The rich. You come from money. A lot of it. It's in every movement you make. It's hanging all over your walls. That's a real Franz Kline out there, isn't it? I thought it was fake until

I came in here and saw that." Evie points at the Christopher Wool *RUN DOG RUN* painting. "I worked the cocktail party at the auction house's sale preview a couple years ago. I remember staring at that painting, fascinated by how sometimes it was just words on a canvas and how sometimes it would dissociate into nothing but shapes and patterns." She looks right at Misha. "I remember what it cost."

She doesn't regret it. For the first time in the interview she feels like she's standing on her own two feet, strong and sure. She knows she's on to something, and it's been eating at her since she first saw Misha: why is a ridiculously handsome rich guy slumming around doing divorce investigations for a bunch of stuffy lawyers?

Misha is just gazing at her, head tilted, face a quiet mask. "Huh. I don't remember you, from that preview."

"I was the help," Evie says. "You're not supposed to remember us."

"Still," Misha says. He indicates the door again. "Thank you for your time, Miss Cross. It was very interesting, meeting you." His expression is still shut down, melancholy, and Evie feels something sharp in her chest that she was the cause of it.

"When I get nervous, sometimes I…" she says, pausing with her hand on the door. She takes a last look at this impossible man and realizes that *he* is the strangest thing ever to happen to her, and in a moment, she will leave and never see him again. "Really, I'm sorry. I was making assumptions and that was wrong of me."

"On the contrary. You were correct," Misha says, as he looks down at her. Evie feels the warmth of him as he reaches past her to turn the doorknob. Just before he opens the door, he leans down to speak softly into her ear.

"But you should be careful, Miss Cross. In my experience, people easily forget wrong answers. But seldom do they forgive right ones."

CHAPTER TWO

EVIE FINDS HERSELF in the front office, heart thundering, as Gemma smiles modestly and brushes past her towards Misha's office. She hears him murmur, "Miss Andrews, is it?" She simpers, "Please, call me Gemma," and then there's the click of the door closing and Evie is left with nothing but the vanishing tracks of Gemma's knock-off Saint Laurent heels on the carpet.

She realizes she's shaking, staring at the vicious brushstrokes of the Franz Kline above the sofa as part of her mind kicks into trauma response, listing all the things she'll have to do to leave New York: call her parents. Tell Claudia. Get rid of everything she can't fit into a couple suitcases. What she can sell; what she'll have to donate or throw out. The orderly list is the only thing that's keeping her from succumbing to the howling sorrow bubbling up inside her. That, and the wounded ache of an empty stomach.

She doesn't know how long she's been standing there, lost in the vortex of her own self-pity, when her phone beeps. Her roommate Claudia's belated good luck message and its string of cheerful emojis are what sends her over the edge. She flees, out of the office, down the corridors, away from the elevators, from any witnesses to her shame, until at the end of a hallway near the bathrooms she finds a kitchenette.

She sits down at its little black table and dials Claudia.

It only takes a couple rings, then there's Claudia's sleepy Puerto Rican accent as she mumbles a "hey, what's up" on the other end of the line.

"I'm not gonna get it," Evie sighs.

"Are you sure?" Claudia asks, sounding a little more awake. "I mean, you were *perfect* for this—"

"I was perfect for *all* of them," Evie says. She leans over and opens the kitchenette's communal fridge as her stomach clenches with hunger pangs. Once when the agency was late paying her, she'd lived for a whole week on packets of powdered hot chocolate from the break room of a large accounting company. "Look, Claudia. I have most of this month's rent, but I... I think you should start looking for someone else for my room." Her voice catches, and the next words come out in a rasp: "Someone with a job."

There's nothing in the fridge except some half-finished hummus that's so old it's gone crusty, and a small box swaddled in a plastic bag. She pulls out the box and unwraps it: sushi, and not even past its sell-by date. Her sushi, now.

"What are you gonna do?" Claudia asks.

Evie presses her palm against her cheek, pushing the tears back in. "I don't know yet."

"You want a shift tonight?" Claudia's voice is soft and kind, and that hurts most of all.

But Evie isn't in a position to refuse her roommate's offer, so she nods her gratitude, even though Claudia can't see her, and says, "Please."

"Okay," Claudia says. "In theory we're fully crewed up, but you know at least one of these idiots will bail at the last minute."

"Where is it?" Evie asks.

"The Met," Claudia says, a little smug. "I mean, it's some fashion couple's engagement party, but Dendur rules and the parking's really easy."

"Well, at least that's dinner taken care of," says Evie, as she tears open the packet of soy sauce and dumps it all over her stolen sushi.

"It'll get better, baby. Something's gonna happen. You'll see," Claudia says. "Oh, I gotta go! Event manager on the other line."

Claudia hangs up, and Evie sighs her "I hope so" into the hum of the dial tone.

She puts her phone down and shoves the first piece of sushi into her mouth. It tastes heavy and bland, but she swallows it, and grabs for the next piece. The chopsticks are halfway to her mouth when she feels the air in the room shift.

Evie looks up, and there's a white woman staring at her, clutching a mug in one hand and a teabag in the other. "Excuse me, is that *my* sushi?" the woman asks, her expression somewhere between shocked and angry.

Evie hunches over the crappy tray of Salmon Lovers' Special. "Can you afford to buy more?" she growls back.

The woman opens her mouth, then hesitates a moment before closing it again and just... leaving. Guilt rolls through Evie, killing her appetite. She forces the sushi down anyway, as a sort of penance. It sits in her stomach like lead the whole way back to Brooklyn.

On the subway, Evie googles Misha.

There are zero results. There's an eighty-five-year-old retiree in Florida and a genetics lab in San Diego with similar names, but as far as the internet is concerned, Misha Meserov doesn't exist. His company has no website, and no entry in the New York State business entity list. She racks her brain to remember if there was even a sign by the door. No social media, either, which strikes her as the most suspicious element of all. The few people she'd ever met who were as good-looking as Misha all loved social media.

It's all very weird, and Evie files it in a box in her mind labelled Things to Investigate Later. There might even be a long-form story in it. She could title it *The Break-Up Artist*; maybe try to track down some of the people whose relationships he tore apart.

Her brief good mood dims when she realizes it would be nearly impossible to write that sort of story from her parents' guest bedroom in Chicago. The things she'd need to ask people for it aren't the sort of things she can ask over the phone. They need to be face to face.

From High Street to Nostrand she idly scans the Wikipedia entry on Georgia, and finds 'Land of the Wolves' a pretty appropriate name for the place that spawned Misha. It's only when the C train pulls into Kingston-Throop station that she feels a stab of anger at herself for spending a whole hour looking up a hot guy she talked to for less than ten minutes.

She shoves her phone in her bag and resolves to consign Misha Meserov to the obscurity he so clearly desires. She has a catering shift to prepare for, anyway. And it will be a good shift, and there will be food, and rich people to mock.

Not for the first time she wonders if she should give up trying to have a legit day job. Maybe if she did something crappy like catering or waitressing it would force her to focus on making her laundry list of journalism projects actually happen. If she could write in the morning, maybe it would be different. Right now, she comes home after a day of temping so tired of screens and keyboards that she can't face writing another word, even if it is for herself. Then she feels like a shitty friend, because for Claudia, catering isn't "something crappy". It's her career. And there's nothing stopping Evie from getting up and writing in the mornings now; she just… doesn't.

Evie pushes herself up the subway steps into the pitiless Brooklyn sunshine, feeling tiny and inadequate and certain of nothing, other than that her dreams are falling apart, right in front of her.

Only ten more hours until the day is over.

THE GALA THEY'RE catering is for a daughter of the Pickford fashion empire, just engaged to some potbellied European who can trace his family back to the Holy Roman Empire. She's rich and slim and her nose doesn't look the same as the rest of her family's. Cocktails and then dinner in the Temple of Dendur, an Egyptian temple ruin housed in a modern, glassed-in courtyard at the grande dame of New York's art museums: the Metropolitan. The courtyard is a spectacular location, made even more so by the event company's uplighting and the four-foot-tall pillar arrangements of pink and white peonies currently being placed on each table.

It's black-tie, but the catering uniform is the standard white shirt, black pants and apron. And, underneath, the blessed relief of a sports bra and sneakers. Evie had wanted to burn her entire interview outfit when she had gotten back to her apartment.

The bar doesn't take long to set up. Behind the main bar are stairs down to a corridor serving as a prep area where their spare supplies and clean glasses are stacked up. Beyond that is a loading entrance where the catering trucks are parked, ready to receive all the crates of dirties at the end of the night. The wealthy don't do disposable cups. The glassware is all real crystal, and the flutes have long, hollow stems that make the champagne in them bubble prettily.

Evie snags plates of canapés for both she and Claudia and then leans against the bar and stares out at the display in front of them. Everything looks peaceful in the late-afternoon light. The May sun is only starting its descent to the horizon, but the canyons of Manhattan would swallow it soon enough. The lighting at the party is set to respond to the gathering dusk and gradually transform as night approaches, sculpting the space into something more intimate. It was already remarkably private in atmosphere for what is fundamentally a large, barn-like glass space. If Evie squints, she can even pretend not to notice the dozens of big guys with glasses and earpieces stalking the perimeter of the huge courtyard, safeguarding the super-rich from the unpleasantness of encounters with common people.

"Not bad, eh?" Claudia says.

"I guess," says Evie, looking out at the golden shafts of sunlight striping the room, illuminating its vast luxury of space. New York was such a bitch. Just when you thought you could give her up, she offers you a glimpse of something magical, and suckers you right back in. But eventually the price gets too high for those slivers of strange joy. The city had her beat, and Evie should have admitted it a year ago, back when she still had savings.

"Hey," she says quietly. "I've been thinking some more and I'm going to head back to Chicago at the end of July. Would you mind if I split my room with someone for the next two months? Then I can pay you back for everything before I leave."

Not that Claudia should be struggling to pay rent. In the few years she and Evie had been sharing an apartment, Claudia had moved up from being a part-time bartender for the high-end caterers to running the entire bar operation and reporting directly to the company's owner. She'd thought up and executed lines of bespoke cocktails for receptions, which had become a major marketing angle for the company, getting them tons of press and lots of new work... and still, Claudia was struggling to make rent in the same neighborhood where she'd grown up.

Claudia slings an arm around her for a sloppy side-hug. "Yeah, you can split your room. Long as she's not a jerk. But don't rush into anything, okay? The city knocks us all down and you know what? It doesn't matter, 'cause we've all been there. The important thing is how fast you get up."

Evie smiles bashfully down at her sneakers, grateful for Claudia's words of comfort even as she doesn't believe them.

The doors open to let in the dozen or so journalists and photographers covering the event, and they immediately clump up by the entrance, jockeying for position and access. Claudia starts lining up glasses of the night's signature cocktails along the bar, the last step to being ready for service. Tonight is something involving watermelon and basil with a little strawberry on a toothpick, very summery and refreshing but very alcoholic. "This weekend, you want to go to McCarren pool if it's nice? We gotta make a plan how you're gonna get up and *stay* up," Claudia says as she nudges Evie affectionately.

"Only if we also plan how you're going to ask for a raise," Evie counters, watching the entertainment journalists flock towards a waiter carrying a plate of hors d'oeuvres. She wonders which of them hadn't eaten that day; how many lived off canapés and cheap wine at the city's endless round of night receptions and openings.

"Deal," Claudia says. The string quartet begins to play, a signal that it's almost go time. Claudia starts lining up coupe glasses and, without looking at Evie, says, "You ready?"

"Hit me," Evie says as she grabs a champagne bottle and strips it of its foil and cage. The catering company Claudia works for sells itself on personalized service, and part of that is the bar staff memorizing each VIP's face, name, and drink preference. Claudia's last-minute pop quiz on those preferences as the doors open is as much a tradition for the two of them at fancy events as Evie slicing her thumb on the lemon zester or Claudia convincing unsuspecting young men to order Flaming Lamborghinis.

Black-clad security guards open the doors officially and the party guests begin to filter in. Camera flashes roll through the enormous space like sheet lightning as each couple poses for the scrum of photographers.

"Peter Pickford," Claudia says, as a short, deeply tanned man in a velvet tuxedo strolls in, arm in arm with a tall, nervous-looking thoroughbred of a woman, whose white silk dress matches his hair. She's half his age, and grips a sparkly clutch bag like it contains the secrets of the universe.

"PATERFAMILIAS," EVIE RECITES. "Started the empire selling ties out of the back of a secondhand Rolls. Manhattan, Maker's, extra cherry. His wife only drinks diet ginger ale but she carries a fifth of vodka in her bag."

"Good," Claudia says. "An ex-cop from New Jersey with a bad leather jacket and a polo shirt buttoned all the way up."

"One, I told you I don't want to talk about my interview," Evie groans, "and two, you couldn't be more wrong."

"You're not talking about your interview. *I'm* talking about your interview, and you're just telling me when I'm right," says Claudia, smugly. "Leah Pickford."

"The middle daughter; it's her engagement party." Evie pauses for a moment to watch Leah do her twirl for the photographers. She's in a long, figure-hugging sequined dress that, combined with her artfully tousled streaked blonde hair, is a little too *Malibu Barbie Goes To The Oscars* for Evie's taste, but it serves its purpose in making her the center of attention. Her fiancé is short, a little stout, and rumpled in his white tie and tails, and he looks up at her with utter adoration. Even Evie's blackened heart melts at his expression, and she silently wishes them happiness.

Claudia elbows her.

"Uh, sorry. Leah runs the perfume business. Krug," Evie carries on. "With Florian, old German family, has a title, works for some big hedge fund. Also Krug."

People are starting to drift towards the bar. Claudia busies herself adding the basil leaves and strawberries to another tray of the signature cocktail. "Correct," she says. "A tall British public school boy with floppy hair and dandruff and no lips but you still would."

"Bzzt," Evie says. "Also, ew."

"Fuck!" Claudia exclaims. "Okay, we got incoming. The rest of the Pickford kids." She hands Evie a bottle of Krug to uncork, and grabs another one herself.

"Eldest daughter runs the cosmetics division and is married to a Russian oligarch, uh…" Evie twists, and the champagne cork comes off into her hand with a muffled pop. She picks out the couple, she in a fluttery, printed maxi dress, with her dark hair in an updo and her face immaculately made up, and him tall and barrel-chested, all in black. The couple exchange a private little smile, and he gives her a little silent-comedy eye roll, *here we go again*, that makes her wrinkle her nose in amusement. She bumps his shoulder and their fingers tangle together, and Evie feels suddenly, terribly lonely.

"Earth to Evie?" Claudia prompts.

"Victoria and Slava. Mojito for her, Armagnac for him. Youngest daughter, Erin, runs the shoe division. Vodka cranberry. She hangs out with Greg Pickford, eldest, only son.

Vodka martini, but no actual martini in it. So just a polite way to ask for a glass of vodka, really. Married to Stewart Jones, the label's womenswear designer, who is actually British, unlike your terrible guess."

Claudia rolls her eyes as, beyond her, Erin Pickford air-kisses her big brother, the heir apparent. Her painfully thin body is tightly wrapped in an aggressively modernist short beige dress. When she laughs, loud and toothy, at something he says, her veneers are so white they're virtually blue. Greg Pickford is in an off-white tuxedo that complements his ruddy tan, with leonine swept-back brown hair peppered with strands of grey. He's almost good-looking; all the individual elements of handsome are there but somehow they fail to come together into an attractive whole. His jawline, objectively fine on its own, comes off in context as heavy, rather than sharp; the same with his lips, whose thickness errs towards the brutish rather than the erotic. His gestures are short and harsh and project a certain insecure power, the kind that needs to be constantly shown off to ensure it remains intact. A signet ring on the pinkie of his right hand catches in the light, and it calls to mind an article Evie once read about the Pickfords. Quite a thing, she thinks to herself, for a man to flaunt the coat of arms his family had bought only a decade before.

"Ugh, okay. Last guess," Claudia says, keeping an eye on the guests, who barely acknowledge her as they grab either a pink cocktail or a glass of champagne off the bar. "An ex-skip tracer, with an undercut and a thing for Puerto Rican femmes. Basically Lucy Lawless but twenty years younger and butch."

"I feel like I've just had this weird glimpse into your libido, but no," Evie says.

"Look, a gayelle can dream. Tell—"

"Um, pardon me?" says a hesitant male voice, and Evie shakes her head, returning to earth. In front of her is Greg's husband, Stewart, the fashion designer, who is delicate and blond and has a sweet smile and the most adorable pair of thick-framed hipster glasses Evie has ever seen. Stewart is wearing a single-breasted, high-necked tuxedo in a dark red velvet, embroidered with a riot of flowers, and a white shirt, also high-necked, with thick French cuffs. It's fun and quirky and suits him, and is so different from the more generic haute-preppy style of the rest of the family.

"Hi, sorry, Mr Pickford-Jones, what can I get you?" Evie says, reaching for the Laphroaig. "Your usual?"

"I'm wondering what *those* are," says the man, indicating the specialty cocktails. Evie can see a hint of multicolored ink at his wrist, peeking out from under the formal white cuff of his shirt.

"I'm not a hundred per cent sure what's in them?" Evie says. "I just know they taste like strawberry-basil gelato and if you have three of them in a row you will feel no pain for the rest of the night. And also might pass out."

"Fabulous," Stewart smiles at her. "I'll take four." As he reaches for the drinks, his glasses slip down his nose and Evie glimpses a heavy smudge of concealer on his cheekbone. She'd assume it was to hide exhaustion, but... it's only under one eye.

Evie suddenly, desperately wants to say something to make this sweet man feel better. She stutters out, "Leah Pickford's dress is very nice," which is a white lie, because she actually thinks the dress manages to be both boring and sparkly at the same time.

"Yes," Stewart says, knocking one of the drinks back. His narrow shoulders slump further. "Her little sister Erin designed it."

"Oh," Evie says.

"Indeed," Stewart whispers, putting the empty glass back on the table. "These really are very good," he says, softly. "I hope your promises come true." Then he disappears into the crowd.

Evie stares after him, trying to process what had just happened. "Did you see that?" she hisses to Claudia.

"The concealer?" Claudia whispers back. "Yeah. Same one I use on my tattoos." When Evie continues to stare into the crowd, Claudia elbows her. "Evie, stop thinking about it. We're the wait staff, that's all. Now either pour more champagne, or tell me about what happened at your interview."

Evie sighs and rips the wire cage off a bottle of Krug with

more violence than strictly necessary. "Ugh, there's nothing to tell. He was kind of an ass, and I wasn't what he was looking for. The end."

"Huh," Claudia says. "That's not all of it, but imma leave you be until you feel like telling me the rest."

Evie eyes Claudia thoughtfully. "You're wasted behind a bar, you know."

"Nah," Claudia smiles. "Best place in the world. You see everything and meet everyone, and they tell you the wildest things."

The next hour is an increasingly busy blur of pouring out drinks, clearing dirties and empties, and bringing up clean glasses from the hallway downstairs that they were using as a staging area. Evie's unwinding the wire cage from the cork of another champagne bottle and telling herself there's only four more hours to go, when an irritatingly familiar voice whispers, "Miss Cross."

Evie glances up and finds herself staring at a broad chest in a very tailored all-black tuxedo. No, not black: a deep, midnight blue. She looks up further.

Right into the amused eyes of Misha Meserov.

"So nice to see you again," he says, reaching over, languid and catlike, and taking the bottle of champagne out of her numb hands. His hair is slicked back, caught in a tidier twist at the back of his neck than it had been earlier. He carries himself as if he was born to wear black tie; like he's walked straight off the set of some *Great Gatsby* remake. In a room full of fashionistas, suddenly everyone else looks like they're trying too hard.

"Uh," says Evie, because she is intelligent and classy.

"Journalism or rent?" Misha asks, cocking an eyebrow at her catering clothes.

Evie feels a furious anger burn through her. She wants so badly to slap his pretty face. "Rent," she hisses, reaching to take the champagne bottle back.

"A shame," he purrs, casually lifting the bottle out of her reach. "There are stories here." He snags two clean champagne glasses in his free hand, inclines his head towards her in the suggestion of a formal bow, and turns back towards the party.

"Wait, Misha!" calls Evie. "You can't take—"

But Misha only raises the bottle in salute as he saunters off into the crowd. Evie watches him join a tipsy Stewart Pickford-Jones, who looks up at Misha like he's the sun, there to warm his bird bones and his short blond duckling hair. Misha runs a hand down Stewart's back and leans in close, whispering something in the smaller man's ear that causes him to smile like he can exhale for the first time all evening.

Evie almost breaks the glass in her hand as Misha's words from earlier in the day echo in her head: *I tear them apart.*

"Who *was* that?" Claudia whispers, awestruck.

"Ex-cop from New Jersey with a bad leather jacket and a polo shirt buttoned up all the way," Evie says, biting down on her anger.

"No shit," Claudia says. "Wow, suddenly everything becomes clear. You think maybe he has a sister?"

"I don't care," Evie snaps.

"Yikes, *chill*," Claudia says.

"Sorry," Evie groans. "I don't know what it is about him. He has a capacity to make me angrier than almost anyone I've ever met. Plus I think he's trying to break up Stewart Pickford-Jones' marriage. And I don't know whether to be mad about that, or secretly happy, because..." She gestures towards her cheekbone.

"... of the black eye," Claudia finishes.

Evie bites her lip and arranges basil leaves in a new round of the pink cocktails, hoping Claudia will drop the subject. She knows it's petty to hate Misha for being smart and hot and completely uninterested in working with a woman on his own intellectual level. But she still can't help the aching sense of shame it causes in her: that she'll never fit in, that nobody will ever want to see what she can do.

Claudia's opening her mouth to ask Evie more questions she doesn't want to answer, but thankfully the husband-to-be's cacophonous coterie of hedge fund buddies descend on the bar. Claudia grins at them, a shark confronting its prey. "How'd you boys like to try some Flaming Lamborghinis?" she purrs.

EVIE SPENDS THE next forty minutes glaring at the crowd, trying to figure out what Misha is doing at the party, and what the deal is with Greg and Stewart. They hadn't talked all night as far as Evie had seen: Stewart (with Misha's help) carefully staying on the other side of the crowded party from his husband. She remembered a few years ago there'd been something in the papers about Greg throwing a phone at his assistant. Tonight, Greg was wound tight, voice loud, gestures bigger than they needed to be. *Look at me, I'm having fun.*

She stops when Claudia elbows her, hard. "Evie, you either start smiling or I'm sending you to collect dirty glasses," she hisses. "You want me to ask for a raise, but how can I do that if the boss gets reports back from tonight that my bartenders are giving everyone the stinkeye?"

"Sorry, Claudia," Evie groans. She grabs a plastic tub. It's a good time to go clean up, anyhow. People will be sitting down for dinner in about fifteen minutes, and it's important that the area is clear of abandoned glasses before it's clear of people. Evie slips in between the laughing, chattering crowds in their $15,000 dresses and hand-tailored dinner jackets. She ghosts past hands wearing diamond bracelets and Swiss watches that cost more than her and Claudia's whole year's rent, more than her college education, and picks up the dirty, lipstick-printed glasses they discard.

Nobody seems to see her; nobody speaks to her. She finds herself at the small standing table where Misha and Stewart had been talking, and she grabs their now-empty champagne bottle and adds it to the tub of dirties to take away. Their two glasses are next to it: one is half-full and shows no sign of having been drunk from. The other is empty, and ringed with the smudges left by a man's lips.

As she hefts the now-overflowing tub back towards the bar, she has a moment of clarity, and in the space of the next few steps she knows exactly what she must do. "Hey, I might be an extra five minutes downstairs after I dump these. Is that okay? I want to make a phone call," she says to Claudia.

Claudia looks around at the party guests slowly filtering away from the bar, towards the dinner tables, and shrugs. "Yeah, sure. What's going on?"

Evie grins as she heads for the stairs. "I figured out a way to get up and stay up."

The wide corridor at the bottom of the stairs is currently serving as the caterers' staging area, and Evie shelves the tub in a tall metal bus cart racked with more tubs of dirties. She slumps against the wall between the bus cart and a wheelie bin of empty champagne bottles, concealing herself enough so nobody will catch sight of her and ask her to help with anything, and then she digs her phone out of her apron pocket. It's quiet in the corridor, but there's still the sound of the string quartet from upstairs, and the buzz of voices.

She scrolls down through her contacts and selects one she never got around to deleting, just in case. It rings and rings, and Evie thinks for one heart-stopping moment nobody will pick up, but then a slightly annoyed female voice says, "Hello?"

"Hi, Nicole?" Evie says. "I'm sorry to call you so late on a Friday. It's Evie, your intern from two years ago?"

"Who?" says Nicole, sharply. Evie can hear the sounds of nightlife behind her; she dimly wonders if it's still the bar at the Soho Grand, or her crowd had moved on to somewhere new. *Gotham*, the magazine for which Nicole Hamilton was features editor, was an incredibly New York-centric hybrid of lifestyle publication and long-form investigative journal, as likely to cover cultural bubbles like rainbow bagels and alpha/omega fanfiction as it was to investigate government corruption scandals and workplace harassment on syndicated talk shows. She'd genuinely loved working there, and she's bitter that Nicole, her old boss, has obviously forgotten her.

"Evie. *Evie Cross*," she says. "Remember the story on the romance writer poisonings? I was the intern on that." The article had won awards. Evie, uncredited, had done all the interviews.

"Oh. I thought you left New York. What do you want? I'm busy—"

"I'm at the Pickford engagement party," Evie says, knowing from past experience that only name-dropping will get Nicole's attention. "So yes, I'm still in New York, and I just saw something that would make a really juicy feature for the magazine. Can we meet early next week? It's time sensitive."

The sound of heavy footfalls coming down the stairs causes Evie to hunker even lower behind the bus cart. Nicole's saying something, frantically trying to recalculate Evie's social worth based on the wildly unexpected information that she's at the party of the month and Nicole isn't. Evie cuts her off. "Look, I don't have a lot of time. Someone's been hired to break up Greg and Stewart Pickford's marriage. I have proof. You want to meet about it or not?"

There's a slow exhale on the other end, and the noise of whatever bar she's at fades away. "I don't know if you heard, but we laid off a lot of staff last week and I can't commission new freelancers right now, it just looks bad. Can you write it on spec? By the time you're done I can probably get budget."

A voice echoes down the corridor, the sort of short, sharp *Hey!* meant to stop someone in their tracks. Evie talks faster, more urgently into the phone. "I can't write it on spec, Nicole. You know I won't get people like this to agree to interviews unless I can use the magazine's name," Evie grits out. She'll be telling the subjects it's for a puff piece on fall fashion, of course, but their PR won't even return her calls if the inquiry isn't backed by a publication they care about. "It's very *Vanity Fair*, though. Maybe they're still commissioning—"

"I don't think you understand, buddy. I ain't askin'," says a harsh male voice down the corridor, and the footsteps that were coming towards her stop.

"I prefer not to. We prefer not to," another voice answers, low, sly and dripping with aristocratic disdain. It's Misha, and he's maybe five feet away from her.

Evie tenses. "I have to go. Do you want this or should I take it somewhere else?" The words come out sharp, the absolute terror of being discovered giving her a confidence she'd never managed while interning.

"I can see you Monday at noon," says Nicole. "At the office. Bring proof."

"Okay. Thank you," Evie whispers, hanging up and pocketing her phone.

She edges forwards, peeking around the bus cart. Two security guards are slowly walking towards Misha, who is standing in front of Stewart Pickford-Jones, blocking the guards from him with his body. Stewart is shaking, white with fear.

Evie quietly reaches into the recycling bin next to her and fishes out an empty champagne bottle, wincing when the ones underneath it shift and clink. If Misha is actually hurting this man, she will—

"Mr Pickford-Jones has gotta go sit down at his family's party," says the lead security guard, a big, bullet-headed man with cauliflower ears. He cracks his knuckles. The second man is wiry, with the intense glint of the fanatic in his eyes.

"I'm not asking, either," says Misha, still blocking the fragile blond from the security team with his body. "Mr Pickford-Jones is tired and I am going to drive him home. He has put in an appearance, been photographed by the right people, and that is sufficient."

"N-no, Misha, it's okay, we t-tried, I'll just go back and do the dinner," says the smaller man, wincing and adjusting his glasses. Evie notices that his bad eye has a cut on the edge of the socket that was hidden by the frames, maybe even an orbital fracture.

The bastard who hit him wore a ring.

Evie's eyes immediately skate down to Misha's hands. He has long, artist's fingers, and wears no rings. Her own hands relax on the champagne bottle.

"I'd listen to Mr Jones if I were you, buddy. Unless you want us to do this by force," says the other security guard. Evie notices both guards have guns in holsters at their waists, hidden under jackets.

"You're welcome to try," Misha says, slipping off his jacket and tossing it onto a pallet of clean glasses. "But let's not do this in front of Stewart, shall we?"

Stewart puts a hand on his arm and Misha picks it up, kissing his knuckles, exactly the motion Evie had imagined when she met him.

Stewart gazes up at him and in a shaky voice just says, "Please, Misha," tugging his hand. Evie realizes he's not just terrified for himself, he's terrified what the bodyguards will do to Misha.

Misha turns Stewart's hand over, and places a set of car keys into it. "If we get separated, wait for me in the car," Misha whispers to him. "I won't be long."

"But—" Stewart says.

Misha presses a kiss to his temple. "Everything will be okay. Trust me." He puts his arm around Stewart and walks him towards the exit, slowly at first, then with more purpose.

Just as they pass Evie's hiding place, the security team breaks into a run. Misha gives Stewart a gentle shove in the direction of the exit. Stewart gets the message and flees, out towards the loading area.

Then Misha turns back the way he came and strides headlong into trouble, a wild glint in his eyes.

Seeing Misha shift into aggressive motion, Evie understands that his body's considerable strength isn't the product of fancy trainers and endless repetitions in a gym. He moves like a fighter, a soldier; like someone who has had a lot of training and even more practical experience in fucking other people up.

The first bodyguard rushes in to meet him, fists up. Thick knuckles and cauliflower ears. He's big, 250 to 280 pounds, but slow.

Misha isn't.

He has the bodyguard down in three moves, dodging the man's opening punch and kicking down to shatter his kneecap, then sending him to the ground with a wicked right hook.

He's still watching the downed guard to see if he's going to get up when, with a splutter of curses, the second bodyguard yanks his gun out of its holster and raises it.

Evie only realizes what she's doing when she's almost on the guy. She intends to shout but instead just manages a startled squeak, and clocks the guy over the back of the head with the champagne bottle.

In her mind this was supposed to result in the guard faceplanting into the floor, unconscious, the unfired gun skittering out of his hands.

But it doesn't.

The gun goes off just as she hits him, frighteningly loud in the hard-walled corridor, and Evie feels terror clutch at her stomach when she sees that the gun was pointed straight at Misha, and it gets worse as the guard turns around to face her, crimson with fury, his gun now pointed at her.

Evie clasps the empty champagne bottle to her chest in terror and backs up straight into the bus cart of empties, which clatters alarmingly. "I'm sorry!" is all she gets out, before the guard's eyes narrow, and—

—Misha's fist crashes into the side of his head. It sends him reeling sideways into the bus cart Evie had been hiding behind. The guard rebounds off it with a crash, then staggers once, as if the floor were doing him a great injustice by remaining still, before he sinks to his knees.

Misha looks down at Evie, his eyes sparkling with amusement, as she begins to unclench from her huddle next to the bus cart. She's panting, terrified, sweating. Misha is none of these things. He's shaking out a blue and white polka dot handkerchief he's pulled from a pocket, and the only sign he's been in a scuffle is a few locks of his hair in mild disarray. As he uses the handkerchief to wipe a smear of someone else's blood off his knuckles, he murmurs, "A for effort. C for technique."

Evie doesn't know whether to swear at him or start crying, but the choice is taken from her by movement in her peripheral vision. The downed guard's hand is creeping towards his gun, half-hidden under the bus cart. She narrows her eyes, raises the bottle, and whacks the guy solidly on the temple. He slumps to the floor and stays down.

"Hmph," Misha says. "B minus."

"Are you okay?" Evie asks, aching from the adrenalin pounding through her body. "The gun, I thought... He was aiming right at you."

Misha shakes his head. But as he goes to replace his handkerchief in his pocket, Evie's eyes follow the motion... and she sees the small hole in his white shirt, no larger than her little finger. "Holy shit," she gasps. "You *were* shot!"

Misha's eyes widen as he tugs at the hem of his shirt, then he chuckles as he finds the hole, a hair's breadth from his waist. "Not quite," he says. "It's merely an old shirt, and it has a hole or two. I'm afraid the Pickfords only merit my second-best clothes." He reaches down and collects his jacket from atop the clean glasses. "Tonight I was lucky. No harm done."

Evie frowns. Misha's remark implied that he'd had unlucky nights, nights where harm *was* done to him. She is about to ask, when hesitant footfalls from down the hall catch both of their attention.

Stewart is stumbling back inside, encouraged by the silence.

"Misha, who is that?" Stewart asks, his voice timorous. Stewart is pointing at her, blinking, unsure.

She's about to snap at him, because he'd talked to her not an hour ago, when she realizes: he's not wearing his glasses. He looks at Misha, then at Evie, with owl eyes, unfocused.

Evie prepares to reintroduce herself to Stewart, or indeed introduce herself properly for the first time, when she feels a warm, muscled arm settle itself over her shoulders. Misha smiles at Stewart, easy and relaxed. The tangible feeling of menace emanating from Misha a moment ago has evaporated, leaving nothing but the society pretty-boy. Evie feels hysterical laughter start to bubble up in her, standing here in a museum access corridor, hanging out with Misha Meserov, a famous fashion designer, and two unconscious security guards. Like they're *friends*.

Then Misha ruins it. "Stewart, this is Miss Cross. She works for me," he says.

"What?" Evie hisses, fluffing up like an angry cat as she wiggles out from under his arm.

"Oh. Hello," Stewart says, then squints at her. "I say, weren't you also working at the bar? You were right about those strawberry things. *Lethal.*" Then he points at her champagne bottle. "That got any left in it?"

Evie tips it upside down. "Sorry." Then she turns and glares at Misha. "I don't—" she begins. But Misha rolls his eyes and jots something on the back of a business card. He extends it to Evie between two long fingers. "Give this to Abi," he says.

She looks down at the card. It's pale blue, with *M.A. Meserov* and a phone number engraved in a simple copperplate. Above his name is scrawled, in handwriting so elegant as to seem old-fashioned: *I changed my mind. Hire her.—M.*

Evie stares at the writing in shock. It is her literal golden ticket. She won; all she has to do is reach out and take it and she can stay in New York. Could it be that easy? In one casual, offhand gesture from a near-stranger, all of her dramas are laid to rest? She could give Claudia everything she owes her. She could pay off her credit card, get back on track with her student loans…

… She could get the proof she needs to sell a feature to Nicole.

But, even though something in her furiously resents the way Misha can just… hand her a job, like it's no big deal to him, she also doesn't feel right taking it, knowing she plans to betray him. She's not that duplicitous. And he's…

… He's tilting his head at her, like a confused puppy. "You are… refusing my number?" he murmurs in bemused shock, like this is the first time it's ever happened to him. It probably is.

His face falls as Evie still makes no move towards the card. "Oh. You are."

She could always bail out of her meeting with Nicole. But if, as she increasingly suspects, Stewart's husband gave him that black eye, she feels it's her journalistic duty to bury Greg Pickford. She can decide how much to reveal about Misha later. She can make it all work out, somehow.

Evie finds she's grinning as she reaches out, and takes the card at last. "No, sorry, I just… It's nothing," she says. "I'll brush up on my…" Evie presses her lips together and swings the empty bottle of Krug she's still clutching.

A genuine smile spreads across Misha's face, and he looks so young, then, carefree and happy. "Ah, well, hopefully we won't have to draw on those skills again. But thank you, all the same." He turns and slings on his jacket, then slips an arm around Stewart's waist. "Goodnight, Miss Cross," he says, and the bastard has the nerve to wink at her. "See you Monday. 9 a.m."

"Evie," she says quietly, to his retreating back. "Call me Evie."

CHAPTER THREE

EVIE IS LATE. She blames the local train that snaps its doors shut in her face at 4th Street as she dashes across the platform from the express train, the next C train for taking twenty minutes to show up, the shuffling hordes outside 49th Street station, the slow elevators at One Worldwide Plaza, and, for good measure, Misha Meserov himself. She's wearing her other decent work dress, a dark grey wool with long sleeves that has turned out to be absolutely the wrong choice for an unseasonably hot late-May day, but she can't help feeling intimidated by Misha's bespoke suits and million-dollar art. Evie doesn't want to be the plainest, sloppiest thing in the office even though she fears that, even on her very best day, she would be.

She rushes through the door of Meserov & Co at 9:20 and stops, shocked, as she sees perfect Gemma Andrews, the girl who interviewed after her, sitting behind the reception desk as if she owns it. Gemma fumbles the giant Starbucks she's drinking and gawps at Evie, like she's seeing a ghost. "What are you doing here?" Evie stutters.

"What are *you* doing here?" Gemma asks, placing her Venti down, her Long Island accent blurring out the ending consonants of her words. She's wearing a tight blue-grey tweed sleeveless dress and pale blue high heels, and she still looks like Sephora threw up on her face. She tucks a lock of her long blonde hair behind her ear. "I thought—"

"He changed his mind," Evie says, sheepishly brandishing Misha's card at her like a fake ID at a college-bar bouncer.

"Um, apparently he hired me?"

Gemma's eyes widen, and she twists a lock of her hair. Evie realizes she's nervous. "But… I already signed my contract," she says, staring down at her gel manicure, baby pink. She is quite pretty: a thin body, delicate face, and big eyes, helped along by considerable effort on her hair and makeup.

And Evie wishes, for one brief shining moment, that she could be a Gemma. That she could be that girl, the one with the good hair and the perfect makeup, who saw her job not only as an opportunity for a career, but as a chance to meet attractive, wealthy men. Men who were very likely to find her attractive in return.

Men like Misha.

It often felt to Evie like every other girl in existence had been sent some secret instruction book on their thirteenth birthday: *This is how to do your hair; your makeup. This is how to make men like you. This is how you settle.* Then there was Evie, tomboyish and adrift and unwilling to hide how sharp she was, and who never received the *How To Girl* manual. Her femininity got lost in the post ten years ago, and she never even got a tracking number.

Gemma knew what she was doing, was focused on her goal, eyes on the prize. She would eventually marry a man a decade older than her, maybe not handsome, but who would keep her in lip filler and handbags and tall suede boots to her heart's content.

And Evie couldn't be content as a secretary, with her day job, but also wasn't getting anywhere with her writing. Abandoned long-form essays cluttered her Google Docs, their titles like memorials to her dreams. *You don't belong here*, the little voice of her anxiety whispers. *You don't belong anywhere.*

"Are you okay?" Gemma asks.

"Yeah, fine. Just trying to figure out what I should do. Sorry," Evie says. She tries to smile at Gemma. "You look really nice today. I wish I was that good with contouring."

"You should go get a makeover," Gemma says. "They teach you really useful stuff."

"Is he—" Evie says, indicating the closed door to the inner office.

Gemma sighs. "Abigail says he doesn't show up until just before lunch," she says.

"Ugh, why did he tell me to get here at nine, then?" Evie flops onto the sofa. She groans, and digs out her phone. "You know the wifi password?"

"No," Gemma grumbles.

"I guess I better go see Abi," Evie says, reluctantly getting up off the surprisingly comfortable sofa. "Make sure this isn't all some weird joke."

Gemma presses her lips together sympathetically. "I hope not. That would be really mean. Besides," she continues, gesturing at the messy stacks of paper on the reception desk, "this looks like a two-person job."

Half an hour later, Evie is camped outside Abigail's office on the twenty-sixth floor, clutching a mug of black coffee from that floor's break-room Nespresso machine like it's the last best hope of Western civilization.

Abigail doesn't seem too surprised to see her when she comes out. Evie's not sure what to make of that.

The HR chief glances at the card Evie presents, gives her a weary but happy smile, and motions her into the office. "Glad he finally saw reason," Abigail says, bending over her laptop and clicking away. A moment later, the printer in the corner chunters to life and begins spitting out pages. "There. That's the contract and the NDA."

Then she settles down at her desk and motions to a comfy-looking chair for Evie to do the same. "Now, honey, sit. We need to talk." Today Abi is in a long, flowing purple cardigan over a taupe dress that's a couple shades lighter than her skin. "First, the contract with Misha is a month temp, with an option to permanent. It's the same as the one Gemma has. Now, she's a very experienced PA who had lovely references, but," Abigail smiles, "I guarantee Misha didn't choose her because he liked her. Speaking of which, Evie, what do you think of him?"

Evie is good at reading people, but Abigail's face is pure innocence. She sips her coffee while her brain scrambles to sort through the complex tangle of impressions she has about the man, trying to present them in a way that won't land her in trouble. She has the sense that Abigail is loyal to him, maybe even considers him a friend, and that is fascinating in itself.

"I think he must be a pretty interesting guy if the HR chief for a top-tier law firm is taking the time to moonlight for him on the side," Evie says over the top of her coffee.

Abigail raises an eyebrow, shooting her an appreciative look. "I see why he was a little scared to hire you the first time around."

She begins to gather the stack of paper that's been spitting out of the printer since Evie sat down. "I want you to keep one thing in mind, Evie, especially in the early days." Abigail looks right at her, warm brown eyes intense. "Misha is infuriating and secretive and doesn't accept help, and at least once a day you'll have the urge to whack him on the head with the nearest heavy, blunt object. But personality quirks aside, you may never meet someone as fundamentally *good* as him again. Even if he has a funny way of showing it."

"Okay," Evie says. She manages to keep her disbelief out of her voice.

Abigail slides the papers into two separate large manila envelopes. One, she seals; the other, she leaves open as the printer continues to spit out pages. "Working for Misha will be the most interesting job you'll ever have. But. *But.* Ultimately it may not be for you, and there's no shame in tapping out. Just come see me if that's the case, and I'll get you back into temping here until something more permanent opens up. Remind me, who'd you temp for, before?"

"Bobbi Huang, up in Corporate," Evie says. She'd spent three enjoyable (and lucrative) months last winter filling in while Ms Huang's secretary was out on an extended Christmas-and-maternity leave. Abigail had given her the opening to Corporate rather than the temp-to-perm in Family Law she'd applied for. At the time, Evie had thought Abi just wasn't listening to her, or she hadn't made her preference clear enough. But then the PA grapevine had been abuzz that the temp they did hire for the divorce specialists had broken down in tears three times in her first week.

Abigail had form, in other words. If she liked Misha, there was a distinct possibility there was more to him than his glossy surface implied. That Evie's first instincts were correct, and this might be a job Evie would enjoy, rather than simply endure. She certainly hoped so.

"Bobbi thought you were great," Abigail continues with a smile, bringing Evie back down to earth. "And she's one picky lady. Good practice for Misha." She hands Evie the first envelope. "It's likely to take him a little while to trust you and let go, so be prepared for that. In the meantime, don't touch anything of his without explicit permission. Investigative snooping around his office would be a terrible idea, even if it's done with the best of intentions." She reaches back to grab the last papers from the now-silent printer. "Speaking of which, he has a temper. His sister's worse. Never piss that woman off. If Misha gets loud, just yell back at him. But if he goes real quiet, the best thing to do is get out of the blast radius as fast as you can." Abigail thrusts the second envelope at Evie. "There. Don't sign either of these until he's gone over them with you. After you and he sign these, bring them both up to me. If you give them to Misha," she sighs, "we'll never see them again."

Evie looks down at the two fat envelopes that contain the best possibility of a future she's had in a long time, and resists the urge to tear them open. "Uh. We never talked about salary?"

"That is something you discuss with Misha." Abigail steeples her fingers and looks at her in clear, if kind, dismissal. "Good luck, Evie. Don't forget to bring those back."

Evie stands, cradling the papers in their manila jackets, and thanks Abigail. She heads back down to the seventeenth floor just as it turns 10am, and there's nothing to do but sit in the front office with Gemma and wait. Evie resumes her place on the sofa, pulls her contract out, and begins to read it.

The phone rings first at 10:30 and both of them reach for it. Gemma gets there first, and hits the caller with a calm, pleasant, "I'm sorry, he's in a meeting, can I take a message?" She looks around on the messy desk for a notepad, unsuccessfully. Evie rolls her eyes and hands her the empty manila envelope from her contract.

Gemma mouths *thank you* and looks almost grateful as she scrawls down the message. There are a couple more, mostly partners from the Family Law floor of Meyer, Luchins & Black, upstairs, chasing Misha for progress updates on casework. In between calls, Gemma rests the envelope with its list of messages on top of the least-messy stack of papers. "If you find an actual message pad in this chaos, let me know," she sighs. "Ugh, why doesn't he have his calls forwarded to his cell, if he's not going to show up in the mornings?"

"Boys," Evie shrugs. "Here, there has to be a notepad under all this somewhere. You take the right half of the desk, I'll take the left." She goes to move the envelope with its call list somewhere safer, but her hand freezes when she sees what's written there. The first message, which Evie reads upside down from Gemma's tidy handwriting, is someone named Octavia Mortimer wanting her call returned. But the second one makes her breath catch: the Pickfords want to pick up their photos ASAP.

Evie pulls out the card Misha gave her. The phone number on it starts with 347, which is more than likely a cell number. The building they were in was old enough that the office phone would have a 212 area code. She pulls out her cell and sends a quick text to the number on the card: *Hi Misha it's Evie you have messages.* She details the two calls and, when there's no response, she tidies up a little more before giving up and sitting back down on the sofa. Just as she sits down, she can feel her phone vibrate in her pocket.

Right. Thanks. I'll be there in an hour, stall them until then.

Evie swears under her breath, and texts Nicole. *Can we meet now? Things changed and I'm only free until 11:30.* The offices of *Gotham Magazine* were in the NMG Building, less than ten blocks away. It was still tight, but she was wearing flats today and if she hurried, she could still make it. She stares at her phone screen, willing Nicole to respond, hoping that she sees Evie's message in time and is in a good mood.

When she sees the three dots of a message being typed, Evie slumps in relief. Nicole can see her early. She smiles at Gemma as she grabs her handbag. "I didn't get breakfast, so I'm going to run out for a snack before he comes in," Evie lies. "You want anything? Another coffee?"

"I want the wifi password," Gemma grumbles.

Evie rushes up Ninth Avenue and across 56th Street, striding into the NMG Building hot and out of breath. She heads straight for the security gates, on autopilot in the familiar space, before she remembers: she's no longer working at *Gotham*. She's a visitor.

The offices on the twenty-third floor are exactly the same as when she interned, though: dark walls covered in glossy blowups of landmark covers from the magazine's first issues in the 1970s through to ones from about seven years ago. A bright red, angular sofa to wait on, flanked by a large fake plant with shiny green leaves. More recent magazine issues scattered on a table near the sofa. The black-painted wall of the reception desk, and the backlit silver magazine logo behind it.

It's all so familiar, so untouched from her time there that when Evie looks up from texting Nicole, she's surprised to see a young Asian-American of indeterminate gender and purple hair behind the reception desk. Before she can stop herself, she asks, "What happened to Damian?"

"Who?" the receptionist asks, tilting their head in confusion. "There's no-one—"

"Damian," Evie says again. "He used to be the receptionist here." Damian was slim and Jamaican and had a wit drier than the Sahara and an unhealthy fixation with pop music. Like her, he had wanted to move into an assistant editor position, existing on scraps, hiding in plain sight in the hopes they'd notice his talent.

"I guess he left." The new receptionist shrugs. "I dunno. I'm just an intern."

They stare at each other, awkwardly, until the receptionist asks, "Were you here to see him, or—"

They're interrupted by Nicole herself clattering in, her long blonde hair a shade paler, her Chanel jacket a season newer than the last time Evie saw her a year ago. She squints at Evie, as if not sure she's the right person.

Evie gives her a little wave. "Hi, Nicole. It's good to see you again."

Nicole beckons at her, exasperated. "There aren't any conference rooms. Come back to my office. I have like ten minutes."

Evie follows, back through the warren of open-plan cubicles she once knew so well, her eyes skimming over empty desk after empty desk, searching out the few staff writers left at the magazine. Nicole is a senior editor so she has an actual office, with a door. It's tiny and messy, a closet-sized space wedged against one side of the building, with a mesh shade drawn over the very window that made the office desirable. Evie knows if she were to raise the shade, all she'd see is the dirty windows of the opposite skyscraper, across 57th Street.

She goes onto autopilot again, her mind glitching back to the days she and Nicole had written the poisoning article. They had worked well together, then. As she pulls out the spare chair, however, Nicole's fancy crocodile-skin handbag tumbles off it, shedding pens and lipsticks and tampons across the carpet.

"Shit, sorry, I didn't see..." Evie says, sweeping everything back inside and placing the bag upright next to Nicole's desk. "... is that a real Birkin?" She'd done an article on those bags, when she was interning. Even secondhand, they cost more than a car. A *good* car.

They cost about a year's salary for an editor.

Evie doesn't miss the tightness at the edges of Nicole's expression when she sniffs, "It was a birthday present." Nicole picks up her phone and starts checking her emails. "Now, I seriously have like five minutes. Pitch me."

"Okay," Evie says, learning forward. The door to Nicole's office is still open, and voices carry in empty spaces, so she speaks softly. "Stewart Pickford-Jones is having an affair. He had a black eye last night, and I'm pretty sure his husband Greg gave it to him. And Leah? The sister getting engaged? Her dress wasn't by Stewart. It was designed by Erin, the youngest sister."

Nicole doesn't look up from her phone, as her thumbs peck out a message. "This is like, TMZ stuff. Juicy, but not a feature."

"No, listen," Evie says. "The Pickfords have hired the guy who's having an affair with Stewart." She sees Nicole's thumbs stop moving, even if the woman continues to stare at her phone screen. "They're trying to get rid of him, so Erin can take over womenswear."

Nicole's brow furrows as she lowers her phone to her lap. "Because if they divorce…"

"… and Stewart's at fault, he won't get any of the company his designs built," Evie continues.

"Is Greg having an affair too?" Nicole asks.

"I dunno," Evie says. "Yet."

"They always are," Nicole sighs. "Trust me." She leans over to her computer, fingers flying over the keyboard as she fires off a message. "Okay, I'm just checking one thing… You can prove this? Receipts, payment histories, photographs? You're not making a case to the reader, remember, they'll believe anything. You need to convince our legal department we can print this and not get sued."

"I can get all of it," Evie says. "Absolutely. I'll need your help interviewing the Pickford family members, though. I'm sort of… undercover right now."

Nicole waves a hand, Cartier bracelets jangling. "I can set up what looks like a puff-piece interview through their PR for the Fall Fashion Special. But we'd need to work out questions based on what you discover. Who's Stewart having the affair with? Can we get to… him? Her?"

"Him," Evie says. "I doubt it. He runs an agency that breaks people up. It's very… discreet."

Nicole's focus is suddenly, and for the first time, completely on Evie. "That's your story. That's the heart of it, right there. Who else have they broken up? Any more famous names?"

Evie's empty stomach clenches in fear. "I don't know. I... I want to focus it more on the Pickfords. The underhand dealings tearing apart America's favorite fashion dynasty; that sort of thing? We can talk to people who used to work for Erin, I bet she's—"

The chime of an incoming message cuts her off, and Nicole swears under her breath as she glances at the screen. "They're *advertisers*. I won't be able to get a scandal article about them past the publisher. We normally stay away from anything negative in retail, especially fashion." She drums her fingers on the desk as she thinks. "You're *sure* Stewart's the innocent party in this?"

"Positive," Evie says.

"Okay, so the Pickfords can't be the primary subject. What's the name of this agency? What's the guy's name?" Nicole asks. Her phone is back in her hands and her thumbs hover, ready to look up Evie's answers.

"I have to handle that part. It stays confidential for now," Evie grits out. Nicole's clearly not about to let it drop, and as she opens her mouth, Evie cuts across her: "I need to protect my source."

"Whatever. You'll have to bring me in at some point, though. And Legal," she says. "But if you can get me a few other names of that agency's victims and we can focus on them too so it doesn't seem too much like a hit piece on the Pickfords, we can do this."

"It *should* be a hit piece on the Pickfords," Evie says.

"And it's going to have to be digital-only. They're just really sensitive about print." Nicole leans back in her chair. "Our digital rate is thirty-three cents a word, and I'd be looking for around five thousand words. Sound good?"

Evie feels nauseous. When she pictured her first feature story in her head, it was a triumphant arrival, a thing to celebrate. But now it's really happening, and all she feels is the sick guilt of someone who knows they're doing something they shouldn't.

"I mean, if it really is what you say it is," says Nicole. "And I get co-credit."

"What?" Evie says. "But it's *my* story—"

Nicole looks at her, serious. "There's a freeze on hiring new freelancers. I'm sorry. It's co-credit or nothing. Plus... I'm not being mean here, Evie, but this is *delicate*, and I'm not sure you have the experience to take on a story with this many complications to it."

"This isn't..." Evie says. She takes a deep breath and chooses her words carefully. "I don't think this is the story I wanted to write anymore."

"Then do it yourself and put it on one of those free sites and pray you don't get hit with a lawsuit from the Pickfords so big you can see it from space. We're not the only legitimate publication who won't touch retail. *Vanity Fair* has even more fashion ads than us. *Atlantic*? *New Yorker*? Good luck, if they'll even talk to you without previous feature credits. Or we can publish it as we discussed, with the full protection of our legal department, and you have a solid first feature with a lot of viral potential."

Frustration and exhaustion prick at the inner corners of Evie's eyes. "...Okay," she sighs. She doesn't believe Nicole, but there's nothing else she can do.

MISHA SLOPES IN ten minutes after Evie gets back to the office, looking like he hasn't slept since the gala. The shadows under his eyes are even deeper, and his hair is loose and messy. He's in a slim light blue v-neck tee that shows off every cut of his absurd body, sprayed-on black skinny jeans that rest perilously low on his hips, and half-laced black tanker boots.

He blinks at Evie and Gemma in his front office, says, "Fuck," goes into his office, and shuts the door. Evie notices he has a large cardboard envelope in his hand, the kind that says *Photographs—Do Not Bend* on the side, and she feels tolerably smug.

The phone rings again. Gemma answers it, then knocks on Misha's door. "Excuse me, sir?" she says, her voice pitched higher and softer than when she speaks to Evie. "Erin Pickford is on the line about some photographs?"

Evie can hear the sigh through the door. Misha comes out and takes the phone from Gemma, leaning against the wall by the desk like it's the only thing keeping him upright. "Yes. Yes, I have them. No, sorry, Greg needs to pick them up himself. No. Absolutely not. It's in the contract. I only hand them over to the named party. And he needs to bring cash."

Misha rolls his eyes wearily as the person on the other end of the line talks for a while. "You *could* do that, but I'd think making this transaction traceable is the last thing you want. Yes. I'll be here until six. That will be fine." He hangs up the phone and sighs in Evie's general direction. "It's like they've never heard of plausible deniability." Then he looks over at Gemma. "Ah. Make all these files go away?" He makes an elegantly dramatic sweeping motion encompassing the chaos scattered across every flat surface.

"Of course!" Gemma chirps, pushing her chair back. "How do you want them filed?"

"Um," says Misha, raking a hand through his hair. "Shred anything over a year old. You'll need to buy a shredder… anything more recent, put in the cabinets in my office, filed by target. Cross-reference them with the client, too, because sometimes I forget. Just put a piece of paper in a folder for the client, listing the target's name. Any receipts, those go on expense reports and get sent to Abi. I have no idea how that works. Ask her."

Then his pale eyes sweep over to Evie. "Miss Cross?" he says, indicating his office. "Bring the contracts Abi gave you."

Gemma picks up the top file of the stack nearest to her and peers at it, as Evie passes her.

Inside his office, Misha shuts the door and indicates that Evie should sit down on the same antique leather chaise longue that she occupied for her disastrous interview the Friday before. He pushes some papers out of the way on his desk and sits on the edge of it, folding one long leg under himself. "Thanks for the text," he yawns, rolling his shoulders to stretch them out. "Sorry. Long night."

"Partying?" Evie asks.

"Working. And insomnia." He reaches out for the contracts, and Evie pulls them out of the envelope and hands them over. "Did you read them?" he asks.

"Not yet, no," Evie says. "Abigail said not to, until I'd spoken to you. And that you'd tell me what the salary was."

"Oh," says Misha, looking perplexed. He gazes down at the fat sheaf of papers in his hand. He blinks, looking exhausted. "I… don't know. What do you want to be paid?"

"Uh. Sixty thousand," Evie declares, fully expecting him to laugh in her face.

Misha shrugs. "Fine," he says. He fishes a pen out of his desk, flips open the employment contract, and amends the final page, initialing it. Evie wonders what would have happened if she'd asked for $75,000; $100,000. Would he have just shrugged and said yes? In Evie's experience, there were two kinds of rich: the ones that didn't really understand money, except as something that was always there; and the ones that resent every cent they have to spend on anything other than themselves. Misha seemed the former, but something ran false about his apparent cluelessness about money. It felt like a façade he put on; an act to lure people into underestimating him.

Misha hands the other sheaf back to Evie. "This is the NDA. Read through it. If you sign it, we can then discuss the particulars of working for me, and whether it's something you wish to do."

"It's fine," Evie says with a sigh. "I need the job." She pulls a pen out of her bag and, as she flips through the NDA to find the signature line, she glances up at Misha. He's watching her, with disappointment in his face.

"What?" Evie says.

"Miss Cross. I expected better of you," frowns Misha. "Never agree to a deal until you know all the particulars."

She glances away to hide the blush of shame in her cheeks. She looks down at the pile of paper in her lap, and starts to page through it. It's a terrible document. The skin at the back of her neck prickles in objection to the pages and pages of punitive clauses and subsections. But in the end, the non-disclosure agreement boils down to an extreme, posh-legalese version of *snitches get stitches*.

She stares at the signature page, her pen hovering over it. She'd spent enough time on the Corporate Law floor of Meyer, Luchins & Black to know that NDAs were mostly scare tactics, messy and difficult to enforce once broken. It still feels wrong to her, to lie that deliberately.

The blank signature line stares back at her.

But then... what if, despite the good money, she's just disposable to him? Another intern, another temp, let go after one month once the office is spotless with an insincere *so sorry* and the promise of a good reference. It's not like the feature's going to net her more than $1,500—or, Evie corrects herself, $750, because she'll be sharing the byline with Nicole.

She signs the NDA, because in the end, what does she have to lose? The only things she owns are some Ikea furniture, some clothes, and a ton of student debt. She hands Misha his copy back. She stuffs the other copy in her handbag.

Misha looks at it, this evil stack of paper in his hands. "It's beautiful, isn't it? Quite perfect in its viciousness. Talk about me, talk about what I do, or the cases we take, and it takes your eternal soul and that of all your descendants, forever and ever, amen." He smiles. It's not a warm smile, but neither is it a mocking one. It brings Evie up short: there's a sadness behind those strange, pale eyes that she doesn't expect.

"Well, not really your soul, but close enough," he says, throwing the document onto the mess on his desk. "Now. Ask me anything. And then you can decide if you want to sign the contract."

"Okay. What do you do that's so awful it requires an NDA with punitive clauses that near as dammit violate the Geneva

Convention? I know you said you tear people apart, but..."
Evie falls silent, thinking about Stewart, how he'd looked at
Misha like he was the one good thing in his life. How Misha
had listened to him, had protected him.

"Exactly that," Misha says. "I break up relationships; destroy
marriages. Want to divorce someone but didn't sign a prenup?
Things get a lot cheaper if that someone has an affair. Or one
person falls out of love but their partner doesn't? I help that
partner start to imagine... other possibilities. Let them down
easy. We make mistresses go away; eliminate the inappropriate
boyfriends or girlfriends of rebellious or naïve young heirs."
He smiles. "It's terribly expensive, of course, but I never fail."

Evie makes a face as she works through this. "I thought...
investigations..."

"I investigate relationships, find their weak points, and insert
myself or one of my subcontractors into them, driving the
people apart. It's fascinating, if you like psychology."

"And hate love," Evie finishes.

"There is no such thing as love, Miss Cross," Misha counters,
calm and quiet. "Sexual attraction, friendship, convenience,
inertia, pride, fear. Yes. All these things and more. Love? I'm
afraid not."

Evie frowns. "But what about if the targets are straight guys?
Or lesbians? Or aren't into white people? Or is this one of those
things where it's never straight guys?"

Misha tucks some of his messy dark hair behind an ear. It
doesn't stay. "It's less difficult than you think. The wealthy are...
inordinately susceptible to the attention of young beautiful
things. I have a dozen people I work with regularly. Between
all of us, I like to think we have someone for every preference.
And I have a twin sister. Masha sometimes handles targets that
prefer women. You'll meet her, if you stick around."

His smile returns, but it's small, hesitant. "If you work here,
you'll have to be okay with seeing photos of all of us engaging in
sexual acts with targets. Some of which will involve significant
kink, and/or are same-sex. You won't ever have to deal with any

of it beyond packing up prints for evidence, but this isn't... a normal workplace."

"I used to work in a strip club in Flatbush when I first came to New York," Evie says. "For rent, and journalism. It was the sort of club where the management turned a blind eye to *extra services* in the private rooms, for a small cut. I've seen most things a couple bodies can do."

Misha tilts his head, and his eyes light up with interest. "You published something about the club? I'd like to read it. I imagine you're quite a good writer."

"Ah... um... no," Evie says, looking down at her hands as a blush heats up her cheeks again. Yet another Google Doc tombstone in her graveyard of abandoned projects. "I wanted to. Had all sorts of plans. But... I really liked the girls. In the end I couldn't take their lives and sensationalize them to benefit myself." Evie smirks. "Besides, who wants to read a story about sex workers and strip club girls being happy and well adjusted?"

Misha chuckles and shakes his head. "Evie, I hate to break it to you, but you're not vicious enough to be a journalist," he says.

"Excuse me, I can be nasty," Evie responds, sitting up straight and wrinkling her nose. "There was this one girl at the club. Called herself Scarlett," and she says it the way the girl did, all am-dram Tennessee Williams. "I suspected she was using my office for some of her *extra services*, so I left a bottle of lube out on my desk. Which I'd filled with extra-strength Purell." She presses her lips together. "Admittedly, that's how I got fired, but it was worth it."

Misha blinks for a moment in surprise, then breaks out into laughter, boyish and light, leaning forwards, his shoulders shaking with it. Evie snorts, then dissolves into giggles herself. Watching Misha laugh is infectious; those eyes have as many moods as the sky and right now they are high summer, when it's still bright at 9pm and everything is possible; everything is forgiven. She wants to hear him laugh like this all the time. He seems so young, so unguarded; like happiness is a thing he hasn't had a lot of practice with.

Misha smiles down at the floor and shakes his head, but then his expression turns serious again, the loose ease of a moment ago vanishing completely into something quiet and sincere. He reaches out and takes Evie's hand, pressing his thumb against the back of her knuckles like he did on the morning they met. His voice is low and measured: "If you work here, Evie, I promise you one thing, and I promise it on the graves of my family: while our work is extremely messy, you will always be safe."

Evie feels pinned by those pale eyes. The intensity of expression in them feels tangible; sharp like a surgical knife, pressing into her, opening everything inside for view.

"You have nothing to worry about from myself, or from Masha, or any of us." He blinks, long lashes fanning down over glacier blue, and he releases her hand. "This business, what I do, can get exceptionally ugly. Last night... last night was only a minor nastiness. It has got much worse. But you will never face that again. Only I take the cases like that. Nobody else is put at risk."

"But who keeps you safe?" Evie asks, before she has time to think about it.

Misha pauses, caught off guard. Then he shrugs. "I get by. You saw, last night..." He trails off, catching his bottom lip in his teeth as his mind seems to drift elsewhere.

"So *about* last night..." Evie starts.

"Yes," Misha sighs. "Stewart is initiating divorce proceedings against Greg Pickford. Which is fair enough, considering that Greg is abusive. Meyer, Luchins & Black is the Pickfords' law firm, and it was suggested Greg hire me to have a rather public affair with Stewart. See, the world, and the family court, will believe Stewart is a cheater long before they'll believe that Greg is the reason Stewart always wears long sleeves and those big glasses, even though he has perfectly serviceable contact lenses. So I seduced Stewart over the course of the last few weeks. And I have the very explicit photos to prove it in court." He looks down. "Stewart was an easy target. People like him always are."

"That's horrible," Evie says. "The poor guy's trying to get out of an abusive relationship, and you, you—"

"Slept with him," Misha says. "And took photos of it without his consent, and soon he will lose his stock in the company his designs built up, and any claim he might have to his rightful share of the Pickford fortune."

Evie doesn't know what to say. An uncomfortable silence descends, the hum of the air conditioning and the overhead lights in the room now painfully loud. She can hear the creak of Gemma's chair and the shuffling of papers on the other side of the door.

Misha starts talking softly, almost to himself. "All those years of getting treated like shit, and Stewart didn't file until Greg beat up their dog." He wipes a hand over his face. "They have this huge grey dog, some sort of mastiff. It's very shy. Greg likes to scare it, makes him feel like a big man, I guess. The dog growled back, so Greg punched the daylights out of it. Stewart... he's passed into that looking-glass world, where it's not abuse because you deserve it, because you aren't as good as when they first loved you. And if you try just a little harder, dance around the landmines just a bit faster, throw the last sorry remains of yourself onto the black altar of your relationship, then you might magically win his affection back, like you had in those first happy days before you screwed everything up."

Evie stands stock still, gripping her handbag to her chest, as Misha pauses, chewing his bottom lip, momentarily lost in thought. He's not looking at her, but she knows he sees her.

"I did what I was paid to do," Misha says. "But I also... I also tried to make Stewart feel good about himself. Realize he was worthy of love, just as he was. He's a really good person, Evie."

"He seemed like it," Evie says.

Misha looks down, his voice quiet and rough. "I want you to remember something, Evie. I break up marriages for money." He moves his hands from his lap to rest on either side of his hips, gripping the edge of the desk. The action tenses the muscles in his arms and shoulders, and Evie is once again all too conscious of the 200-odd pounds of solid bulk that makes up his body; of the ruthless, practiced efficiency with which he had taken down the two bodyguards the previous night. He looks up at her, his eyes twin chips of Arctic ice. "But I ruin abusers for free."

Evie stares at him, frozen, like a rabbit caught by a hawk. Questions crowd her head, but before she can sort through the tangle of her thoughts to get one out, the dull trill of the office phone cuts through the room.

Misha stands up. He's still tense, and he turns to the ringing phone on his desk just as it stops. He stares at it for a moment, then turns back to Evie. He holds out her contract. "Here. Let me know what you decide by the end of the day."

Evie takes it just as the door opens.

Gemma sticks her head in. "Misha? It's Octavia Mortimer again," she says.

Misha waves her off. "I'll take it." Then he looks at Evie, standing awkwardly near the chaise longue, and motions for her to leave his office.

Evie goes out. As she shuts the door behind her, she hears Misha growl into the phone, "Yes, I will take care of it for good. Tonight."

THERE'S NOT MUCH to do, beyond helping Gemma out. Evie grabs the nearest stack of papers and sorts through it. Gemma's set up piles along the wall behind the reception desk: one for expense reports, another for papers to file, a third for papers to shred. As they work side by side to tidy the reception area, Gemma says quietly, "Did he give you the speech?"

"Yeah," Evie says. She's staring at the stack of papers to be shredded, wishing Gemma wasn't there so she could stop pretending she wasn't desperately interested in what was on them.

"You going to take the job?"

"Yeah, I think I will," Evie says. "It's good money, and I really need it." She picks up a blank envelope with the logo of a luxury hotel on it. In it is a receipt for a two-night stay; each night cost more than her monthly rent. She drops it on the expense report pile. "This is gonna sound weird, but you seem too good to be working in a place like this. Like, I see you at some big investment bank or something."

Gemma falls silent. "I was at one of the banks downtown," she says quietly. "For five years. I decided I wanted to work somewhere smaller, where I wasn't so... disposable."

"Yeah, no wonder he hired you, like, immediately," Evie says. "I mean, I almost turned around and walked out again when I saw you there at the interview."

She doesn't expect Gemma's bright bark of laughter. "I thought I tanked it. It was my first interview since my old job and... I don't know, I just started *talking* about it to him. I left the bank because... something happened, and... oh God, I was just saying all this stuff, *bad stuff*, about my old employer." She stops herself, shaking her head. "He hired me anyway."

"If it's any consolation I said a bunch of dumb stuff too," Evie says. "He's scary good at getting people to open up. I have a journalism degree and I'm mad about how skilled he is at it."

"Well, at least we know his weakness," Gemma snorts. "He sucks at filing."

"I resemble that remark," Misha says, coming out of his office. He leans against the door jamb, fists shoved into the pockets of his skinny jeans. "And you're absolutely right. When I'm not here in the mornings, you can start on the piles in my office, too. Same thing." Then he blinks, and looks down to where Evie is kneeling in front of her and Gemma's paperwork triage unit. "So, uh," Misha says, suddenly shy. "You're staying?"

"I think so," Evie says, getting to her feet and cautiously approaching the contract where she'd left it on the sofa. "The first month is basically probation, right?"

"Yes. You can leave without notice if you hate it here. Both of you can. Which is," and Misha raises his eyebrows in considered assessment, "quite likely. Especially as we're in in the middle of one of the ugliest cases we've had in years. I hate to say it, but the business of breaking people up is usually far more mundane."

Evie digs a pen out of her bag and, before she can overthink it, signs the contract. *Evangeline M. Cross*. "Let me guess. This goes back to Abigail?"

Misha nods, then he smiles, quiet and genuine. "Welcome to Heartbreak Incorporated, Evie."

"Thank you," she replies.

He wipes a hand down his face. "Now, speaking of ugly, Greg Pickford is on his way to pick up his photos. This has the potential to become very unpleasant, so I need to ask you a favor." He reaches into his back pocket for his wallet, pulls out $100 and holds it out it to Gemma, who stares at it in surprise. "Take a long lunch. Don't come back until 2:30."

He hands another $100 to Evie. "Go buy a photo envelope like the one I brought in this morning. Fill it with about twenty-five sheets of blank photo paper and seal it shut. There's an office supply store—"

"—over towards Grand Central, yeah, I know," Evie finishes. "When do you want me back?"

"I need you to drop the envelope off here. Write *Pickford* on it, and leave it on the corner of the reception desk. Do not come into my office under any circumstances, no matter what you hear. Then," he says, producing another $100 and giving it to her, "you go to lunch too."

Evie takes the bill, and immediately Misha's hand goes to rub his eyes. He doesn't look like he's in any shape to remain standing, much less deal with Greg Pickford. Evie's stomach roils in unhappiness at the memory of the thick, nasty brute from the party at the Met, the way his heavy hands liked to curl into fists. "Do you want me to get you some coffee before I go? Or bring you back something for lunch?" she asks.

Misha shakes his head. A small, predatory smile tugs at the corners of his mouth, and his eyes are the colorless grey of a winter sky before a storm. "No need. I'm getting delivery."

CHAPTER FOUR

EVIE IS ACROSS the street from the office, her purchases tucked under her arm, when she sees Greg and Erin Pickford step out of an Escalade.

She runs.

Greg is talking on the phone. He's in a grey double-breasted suit that's two shades too pale for him, accentuating his ruddy complexion, and he's toting a hard-sided metal briefcase in his free hand. Mint-green tie; Windsor knot. Erin crosses her arms and seems to be mentally urging Greg to finish his call so they can get this over with. She's in wide-legged white trousers, a navy wrap cardigan and red boots, with a little matching handbag dangling off her wrist. Neither Erin nor Greg notice Evie's messy curls and clearance-sale flats as she slips past.

Evie hurries inside the building and sprints towards the elevators, elbowing her way upstream through the bodies pouring out on their lunch breaks, ignoring the nasty looks she gets. There's an elevator about to close and if she can just slip inside it, she'll beat the Pickfords up to Misha's office by a couple minutes at least.

As Evie flat-out runs up to the elevator, she notices it's not empty: there's a stout middle-aged man in a suit inside, occupying as much space as he can. As the doors begin to close she can see the frown on his face, and the way his right arm is jabbing the "close" button. She jams her leg into the narrowing gap of the doors. They slide open again with an unhappy chime, and Evie smiles her sweetest smile at the man in the suit as she steps inside. He harrumphs under his breath. Evie can feel his eyes on her, disapproving, as she presses the button for Misha's floor and then roots around in her shopping bag. She tears open the box of photo paper and the lid comes fully off, cascading paper onto the floor. As she curses under her breath and kneels down to pick up the spilled pages, she can feel the man's displeasure turning glacial, his hooded glare reflected back at her from a thousand incidental shiny surfaces in the elevator. Something in her mind tugs at her. She remembers him, dully. She glances up: he's going to the twenty-ninth floor, which is one of the law firm's floors.

As Evie scoops the rest of the paper back into her carrier bag, she catches sight of a long black smudge on her skirt, left there by the elevator doors. She straightens up, uncomfortably aware of the mark, and of the cooling sweat stains under her armpits from her crosstown dash, and all she can think about is Erin Pickford's white silk trousers, pristine as new snow in the middle of the city's dirt.

The elevator chimes as it stops at her floor. As the doors open Evie starts to smile appeasingly at the lawyer, in the way that women are taught to do in the presence of powerful men, and suddenly, fiercely, she hates that everything is so much easier for people like him, and people like the Pickfords, and how, worst of all, she's expected to be polite about it to keep their favor. Be nice and smile, or you might not get a tip, get a permanent job, get the crumbs you need to survive. So she does smile at the nasty man in his suit, but it's a thing of teeth, and she trails her hand down all the buttons between his floor and hers, lighting them up.

Evie rushes into the reception of Meserov & Co and wordlessly holds up the office supply store bag. Gemma is still out, but Misha is leaning against the doorway of his office, distinctly nervous. "They're on their way up right now," Evie huffs, still catching her breath.

Misha nods. "Good job," he says. "The envelope?"

"Doing it," Evie says. She sits down in Gemma's chair and pulls out the paper and the cardboard envelope, swiftly assembling a dummy package of blank photos under Misha's instruction. She labels it discreetly in her messy, all-caps handwriting, *PICKFORD*, and then glances up at Misha to ask what she should do next.

He is still leaning against the doorway of his office, his gaze unfocused, lost in thought. He looks like he's being sent to his own funeral. No, worse, Evie thinks: he looks like he's halfway into the casket. His eyes are darkly circled with exhaustion, the hollows under his sharp cheekbones more pronounced than ever.

"Misha?" she says. It's unsettling her, seeing this crack in his polished exterior. A tendril of fear uncoils within her, that he may not be strong enough to get through this.

He blinks, and looks down at her, as if just noticing her. "You should go, Evie," he says quietly. He reaches forwards to take the envelope and stumbles, his legs failing to support his weight.

Evie is half out of her chair—she has no idea what she's going to do, he's way too heavy for her to support—when he catches himself on the edge of the reception desk and leans there, eyes squeezed shut.

"Are you—" she starts.

"I'm fine," he grits out. His face is hidden by a curtain of dark hair.

"You're not fine," Evie says. "You look like you fell face-first out of an Aubrey Beardsley drawing. Are you sick? Should we tell the Pickfords to come back tomorrow?"

"No," Misha snarls, flicking his hair out of his eyes. Evie flinches in shock, and Misha softens almost immediately, an unspoken apology swimming in his pale eyes. "It's nothing. Just a dizzy spell," he says. "I'll be all right soon." He reaches out to touch her forearm, or at least she thinks that's his goal, but he stops, his hand inches from hers. Instead, he taps the surface of the desk, twice, with a knuckle as he averts his gaze. "I'll be in my office."

He pushes off from the desk and shuffles into the other room, his shoulder brushing against the doorway. If Evie didn't know how gracefully he usually moved, she'd think nothing was wrong.

But no, something was definitely off. She figures she'll give him a last minute or two of privacy before the Pickfords arrive, and she starts to pull the double doors to his office closed.

Just as the doors are about to shut, Misha says her name. She stops, and looks into the office. He's sitting on his desk, head bowed like a penitent schoolboy.

He runs a hand through his hair. There's nothing but awkward silence for a moment, as he stares down at his half-laced boots. "Evie," he says, finally, hesitation softening his voice to barely above a whisper. "I'm sorry. I'm not fine. But I will be. Trust me. I'm sorry. You were…" He makes a vague gesture with his hand and looks away, still unable to meet her eyes. "It's very kind of you, to care. I'm not used to it."

Evie tries to think of something better to say than *okay*. But all the easy words have fled, and ones left behind are too clumsy, too likely to shatter an already fragile moment. She takes the route of all cowards and turns it into a joke. "Don't be vulnerable. It freaks me out." The jest sits hollow in her. She swallows. "I'm staying," she adds.

Misha rolls his eyes, but before he can editorialize on Evie's choices there's the sound of footsteps approaching down the hallway: the heavy and purposeful tread of a man in dress shoes, and the staccato clip of a woman in heels.

Greg and Erin Pickford breeze in past Evie, not even acknowledging her existence, and march straight into Misha's office. Misha glances down at the metal briefcase Greg is carrying, then indicates he should put it on the desk next to him.

It all happens so quickly. The scent of Greg's aftershave, the breeze of their passage, doesn't even hit Evie until after the doors to Misha's office click closed behind them.

Evie hears the *klak* of the briefcase being opened, and the harsh twang of Greg's voice. "All there."

She backs up Gemma's chair against the wall dividing the reception area from Misha's office, hoping she can eavesdrop on what is being said. She tells herself it's important, it's for the article, but she can't quite bury the fact that she's worried about

Misha. Even if he can find the energy to fight, Greg Pickford is not a problem Misha can punch his way out of. There are consequences for striking a man that powerful.

Just as she sidles her chair up to the wall, her phone trills with a series of incoming text messages. Evie swears under her breath and throws herself across the office to her handbag, forgotten on the sofa, scattering its contents in order to grab her phone and put it onto silent mode. Six messages from Claudia. She'll deal with them later.

When Evie gets back to her listening post, still clutching her phone, there's nothing but silence from inside the office. Her heart beats double-time: did they hear her? Do they somehow know what she's doing? What has she missed?

She would never characterize Greg Pickford's voice as calming, but she sighs with relief on hearing his low chuckle and a teasing, "Do you want to see, Erin?"

She thumbs open Voice Memos and starts recording, holding the microphone end of her cell to the wall.

His sister snorts derisively, and says, "Pass."

Misha's voice, soft and low, carries the least well, but she can just make out his words: "Once you're done looking through them, my assistant will provide you with your copies. These stay in my safe until the case is over."

There's nothing but silence, then Greg's drawl, self-assured and patrician. As if their family had sprung up fully formed in an Upper East Side mansion, rather than a tatty South Jersey development. "I can't believe I hired a rent boy to seduce my husband."

"I'm not a rent boy," Misha says, his tone the sort of glacial, deceptive calm that lures the unwary out further, to where the ice is thin.

Erin's waspish sigh cuts through the tension. "What was the alternative, Greg? Give that little shit half of womenswear? Womenswear is *mine*. Daddy *said* if the sales fell again this year I could have it."

"And you shall," Greg hums.

"Ugh, let's *go*," Erin says.

"You go," says Greg, distractedly. "There's something else I want."

Evie startles hard as the door to Misha's office opens. She only just turns around and pretends to be busy at Gemma's desk in time. Her phone's in her lap, still recording, and she prays Erin doesn't notice her, doesn't look down.

Erin pauses in the doorway and sniffs at Misha, "Thank you for your... *services*." The derision-filled emphasis on the final word is not lost on anyone. Evie's ears burn with it. She will bury this woman. She will claw herself into the journalism career she's always wanted, *specifically* to burn Erin Pickford to the ground.

Erin turns to Evie and glares at her, and for a moment Evie is gripped by terror, convinced Erin can see right through her. But then Erin extends one manicured hand towards the cardboard envelope Evie prepared and says, "I'll take those." When Evie doesn't comply fast enough, she snaps her fingers at Evie, like she was a dog. "Now-now."

"I, I can't," Evie stutters. "I'm not allowed." She takes the envelope of fake, blank photos and puts it in her lap, hiding her phone. "I'm new, I just started, and Misha said to only give them to Greg Pickford and I don't want to get in trouble—"

"I'm his *sister*," Erin sneers. "Give them to me."

Evie hunches her shoulders and tries to look cowed. She's pretty sure that whatever Misha's plan is, this isn't it. "Um, if Misha says it's okay?"

Erin flips her hair in annoyance and marches back into Misha's office. Evie palms her phone into her pocket then peeks in too, hoping Misha can give her some sort of signal what to do.

It takes both women a few seconds to process what they're seeing. Greg has crowded up against Misha on the desk, standing in the V of Misha's legs. He has a fat roll of money in one hand, and the other, the right one, the one with the big signet ring that marked up Stewart's face, is on Misha's upper thigh. His brutish lips are close to Misha's ear, and he's purring, "Let's just say I'm jealous. This enough?"

"For what?" Misha says, batting his eyelashes in coy, if false, innocence. He's leaning back, abs taut, forcing Greg off balance over him. Greg doesn't seem to care and just leans in closer.

His hand moves further up Misha's thigh. His voice is thick with lust as he leans in to brush his mouth against Misha's ear. "For what Stewart got."

"Ew, Greg," Erin says, stepping backwards and shutting the door. "*Ugh.*" She curls her lip into what would be quite a sour expression, if the Botox allowed her to have those. Then she glances down at Evie, who is clutching the photo envelope to her chest so hard her knuckles are white.

Something crashes to the ground inside Misha's office, and there's a laugh, low and wicked.

Erin shivers and yanks a phone out of her little red handbag. She starts texting one-handed, walking out of the office without another word.

Once Evie's heart stops trying to thunder out of her chest, she places the decoy photo envelope back on her desk and checks her phone. After a moment's hesitation, she stops the recording. There's another sound from inside the office, the dull thud of a body being pushed heavily against furniture. Evie glances around for a weapon and there's nothing, not even a pair of scissors in the desk drawers.

Greg saw her when he came in. He wouldn't assault Misha with her right outside as a witness, would he? But then... *did* he see her? Or were people like her just invisible to people like him?

Then there's a long, low moan, and Greg's voice, raspy with pleasure, hissing, "Oh, *fuck.*"

And Misha... Misha laughs.

Suddenly, Evie understands why he didn't want her to stay. She fidgets, deeply uncomfortable, and weirdly aroused.

"Jesus Christ," Greg grunts.

Red with embarrassment, Evie grabs her bag and flees.

* * *

Evie sits at the rickety little two-person table in the floor's shared kitchenette and cradles her head in her hands. She feels like an idiot for freaking out. Misha told her this wasn't a normal job. And he told her he was going to do something to Greg Pickford. But all she can hear is the sound of Greg shoving Misha into his desk. It brings back dozens of shady experiences she's had: drunk boys in college leaning all their weight on her, not stopping when she wanted to stop; guys grabbing her at parties or saying gross things to her and then telling her that it's her fault for not being able to take a joke.

Misha said he could take care of himself.

She pinches the bridge of her nose, trying to pull herself back into the present moment. She listens to the hum of the refrigerator, the rumble of the air conditioning.

And then, out of the corner of her eye, she catches a flash of movement, an obscuration of the light from the hallway. Evie tenses and looks up.

It's the same middle-aged white woman from Friday, the one whose sushi Evie had stolen. Her brown hair is up in a sensible twist, and she's in office-casual gear of a long striped shirt and an even longer black cardigan. Her eyes are wide and startled.

"Um—" Evie says.

"Uh, I'll come back," the woman mutters, glancing down at the mug she has clutched in one hand.

"No," Evie says, half-standing. "Hey, I'm sorry. About Friday." She digs into her handbag and pulls out a leftover $20 bill from the money Misha gave her. "Here," she says, holding it out to the woman. "For the sushi."

The woman hesitates, her demeanor relaxing. Rather than reaching out to take Evie's money, she laces her free hand around her coffee mug. "Could you really... not afford lunch?"

"Lots of people can't," Evie replies gently. "People in this building." She smiles, and wiggles the $20. "But today I can. So here."

The woman smiles back. "Keep it." She walks over to the coffeemaker on the counter and fishes a key out of her pocket.

As she unlocks a cabinet over the Keurig machine, she asks, "Want a coffee?"

"You buying?" Evie says, unable to keep the teasing note out of her voice.

The woman laughs. "I'm Diane. I work at the architects, down the hall." She pulls down a box of Keurig pods from the cabinet and offers them to Evie.

"I'm Evie. I just started at the... little consultancy. Meserov." She grabs a French Vanilla pod out of the box.

"Well, welcome to the seventeenth floor," Diane says. She replaces the coffee box and takes a bag of jasmine tea out of another box. Then she opens one of the other kitchen cabinets, this one without a lock. "There are a whole bunch of random mugs in here anyone can use," she explains. "Just put them in the dishwasher when you're done. The janitor runs it overnight." She goes through the small, domestic motions of making hot water, and then coffee, in the machine. The everyday sounds—the bubble and hiss of the water, the clinking of the mugs—come as a balm to Evie, sloughing the tension of the morning off her shoulders. "Meserov," Diane says. "Is that where... the guy..." She places Evie's mug on the table in front of her.

"Uh-huh," Evie says. "That guy."

"Okay," Diane says. She tosses her wet teabag into the trash.

"Yeah." Evie pulls out her phone, guilty. She should probably check how *that guy* is doing. "Thanks for the coffee."

Diane raises her own mug in quiet salute and then departs, back to work.

Evie dashes off a quick text to Misha—*you okay? I'm around the corner, in the kitchen*—then scrolls through all her missed texts from Claudia. It's mostly cute memes of congratulations, plus the inevitable *so how's day one with your super-hot new boss?* and then a final text that's just every remotely rude emoji there is and a few that become rude simply by proximity to others. She sips her coffee black, typical watery Keurig stuff but fine for an early-afternoon drink, and texts Claudia back: *this is either the best job or the worst job I've ever had and I'm not sure which yet* and *it's not boring tho*. Claudia likes the message almost instantly. Her inevitable *lol* reply causes a big smile to spread across Evie's face, and she realizes, in that moment, that somehow, despite everything, she's happy.

She decides to get her chores out of the way while the feeling persists. The audio on her recording isn't great, but it's still clear enough to hear with the volume up. She sends it to Nicole, with the short message, *here's your proof*. Then, because she's not convinced Nicole will actually listen to the recording, she adds, *Greg confesses to hiring someone to seduce his husband. Erin to taking over womenswear.*

The dancing dots of a message being composed come swiftly. Then, from Nicole: *Her designs suck tho*. A second text follows: *So we need to interview her, Greg and ??*

Evie thinks. *And Daddy Pickford. And Stewart if we can. Plus a few people who used to work for them.*

I'm serious tho, we need to bury this around at least two other cases from this breakup agency to get it published, Nicole responds.

Im working on it, Evie types back, bitter. She expected a "thank you" after handing over actual recorded proof to Nicole, not a "why haven't you done more?" *Do u know where Greg lives? I need to figure out who their vet is.*

West Village somewhere, Nicole texts back. *Why vet?*

Someone clears their throat from behind her and Evie startles, cursing herself for getting so annoyed with Nicole she wasn't being aware of her surroundings.

"All clear," Misha says. He's lounging in the kitchenette doorway, thumbs hooked into the pockets of his black skinny jeans, dragging the already low waistband so it hangs under the sharp points of his hips. His hair is a mess, out of its tie and cascading around his face. But the most surprising thing is, not only are there no signs of abuse, but he somehow looks much fresher, less exhausted. The circles under his eyes are gone.

Evie grabs her bag and her coffee and gets up. "Are you all right?"

Misha snorts, falling into step next to her as they head back to the office. "Disgusted with myself and fighting the urge to bathe in bleach, but other than that, Miss Cross, everything is delightful."

"Okay. I was worried," Evie admits.

Misha sighs. "Told you I can take care of myself."

"Sure," Evie says. "Your shirt's inside out."

Some people have beautiful smiles. Misha doesn't; the goofy grin that spreads over his face is too wide, too gummy. It dissolves the fine perfection of his features into something else, something young and honest and carefree. He isn't handsome in that moment, but he is profoundly attractive. "I can *mostly* take care of myself," he amends.

Evie realizes she's grinning back at him, her heart all but glowing in her chest. The urge to reach out and touch him— bump his shoulder, poke him in the side to see if he's ticklish— is overwhelming. Evie has to dig her nails into her palm to stop herself. She falls back a step as Misha unlocks the office and tries to deal with this new, awful thing her feelings have gone and done without her permission. He's *her boss* and having a crush on the person who is, one, wildly out of her league, and two, a professional seducer, is, in her heart's long history of terrible ideas, very possibly the worst yet. Plus, whatever the fallout is from her article, it's not likely to end up with them remaining friends.

He wanders into his office, which is as much of a wreck as Evie thought it would be, the floor a mess of papers and bundled $100 bills fallen out of the briefcase Greg Pickford had brought. "I'm going to take this cash to the bank and then go to the gym and shower," he says as he picks up the briefcase from where it lies upended on the floor. "Then I'll introduce you to the Tweedles."

"The who?" Evie says. She realizes she's trailed after him like some sort of lovestruck duckling, so she starts gathering up bundles of money to make it look like she had some purpose in following him.

"The law partners I work with," Misha says. He clucks his tongue as his foot dislodges the rolled-up wad of bills Greg had given him for *extra services* from its resting place half under the desk. "They can be... hm, how to say it? Hard work," he continues, bending down to pick up the roll. "I'd prefer to shield Gemma from them for now, if you don't mind. She deserves a break from terrible bosses."

"No, sure, that's fine," Evie says. "What happened with her?"

"Not my story to tell," Misha replies. He closes the briefcase. "I'll be about an hour."

"Uh, shirt," Evie reminds him.

"Shit, yes," he says. He grabs the hem of his shirt and just... strips it off, right in front of her.

Evie lets out a choked-off squawk of surprise and turns her back, the blush hitting her cheeks like a slap. She squeezes her eyes shut.

"Sorry... I..." Misha says. "I'm dressed again, you can..."

Evie opens one eye and slowly turns around. Misha has backed away. Holds his hands up, palms facing her in a gesture of surrender.

"Evie, I'm sorry," he says. "I didn't think."

She glances away, because if she tries to look at him she's going to stare at his abs. "It's fine."

"It's not fine," Misha replies. "I know that..." He presses the heels of his hands over his eyes and huffs in frustration. "I know that other people's bodies aren't public property. I just sometimes forget mine isn't, too."

"I get it," Evie says. "It really is fine. Besides, like you said, I'm going to see photos of it. I mean, you. Just... give a girl some warning next time."

"It won't happen again, I promise," Misha says, solemn. "I'm not used to having people around. It will do me good to curb my bachelor habits." He grabs the briefcase of money off his desk.

"Want me to tidy up in here?" Evie asks.

He looks around his disaster of an office, as if seeing it for the first time. He sighs, and wipes a hand down his face. "Do it tomorrow morning. It'll keep." Then a smile quirks at the corners of his lips. "Oh no," he says. "Greg forgot his photos."

Misha points at the reception desk. The decoy envelope of photos is still sitting in pride of place where Evie left it, on the chair.

"What do I do if he comes back for it while you're gone?" Evie says. She does not want to have to deal with a furious Greg Pickford by herself.

Misha smiles. It's his wolf's smile, the one that doesn't reach his eyes. "I wouldn't worry about that, if I were you." He throws her a rakish salute, and leaves.

Evie stands in the quiet, empty office for less than a minute before she decides that, whatever Misha says, discretion is the better part of valor and she should lock the front door against Greg returning. She peeks outside and sees Gemma hurrying down the hall, a carrier bag bumping against her leg, so she waits until the other girl is inside before shutting the door and throwing the latch.

"What's wrong?" Gemma asks. "Where's Misha?"

"Everything's fine," Evie says. "Misha ran to the gym. But Greg Pickford left his photos here, and I kinda don't want him to come get them while we're here by ourselves."

"Oh," says Gemma. "Is he...?"

"Not the sort of guy who takes no for an answer. About anything," Evie says.

Gemma nods. "Let's keep the door locked, then." She goes to sit down in her chair and sees the envelope there. "Are these..?" she asks.

"No, those are nothing. You can chuck that in the trash," Evie says.

"Okay. Oh, I ordered a shredder while I was out," Gemma says. She tosses the envelope in the trash and then sits down and starts taking her shoes off. "It'll be here end of the week and then we can start to get rid of all these old papers." She reaches into her carrier bag and pulls out a pink rectangle. "And we have message pads now. Also, I got these," she smiles shyly, holding up a soft-looking pair of ballet slippers for Evie to see. "I was so jealous when I saw you in flats. We weren't really allowed to wear them at my old job."

Evie realizes, despite herself, that she actually likes Gemma. "Want help filing?" she asks.

"No, let's leave that for now." Gemma holds up a fat folder of receipts. "I thought I'd spend the afternoon figuring out how to do the expense reports and then take them up to Meyer, Luchins & Black. He must have two years' worth that he hasn't turned in."

"Ugh, why are boys," Evie mutters, as she grabs a stack of papers anyway. With luck, something in it will help her satisfy Nicole's demands for a broader story focus.

MISHA SLINKS IN an hour later like some sort of off-duty and way-too-tall ballet dancer, in a sailor-striped long-sleeve tee and slim black dropped-crotch sweatpants, his hair freshly washed and twisted up. Nobody should be able to look that good. There's no trace of the morning's exhaustion on him; he positively glows now. Evie is torn between staring at him to verify that he is real, and looking away, because his is a sort of loveliness so sharp that it hurts.

It makes her feel better to see that Gemma's temporarily lost the power of speech, too.

Misha tosses a small duffel bag into his office then leans over and taps Evie on the shoulder. She just about jumps out of her skin.

"Come on. Let's take you up to meet Don and Dee, and then we'll have all the unpleasant things done before tea-time," he says. "Bring your contract." He walks out, assuming Evie will follow.

She does.

The elevator, when they reach it, is too small. Of course, it's the same size elevator it's always been, the one that brought her up to the seventeenth floor this morning, and back down at lunch. There had been enough room in it when she shared it with the stuffy, disapproving lawyer coming up again with her shopping. But there is not enough room in it now. Not with Misha leaning against the center of its back wall, hands spread out against the chrome rail. Evie has squashed herself in next to the buttons. She still can't escape the subtle smell of him, old leather and limes and juniper.

And he's *singing*.

It's soft; she can barely hear it, but Misha is gazing up at the ceiling and singing to himself, his quiet baritone shaping words in a language she doesn't recognize. The fingers of his left hand tap a simple rhythm on the rail.

She almost leaps out of the elevator when they reach the twenty-sixth floor.

If Misha notices her discomfort, he is too polite to say anything. He steps ahead of her and opens the door to HR, holding it for her with a courtly little bow. She wants to tell him to stop it, stop the manners and the singing and the strange vulnerability and everything else. But instead she just mutters *thanks* and steps inside.

Abigail smiles up at them when they appear outside her office. She beckons them in, and shoots Misha a knowing look. "You're cheerful, Misha. What have you done?"

Misha exaggerates a feigned, wounded innocence. "Moi?" he drawls.

Abigail rolls her eyes at him in response. She switches her attention to Evie. "He didn't manage to scare you off in the first day, then?"

"He tried," Evie says. She looks over at Misha, who is still pretending to be the paragon of blue-eyed virtue. "A for effort," she says.

Misha snorts and covers his mouth, giggling like a schoolboy.

Abigail sighs and puts her hand out, wordlessly asking for Evie's papers. "Don't encourage him," she mouths. Then, as she checks Evie's contract and the NDA for signatures, she says, "I'm glad you two seem to be getting along. You taking her to meet the Tweedles?"

Misha nods.

Abigail lets out a long exhale, and her look is serious when she turns back to Evie. "They are very important, profitable partners in the firm," she says, narrowing her eyes. Then her mouth pulls into a small smile. "You almost ended up working for Don, last year."

"Ugh," Misha says. "You dodged a bullet. He goes through assistants like tissue paper."

"Out!" Abigail orders, making shooing motions at him. "No disparaging of the firm's employees in this office unless you're here to report something."

"Thanks, Abi. I owe you," says Misha, turning to go.

"I'll add it to your considerable tab," Abigail grumbles, tapping at her computer. "And stop being so cheerful. It's disconcerting."

Misha cackles, putting his hand on Evie's shoulder blade to guide her out of the office.

They head up to the twenty-ninth floor. Evie is at first thankful they're not alone in the elevator this time, but then as more and more people get in, she is increasingly wedged into Misha's space. There's still breathing room, though, or at least there is until a red-headed man squeezes himself in through the closing doors. He's got a full backpack slung over his shoulders and he's utterly unaware of how much space it takes up behind him, which is made clear when he turns and nearly smacks Evie with it.

She lets out a startled curse and tries to step backwards, but there's no space, she stumbles—

—Misha's hand whips out and stops the backpack before it connects with her face.

She hasn't quite fallen into Misha, but it's a close-run thing, and she can feel the warmth of his body on her cheek, the clean cotton smell of his shirt. And she sees the shift of lean muscle in his arm as he wrenches the backpack half off the man's shoulder.

"Hey," the guy says, bumping into the woman next to him as he shifts to glare at Misha.

"Your bag," Misha says, his voice icy. "You nearly hit the lady with it. Take it off your shoulder."

The man opens his mouth to argue, masking his embarrassment at being called out in public by pivoting swiftly to rage.

Misha leans forwards, into his space, and twists the strap of the backpack still in his hand. Evie thinks she hears fabric rip. "Or I will," he says, quietly.

Evie stares at the floor, sending up silent prayers to whoever is listening that Misha doesn't get into a fight in the crowded elevator. She knows empirically that Misha is trying to be kind, that it's just a misplaced protectiveness, but the way he goes about it is so old-fashioned that it feels patronizing.

The man mutters something to himself, sniffs, and slides the backpack off his shoulder.

Evie exhales in relief.

The doors open on the twenty-ninth floor and she squeezes out into the blessedly uncrowded space of the elevator lobby. She glances back to check that Misha is following her, in perfect time to see him blatantly shoulder-check the ginger with the backpack as he exits. The door closes on the guy's angry protestations.

"Misha," she mutters as he swipes an ID card at the floor's glass entrance doors, the firm name painted across them in a tidy copperplate. "I know you meant..." She sighs and tries again. "You don't have to do that."

Head tilt. "Why not?"

"Because you're not the only one who can take care of themself."

"He was much bigger than you," Misha replies. He moves forward, and holds the door for her. His lips twitch in amusement. "And you lacked your trusty champagne bottle."

"Yes, but if you hadn't barged in like that, I could have stepped on his feet on the way out," Evie says.

A smile spreads over Misha's face like sunshine as they wind their way through the law firm's corridors. "Miss Cross, you are incorrigible."

"Says the man who almost started a fight in an elevator," Evie says.

"Would have won it, too," he says idly. He stops at a corner office, its door shut, and addresses the harried-looking middle-aged woman whose open-plan desk is closest to it. "He in?"

She nods and reaches for her phone. "Who shall I say is…?" Her words tail off in shock as Misha opens the door and walks inside. "You can't—"

Evie dutifully follows.

"Don," Misha says. "I wanted to introduce you to—"

Evie freezes. She knows the portly man in the suit glaring at her from behind his desk. She'd run into him that very day. In the elevator, on her way up ahead of the Pickfords. "Uh, we've already met," she says.

Misha raises an eyebrow at her.

"I should have known this one was working for you," Don Kieselstein says. "She has your manners."

"My manners are delightful," Misha responds.

"Hi, Evie Cross," Evie says, holding out her hand. "I'm sorry about earlier. I was really stressed."

Rather than reaching out to shake her hand, the man smooths down his Hermès tie and switches his attention to Misha. "What's going on with the Pickfords? You done with that yet?"

Evie retracts her arm, feeling like an idiot.

Misha ignores him. "Evie, this is Don Kieselstein. He and his cousin Dee handle most of the divorce cases at the firm. While we don't work directly for them, they do send us a lot of clients." Then, to Don, he says, "Evie will be acting as an intermediary and helping you and Dee get documents or status reports when I'm not available."

Don grunts in her general direction, but his attention stays on Misha. "I want a status report on the Pickfords."

"Ah," Misha says. "Yes, that's all finished. Greg even came to pick up his photos earlier, but we got to talking and he left them in the office."

"Bring them here. He's coming in Wednesday morning to

finalize our counter-offer to his husband's counsel."

"Don, you know I don't do that," Misha says. "Now that you've met Evie, I'll send her up with them. When's the appointment?"

Don leans to the side and bellows past them. "Patricia! When am I seeing the Pickfords?"

The secretary sticks her head around the door. "10am on Wednesday, Mr Kieselstein."

Misha twists his mouth into something approximating a smile. "I'll send her up at 10:05, then."

"You better have done a good job, Meserov," Don says as he ushers Evie out.

"I always do," Misha parries back.

The other Family Law partner, Don's cousin Dee, is in a meeting, so they put off that introduction until tomorrow. As they head back down to Misha's office, he whispers, "What did you do to Don?"

"He tried to shut the elevator doors on me when I was running to beat the Pickfords up to the office. So when I left, I lit up every floor between ours and his," Evie admits.

"You're a menace," Misha hums, amused. "But I've no doubt Don deserved every bit of it and more."

It's almost 5pm when they get back to the seventeenth floor. Misha saunters into his office, leans down and plucks a file unerringly out of the disaster zone on the floor. He waves it at Gemma. "Tonight, I will get Octavia Mortimer to stop calling us, *finally*."

"How did you know she rang back again?" Gemma says, holding out a pink missed-call note to Misha.

He shakes his head, exasperated, as he takes the note from Gemma. "Lucky guess. She is exceptionally high-maintenance." He dials the phone in his office, punching the keys as if they'd personally offended him. But when he speaks into the receiver his voice is a teasing mix of silk and steel, as if he had been looking forward to nothing more all day than speaking to his difficult client. "Yes, Octavia. The plan is still the plan. No, I would love to see you tomorrow. We can wrap things up." He smiles at something Octavia says, then responds, "I am quite sure of myself. But I never lose. Not at this game." He arranges for her to come in the next morning, and only manages to end the call by reminding Octavia several times that if he is to do his work for her tonight, he has to leave immediately. When he hangs up, he runs his fingers through his hair and squeezes his eyes shut, visibly pulling himself together. "Some jobs," he grits out, "are just terrible people all the way down, and hers is one of them."

He grabs his gym bag and another folder from the mess on the floor, and as he leaves the office, he hands the second folder to Evie. "I'm running late. Can you do me a favor and burn these? Lighter's in the top desk drawer, and I disabled the smoke detector years ago."

"Uh, sure," says Evie. She takes the folder and glances inside, only to be confronted with an image of Stewart Pickford's face, contorted in ecstasy. She shuts the folder quickly, and for a moment, her eyes slide to where her handbag lies on the sofa.

"And please be assured I know exactly how much ash is produced by burning a dozen photos," Misha says, low and cool, only to her. "I normally use the metal bin under the desk. I suggest you do as well."

In that moment, Evie realizes she has greatly underestimated Misha Meserov. That, like the silences in conversations he leaves as traps for the unwary, his air of posh disorganization is merely there to obscure his strategic genius, like a pool shark playing at drunk, content to let his opponent get a few balls in the pocket before he casually runs the entire table.

"Wait!" Evie says. "Are there any other copies? Won't we need these for Don's meeting?"

"Oh," says Misha. "Greg won't be at that meeting." He flashes a smile at her and Gemma. "Good first day, the both of you. See you tomorrow."

Evie tries to ignore the shiver of dread that trickles down her spine as he leaves.

CHAPTER FIVE

THE A TRAIN at rush hour is a nightmare. Evie gets a seat in a packed carriage near the front, squished between a woman with a half-dozen shopping bags and a man who is apathetically taking up all her legroom with one spread knee. She doesn't even pull out her phone. She just watches tired bodies sway to the atonal lullaby of the subway tracks.

When she shuts her eyes, she sees other bodies swaying in naked embrace, spread out across rumpled white sheets. Fingers entwined in the throes of passion on a sofa. A tender kiss in the dim lamplight of a cocktail bar, immortalized in a covert photograph. She had burned every one of them as directed, unable to look away as the flames twisted black streaks across Stewart and Misha's skin, until no evidence was left of their affection but a pile of ash.

And the three stolen images on Evie's camera roll.

Her phone seems to burn in her bag; she touches the ribbed edges of its case to reassure herself it's still there, but she doesn't dare look at it, at her crime. Not until she gets home.

As Evie hurtles through the darkness under Brooklyn, she flushes with shame at the deceptions she's used to get her story. Back in college, when everything was simple, she'd been a confident absolutist in class debates over ethics. The profession of journalism was one of bringing out reluctant truths. Lies from the reporter to sources were only permitted when lives were at stake; when the story was of profound or national importance.

This feature was profoundly important to nothing but her career. No lives were in danger; just reputations.

And theft... theft was so off-reservation they'd never even discussed it in class. Your sources, who knew you were a journalist, they brought you proof, if you could make it safe for them to do so. But then again, these hypothetical discussions of ethical dilemmas had always begun with a phrase like, "you are a reporter at a local TV station", or "you are on the city desk of a large newspaper". You have a job with a monthly salary and benefits, and an infrastructure that will shield you from any blowback your story creates.

You are a freelancer who is drowning in student debt from a degree which carefully prepared you for a profession that no longer exists. You are offered one last opportunity to break in, but it involves violating every principle you were taught. Do you take that shot in the dark? Or do you give up and become a normal, civilized person from 8 to 5, accept the snail's pace of working life, dutifully filling in the hours of your existence like a coloring book you've lost interest in but which still must be completed to get a passing grade at adulthood?

You are a foreign correspondent dispatched to report on the repressive, insular nation of the extremely wealthy. You believe that if you disclose your identity as a journalist, at best you will be permanently exiled to the refugee camps of the gig economy, and at worst your life will be at risk.

Evie stares out the window at the blur of Lafayette Avenue station as the express train thunders through it without stopping. Did she really think she was in danger?

Misha's tightly focused explosion of violence against the security guard at the Met; the controlled menace he'd exuded in the elevator; his casual assurance that he would ruin Greg Pickford.

Evie shivers. And, for the first time, she is truly afraid.

HALF AN HOUR later, she trudges up the four flights of stairs to the tiny apartment she and Claudia share on the top floor of a

Bed-Stuy brownstone. She has a six-pack of beer she bought at the corner bodega; it isn't the smartest use of her remaining lunch cash from Misha but she can't find it within herself to be sorry.

Claudia's sprawled on the two-person sofa that takes up most of the minuscule living room, poking at her phone. Evie grunts a hello as she stops briefly to shove a couple bottles of beer in the freezer before continuing into her room and collapsing on the twin bed. She wants to get out of her dress and tights and into something comfortable, but she has bigger concerns first.

She pulls out her phone and quickly sets up a cloud folder into which she moves her stolen photos and the covert recording. She sends a link to Nicole via text, deletes the evidence off her phone, and then, finally, she allows herself to relax.

"Are you dead?" Claudia calls out from the other room.

"Yes," Evie says. She dumps her phone on her dresser; she doesn't need to move to do it, the room's so small she can reach out and touch the opposite wall from where she's starfished on her mattress.

"Okay, so dead people don't need tacos, right?" Claudia says, sticking her head into Evie's room. "Because I'm ordering."

Evie slowly raises her hand off the bed, middle finger up.

"It's a miracle," gasps Claudia. "She lives!"

"I have money," Evie mumbles into her pillow.

"I have gossip," Claudia teases back.

Evie levers herself up onto one elbow, confused. She can't think of any mutual friends on the edge of scandal. "Is this your cousin again?"

"No! You know that rich guy from the party on Friday night? One of the family. Vodka martini, no tip."

"... Greg Pickford." Evie sits up all the way and starts to grab her phone, but realizes she doesn't need to.

"Yeah, that's the guy. He—" Claudia starts, before Evie says, "He's dead."

Claudia deflates. "Oh, you already heard."

"Not really," Evie says, as her stomach sinks within her like a stone. "Just a lucky guess. Tell me how it happened?"

Claudia sits down on the edge of the bed and begins to gesture excitedly. "Okay, so apparently? He was in his office yelling at someone on the phone and then his assistant heard this loud thud but she didn't go in because he's, like, super mean if his calls get interrupted? She finally gets up the courage to go in an hour later and there he was on the floor, all stiff and dead." She wakes up the screen on her phone and shows Evie the article. "He wasn't very old, just forty-eight, and they say he was dead from heart failure before he hit the ground, which, like, that poor secretary, at least she doesn't feel like it was her fault—"

"Uh, Claudia?" Evie interrupts. "I'm really sorry, I gotta make a phone call."

"Okay, be weird," Claudia says, pushing herself off the bed.

"There's beer in the fridge if you want some? I'll be out in a sec," Evie says. "And be nice to me, I'm a weirdo with a salary now." She reaches through her phone and starts scrolling through social media reports of Greg Pickford's death. There was the usual clutch of official hagiographies of An Impressive Man Gone Too Soon, and Stewart had posted on his Twitter account a simple, candid photo of Greg and a little broken-heart emoji. But elsewhere, the knives were already out: people who had been fired by Greg, or who he'd treated terribly at fashion shows or while travelling were recounting their stories. There's nothing more on his cause of death other than unexpected and catastrophic cardiovascular failure, no previous history of heart trouble.

She kicks her door shut (or as shut as it will get with her towel hanging over the top of it) and dials Nicole. It rings and rings, to the point that Evie thinks it's just going to go to voicemail, but then Nicole picks up.

"What," Nicole barks.

"Nicole, it's me, did you see—" Evie begins.

"Evie?" Nicole says. There's rustling in the background. "I can't talk now, I'm getting ready to go out."

"Call me tomorrow morning?" she asks. "It's really important. I think our story's just turned into a murder investigation."

The rustling stops. "What?" Nicole says. But before Evie can answer, there's the rough alarm of Nicole's door buzzer. "Shit, I'm not ready," Nicole whispers.

"Look at the folder I sent you—" Evie says, but she's not sure Nicole hears her. There's the muffled sound of swearing, and then a clatter as Nicole's phone slips out of her hands. The call drops.

Evie stares at the screen until it goes black. She wakes it up again, creates a new document in her folder, and starts to type out her suspicions. She hopes, by writing them down, she'll see how thin and inconsequential they are. But the more she types, the more she becomes convinced that Greg Pickford's death was no accident.

THE NEXT MORNING, Evie gets to Worldwide Plaza nice and early, and even indulges herself in a coffee from one of the bodegas near the subway station. But instead of going up to the seventeenth floor, she ducks around to the back and finds a place to sit in the little piazza that separates the building from the ramshackle beginnings of Hell's Kitchen. She sits with her back to the wall, so she'll be able to see anyone coming. And she types in the first of a few numbers she's scrawled on a slip of paper.

"Hi, I'm the new intern on the city desk at the *Post*," she says brightly to the tired voice on the other end of the line. "My editor wants to know if the Chief Medical Examiner is going to look into the sudden death of Greg Pickford yesterday?"

The man who was stuck on phone duty at the coroner's office mutters at her to wait. Evie can picture the institutional beige keyboard he's poking to pull up Pickford's file, each key clacking resentfully as the ancient machine grudgingly coughs up the requested information. "Nah, miss," the guy says, his Queens accent thick. "No inquiry. EMTs declared him at the scene and then the family took over."

"Oh, really? Huh, my editor heard a rumour that it wasn't natural causes," Evie says.

"If EMTs took blood to run a tox screen, it won't be back yet, but we wouldn't have a record of that. You'd have to talk to the hospital they were dispatched from, but—"

"—they'll only release to family. I know. Thanks." She hangs up and tries her next number. Almost immediately it's picked up, and a woman chirps out the research institute's name and a cheerful "How may I direct your call?"

"Toxicology, please. I'm looking for Dr Danishta Chaudry?" Evie says. There's a pause, the sound of a ringing phone, and then another woman says, "Tox lab."

"Dr Chaudry?" Evie asks.

"She's in a meeting. Who is this?"

"It's Evie Cross, I'd spoken to Dr Chaudry a couple years ago for an article I wrote about the romance novel poisonings? And I was wondering if I could take up a little more of her time for another murder case that's come up."

The woman on the other end of the phone becomes noticeably more friendly. "Oh, yes! Dr Chaudry has that article framed in her office. But wasn't it written by someone named Nicole?"

"I was her intern," Evie says. "I actually did most of the interviewing."

"Oh, really? I'm an intern here too, doing my graduate project," the woman says.

"Is it on nerve agents, by any chance?" Evie asks.

"Yes!" the woman says brightly. "Well, it's on combatting and detecting slow-acting organophosphate compounds—"

"Please let me email you," Evie begs. "I have someone who died four to six hours after suspected exposure and I need to figure out if I'm being crazy or not."

"Haha, if there is any chance the Russian government is involved, you're probably not crazy," the woman says. "My name's Ireshi. Dr Chaudry's the PI here so obviously she's the real expert, but I should be able to help." The woman spells out her email address for Evie; she jots it down under the lab phone number and promises to email that evening.

* * *

WHEN EVIE GETS up to the office, there's already someone on her sofa. A petite Latina with long, honey-blonde hair and hazel eyes is reading an actual paper book, which Evie recognizes as the big literary novel-du-jour from a few years back. The woman's in a buttery-soft leather biker jacket in a dark hunter green with gold zips, a slim white tee, and fashionably torn skinny jeans, and she has her legs tucked up on the sofa like a little girl.

"This is Beatriz," Gemma says, as the woman glances up and smiles at Evie. "She's one of Misha's freelancers." Gemma is dressed more casually in a light blue blouse and dark skinny trousers, and while her makeup is still perfectly executed it's veering towards what Evie assumes must be a natural look for her: foundation, mascara, brow pencil, contouring, lipstick, and subtle touches of sparkly highlighter at the inner corners of her eyes.

"Hi," Evie says. "Are you waiting for Misha?"

"Yes, but he knows. I texted him," Beatriz says, moving over on the sofa to give Evie room to sit down.

"Oh, good," Evie says. Then, "Oh God! His office is a complete disaster."

Beatriz just laughs. "It's fine. It's always a disaster."

"No," Evie says, her eyes widening in horror. She turns to Gemma. "We need to buy sanitizing wipes." Then, as soon as the words are out of her mouth, she realizes that she has the perfect excuse to go into Misha's office and poke around what very well could be the scene of the crime, if her instincts are right. "I'll just... go straighten up in there. Trust me, it's necessary."

Gemma doesn't even look up from the pile of receipts she's sorting, and Beatriz has returned to *Vernon Subutex*, so Evie slips into Misha's office before anyone can question her unseemly haste. She knows there's nothing in the trash can but ash; nothing in the top drawer of the desk but pens, the lighter, and a pack of playing cards. The top of the desk is bare, the files that used to cover its surface shoved heedlessly onto the ground.

The Christopher Wool painting on the wall stares down at her in silent ultimatum: *RUN DOG RUN*.

But she doesn't run. She straightens the desk and gathers the files on the floor, and she thinks. Greg had sex with Misha in here. There would have been a condom; Greg's not that stupid, especially with someone he viewed as a sex worker. It would have most likely been in the trash, but she knows for a fact the bin was empty when she burned Misha and Stewart's photos.

Misha left soon after Greg did; to the bank, and to the gym. If he took the evidence of the sex with him, he would have taken evidence of any poison, too. It would have been so easy, Evie thinks. Couple street-corner bins, a few streets apart, and a used condom and a small glass vial disappear into the city's 7,000 tons of daily garbage.

Evie stacks files underneath the *RUN DOG RUN* painting, out of spite. She makes a separate file for anything over a year old, or anything that's mostly receipts. Those can go out to Gemma. As she tidies, she admits to herself that if there was foul play, Misha is more than smart enough to cover his tracks flawlessly. Part of her still hopes that he's been careless enough that she can discover something conclusive, that will tell her one way or the other if she is correct. And another part of her hopes against hope that she is merely a modern-day Catherine Morland, creating gothic follies of the mind out of plain and innocent country houses.

Still. She checks along the skirting boards and under the chaise longue, just in case.

She finds thirty-five cents and a box of matches from Pravda.

By the time Misha swans in half an hour later, she has at least taken all the small piles of paper cascading across every flat surface and condensed them into three big piles. It is entirely worth it, to see Misha's expression when he looks around his office and realizes that, for possibly the first time in recent memory, it's tidy.

Beatriz is positively awestruck, and whispers, "Misha, you should have gotten help *sooner*."

"Yes, well," Misha sniffs, with an air of wounded pride. Then he turns to Evie. "Thank you. This was unexpected."

"Okay. I'll just…" Evie picks up one of the piles, the one of everything over a year old, and gestures with her chin towards the door. She leaves them, nudging the doors mostly closed as she goes. They're still open a crack, and she expects Misha or Beatriz to shut them all the way, but they don't. She settles on the sofa as close to the doors as she can, and starts sorting receipts.

By the time Gemma's shown her what to do, she's missed the first half of the conversation in Misha's office. But Beatriz's next words are easily audible over the quiet rustle of paper: "I really like him."

Misha is silent for a while. Evie can imagine him pacing; he strikes her as a kinetic thinker. Then, finally, he says, "We can't pull the job, Bea." His voice is apologetic.

"I know," Beatriz says.

"And your relationship may not survive the scandal."

"Well," Beatriz replies, in the too-high voice of someone trying to make an unfunny thing funny, "at least it's not his first."

"Quite," Misha sighs. "I need time to think this through properly. How we can make you look as innocent as possible. I get some street photos of you two together, and then… I still need you two to have sex in the store. That's the main thing, for the client. But rather than you going public…" Evie can definitely hear Misha's footfalls now, as he paces. "Okay. I get the footage from the store security cameras. Maybe we ask Dani to work at the store, she can pretend to have a grudge against you because you're having an affair with the CEO…"

"Oh, no need, there are absolutely girls at the store who resent me already," Beatriz says.

"Hmmm," Misha says. It's a pleased sound. "I can work with that. Send me their Instagrams and let me know when they're headed out for drinks after work, and I'll do the rest."

"I'm sorry," Beatriz sighs.

"Don't be," Misha replies. "This job has an expiration date. Nobody does it forever. If you're happy with him, if it lasts, then I'm glad for you."

"You don't think it will last." Beatriz's tone is sad, like Misha is confirming something she already fears.

"It isn't an angry wife that hired us, Bea. It's a competitor. They're trying to take his company. He won't sell and he won't step aside, and they're trying to get him on character. Having affairs with the flagship store's young female staff, which he promised he'd stopped. And..." Misha pauses, and when he speaks again, his voice is softer, less argumentative. "I hope you get your happy ending. That's all."

"Yeah. Me too," Beatriz replies.

Their voices are getting closer; the meeting coming to an end. "And if it doesn't work out, or if Freedman ever doesn't treat you right, you know you're always welcome here. As a friend."

"Thanks." Beatriz comes out of the office first, Misha just behind her. She turns and hugs him, and he takes a moment to reciprocate. "Really. Thank you." They separate, and Beatriz still has her hands on his shoulders. "He's back in town next week, and it's been a while because of his Asia trip, so... I should be able to arrange what you need to finish this."

"Okay. Be safe, Bea." Misha cups her cheek in his hand, fondly. He watches her go, smiles back at her cheery wave, and stands, eyes fixed on the middle distance, until Beatriz is long gone. Then he sits down with a sigh on the sofa next to Evie, tilting his head back and closing his eyes. "That's going to end in disaster," he mumbles. "Poor Bea."

"Does this happen often?" Evie asks, after a moment. "People leaving? Falling in love with their targets?"

Misha shrugs. He's in a loose-knit black sweater over a tank top and skinny black jeans, and Evie can see the play of his muscles through the holes in the knit. She looks away. "It's better when they leave for someone outside of work," he says. His lips twitch in amusement. "Less effort for me, shoring up their fake identity enough to make it permanent."

Evie risks one more question, seeing that Misha is in a reflective mood. "Doesn't it wear on you, that so many of the clients and targets are bad people?"

Another shrug. "In some ways it's easier. Less guilt," he replies. He sits up. "What time is it?"

Evie glances at her phone. "Uh, almost 11am."

"Fuck. Octavia Mortimer's going to be here any minute. Gemma, there's some tea in the bottom drawer of your desk?"

Evie hears the rumble of the drawer being pulled open, and then Gemma's whispered, "Why are boys allowed to be in charge of anything?"

She's on her feet before she can think twice, eager to see what is putting that expression of bemused horror on Gemma's face. In the drawer is a pile of unopened mail, a dead plant, and an untouched box of fancy chocolates, its cellophane thick with dust.

"Oops," Misha says from over her shoulder. Then he reaches around her and opens the next drawer up. "I meant the other bottom drawer." He pulls out a tin of Japanese tea and passes it to Evie. "She only drinks this. Would you mind awfully being the tea lady?"

"No, it's fine," Evie says.

"What?" Misha says, when he realizes that both Evie and Gemma are staring at him. "There is a system."

Gemma raises the dead plant. "Does that mean... you want to keep... this?" she asks.

"Don't be ridiculous, that's clearly the trash drawer," Misha says. He prods Evie's shoulder. "Tea. Please hurry. She's never late, unfortunately."

Evie heads out to the kitchenette, Gemma's soft, shocked recitation of the phrase *trash drawer* floating in the air behind her.

WHILE THE WATER heats, Evie looks up Beatriz's target. It's not a difficult search: Ron Freedman, CEO of luxury furniture empire Aesthetica Moderne, with a giant flagship showroom down in the Meatpacking District. Left his wife after a scandal a decade ago with a young store employee; currently in a long-term relationship with a model who is not Beatriz. It's something. It's still retail, but it's another case to slot into the article, if Nicole doesn't see it as a murder story.

Evie gets worried. With Greg dead, if she can't sell the article to Nicole as a murder story, she's not likely going to want to pursue it any more. Greg might have been a terrible, abusive person, but putting out a hit piece on the newly deceased isn't even something the *New York Post* would stoop to. And *Gotham* likes to pretend it's classy.

She quickly dials Nicole's cell, but rather than getting her, it's the receptionist. "*Gotham Magazine*, how can I help you?" Nicole must have forwarded her calls.

"Uh, Nicole Hamilton, please," Evie says.

"I'm sorry, Nicole's not in yet," the receptionist says. "Do you want her voicemail?"

"No," Evie says. "It's fine. Thanks." She ends the call and looks at her phone screen. 11:05. That's late, even in the notoriously casual *Gotham* office. She fires off a text, hoping it will get through to Nicole: *hey u ok?*

She finds two nice, handmade-looking mugs in the cabinet that are like the ones you get in Japanese restaurants, without handles, and pours the tea. There's a little tray too, so she puts the mugs on those and carefully walks them back to the office. When she gets there, she is amused to see the dead plant and the chocolates already in Gemma's bin, while Gemma herself sifts through the pile of five-year-old unopened mail.

The door to Misha's office is open, and Evie can glimpse an extremely well-preserved brunette in her fifties perching on the edge of the chaise longue, her ankles crossed, her posture immaculate. An off-white goat-hair jacket and a lavender, ostrich-skin Birkin bag lie next to her. Evie hesitates in the doorway, not sure whether to interrupt.

"You're *positive*?" the woman asks, in a clipped, upper-class British accent.

"I obviously can't guarantee your husband won't try to take another mistress, Mrs Mortimer," Misha says, gesturing for Evie to come in. "But I can assure you that Nicole Hamilton will not be coming back."

Evie can't help the small squeak of shock she lets out, her grip on the tea tray going white-knuckled in an effort not to drop it.

Misha glances over at her and smiles, ignoring—or even worse, possibly enjoying—what she assumes is a look of utter terror on her face. "Ah, Evie," he purrs. "You even used the right cups."

CHAPTER SIX

THE REST OF the day passes in a blur of low-key panic. Gemma and Misha snipe at each other over her attempts to set up standard office procedures like electronic calendars, contact lists, and databases, Misha insisting that none of that was necessary because he had all the essential information in his head.

Gemma gestures at the piles of papers awaiting the delivery of the shredder. "A database would be more secure, more easily searchable and a lot less wasteful than this," she says.

"I don't have time to type everything in," Misha counters. "And I viscerally object to anyone knowing where I am, so no calendars."

Gemma rubs her temples in frustration. "Okay, let me start this another way. I've found two freelancer contracts in this mess. How many more are there? Can I at least have all of their contracts and phone numbers so I can make sure they get paid?"

Misha starts to refuse, but shuts his mouth when Gemma adds, "And get them their expenses?"

They stare at each other for a long moment, before Misha grits out, "Fine." He walks into his office then walks out again, throwing up his arms. "Of course I don't know where anything is any more," he pouts.

Evie sighs and gets up. "Do all of them have contracts?" she asks.

"Yes," Misha says, too quickly. "… Maybe."

Evie sits down in Misha's office on the floor next to *RUN DOG RUN*. She grabs one of the piles she made this morning and hefts it into her lap. "Why don't you make a list of every active freelancer, and we'll try to find their contracts?" she suggests.

Misha doesn't say anything, but she hears him cross the room and sit down at his desk. The office is quiet but for the rustle of files and the dull staccato of a ballpoint pen on paper.

Evie's back is to the room. It makes her braver, not being able to see Misha's face. She breaks the silence. "So who was Octavia Mortimer?" she asks, aiming for casual disinterest. It's undermined by the way her voice cracks halfway through.

"She's the younger daughter of a British viscount. Usual story: old title, no money." Misha taps the back of his pen on the desk. "Husband's August Mortimer, the second generation of a big American publishing family. No title, piles of money. He had a... young protégé, at work." Misha huffs out an amused breath. "Not his first. And not even someone he was having sex with, which by his definition meant he wasn't cheating, not physically. Only emotionally. But he made the mistake of giving the mistress a nicer handbag than he gave his wife. So on that exceptionally petty basis, I was tasked with banishing the mistress."

Evie turns to look at Misha, at once filled with both relief and terror. He doesn't suspect her. At least, not yet. Not fully. "Which, uh, which publishing company?" she asks, even though she knows the answer.

"The one just up the way." Misha gestures vaguely towards the window. "National Magazine Group, or whatever they're called since they were taken over." He pushes his chair back and runs his hands through his hair. "The whole thing was a spat over handbags, Evie," he says. "And those handbags. They were so *ugly*. Both of them."

Evie remembers Nicole's beige and white ombré crocodile-skin bag, and can't help the hysterical snort of amusement that bubbles up within her. Misha cracks up too, his shoulders shaking with it, bright peals of laughter filling the room.

"What's so funny?" Gemma says, appearing in the doorway.

Unable to talk for laughing, Misha motions her over. He shows her an image on his phone screen.

Gemma bends down to squint at it and then straightens, disgust written across her face. "That's... that's the grossest bag I've ever *seen*. Ew."

"It costs a hundred thousand dollars," Misha says.

"Why?" Gemma groans.

Evie laughs so hard she can feel tears gathering in her eyes, until she feels like she's going to be sick with it, because everything is falling apart, but for the moment, she's safe.

CLAUDIA IS OUT at work when Evie gets home. She makes herself a bowl of cereal for dinner, then curls up on her bed, scrolling absently through social media. Usually it's some comfort, burying herself in the bustle and noise of friends' conversations, but tonight it holds nothing but outrage and the same old gifs she's seen a hundred times. The same seven joke structures, all applied repeatedly to the topic of the day. She closes Twitter down and tries to get through to Nicole again.

The text comes back as undeliverable.

She hopes that Nicole's simply turned her phone off for a couple days. It's certainly not unreasonable, given that her affair has just ended. But it still makes Evie uneasy.

She can't get out of her head how sure Misha was that Greg Pickford wouldn't make it to his meeting with his lawyer. And she just needs to know that whatever happened to Greg didn't also happen to Nicole.

She sits cross-legged on her bed and opens up the cloud document she'd shared with Nicole, leaving a big 24-point message across the top, *Nicole if you get this text me so I know you're okay* followed by her phone number. She stares at the blinking cursor for what feels like an eternity, surrounded by the low electrical hum of the building, and the muffled sounds of the street outside. She knows she should make notes on the other Meserov & Co cases she's learned about: Beatriz and Ron Freedman of Aesthetica Moderne. Nicole and August Mortimer. She remembers her last conversation with Nicole: the other woman was prepping to go out to dinner with someone. And, with a painful certainty, she realizes who Nicole's date was.

She can't bring herself to close the circle, to let Nicole know she's been had by the very same agency they're researching. Nicole could work it out for herself, of course, as soon as she sees the photos of Misha. But it feels dangerous, spelling it out. And she thinks of Beatriz, hoping for a long-term relationship with her target, how Evie stands to destroy that too in the name of furthering her career. She finally closes out of her research notes, having accomplished nothing but tying herself up in knots of anxiety and self-doubt.

In order to feel like she's done some work, she types a quick email to Ireshi, the friendly postgrad from Dr Chaudry's lab, giving her as many details as she can about Greg Pickford's death short of actually naming him. She asks if there's a poison that can be administered with no immediate effects, but will result in untraceable cardiac failure six hours later. She hopes Ireshi will email her back and tell her no such poison exists. She can't reconcile Misha, the person who laughs about tacky crocodile handbags, with someone who would premeditatedly murder one of his own clients.

Evie squeezes her eyes shut and prays that Nicole is alive and unhurt.

THE NEXT MORNING, Evie wakes up to the news that *Gotham Magazine* is ceasing print operations and going purely digital under a new managing editor: some white guy who had previously been a deputy at the *New Yorker*. Nicole is not mentioned anywhere, and when Evie checks the magazine's digital masthead, she's been scrubbed from there, too.

Nicole's fall from August Mortimer's good graces was fast and far, it seems. Even her articles have been pulled from *Gotham*'s site; a search for her byline shows no results. And just as Mortimer paid for her handbag, *Gotham* probably paid for her cellphone, and cancelled it as soon as the magazine showed her the door. Hence Evie's texts coming back as undeliverable.

Evie never liked Nicole. She was unquestionably shallow, pretentious, and manipulative, and never had to pay for a thing in her life. But while Evie's riding the subway into work and a melancholy song comes on her playlist, she still finds herself feeling sad for how quickly the knives came out for the other woman. She finds Nicole's Instagram after a swift search, and is a little relieved to see a photo of her, smiling and blonde and flashing a peace sign, at JFK airport from earlier this morning. *Going home 2 Cali for a sabbatical!!! I'm writing a book xoxo stay tuned for exciting news my lovelies!*

She snorts and puts her phone away, a little less sorry for Nicole now that she knows the woman would be sitting out her scandal on the beach, looking for the next man wealthy enough to keep her in ugly luxury.

Wednesday is a dull day. The shredder arrives, as does a brand-new laptop for Evie's use, courtesy of Gemma's organizational skills.

Evie spends most of the day feeding old printouts and cryptically annotated articles into the shredder. There's frustratingly little information about Misha's cases in his files. Here, a wedding invitation; there, a pair of tickets to a play. Whenever Evie does find handwritten notes, they're all in a mix of Cyrillic and the strange, curlicue script of the Georgian language. No wonder Misha was relaxed about leaving files around.

There are no photos, incriminating or otherwise. Evie presumes that he's careful enough to burn those.

Misha spends the day alternately reading on the chaise longue or looking things up on his phone. She or Gemma check with him about anything handwritten. Misha waves each one away with a muttered "that's old" or "I don't need those any more", and into the shredder they go. There are no calls from the lawyers upstairs, no demands for the Pickford photographs.

At 4pm, Misha announces he's leaving, and gives the girls the rest of the day off.

"Resting before another night out?" Gemma asks.

Misha groans. "Both my sister and I have work tonight." He glances at Evie, eyes narrowing. "With different people."

"I said nothing," Evie squeaks.

"Your face said everything," he replies. He ushers them out and locks the door. "Masha takes forever to get ready, and she likes me to be home to help her. She is going to be intolerably smug that I took her advice and hired you two."

"Too right," Gemma replies. "She sounds wonderful, and very smart."

"You two will never be allowed to meet," Misha grumbles. "My life is hard enough without you teaming up with my sister to make it worse."

They take their leave outside the building, Gemma heading for the subway back to Long Island City, Misha hailing a cab, and Evie with nowhere to go.

The afternoon is one of those beautiful early-summer New York days, when the sky is pure blue above the high towers of Midtown, the air is warm, and it feels like anything is possible. It will stay sunny until 8pm, and Evie doesn't want to go home. She wanders down to the High Line and sits on a bench to the side of the elevated path, watching strollers and runners go by. She likes the High Line better than she likes parks. A park has regulars, even cliques. The High Line is a purely liminal space: peaceful, attractive, and meant to be passed through.

She considers her options. Her first paycheck won't hit her account for another ten days, and between the tips from Friday night and what she still has left over from Misha's largesse on Monday, she has about $62 to her name. There will be no indulgent afternoon movie, or leisurely solo dinner in a Chelsea café with a glass of dry white wine.

There might be an evening's work, however. Evie texts Claudia to ask if she's working an event later. Claudia texts her back too fast for it to be good news: *nah working next 3 nights straight but tonight is TV n chill.*

Evie walks the rest of the way down the High Line and hops the A train home at 14th Street. At the bodega on the corner she drops $7 on her breakfast for the next ten days: an economy-size tub of instant oatmeal and a box of brown sugar. She watches reality TV with Claudia for a couple hours before the stress of the week gets to her and she crashes out.

THERE'S A HORRIBLE trilling sound and it won't go away.

Evie reaches one arm out from under the duvet and flails for her phone on the dresser. She knows it's not her alarm because it's still way too dark outside. Her alarm also has the good grace to start softly, while this is blaring at full volume, like it's stabbing at her.

She lunges across her bed towards the rectangle of light and noise she can see vibrating on top of her dresser.

This is a mistake, and causes several things to happen in short succession: she almost falls out of bed, bangs her knee on the dresser, and then manages to knock both her phone and her iPad onto the floor, along with her hairbrush and a bowl of hair ties.

Evie sits back down on the bed swearing at the truly apocalyptic pain in her knee. She grabs her phone off the floor and swipes at it once she realizes that it's still ringing, more to make the sound stop than with any actual intent to speak to whatever Satanist or drunk is calling her at (she checks) 3:14.

"Hello?" says a woman's voice, soft and hesitant. "Is this Evie?"

"Mmuh," says Evie. "Whozzis."

"This is Maria Andreyevna. Misha's sister? I am sorry to bother you so late, but there is a situation…"

At that, enough of Evie's brain judders online that she can at least string together sentences, even if they're not very rational ones yet. "Where's Misha? What's wrong?" she mumbles.

"Oh, Misha is fine. He's out. But not answering his phone." The sister's accent is stronger than Misha's, and she's speaking quietly, as if she doesn't want to be overheard. "The situation is with me." There's something vulnerable and scared in her voice. That, more than anything else, gets Evie moving.

She flicks on her bedside lamp and blinks as her eyes adjust to the glare. "Okay. Okay. What's up?"

"Is there any way you could come pick me up in Park Slope? I had to leave somewhere—a target's—very quickly. I don't have any clothes." Her voice drops even lower. "I am hiding behind some bins and, ugh, there are rats."

"Don't worry, Park Slope rats won't touch you. You're not organic enough for them," Evie says, stepping clumsily into a pair of sweatpants. "Now, a 138th Street rat, they're something to be concerned about."

Maria—*Masha*—giggles. "Thank you," she says, giving the address. "Misha said you were kind."

Great. Misha had told his sister about her. Evie can't help the little swoop in her stomach that the woman's words cause, and wishes it hadn't been so long since anyone had told her she was doing a good job. A few compliments from Misha in the desert of her existence, and she is willing to accept all his mirages as real. She shoves her sneakers on and grabs Claudia's keys out of the bowl by the door.

Evie rolls into Park Slope in Claudia's beat-up little Honda Element twenty minutes later. She pulls over under a streetlight and throws her hazards on, across from the address Masha gave. It's a tall brownstone half a block from the park, indistinguishable from any of its neighbors. Each is a beautifully maintained family home, every front stoop ending in only a single bell next to the heavy wooden front door. Underneath the stoop, at street level, are a line of tall black trash bins: one for garbage, one for plastics, one for cardboard.

There's no sound but air conditioners on high and the scuttle of vermin below. A cat saunters noiselessly across the street, its eyes flashing yellow in the Element's headlights. Evie shivers, and clambers out of the car. "Masha?" she whispers.

"Evie?" A figure steps hesitantly out of the shadows, arms wrapped around herself. Evie waves, and the woman hustles towards her, shoulders hunched. As she crosses into the light of the streetlamp, Evie can tell she's Misha's twin. Like her brother, Masha hit the white-beauty-standards genetic jackpot. She shares his pale eyes, hers made even more unsettling by the smudge of mascara around dark, dark lashes and a mess of long almost-black hair. She is tall, maybe five ten, with long muscular legs and a slim waist; like Misha, she has an athlete's body. It's perfect, except for what looks like a small scar on her sternum that disappears under her left breast. Evie only glimpses it in the half-light; Masha is clutching a handbag and between that and her arms, she's doing an okay job of covering the private parts of her body.

"Here. This should fit, and it's easy to get on," Evie says, thrusting a paper shopping bag full of cloth at Masha and looking politely off to one side. Then her gaze lands on a rat and she looks back.

Masha takes the bag out of her hands. She digs out the huge bundle of blue and cream fleece from it, and stares at it uncomprehendingly. "What... is this?" she asks.

"It's, uh, my Snorlax onesie. I didn't know what would fit you. Claudia and I are kinda short and, uh, Misha isn't, so..." Evie waves her hands around. Did they have a robe? Shit, there was a robe in the bathroom. Oh well. "Um, there are some pool slides in there too. Because no part of anyone's bare skin should ever touch New York streets."

Masha is smiling, and it's that same warm, too-big grin that Misha has, the one that verges on being goofy. She steps into the onesie and zips it up. "What do you think?" she says, striking a pose. "*Paris Vogue*? Or no. I think maybe *Vogue Italia*. They are more avant-garde."

"Ugh. You make that look good. I hate you," Evie grumbles, getting back into the car. She chucks Claudia's jacket and work shoes off the passenger seat into the back, and double-takes in horror at the mess of cocktail lists, parking permits, and menu printouts revealed underneath them. She sighs and just shoves them into the footwell.

Masha folds herself gracefully into the car, and gives a Manhattan address that Evie plugs into her phone. They're almost to the Manhattan Bridge when Evie, who has been stealing glances at Masha, finally gets up the courage to ask what happened for her to end up minus her clothes in a Brooklyn street at 3am.

Masha groans and runs her fingers through her hair, in a gesture she must have picked up from her brother. "The wife was supposed to be out all night. She was not."

"Isn't the wife your client?" Evie asks. "The one who hired you?"

"Yes. But unexpected meetings are... discouraged." Masha shoots her an exasperated look. "The involved parties will blow it. They can't act. They either react too much or too little, or worst of all they say your name. But her coming home to another woman's lingerie on her bedroom floor? Very effective." She sighs, wearily. "If only it had been planned. Still, she got her money's worth."

"Why do you do this?" Evie asks.

"Do what?" Masha replies.

"The whole Heartbreak thing. I mean, why aren't you a model?" Evie blushes then, remembering Masha's jokes about *Vogue*, and regretting that the last time she'd looked at a fashion magazine had been before college. "Um, or *are* you a model?"

"Not a model," Masha mutters. "I don't like having my picture taken. And I don't really need to work, but it's nice to help my brother out." She looks down at her nails, painted a dark metallic blue, almost black, that shines as the tunnel lights go past. "As for why Misha does this, it is more complicated. You will have to ask him yourself."

There are hardly any other cars on the road at this hour, and Evie forgets just how small Manhattan is when it's empty. They're only on the island for about ten minutes before they turn onto a cobblestone West Village street and Masha indicates an elegant 1800s brick townhouse. It's only three stories, but Evie can tell from its tall windows that the rooms must have high ceilings and elegant proportions. "Wow," she breathes, looking up at its perfect white lintels. "Is that... Do you..."

"Our house," Masha answers. "It has been in the family for a while."

"It's just, I didn't think real people actually lived in the West Village any more." Evie cringes as soon as the words are out of her mouth. That sounded… bad. Sue her, she's not the best conversationalist at ass o'clock in the morning.

But Masha just smiles, small and private. "We never said we were real people."

As she gets out of the car she reaches in and squeezes Evie's hand. Masha's skin is hot, in a way she didn't expect given how perfect and statuesque the woman is. Evie expected her to be cold, like marble. "Thank you for my rescue," she says. Then she indicates the blue and cream fleece enveloping her. "I'll wash this and send it in with Misha later in the week." Then she gets a wicked gleam in her eyes. "Or maybe I'll keep it for a while and wear it around the house to horrify him."

"If you get a pic of Misha's face when he sees you in that onesie, you can keep it forever," Evie says.

The bright peal of Masha's laughter is the last thing she hears as she drives away.

THE NEXT MORNING—or, in fact, later that same morning— Evie sleeps through her alarm and her second alarm. She only wakes up when Claudia shakes her. Claudia, who is never up before 9:30.

Evie yanks on the first decent dress she can find, washes her face and brushes her teeth, slaps on the bare acceptable minimum of makeup, and heads into work. The one advantage of being ridiculously late is she's missed the A train's morning rush hour, but she still doesn't get into the office until almost 11.

Gemma is on the phone when she arrives, dealing with some aspect of the expense reporting, but she waves her a cheery hello. Evie slouches onto the sofa, wondering just how unprofessional it would be to fall asleep on it. Misha's office door is closed. She presumes that means he isn't in yet.

She hears the landline click back into the receiver, and Gemma's groan. "The good news is, it's like the expense tracking software I used at my old job," she grumbles. "The bad news is, I have to photograph every single one of these and upload them in batches by job." Then she fully takes in Evie's disheveled state. "Are you okay? I was worried when you were late... Do you want to trade numbers in case something comes up?"

Evie sighs. "How are you so organized all the time?" she asks, sitting up and fishing out her phone.

"Oldest of five," Gemma grins. "The rest are boys." She takes Evie's phone, puts her number in, and sends a text to herself before handing the phone back. "And then four years as a PA at an investment bank looking after forty-year-old children."

"Ugh, I temped a little bit at a bank. It was... bad," Evie says, saving Gemma as a new contact. "That why you're so good at standing up to Misha?"

"Probably. He's stubborn, but he listens to reason. I had one managing director who wouldn't read his emails unless you printed them out for him and folded them vertically," Gemma says. "Ver-tic-al-ly."

"I had a bond trader shit his pants and then hand me those pants for dry-cleaning," Evie says. "He still had a gram of coke in one of the pockets."

"Children," Gemma sighs. "Literal children, in charge of the financial system."

"Is that why you left that world?" Evie asks. "I mean, the people suck, but it pays well."

Gemma waves a hand in dismissal. "I don't tell that story sober, and I'm a crybaby when I drink." She smiles, small and brittle. "So I don't tell that story at all."

Evie raises an eyebrow. "Who do I have to kill? Just, y'know, for the record."

"His name was Justin Koh," Gemma says. "The irony is something he did six months before... well, before he was bad to me, the girl sued, and the firm forced him out less than a month after I was pushed out for trying to report him."

Gemma's expression is tight. "She didn't work there, so they couldn't force her to be quiet." Her voice takes on a deeper timbre, a mocking impression of an older, patrician man. "He has a bright future at Goldberg's, do you really want to ruin that for one regrettable incident after work hours, at a bar you were at voluntarily? Are you sure you didn't have too much to drink and initiate things yourself? Do you normally wear skirts this short to the office?" She blinks and presses the heel of her hand against her cheekbone to stop a tear. "Sorry," she says, her voice cracking. "I'm still just… very angry. I was so shocked throughout the time it was all happening, I couldn't think clearly or, or answer their questions very well. And looking back on it now, I *know* I was railroaded, but also… I don't want to go back and fight them again. I just want to forget about it."

"Misha knows?" Evie asks.

"Yes," Gemma smiles. "That was my big interview faux-pas."

"Well," Evie says, "you never know, Justin Koh, he might just drop dead one day soon, like Greg Pickford." When lightning doesn't strike her down for voicing that out loud, she gets up and grabs her bag. "I desperately need caffeine and, honestly, you need sugar. I'm going to hit up the soda machine. What's your poison?"

"Cherry Coke, please. And, thanks, Evie," Gemma says. "I'm glad I'm not here alone."

"I met Masha last night," Evie calls over her shoulder as she heads out the door. "I'll tell you about it as soon as I get back!"

Misha rushes in moments after she returns with the sodas. He's flustered, and in a casual-Friday pair of skinny jeans and an almost indecently form-fitting T-shirt under a leather jacket. "Did either Don or Dee's offices call down?"

Gemma shakes her head. "No calls yet this morning," she says.

Misha sighs in relief. He digs around in the pockets of his biker jacket unsuccessfully, pats his jeans absentmindedly, and then pulls out a slightly crushed letter-sized envelope out of his back pocket with a quiet "Aha". He turns it over in his hands. "I'm not too late, then."

Evie stares at Misha's hands, because he's wearing nail polish, the same dark navy shade Masha had been wearing before.

"She uses me as her guinea pig," Misha murmurs, a blush coloring his high cheekbones. "To see if she likes the shade."

"Oh," Evie says, embarrassed that she's been caught looking.

"What? Who?" Gemma says.

"My sister," Misha says, holding up the back of one hand to Gemma so she can see the polish.

"Do you want me to pop out and get some remover over lunch?" Gemma asks.

Misha shakes his head, a smile tugging at the corners of his lips. "No. Don once asked if the nail polish was part of my 'gay agenda'"—he uses actual air quotes, like a dork, the envelope in his hand braced against his palm—"so ever since, I make sure to wear it at least once a week."

"It's nice," Gemma says. She glances down at her own nails with their conservative French manicure, and smiles to herself. "I think I'll try something a little more daring next week."

Misha holds out the envelope to Evie and says, "Run that up to Dee, would you? It's Masha's recording from last night."

"Right now?" Evie says. This is not a morning where she feels up to dealing with condescending law partners. She shakes the envelope. It's nearly empty, just a small flash drive or something similar rattling around inside.

"Right now. I'd avoid Don if you can. He's going to be in a mood about the Pickford case for the rest of the week," Misha says. He slips out of his jacket and slings it over his shoulder as he heads into his office. Evie tries not to stare at the little slip of bare skin visible between the top of his low-slung jeans and the hem of his shirt. "I'll be in my office contemplating the futility of existence for the next hour or so," Misha says, wearily. "This week has been entirely too full of awful people for it to be only Thursday."

"I'll hold your calls," Gemma says, primly.

"You are a saint who is too good for this world," Misha mumbles. "You both are."

Evie heads up to the Family Law floor at Meyer, Luchins & Black. As soon as she gets into the blissfully empty elevator, she sighs and bangs her forehead against the wall. She needs to get over her ridiculous infatuation with her weird boss. She's going to blame the striped tee he was wearing that first day. It had a wide neck, and slipped down over one shoulder when he dropped his bag. There needs to be Queensberry Rules about crushes, and unexpected bare shoulders, or indeed shirtlessness in general, should be cause for an automatic disqualification and rematch.

She buzzes to be let in at the twenty-ninth floor and Dee's executive assistant, a rather butch South Asian girl, appears a few minutes later to open the door for her. "Hey," the girl says. Then she looks Evie up and down appreciatively, taking in the somewhat-untamed curls and the dark purple eyeliner and the navy striped tunic dress she'd borrowed from Claudia in the morning's panic. "Heyyyy," she drawls, several degrees warmer. She beckons Evie to follow her through the cubicle farm towards the partners' big offices along the wall overlooking Eighth Avenue, chattering away as she walks. "So of course you work for Misha, because that office *needed* more hot people in it. C'mon. Dee's expecting you. Oh, my name's Dimple. You're Evie, right?"

Evie smiles to herself as she navigates past harried law clerks and juniors, and blushes for what feels like the third time that hour. If Dee is anything like her executive assistant, this isn't going to be as bad a trip as she feared. They arrive at the office next to Don's. Dimple sticks her head in, then waves the all-clear, ushering Evie inside.

Dee is, unfortunately, anticlimactic.

She's in her fifties, a little heavy, rumpled in a navy suit, with chin-length hair dyed a light brown that was clearly seen as an acceptable compromise between the dark brown of her youth and the skeins of silver and white that had emerged in middle age. She glances up at Evie, gives a distracted twitch of her lips and holds out her hand for Misha's envelope.

Evie gives it to her and Dee checks inside, prodding the little red flash drive with a finger. "What's the story?" she says.

"Uh, I dunno?" Evie says. "Masha had to leave pretty quickly because the wife came home early, so there's apparently lingerie—"

Dee looks up at her, small but fiercely intelligent hazel-green eyes meeting hers. "No. I mean, how did this tape come into our hands?"

Evie is about to stutter out another "I don't know?" when Dee makes a questioning noise and pulls two pieces of paper out of the envelope. One is an Airbnb reservation receipt and the other is a printout of an online review posted that morning, about how the renter couldn't sleep because of the noisy sex happening in the building next door.

Dee holds them up for Evie to see. Her eyebrows are raised, and she's fighting a smile. "Tell him well done, as usual."

"I will," says Evie, grinning and bouncing slightly on her toes.

She has a moment of low-key internal panic: when had Misha's victories become hers, too? She needs to figure out what side she's on. With Nicole in the wind and *Gotham Magazine* under new management, her feature was as good as spiked. Does she keep investigating, keep adding to her file? Or, once she establishes Misha's not an actual murderer, does she just let herself enjoy what so far has been a pretty terrific job? She is finding it increasingly hard to evaluate her choices rationally. She wants to believe that someone as ethereally beautiful as Misha is a good person and, from the glimpses of him that she gets, he really is. The coming weekend will help. She can get some distance from the situation; hopefully hear back from Ireshi...

She realizes she's still in Dee's office, still smiling and bouncing like a loon. "Okay, uh, it was great to meet you, I'll just..." She turns to go—

—and smacks straight into Don.

"I still need the Pickford photos," he says, his voice heavy with condescension. "You promised them yesterday by 10am. Not that I expect anything like punctuality from that lazy whore, but I assumed Abigail had at least set him up with competent help. Am I wrong?"

Evie had already antagonized this man once, and she knows he's responsible for the majority of Misha's work. Much as she wants to antagonize him again, she knows it won't help anyone. Instead, she plasters a hopefully sincere-looking expression on her face and says, "I'm so sorry, Mr Kieselstein, Misha said you wouldn't need them any more because…" She waves her hand in the air. "Because your client is, uh… dead."

Don glances over at his cousin, and one of his sausage fingers flicks out in Evie's direction. "Has she seen the ad? Did you show her what Misha looked like before we set him up in that business? She should know what she's working for," he says, his voice edged with acid.

"Don, I don't think that's necessary," Dee starts, placing down her paperwork with an aggrieved look.

"Oh, but it is," Don says. He waddles past Evie towards a cabinet in Dee's office that is locked with a keypad. "Same combination?"

Dee rolls her eyes. "Same combination."

Don punches in a passcode and opens a drawer, flipping through files before making a pleased little grunt. He thrusts a large manila envelope at Evie.

She takes it. Dee shakes her head slightly, letting Evie know she doesn't have to look at what's inside.

Evie looks anyway.

There are two pages. The top is a printout, like a contact sheet: several small photos of male escorts. One photo in the second row is circled with faded blue highlighter, and Evie's heart skips when she recognizes the long dark hair and unreal body in the picture. The second page is a high-quality 8x10 blowup of that picture.

It's an erotic photo of Misha. He's sprawled on his back across a bed, head towards the viewer, face turned to the side and covered with loose waves of hair. One leg is hitched up, bent; the other is extended. He's not naked. It might be better if he was, Evie thinks. One hand is on his massive, muscular chest, over his heart. The other…

… The other is further south.

Misha is wearing what looks like women's panties. Pale peach, silk, and nearly transparent. He's hard, and the panties do not in any way contain him. The silk strains over the base of his arousal, his cock pushing out from underneath the delicate fabric and up onto his perfect abs. He holds himself through the silk, loosely, with his left hand, which only serves to emphasize how much of him there actually is. Evie swallows, deeply uncomfortable with her own levels of arousal as she stands in a Midtown office, observed by two middle-aged divorce lawyers.

She squeezes her eyes shut and shoves the photo back in the envelope.

Don takes her response for disgust. Which is for the best.

"A decade ago he was just a pretty rent boy at a high-priced escort agency we hired," Don says, "to see if the Petitioner was as holy as she seemed. We *made* him. He'd still be shaking his tail at rich Arabs if it wasn't for us. He needs not to forget that."

"Don," Dee counters. "That's not fair. We hired an escort who turned out to have a hell of a head for business and an uncanny ability both for subterfuge and for charming people. You remember, Uncle Myron wanted to recruit him into the CIA at the office summer picnic. And when Masha showed up—"

"He's still a whore," Don says, cutting off his cousin with a gesture of his swollen fingers. "When she showed up, all we found out is that it runs in the family." He turns to Evie, boxing her in near the doorway. He smells aggressively of a soapy, musky cologne. It tickles Evie's nose and makes her want to sneeze. "We need the photos," Don says, his tone laced with finality. "The family is contesting Greg's will."

Evie wants to say a lot of things. She wants to say *your services are bought and sold too, you're just a fancier kind of whore. Apparently you can't win cases without Misha so maybe if you want to insult him you should get better at your job first. At least Misha is honest about what he is.*

But instead she says, "Does this happen often? Young clients dying in the middle of the divorce?"

Don's eyes widen. He opens his mouth, then snaps it shut. Evie glances over at Dee, who is suddenly very engrossed with paperwork on her desk.

She has her answer. It's the very last answer she wanted. Greg Pickford's death was not an isolated event. Someone is murdering the Kieselsteins' clients, and there's only one person it could be.

Evie's mind races: she can build up a list of Don and Dee's clients and trace cases back to when Misha began working for them. She should be able to create a mostly comprehensive list of unusual deaths within a day or two. Misha started with the Kieselsteins ten years ago. How many have died in that time? Is he a one a year guy, or does he get greedy?

Part of her is screaming *stop poking at this, danger, danger, this is how girls get themselves killed*. But the more rational part has to look, has to find out. If nothing else, because working for him makes her an accomplice. Because that level of charm combined with casual, remorseless murder is classic high-level psychopathy. She needs to know that it's not true. That Misha isn't a sociopath. If he is… she'll find a way to expose him. It's what she was trained to do. Even if it is on a citizen-journalist site like Medium rather than a *real* outlet.

Evie makes her excuses to Don and Dee, and leaves.

Dimple takes one look at Evie's red eyes as she heads out of Dee's office, and hands her a mini-pack of tissues. "Welcome to the Don Kieselstein Experience," she whispers, her expression sympathetic. "We have a therapy group that drinks and bitches on Wednesday nights, if you're interested."

Evie nods her thanks and takes the tissues.

As she reaches the elevator, she hears a pair of low heels clacking along behind her. It's Dee, in her sensible black patent Ferragamo pumps. She carries a fat, beat-up leather satchel under one arm.

"Ignore my cousin," Dee says as they wait for the elevator together. "When he's disappointed, he lashes out." She straightens her skirt and continues. "Do you mind if I walk you back? I have to see Misha anyway."

Evie shrugs. And realizes she's still clutching the manila envelope with Misha's photo in her hands.

EVIE TRAILS DEE back to Meserov & Co. As Dee moves to open the closed door to Misha's inner office, Evie remembers Misha's comments about wanting an hour to himself and touches Dee's forearm to get her attention. "Um, let me just see if he's ready."

Dee steps back, and smiles at Gemma as Evie slips into Misha's office, closing the door behind her.

He is lying on the chaise longue, his eyes closed. He doesn't move or acknowledge her presence in any way, other than saying, "Dee's here, isn't she?"

"Yes," Evie says. "She didn't say what for, but she's... nice?"

Misha sits up. "She is definitely the preferable of the two Tweedles." He still looks exhausted, staring dully at the floor, but he makes a beckoning gesture. "Once more into the breach," he sighs. "Let her in."

Evie opens the door. "Dee? He's ready for you now."

Dee steps inside, her expression quickly morphing from one of impatience to one of confusion and wonder. She stares at Misha's desk, which has nothing on its surface except Misha, sitting cross-legged and smiling. Then she turns to Evie, and stares at her. Evie smiles back.

"Misha," Dee says, pointing at Evie and then at Gemma. "These women are miracle workers." She walks over and prods the bare surface of the desk, as if verifying it's not an illusion. "I haven't seen your desk clear... ever." She looks over at Evie, her voice full of disbelief. "How?"

Misha is trying to look affronted, but it's undermined by the fact that he can't stop grinning. "I am organized," he says. "It's just... nobody else understands my system."

"Then find me the Miyamoto file," Dee says, raising her chin in challenge.

"Uh," Misha says, glancing over at the neatly stacked files below the Christopher Wool painting. "My system is currently undergoing routine maintenance."

Dee shakes her head fondly and sits down on the chaise longue.

"New case?" Misha says.

"New case," Dee responds.

"I'll just…" Evie starts, stepping towards the door. She's surprised when Misha waves his hand at her, indicating she should sit too.

"Stay," he says. "I want you to start helping me with the research phase of my work."

She nods and plops down next to Dee on the chaise longue. The irony doesn't escape her: she's finally getting to use the skills she went to college for, but for someone who is increasingly looking like he might be the bad guy.

"This place needs another chair," Dee says.

"Baby steps," Evie replies. "We only just found the floor."

"Now," Dee says, pulling a file out of her document bag and handing it to Misha. "This is an interesting one. California couple, but claim residence in New York for tax and legal purposes. You know StarTech?"

"The cellphone people?" Evie says. She has a StarTech 7 in her bag; she had hoped when she was all caught up on rent to buy herself a secondhand StarTech 9 or 10.

Dee nods. "Selene and Eric Overstreet. He started the company soon after they were married. Without a prenup," she continues, her voice dipping into registers of disapproval. "Now Selene is getting older, and Eric wishes to marry some girl from StarTech's PR department." She sighs. "And we need to keep him from losing half the company in the divorce."

"They're in San Francisco?" Misha asks, flipping through the files.

"For the spring. They'll come back to New York in July, and that's when Eric wants to begin proceedings."

"That's not a lot of time," Misha says.

"Please, Misha," Dee groans. "I've seen you pick someone up within twenty-four hours."

"Well, indeed, but I don't like cheating."

"Define cheating," she says, ever the interrogator, her eyes narrowing.

Misha grunts and makes a dismissive gesture.

Dee sighs. "There's a party at their place in Palo Alto next week, an annual thing they do. You'll be invited."

"Oh?" Misha asks, something playful sneaking into his expression. He passes the file to Evie. "Evie, everything about the Overstreets that's not in the file. Interests, scandals, rumors, no matter how trivial. Her favorite color. Her favorite flower. What sort of man or woman she's seen with, when not with her husband. What sort of movies she goes to. Books she likes. *Anything.*"

Evie nods. "I can do that."

Dee smiles. "Well, I'll leave you to it, then," she says, smoothing her skirt as she stands.

Dee leaves, but Evie remains, her fingers tracing over the manila envelope next to her. Wondering what to do with it, how to bring it up. She's aware of Misha watching her.

"How much can you have by the morning?" Misha asks. And he's right there, standing in front of her. She hadn't heard him get off the desk.

Her breath catches in her throat. "Enough," she says.

And she knows she's being incredibly obvious. Easier to read than a billboard, especially to Misha, who seduces people for a living. She sighs and thrusts the envelope at him. "Don called you a whore and made me look at this. And I accidentally didn't give it back to him. I'm glad, because he shouldn't have it. You... you should have it."

Misha raises an eyebrow, and takes the envelope. Evie can tell from his amused expression that he knows exactly what it is. "I wanted to tell him to fuck off, so badly," Evie whispers. "If you weren't around, he wouldn't win half as many cases, would he? And he still insults you."

She gasps as Misha puts his thumb under her chin and presses gently, tilting her head up to meet his gaze. As she drowns in the glacial blue of his eyes, he whispers back, "I don't care what anyone says about me. It's very sweet of you to stand up for me, and this is the second time you've done it, which is two more times than anyone else ever has. But I have a tendency to make very dangerous people angry, and you shouldn't get between me and my bad habits. I can defend myself. Against anyone."

"You shouldn't have to," Evie says, turning her face aside, away from his hand, because she's going to embarrass herself if she has to look at him any longer. "You deserve friends. You're..." She swallows. "You're a good person," she says. *I want you to be a good person.*

Misha withdraws his hand; he runs his fingers over the top edge of the envelope, contemplating its contents. "I'm not, but I thank you. That means a lot."

They stare at each other, and the moment stretches. Evie realizes she needs to leave Misha's presence now, before she says something really stupid. She clutches the Overstreet file for dear life. "Okay," she says, her voice coming out high and cracked. "I'm going to start on this now." And then, mere feet from the door, she says something really stupid anyhow. "Nice picture, by the way."

Misha shrugs, and tosses the envelope onto his desk. "It's Photoshopped."

He catches the blush that races across Evie's cheeks as she imagines what part, and he laughs. "Keep your eyes open this time."

And then he's pulling up his shirt.

Evie is pretty sure she stops breathing. She needs to have a serious word with Misha about his body and its status as a weapon of mass distraction, because—

—there's a scar on his chest, a foot long, nasty and jagged, over his heart.

Misha smiles ruefully as he touches it. "Not the most attractive thing, is it?" His eyes, always so expressive, shine with vulnerability and regret. "Luckily, quite easy to get rid of in photographs, if not in real life."

Evie wants to hug him and tell him it's okay, he's still the most beautiful thing she's ever seen, but instead she just grips the Overstreet file tighter. "Heart surgery?" she squeaks out.

He nods. "Yeah." A sour flicker of amusement tugs at his lips as he pulls his shirt down again, covering the scar. "I have a rare condition."

Evie wants to say something to take away the pain in his eyes. To make that sunny, too-wide grin come back. "The, um, the Japanese have this idea that nothing is truly perfect until it has an imperfection. They'll rub gold into the cracks when they repair something broken, because the break is an important part of the object's history, not something to be disguised."

Misha smiles then, warm and sad, but Evie still counts it as victory. His eyes are wet with emotion and she realizes he's about three breaths away from crying. He steps into her space and moves to hug her, but stops, his hands held awkwardly a few inches from her. "I can…?"

"Yeah. Okay. This once," Evie mock-grumbles. "But don't make a habit of it."

Then two strong, impossibly warm arms are circling her and she finds her cheek pressed against Misha's chest. She can't hear his heart beat over how loud hers is. She has *definitely* stopped breathing. He's so warm and solid. She feels like nothing could ever hurt her again, safe in his embrace.

He rests his chin on the top of her head, and whispers a thank you into her hair. "Maybe one day I'll have the courage to paint it gold," he says.

Misha steps away from her and turns, embarrassed. His departure is swift and she feels cold suddenly, aware of every inch of his absence. He shoves his hands in his pockets and pretends to be interested in something out the window. She takes a deep breath and walks to the outer office…

… and sashays suavely into the corner of the reception desk, because she isn't looking where she's going.

She swallows the twang of pain in her hip and sits down, her smile only slightly dimmed. She flips open the Overstreet file and sets up a fresh Google Doc.

And because she can't stop herself, because it's like picking a scab, she opens up the document of notes she's already made on Misha and begins a new search: *Kieselstein divorce heart attack.*

What she finds terrifies her. As the saying goes, once is chance, twice is coincidence, and three times is conspiracy. In the decade Misha has been working with Meyer, Luchins & Black, six people have died of heart failure within a year of their divorce. Some were the client; some were the other side. Two more people have unreported, but non-violent, causes of death.

Evie notes down their names and writes up a couple lines on each of them from publicly available information. Over the weekend, she'll research them to try to distinguish a pattern across the deaths, a link, other than the obvious: Misha. But for now, she needs to focus on Heartbreak Incorporated's next target.

CHAPTER SEVEN

BY FRIDAY MORNING, Evie knows that Selene Overstreet is forty-seven, has had a light, well-done face lift recently, likes the color blue, last read a book called *The Command to Look*, prefers spicy, floral scents and natural fibers. No rumored affairs, but she has a pinched, distracted look that wasn't there five years ago. She tends to wear skinny jeans and expensive coats, paired with $5,000 Dior heels. She's into ballet, and oversees her husband's rare book collection. She helped fund a documentary on a male ballet dancer with dark hair and light eyes.

"I think you're in," Evie calls out, leaning forwards on the sofa so she can look into Misha's office. "She likes hot blue-eyed Russians with good bodies."

Misha comes out to see. He leans down and braces his hands against the sofa's arm, getting into Evie's space so he can look at her screen. Normally this would make her profoundly uncomfortable—she hates people looking over her shoulder—but her internal proximity alarm seems to be on permanent snooze for Misha. "Only one problem," he says, and she can feel the smile on his face. "I'm Georgian. We're not Slavic peoples. Not Russian."

"Ugh, potayto, pohtahto. If Americans don't commonly know a fact, it doesn't actually exist, you know that, right?" Evie says.

Misha makes an unhappy noise at the back of his throat. One hand moves off the sofa and Evie feels herself poked in the ribs, hard. She squirms, lets out an annoyed "Ow!" and wrinkles her nose at Misha.

Misha wrinkles his nose back. "Russians have a long history of committing massacres in my country."

"Oh," Evie says. "I'm sorry."

"But we gave them Stalin and Beria, so I suppose we're even." And Misha smiles absently and looks back at the screen, letting it all slide off, in the way of old wounds that will never stop hurting. Things that you joke about, because it's all you have left, laughing and pointing at the absurdity of it all, too tired to spar with the anger and the sadness that ride with the real memories.

He leans over Evie again. "Let me handle the strategy part. It's what I'm good at. Now, what else does she like, other than dancers? What was the last thing she bought?"

Evie rolls her eyes and moves over, patting the sofa to indicate that Misha should sit down and stop looming. "Let me see," she says, as she clicks through tabs. She comes up to an ArtWire report from a Swann's auction. "The last big-ticket thing they both bought was for their collection. They're into rare books and manuscripts. They paid about fifteen million dollars for some old Book of Hours—"

Out of the corner of her eye Evie sees the muscles of Misha's forearms tense. Then one hand is on hers, pushing it aside, taking the laptop from her. He enlarges the photos that accompany the auction report. Misha leans in close to the screen, body taut as a bowstring, as he pages through photos of a tattered old vellum book, its script archaic and incomprehensible.

"Fuck," he says. "They bought this six months ago." Misha turns to face Evie, and she gasps. He looks dangerous, that same focused, panther-like viciousness she'd seen when he took down the two security guards at the Met. But underneath it, she can see a flicker of something new: pure, white terror. "I need to know everywhere they've been, separately or together, since buying that book," Misha says, his voice an urgent rasp. "Everywhere. Bring the list into my office when you have it."

Then he's gone, doors slamming shut behind him.

Evie begins typing Selene Overstreet's name into a new search. She gets as far as *SELENE OVE* before the search bar autofills and her photo pops up. Evie stares at it, idly weighing up who is the worse off: Selene as the first wife, looks fading while the wealthy businessman—never very attractive in the first place—transfers his affection to a younger model. Or the younger model, enjoying the attentions of a balding, ferret-faced tycoon. Fucking for handbags. What happens, Evie wonders, when your only currency is a rather commonplace sort of beauty?

Evie looks down at the keyboard of her laptop, her unremarkable hands hovering over the keys. What happens when you don't even have that? she thinks to herself. When does she stop being full of potential, and start being a has-been? At thirty? At forty? Right now? When will she wake to find that her tomorrows have dried up?

What will *any* of them do? Misha when he gets too old and has no hearts left to break but his own; Gemma with plenty of boys to organize, but none who see her and love her for more than that. Evie herself, hopping from job to job, fifty years old and with no savings, still living with a roommate in an unfashionable part of Brooklyn.

She takes a moment and just breathes. She can't bring herself to sniff around on the trail of the uber-rich quite yet, and tabs back instead to the old book. Books have never let her down, and this one is no exception: she finds a kind of peace in staring blankly at its meaningless words in their decorative red and black ink; its menagerie of gilded beasties curling around illuminated capitals. Someone painted every letter of that book, and 700 years later, it was still being cherished. What had she ever made? What would she leave behind?

Evie shifts, and closes her eyes. It had been a long and overly exciting week and she was full of leftover emotion and the dry residue of too much stress. She needs to sleep the weekend away, and then everything will be fine.

She does the search. Like most avoided tasks, once begun it turns out to be distressingly easy. The Overstreets hadn't actually travelled much: Sundance, LA, New York, LA again, a party up in Seattle. All depicted in their own social media posts and others'. She scrawls down the approximate dates and knocks on Misha's door, getting a mumbled *come in* as a response.

Misha is leaning over his desk, tapping at his phone while also scrolling through search results on his laptop. He looks like he's about to go to war.

Evie shuts the door behind her, then walks over to the desk. She puts the paper with the Overstreets' travel history in front of Misha. Something occurs to her. "You were a soldier, weren't you?"

"Mm," he says in confirmation, pulling the paper towards him. He looks up at her, almost apologetic. "Russian cavalry."

"Nothing about you is simple, is it?" Evie says.

"No." He starts typing dates and locations into his phone, and... he's looking at star charts. The night sky, on those dates, in different parts of America. "But we need to pretend it is. I am here, you are here, and we are going to destroy a book."

Then he turns his attention to the laptop. "Let's see how stupid you are, Eric Overstreet," he whispers as he types in another search. It's for missing persons.

"Why are we destroying a book?" Evie asks, leaning on the desk. "It's just a Book of Hours."

"No, it's not," Misha murmurs, the glow of the laptop screen making his eyes even more eerie than normal as he reads the results of his search. "There is a second book inside of it. Take all the red letters and put them together. That second book... it's a thing of great evil."

Evie scrunches up her face. The conversation is making less and less sense, but Misha seems utterly certain of what he's saying. "What does it do?" she asks, her voice hesitant.

"Wrong question," Misha says, distracted. "It does nothing. It's just a book. But through it you can learn..." he wipes a hand down his face, "... bad things."

"How do you know..."

Misha smiles. There's no warmth in it. "Rich family. Misspent youth."

"So, uh, can we define evil? Because you're casually making me an accessory to something that's sounding extremely criminal and I'd like more information." Evie hesitates. "Uh, you're not going to kill me or anything if I don't want to be a part of this, are you?"

"What? No. Don't be ridiculous," Misha snaps. He shivers, as if shaking off something unpleasant, and looks at her. "You're right. You shouldn't be a part of this. Go home. Have a nice weekend, Evie. I probably won't be in next week. You're... you're a very unusual person, and I'm glad you're here."

"Okay," Evie says.

She gets halfway to the door.

"I need to know," she says.

Misha abandons his desk and leans against the window, staring down onto Madison Avenue, seventeen stories below. The low afternoon light silhouettes him, bathing him in rose and gold. "It's better if you don't, Evie. Trust me." He runs a hand through his hair. "I needed to know once, too. Go home, Evie. Watch Netflix."

She sits down on the chaise longue, its worn old leather warm and comforting. She feels tears prick at the corners of her eyes. "I..."

She's crying. She can't pull the emotion back. The façade is fatally cracked, and there's nothing left now but for it to fall apart. "I don't know what I'm doing," she snuffles out between gasps, the words raspy with anger and despair. "I don't know. I don't want to watch fucking Netflix. I don't want to sit at home and stare at the walls. I'm tired of nothing *meaning* anything." Evie exhales, ragged and messy, and she pushes the palms of her hands against her cheeks to try to make it all stop. "I'm tired of just... existing."

She feels Misha's weight as he sits down next to her. He leans his shoulder into hers, a wordless support. "It is hard. I know."

"How would you know?" Evie snuffles sourly through her sobs. "You have a ton of money and you're gorgeous. You own a house. A house! In *Manhattan*. That you inherited. I, I have a room barely large enough for a twin bed and a dresser, there's two feet between my mattress and the wall, and I have to hang my clothes on a rail in our so-called living room. We have *cockroaches* in the kitchen. And I can still barely afford rent. What sort of problems can you have?"

Misha exhales, shifting away from her. "I've made a lot of bad choices. Very bad ones."

"Like *what*?" Evie frowns. She knows she's being petty but something small and nasty in her can't help it. She wants to lash out at Misha, because there is a sick pleasure in dirtying pretty things.

"If I told you, you'd never speak to me again," Misha says quietly. "So I don't want to tell you. You think I'm a good person, and I know it's a lie, but I just want to pretend for a little longer."

Misha doesn't say anything else. He just passes Evie a red and white handkerchief, and sits next to her as her tears die down.

Once she is sure her voice won't crack with fresh sobs, she says, "I'm sorry. It's been a long week."

Misha doesn't respond with words, just bumps his shoulder gently against hers again.

"Look," he says, as the light of the setting sun bathes the canyons of Midtown in orange fire, "if you... if you help me with this book... it's like going through a looking-glass. You can't go back. Things won't be the same, ever. It's very dangerous. And at the end, you won't be able to tell anyone. This won't launch your journalism career."

"But the book is something bad?" Evie asks.

Misha nods. "It makes monsters, of a sort."

"You're sure?" Evie says, because the rational part of her is whispering that this is nuts, she should run, and another part of her is rooted to the spot, knowing that it might take only the slightest push right now to find out what she needs to know about Misha.

Misha stands up and paces, catlike, towards the laptop on his desk.

"It made me," he murmurs.

And there it is. "You killed Greg Pickford," Evie says.

Misha is watching her, over the desk. In his absence, it was easy to think of him as a cold-blooded killer. But in the same room as him, it's almost unimaginable: his slightly-too-big features telegraphing every emotion he felt, his strange eyes shifting through their remarkable range of color, from bright summer skies to the grey storm of a winter sea. He looks away, but the corner of his mouth twitches into the beginning of a smile. "And what led you to this conclusion, little investigator?"

Evie opens her mouth, and closes it.

"You have proof? I'd be interested to hear it," Misha continues, leaning forwards, arms braced on the desk. It's relaxed, easy, but serves to emphasize how wide his shoulders are.

"I have no proof," Evie admits. "Just a feeling."

And Misha just... watches her, leaning on that stupid desk, head tilted slightly, a quiet amusement playing lightly across his expressive features. It's like being watched by a jaguar, the lazy curiosity of the apex predator wondering if its prey will do something more interesting than freeze or run.

Evie stares back. She's on to how he uses silence now. After enough time passes that her heartbeat has slowed down, she raises an eyebrow at him.

"I did not, actually," he says, looking down to trace a finger over the newly clean top of his desk. "He really did have a weak heart. If he had managed to control his temper then he still might be among us, but alas." He looks at Evie again. "I can't say I'm sorry he's dead."

"But you knew he wouldn't come back for his photos," Evie says, doggedly. "You knew he was going to die."

"Yes. And I know if I don't destroy that book, many more will die," Misha says. "Go home, Evie. I must deal with this." He turns away from her to face the setting sun through the windows, and stretches his arms above his head, as if limbering up for a fight. "Next one, perhaps. But not this one."

Evie nods and stands up.

She needs space. She walks out of the office without a backwards look at Misha, grabs her bag, and mutters *have a nice weekend* at Gemma.

The headache hits her on the subway ride home to Brooklyn. Post-tension migraine, her doctor calls it. She presses her eyes shut and tries to shove down the nausea, not helped by the mingled scents of old piss and takeout curry in the confines of the ancient subway carriage. It feels like needles are being driven into her brain.

All she ever wanted was a mystery. The chance to solve a murder, to make the world a better place by dragging something sinister out into the light. Now she has it, and all she wants is to throw up. All she's done is run away.

In her mind, in the fine country of let's-pretend, where she Woodward & Bernsteined her way to a Pulitzer in her first investigation, everyone involved had been sinister. The villains who needed to be taken down, they were men she knew on sight were not on the side of the angels. Nowhere in those fantasies had been six feet of blue-eyed trouble who…

… who somehow, despite being *shady as fuck*, didn't seem like the bad guy.

That's the problem. All the evidence—circumstantial though it is so far—points to him being a killer. But her instincts, her gut, won't stop telling her that Misha is a decent human being. He hired Gemma, not only because she was an excellent secretary, but also because she'd had something awful happen to her and needed a place to go. He was genuinely kind to Stewart, and respected Beatriz enough that he would try to help her make a life with her current target.

But what if she's wrong? What if this isn't her gut talking?

Would she be so willing to believe in Misha if he were ugly?

SHE CHECKS HER email on the walk home. There's a message from Ireshi, Dr Chaudry's intern. She sits on her stoop and reads it.

Hello Evie! Sorry to take a few days, we got really busy here. I'm not sure what I can tell you to help with your investigation, other than I think it was unlikely that a nerve agent was used. While an acetylcholinesterase inhibitor is one of the few poisons that can cause the sort of cardiac arrest your victim suffered, they are profoundly (and thankfully!) impractical to use, and your victim would have had to have been exposed to the agent almost immediately prior to his death. Which means your suspect would have to have given him something that he would not touch for six hours. He touches it, or sprays it on himself (there was quite a famous case with a cologne sample!), death follows swiftly if it is of the newer, Russian-developed organophosphate AChEI agents.

The problem is, nerve agents don't go away. They're quite oily and adhere to surfaces. And only a tiny dose is needed to produce an effect. You said he died in his office? There would have been secretaries, friends, colleagues, EMT staff, perhaps even family, handling almost everything in his office and on his person, especially if poisoning was not suspected. Even if it were, say, a small vial of perfume slipped in a pocket, or a card soaked with the agent while the victim was out of the room, the likelihood of someone else touching it is extremely high. There is another case of a man's phone being coated with a nerve agent; he died, and then the poison harmed his secretary a month later from the same phone!

I would say in a situation like this, where you will not have access to the victim's autopsy records and the family is not investigating, the only indication that a nerve agent is involved could be a sickness or death of someone who also handled the victim's belongings. Unfortunately, that person may not be someone in your victim's circle: four months after the case with the cologne sample, a couple found the bottle in a park some distance away, sprayed it on themselves, and one of them died. Your collateral victim may be a janitor, or someone who simply finds an interesting little bottle in the grass.

I'm sorry I can't be more help. While this is truly not our area of specialization in the lab (we are working on targeted use of acetylcholinesterase inhibitors to increase neuroplasticity in certain neurodegenerative conditions), we are of course a little fascinated by the more sinister uses of the compounds, and Dr Chaudry is frequently called in to provide expert analysis on cases involving suspected organophosphate AChEI poisoning. I wish you luck with your investigation.

Also, please do not ever spray anything on yourself that you find on the ground.

Kind regards, Ireshi R.

Evie tucks her phone in her pocket and begins the long slog up to the fifth floor.

CLAUDIA IS HOME. Although Friday nights are busy, Saturdays and Sundays are downright hell for caterers: up at dawn, in bed at 2am, do it all again the next day. Claudia had gotten into the habit of letting her assistant handle Fridays so she could rest up before the weekend assault of bridezillas, bar mitzvahs and charity galas full of nervous, birdlike women who, when they thought nobody was looking, would stare at the food with a terrifying longing.

Most Fridays, Claudia will tend to watch one of the calmer reality-TV shows and play with her phone at the same time, and then go to bed by 9pm. This one is no different. She looks up from the TV, already in her sleep shirt and shorts, as Evie slumps in. "How's the new work?"

"Ugh," Evie says.

It's too late for rizatriptan to stave off her headache, but Evie goes into the bathroom and swallows one dry anyway, a hail-Mary to the migraine gods. She flops next to Claudia on their tiny sofa. Their clothes overhang the sofa arm, a fuzzy raspberry coat she'd gotten on clearance tickling Evie's hand. "I can't believe you're watching a cooking show on your day off," Evie mumbles.

"It's the British one," Claudia smiles. "They're so *niiice*. You can't not watch this show and feel good. They help each other!

And cheer each other on!" She gives Evie an assessing look. "Speaking of help…"

Evie groans and makes an operatic gesture.

"Ohhh," Claudia says. "You have a crush on him." She shrugs. "He is stupid levels of hot."

"That is maybe ten percent of the problem," Evie says, her voice sharp.

Claudia looks at her severely.

"Okay. Thirty-three percent."

"Is he a jerk? Because if he's mean to you I'm gonna come down there," Claudia says. Her eyes are already back on the baking show, where someone is making disasters out of macarons.

"No," Evie replies. "Which makes it worse. He's nice. In a weird way." She picks at the fraying beige tweed of their old Ikea sofa. "He's either been quietly killing off the firm's worst clients for years, or I just threw over the best chance I ever had at firsthand investigative journalism. Or, y'know, both."

"Wait, back up to the killing part?" Claudia says, muting the baking show.

"Every couple years, one of his clients dies. Usually something related to heart failure, usually a few months after meeting Misha."

"Like the Pickford guy died!" Claudia says.

"Yeah, like Greg Pickford." Evie twists one of her curls around a finger. "He's the only one to die so close to being seen with Misha… but statistically, it can't be just chance."

"But how? Poison?"

Evie shakes her head. "It would have shown up. He said he had a rare medical condition, so I looked that up too… and if it was infectious, that would have appeared in at least one autopsy result too. His clients are wealthy, powerful people, Claudia. If they die unexpectedly, the family looks for reasons." She rubs the bridge of her nose. "And there aren't any. Nothing out of the ordinary, in any of those deaths, except people's hearts giving out much earlier than they should. So now I'm wondering if I'm crazy."

"You're not crazy, Evie. You have great instincts. If there's something strange about him, you should believe yourself," Claudia says, her voice firm.

"But I don't know *what* I believe," Evie sighs. "My gut says trust him. But then this afternoon he kind of freaked out about an antique book and he's flying off to California to break into some tech billionaire's house and burn it. And I think he wanted me to go with him."

Claudia glares at her. "No. The end." She turns up her TV show again. "When you said you were finally going places, I didn't think you meant jail, or the hospital. Because that's where you will end up."

Evie decides not to mention the part about monsters. She grabs her iPad from her room and does the same search as she saw Misha do earlier: missing persons, reported while or soon after the Overstreets had visited their city. Luckily, her memory is nearly photographic, so it wasn't hard to recall the right dates and cities.

"Ooh, macarons. Those are tough," Claudia mutters from next to her.

"Holy shit!" Evie screams, nearly dropping her iPad as her blood turns to ice water. Claudia leans over Evie's shoulder to see; her curiosity rapidly turning into a hiss of shock. *Inland Empire: Ritual killing suspected in homeless man's murder.* Evie feels faint as she clicks on the next results tab. *Missing hiker found near Aspen, partially eaten.* She moves east, to New York, where the Overstreets had spent last May and June. *Body in East River missing internal organs.*

There are almost 17,000 people murdered every year in the US. Evie knows her crime stats. Three hundred and fifty of those are in New York and about three hundred in LA. Someone dies violently every day. It could all be a coincidence.

… There were too many goddamn coincidences.

Evie is in her room and dialing her phone before she can allow herself second thoughts. It rings twice, then there's a little questioning noise of surprise from the other end.

"What's the deal with the missing body parts?" she asks.

"Evie, I'm standing in the middle of JFK," Misha mutters low into the phone. "This isn't the time to explain."

"Fine," she says. "I'm coming with you." She looks around for something to pack clothes in.

"I'm on the last flight out. It leaves in an hour. You won't make it."

"Watch me," Evie hisses. She grabs her handbag, stuffs a change of underwear in it, and heads towards the door.

"Okay," Misha murmurs, barely audible over the background noise. "I'll get you a ticket. Delta. Terminal Four. I'll meet you by the coffee shop, before security."

"On my way," she says, and hangs up.

"Where are you going?" says Claudia, standing up, as Evie is halfway out the door.

"San Francisco," Evie shouts. "I'll text you tomorrow!"

Claudia comes barreling out after her and grabs her arm. "Evie, this is *not* safe."

"I know." Evie takes a deep breath and pulls her arm out of Claudia's grasp. "But you said to trust my instincts."

CHAPTER EIGHT

EVIE TUMBLES OUT of her taxi at the airport ten minutes before boarding closes. Misha is waiting, strangely alert as he lounges against the entrance of a Starbucks. He's thrown a black velvet blazer and a long grey scarf on over the lavender T-shirt and black skinny jeans he'd worn to work, and he looks like the world's most fashionable panther. She only sees him at rest for a moment before he spots her and prowls over. His face is indecipherable; she can't tell whether he is pleased to see her, or resentful of her intrusion.

He takes her arm, gently but firmly, and leads her through some special part of security where there is no line, and she doesn't have to take off her shoes. Then it's the walk to their gate, and Evie struggles to keep up with Misha's long stride but she's not going to ask him to slow down. She'll die before she lets on that she can barely keep up.

They go straight onto the plane and within a few steps of the entrance, Misha is tugging on her arm again, turning her towards a seat. *Oh.* They're sitting in First Class. He tosses his small duffel bag under the seat in front. "Do you mind taking the window seat? I don't like to be boxed in," he says.

The First Class seats are huge, as big as an armchair. Evie shakes her head—the window is just fine—and slides in.

Misha lowers himself down next to her and looks at her, his gaze cool and assessing, but there's still a hint of surprise in it. Evie likes that she's managed to confound his expectations somehow. It makes her feel like she's won.

"You should get some sleep," Misha says. "We don't get in until 2am." His eyes flick down to her handbag. "Masha flew out earlier. She can go with you and get clothes and things you need for the trip tomorrow." His eyes crinkle. "She has to get things for me anyway, so."

"Do you always…" Evie starts, pointing at his tiny carry-on bag. Then she sighs. "Of course you do."

"Don't you know?" Misha teases, deadpan. "I have a house. In Manhattan. That I inherited."

Evie flips him off.

Misha cracks up, his laugh bright, body folding with the energy of it. "Welcome to the lifestyles of the rich and disorganized. Besides," he says, "we have a party to go to. A party full of judgmental tech entrepreneurs. Whatever you have in that handbag will not suffice."

"All I have is some underwear," Evie admits.

Misha tilts his head, considering. "Well, it *would* cause a distraction, but it gets rather cold in San Francisco at night. Goosebumps would ruin the look."

"I hate you," Evie says.

Misha just looks at her with an expression that makes it clear he's pretending to think about her in her underwear.

"Uugh," she groans, and lifts her lip in a snarl.

"I'm glad you came, Evie," Misha says quietly, staring down at his lap. "It's nice having someone to talk to. To have a friend."

"You have Masha…" she says.

He shrugs as he settles into a comfortable sprawl in the First Class seat, his half-laced boots braced against the footrest in front of him. "Family is always less of a consolation than you'd expect."

Evie watches out the window as they take off, New York shrinking to a dazzling tapestry of lights below them. The flight attendant comes past, bringing champagne. Misha looks questioningly at Evie. She nods, so he takes two glasses, and gives them both to Evie. He has a cheap paperback sci-fi novel open on his lap; the title is in Russian.

She sips the champagne and the bubbles burn against her tongue. The acidity gives her the little push of courage she needs. "So. Body parts."

Misha shoots her a glance that conveys his amusement at her tenacity, then he sighs. He leans in towards her. Their faces are very close; cheekbones almost touching. "It's practice," Misha says, finally. His eyes go distant for a moment. "The book… it teaches a ritual. But it's very difficult. If you mess up, you die. So… some practice with a knife is useful."

"What if you don't mess up?" Evie says, whispering. "What happens?"

Misha exhales, long and slow. "Remember when we first met? I asked you if you believed in the supernatural, and you said you didn't logically believe those sorts of things existed."

She nods.

"You were wrong."

Evie's brows furrow. Questions tumble forth in her mind, but as she opens her mouth to ask the first, Misha puts a finger on her lips and shakes his head. He returns to his sci-fi novel and doesn't meet her eyes for the rest of the flight.

A BRIGHT YELLOW muscle car is waiting for them right outside Arrivals. Evie had always wondered what kind of jerk drove a yellow sports car, and now she knows. She has to admit to herself, though, that the low, sleek, powerful car suits Misha, and even the flashy color works with his look in the way black or red wouldn't.

As he opens the passenger door for her, Evie watches a passing woman walk into a cement bollard, so distracted is she by the combined sight of Misha and the car. Evie has never met anyone who could weaponize their sexuality as well as Misha could, and as effortlessly.

And yet, no photos of him exist online. No Facebook, Twitter, Instagram. Nothing. Search results for any variation on Mikhail Meserov comes up with nada. Evie had originally found that unremarkable: he was careful, old-fashioned, or both. But since his hints about the supernatural on the plane, it had begun to gnaw at her. Why does someone so beautiful not want to be seen?

No, she thinks. He *loves* being seen. Hence the skinny jeans and the thin T-shirts that show off his form.

Misha doesn't want to be *recorded*.

Because of a link to the supernatural.

Evie thinks of all the trashy novels that Claudia reads on her phone: vampires and werewolves and fallen angels and fairy knights. All manner of nonsense.

The world could not contain that sort of strangeness. It was impossible. It would be noticed, photographed, captured. Experimented on, or celebrated, or both.

But what if there weren't packs of werewolves or covens of witches or... whatever the collective noun for a group of vampires is? What if there were only a handful of supernatural beings, and they were very, very careful? And part of that care was avoiding being recorded.

She glances over at Misha as he drives them south through the California night towards Palo Alto. He catches her eye and smiles, weary but reassuring. Suddenly she feels very ridiculous indeed. He's so normal in that moment, stifling a yawn, fingers on the steering wheel tapping along to a song only he can hear. There are a few hairs caught on the velvet of his jacket.

She stares a little too long and his gaze flicks to the corners of his eyes, to her, and he says, "What?"

"You tired?" she asks.

"No. I'm fine. Don't sleep much anyway." He checks the GPS. "Almost there. How are you holding up?"

What Evie doesn't say is: *I'm so exhausted I seriously just had a fifteen-minute internal conversation with myself about whether you're a vampire.*

What she does say is: "I could go to bed." It comes out low, husky, and sly.

Then Evie realizes how much accidental innuendo was in that

statement. She flushes bright red, and squeaks, "Sorry, I didn't mean—"

Misha laughs, bright and happy. The thing about Misha is, he laughs with his whole body. He shakes his head, leans forward, flexes his arms as he taps the steering wheel in amusement. His eyes are positively twinkling as he glances over at her, his mouth set in a naughty smirk. "I know. But your delivery was perfect. I might have to steal that."

He tucks his chin, hair falling over his face, and stares out at the road. When he speaks, he's dropped his voice a couple registers to something smoky and whiskey-rough, but still playful. "I could go to bed," he growls, and it comes out not as a statement, but as a promise. He raises an eyebrow at her. "Hm?"

Evie shifts in her seat. Damn him. "Stop it."

"What?" he says, innocently. And then he makes a teasing, questioning noise that seems to run on some magic frequency direct to her groin.

Evie shuts her eyes. Because nice as it would be to believe that Misha means a word of what he's saying, she knows he doesn't. "You're over the line," she says. "Put it away. I'm not here for you to practice on." She moves as far away from him as she can in the passenger seat, and rests her head against the cool glass of the window. "It's shitty and manipulative," she mutters, but the anger has bled out of her words and now she's just tired, and this is all so much more than she wants to cope with after being awake for almost twenty-four hours.

Misha doesn't say anything for a moment, then he stutters, "I, I'm sorry." In her peripheral vision she can see his right hand lift off the gearshift and hover near her, wanting to touch her arm, reassure her, but then he thinks better of it and awkwardly moves his hand to the steering wheel. "I didn't mean to make you uncomfortable, I was just…" He exhales, frustrated, lost for the right words. "I think this is all I know how to do any more."

"It's okay, Misha," Evie says, watching the night speed by out of the passenger window. "I know."

The freeway rolls by underneath them for a few silent minutes, dashed yellow lines appearing in the headlights' glow and disappearing again, before Misha says, "You should get some sleep. It's another half hour until we get to the hotel."

Evie puts her seat back all the way, if for no other reason than to better ignore Misha. She doesn't think she'll fall asleep but the rumble of the engine and the hum of the road under their tires must send her under almost immediately.

She half-remembers Misha saying her name, leaning over her to unbuckle her seatbelt. The car isn't moving, and the air around her is cold. She mumbles and snuggles closer towards Misha's voice. He says something else and when she doesn't reply, she's wrapped up in something warm and she's moving again. The warm thing smells wonderful. She curls up closer to it.

THERE'S A KNOCK at the door.

Evie sits up. She's awake and panicking in the same breath, utterly disoriented. She is on top of a king-size hotel bed, still in her travelling clothes. Her shoes are off, and her bag is on the bedside table. The room is pleasant, in that anodyne version of modern that rich people mistake for style: muted colors, empty spaces, natural light.

She remembers the sports car, the rhythm of the freeway lane markers disappearing into the night past her window, and then… nothing.

The knock comes again.

"Evie?" says a woman's voice. "It's Masha."

"Just a sec," she grumbles, rolling out of bed. She pads into the bathroom and looks at herself. She's a disaster. Her curls are in full riot mode; her meticulously applied green eyeliner and mascara have smudged all around her eyes while she slept, and now she looks like some sort of tropical raccoon.

Ugh.

Well, she's seen Masha naked in a rat-infested Brooklyn street, so.

She opens the door. Masha is standing there in a casual, floral-print dress, sunglasses pushed up into her hair. Masha clears her throat and Evie looks down, only noticing then that the woman is holding out an extra-large coffee and a paper bag that has warm, toasted-bagel smells coming from it. Her nails are painted gold. "Good morning. I thought you might be hungry? Misha said your flight arrived very late," she says, her light accent adding a gentle music to the words.

Evie clutches the offerings like a lifeline and mumbles, "For the record, I like you a lot better than your brother."

Masha grins. "You slept well?"

"Yeah," Evie mutters, padding towards a small round dining table in faded wood and distressed silver lacquer. The hotel room is bigger than her and Claudia's whole apartment, and once she's more awake she will work up the energy to resent that more properly. "Um, how did I get here?"

Masha eases herself into one of the chairs at the table as Evie flops down in the other. "Your least favorite Meserov carried you up. You were completely asleep, apparently."

Evie groans into her coffee.

"Oh!" says Masha, digging in her bag for her phone. "I have something to show you." She keys it open then swipes the screen a few times before pushing it over to Evie. "I'm afraid you're never getting this back."

It's a photo of Misha, in the stupid Snorlax onesie, making a face at the camera as he leans in an open doorway of their house. The onesie is mostly unzipped, because of course Misha's default state is half-naked.

"It's his favorite thing now," sighs Masha. "I think he does it just to annoy me."

"Well, y'know," Evie drawls, "must be a novel experience for him, wearing something that isn't so tight it nearly cuts off his circulation."

Masha's eyes widen in shock, and Evie becomes worried she's violated some unspoken protocol of the *only family is allowed to insult family* variety. Then Masha bursts out laughing. "I'm stealing that," she says. "Thank you." She looks at Evie fondly, which is slightly poor timing as at that moment Evie is trying to cram as much bagel in her mouth as possible. "Misha said I am to take you shopping, as you two are going to a party tonight."

"Mmf," Evie says, trying to communicate a sufficient amount of discomfort about the idea of having clothes picked out for her while also inhaling her bagel.

"Obviously, you are completely able to pick out your own clothes, but Misha thinks if he just gives you money you'll feel guilty about spending it and will buy something cheap. So I am here only to bring you to the right shops and make sure you take advantage of my brother for everything he is worth," Masha says. She tilts her head. "And he's worth a lot. Besides, I'll be busy picking something out for him to wear, so do not think of it as us choosing for you. You will be helping to choose for him."

"Where is he?" Evie says. She feels considerably more alive after half a cup of coffee and most of a sesame bagel.

Masha shrugs. "Off doing Misha things. I don't ask."

Evie begs off for an hour, enough time to take a shower, sort out her hair, and make herself feel like she's returned to some semblance of human. They taxi over to an open-air luxury mall, all warm stone, fountains, and lush greenery. It's bustling, full of a Saturday-morning shopping crowd: healthy, affluent-looking people in khakis and cheerful pastel colors. Evie's inner New Yorker wants to burn them all to hell.

Masha has already put on her sunglasses. Like her brother, she has the gift of looking effortless in the outfits she chooses, which are never remarkable, but achieve a remarkableness on her. A simple Liberty-print silk tea dress, brown leather sandals with high wooden heels, a woven-leather bag, and big tortoiseshell sunglasses, and she is unmistakably the best-dressed woman in the whole shopping center. She is also just about dragging Evie through the quietly jealous throng to the shelter of the most expensive department store in the mall.

Masha is just as tactile as her brother: little touches to Evie's arm, back, or shoulder, taking her hand to guide her through the crowd. Evie never had siblings, so isn't used to the physicality of a large family. Or maybe… she thinks of street-style pictures she's seen of Italian girls, their hands entwined, and she wonders if it's a European thing. It's not unpleasant, it's just… different.

Evie wonders what else is different about the twins. If Misha has some sort of ties to the supernatural, does Masha, also? It seems impossible that Misha would (or could) hide anything from his sister, so Evie has to assume Masha is part of it as well. She is less guarded than her brother, though. If Evie is lucky, maybe Masha will slip up somewhere, let out a clue.

The department store has a lounge area on the top floor. They seem to be expected, as a trim, petite, silver-haired man greets Masha (as a "Miss Vronsky") at the elevators, introducing himself as Alan. Masha folds herself down onto a cream-leather sofa and indicates Evie. "My friend needs an outfit and shoes for a party, and then some daytime things, too," she says, and Evie is surprised by how reserved her voice and posture are around strangers. She's closed off: ankles crossed, arms in close to her, cellphone held up to her chest like a shield. "Evie, tell this gentleman your sizes and preferences, and he will pull things for you." Masha refocuses her attention on the shopper assisting them. "What men's collections do you have? I need some outfits pulled for my brother, too."

"Ah, most of the major ones. We just got in the new pre-fall collections from Tom Ford, Gucci, and Dolce & Gabbana which is *faaabulous*, and some amazing key pieces from Celine, Rick Owens and YSL."

Masha raises an eyebrow and makes an approving noise. She becomes engrossed in her phone, calling up a fashion site and paging through runway photos of men's collections.

Evie realizes Alan is watching her, waiting for her instructions. "Uh," she says. Though she likes looking good, the closest she got to high fashion was discount stores and secondhand sites. And given her dubious financial situation, not even that for a long time. "What do people wear to parties around here?"

"Depends on the party," Alan says. He's surprisingly non-judgmental—well, not surprisingly, Evie thinks, he works on commission—but he still manages to be reassuring. "You can get away with almost anything, but I always suggest sticking with a look you're comfortable with. Let's start this way: skirt or pants?"

"Skirt, I think," Evie says. "But not heels with it. Or flats." She's way too short to wear flats. "Maybe boots? Something easy to stand in." Boots won't do her short legs any favors but they'll make her feel better, and sometimes that's reason enough.

"Oh, we have a lovely Rick Owens boot with a wedge heel. I'll pull that for you. Preference on colors?"

"Um, prints are usually a no. I always say I love black, but I end up wearing rich, deep colors?"

Alan nods. Everything about him is neat and tidy, from his slim, simple grey suit with a pink checked shirt and tie, down to his brown cap-toe brogues that are polished within an inch of their lives. "How bare do you like to be on top?"

"Er. Not very," Evie says.

"Right, then," Alan says with a bright smile. His teeth are unnaturally white. "Something pretty you can wear a bra under. We have some lovely things; you're going to look great. And you're about a size... eight? Yes?"

Evie nods. Alan is about to head off when Masha waves him over, somewhat imperiously. Evie realizes she's only seen the twins with people they know, or with targets. Were they always this removed with strangers? Was Misha as on guard as his sister in new situations, or is it just the nature of being female? That even with a personal shopper who seems a hundred percent not interested in women, Masha is still automatically throwing up walls, trying to keep men from assuming a closeness that doesn't exist.

She glances over at Masha, who is showing Alan pictures on her phone. "... and this from YSL?" she says.

Alan nods, adding a quiet, "Yes, that's gorgeous."

Masha swipes the phone screen and extends it to Evie. "What do you think?" she asks. "Misha, for the party."

It's a runway photo of a slim male model with lank, dirty-blond hair, concave chest and vacant expression, stomping down a catwalk. He's wearing long, tight dark brown leather trousers and a white-on-white patterned shirt open to the navel. A grey-blue military jacket, all gold frogging and touches of velvet, is slung over his shoulders.

Misha is much better looking than the model. Evie pictures how much sexier the skinny trousers would look wrapped around Misha's muscular physique, how well the jacket would hang over broad shoulders that narrow down to a thin, strong waist. She feels herself flush. Masha is still looking at her, waiting for a response. "Er," is all Evie manages.

Masha grins. "If it has that effect on you, and you don't even like Misha, we are *definitely* getting it for the party."

Masha's offhand comment shocks Evie into silence, but before she can respond, Masha is already deep in conversation with Alan, both of them looking at the outfit photo. Once she's finished rattling off her brother's measurements, Alan says, "Very good," inclines himself into a polite bow of acquiescence, and heads towards the elevators.

Once the elevators shut and they're alone, Evie turns to Masha. "Wait. Misha thinks I don't like him?"

"You confuse him," Masha says, tucking her phone away. "Which is not something he's used to."

Evie slouches down on the sofa and rubs her face with her hands. "Ugh," she groans. "Your brother is an idiot."

"I know," hums Masha. "In so many ways. But enlighten me."

"I don't... *not* like him," Evie begins, cautiously. She's pretty sure anything she says to Masha will get back to her twin sooner rather than later. "He confuses me, too." Evie looks down at her fingers. She should probably do her nails before tonight. "He's very attractive," she mutters. Then a little flame of annoyance sparks up in her. "But I'm his assistant. I'm not some toy for him to practice his flirtation skills on. Men who look like your brother don't hit on girls who look like me, and it's just... he needs to think. What he's doing is mean. It's not friendship."

She looks up at the end of her little rant to find Masha staring at her in shock, eyes wide and wet. "No... that's not..." Masha starts. Her hand moves to Evie's. "I know he doesn't think that. He doesn't really have friends, Evie. Both of us... we push people away. Most people see us as playthings, as conquests. You are so rare. You see Misha as he is—"

Evie snorts. "Yeah, *about* what Misha is—"

"—*Evie*. He has let you closer to him than anyone else in a very, very long time," Masha says, her voice sharp. "It's huge."

"I don't know why," Evie says. "I'm not special. Or even pretty. I'm a failure, really."

Masha raises an eyebrow, looking down her nose at Evie. "Nonsense. You're good and honest and very funny, and you *are* pretty."

Thankfully, the elevator dings and Alan steps out, pushing a full garment rail. Over the swish-swash of the approaching clothes, Masha leans in and whispers one last thing to Evie: "And know this. My brother overthinks *everything*. If he does something, he intends every part of it."

Evie feels like her veins are full of champagne. Everything fizzes, an almost unbearable sense of hope and joy building up inside her. She closes her eyes and rubs the bridge of her nose, indulging in a brief fantasy of what it would be like to kiss Misha. She knows it's ridiculous, but for a few short seconds, she allows herself to dream.

When she looks up again, Masha is gracefully pretending to be fascinated by the contents of the clothes rail.

Alan turns out to be some sort of genius. He finds a dusky purple Vivienne Westwood dress that curves and drapes in all the right ways over a black slip that makes her cleavage look better than it ever has in her life. And then there are the boots, tall silvery-pewter and a magic combination of comfortable yet sexy. In them, she's nearly as tall as Masha.

The boots alone cost three months' rent.

She nearly chokes when she sees the price, but Masha just waves a dismissive hand at her. "Your entire outfit isn't going to add up to half of what his jacket costs. Don't complain. We're doing this."

Masha and Alan conspire to throw in jeans and skirts and tops for her. Fancy new sneakers. Underwear. Silk pajamas. A pair of sunglasses, which Evie immediately puts on. There's a week's worth of clothes for her folded up in shiny paper shopping bags by the time Masha hands over a credit card and they're done. It's probably the most efficient shopping mission Evie has ever been on: they leave the store barely an hour after arriving.

Masha dials up an Uber as they walk back through the open-air mall, heavy bags banging against their knees. People in the crowd of shoppers now look at them as if they're something special, the two women in the sunglasses with all the fancy carrier bags. At first, Evie is quietly delighted by the attention, but then feels more and more disgusted as she realizes that it's their very consumption that's making them notable to people. Nothing they've done. Just that they've spent a lot, and someone with that much money has to be worth looking at, maybe knowing. She goes back to wanting to burn the whole mall down, and the entire concept of capitalism along with it. And she begins, in a small way, to understand why the twins place so many walls between themselves and others.

Evie is about to say something about it when Masha swears in what Evie assumes is Georgian and yanks her into a sporting-goods store.

"Ow! What?" she says, glaring at Masha. The taller woman is looking over her shoulder, past a rack of clothes and out the window, where two priests in scarlet-lined robes are taking a selfie in front of an ornate fountain. One is tall but stocky, Korean-looking; his friend is shorter, with olive skin and a distinct curl to his dark hair. "Sorry," she murmurs. "Didn't want them to see me."

"You have something against priests?" Evie asks.

"Not all priests," she says, moving towards the back of the store, further into cover. Her shopping bags tangle against racks of sweatpants. "Just those kinds."

Out the window, the priests look at the selfie on the taller one's camera, and a passerby asks if they want their photo taken. But for a small design of an eye on the left shoulder of their cassocks in crimson embroidery, they're just... Catholic priests. Evie wanders back to where Masha is pretending to be interested in football shirts.

"Misha was in love with a priest once," she says, wrinkling her nose at the color combinations on a Miami Dolphins shirt.

"Wait, Mr Love-Doesn't-Exist has actually fallen in love?" Evie says, putting down her shopping bags and rubbing the ridges in her palms their handles had left. "I'm shocked."

"He was right, in this case." Masha gives her a melancholy smile as she puts the shirt back on the rack. "It turned out to be an infatuation. The affair ended. Our country fell apart." She rakes her hands through her hair, letting it fall over her face when she finishes. "Everything fell apart."

"Tell me?" Evie says. "I wondered. You don't get that cynical unless you've fallen hard and been badly hurt."

"I wouldn't say he's a cynic," Masha says, looking over running shoes with a disinterested air. She doesn't seem like the fitness type. "He thinks he is, of course. But he's more... a very sarcastic romantic." She glances towards the window. "He falls a little bit in love with all his targets, you know." The priests are still out there, thanking the woman who took their picture. "As for Pavel... There's not much to tell. Misha was young, and very spoiled. We both were. And he thought... he thought if you loved someone enough, you could make it work. Be what they wanted. Nothing had ever *not* worked for him." Her next words come out quiet and scratchy, as if the words are rough from disuse. "He did some very stupid things. It wasn't our finest moment."

"I'm sorry," Evie says.

"Yes, me too. It wasn't the priest's fault," she snorts, a mocking, self-hating sound. "That honor was all Misha's."

Masha clears her throat, then flashes a grin at Evie, but it's a pantomime, a mask hiding a tightly controlled, inwardly directed fury. Evie can see it in her eyes, their pale blue hardening to the color of steel. "Anyway. What do you think?" she asks, holding up a 49ers jersey. "Should I change my look?"

"It depends on whether you think it's adequate revenge for Snorlax," Evie says.

Masha hiccups with laughter, awkward and dorky.

EVIE RESTS AT the hotel for the rest of the afternoon. Every so often she gets up and pokes at the piles of new clothes sitting on her bed, as if, like Cinderella's, they are only borrowed against the stroke of midnight. She has an urge to save the tags. She keeps picking them up to look at them, to gaze upon numbers so high they cease to have rational meaning. $3,000 boots. $2,900 for a dress. $750 for jeans.

She texts Claudia with a pic of her haul: *Still alive. Have lots of new clothes.*

Claudia texts back about twenty minutes later: *Rub lipstick all over them so if he kills you and dumps you in a ditch he can't return them.*

Evie tabs over to Google Docs on her phone and opens up her abandoned notes for the article that vanished when Nicole did. She doesn't lie to herself that she's going to resurrect it somewhere else. It feels too private now, too dangerous; she is no longer reporting on the story, but has stepped into it, become a part of it.

But writing things down has always helped her to organize her thoughts. She stares at the blinking cursor and then, slowly, begins to list the things she doesn't understand. The priests, with the strange little eye symbol on the left shoulder of their cassocks. Masha's fear of them. The book, and what its red letters spell. She wonders if she can trace the book's provenance, to see where Misha might have crossed paths with it.

Jet lag numbs the corners of her mind, making her slow and dull, and after a weary hour of staring at her list she gives up on getting any research done. She curls up on the giant white bed with the fine Egyptian-cotton sheets instead, and dozes.

Misha knocks on her door around 4pm. He's barefoot, in his gym clothes: the striped shirt, the trendy black sweatpants.

Evie opens the door for him and then slumps back over towards her bed. "You going to tell me what's going on?"

"Wasn't planning on it," Misha says, prowling after her and leaning against the dining table.

"I can't help you if—" Evie begins, at the same time as Misha snaps, "This is not a game."

He shuts his eyes and puts a hand up to stop further discussion. "This book in the hands of an amoral tech billionaire is the worst situation I can possibly imagine. I don't know how far along Eric Overstreet is with deciphering it. Not all the way, I'm fairly certain. But still. There's a chance he will... *understand* what I am. And then things could get very ugly, very fast."

"What are you, Misha?" Evie says, her voice flat.

Misha tilts his head and, just for a moment, goes unnaturally still, like a cobra before it strikes. A deep, animal part of Evie's brain begins to whine in terror. "I'll be the nastiest thing at the party, by a long chalk," he says, and Evie can believe it. He moves then, but it's not towards her: it's to shove his hands in his pockets, and pace, restless. His bare footsteps make almost no sound on the thickly carpeted floor. "I can't—" He stops and turns to her. His posture sags. There's a plea behind his eyes, as he says, cracked and small, "I can't." He wipes a hand down his face. "Not yet."

"Maybe tomorrow?" Evie asks.

"Maybe never," Misha says, slumping down into a chair. "I don't know." He drums his fingers on the arm of the chair and looks anywhere in the room other than at her.

Evie decides not to push her luck, lest he shut down any further. "So. Do you have a plan?"

"We leave at eight," Misha says, his confidence returning. "When we get there, I'll flirt my way around the party and try to locate the book. I don't need to see it. I should be able to *feel* where it is. We... exist on the same frequency, so to speak, it and me." He runs a hand through his hair. "Then I'll find Selene Overstreet, see if I can make Eric jealous. Or at least curious enough about what he's paying for to watch. While I have their attention, I need you to get the book. Burn it, if there's an open fire. If not, leave immediately and come back here with it. They won't expect you. With me..." Misha hooks the wide collar of his shirt with one finger, pulling it down far enough to show his scar. "... as soon as they see this, well..." He grins, toothy and mean. "I'll know who has read to the end."

He gets up and paces towards the window, shirt riding up as he reaches his arms over his head, lengthening and stretching his back. "Oh, our legends: I'm a model/DJ/whatever. You're a writer. Fiction." He smiles. "Your debut novel will be out next year. We're trendy in New York, and we're at the party to make it more decorative, and cultural."

"Can I ask one question?" Evie says.

Misha angles his head, his expression becoming more guarded. It's a simple, eloquent gesture: *Perhaps*.

"Are you the only one... of what you are?"

"No," says Misha, his tone cautious, his eyes once again sliding away from her. "But there are very few. The world is not full of the hidden supernatural, Evie. Just a handful of abominations and crooked mistakes, with our numbers growing fewer every year."

"What happens to them?" She expects Misha to shut the conversation down, or to sass her about two-part questions.

But instead his eyes flash to hers, startlingly raw, pinning her. A smile that is not a smile picks at the corners of his mouth like a scab.

"Those priests you saw? They kill us."

CHAPTER NINE

THE OVERSTREETS' ATHERTON mansion looks like a Case Study house that came down with gigantism. It's a tumorous monstrosity of white planes, jutting cubes and walls of glass, its bright glow clinical rather than inviting. As she and Misha languish in the valet parking queue, Evie keeps her eyes on the hard lines of the house as it emerges past the treetops like it holds the key to her salvation. It doesn't. It just keeps her from staring at Misha.

It hurts to look at him.

It hurts *not* to look at him.

He'd knocked on Evie's door an hour prior and she'd opened it and there he was, in the tight leather trousers and the fancy military jacket, leaning against the wall. He'd smudged a little dark liner softly around his eyes, and the tops of his already ridiculous cheekbones shimmered in the hall light.

It's at that moment Evie realizes she'd never really seen Misha make an effort with his appearance before. Every time she'd seen him, he'd just rolled out of bed like that. Even his tuxedo at the Pickford engagement party he'd probably just thrown on after work. But this...

"What do you think?" Misha says, pulling his plush lower lip between his teeth.

Evie slams the door in his face and goes and hyperventilates in the bathroom for a good five minutes.

She removes her hands from the cool marble of the sink reluctantly, and returns to the bedroom. Calmly, a little numb, she picks up her bag (oversized; large enough to hide a hardback book) and puts on some lip gloss. Then she opens the door again.

Misha stands up quickly from where he's been slouched against the wall, like a scolded schoolboy.

Evie doesn't especially notice. She keeps her eyes firmly locked on the hallway's pale grey striped wallpaper and its minimalist black and white photos of ocean horizons.

"Very Ballets Russes. Selene Overstreet should love it," Evie says as she fiddles with the contents of her handbag: room key, wallet, phone, lipstick.

She definitely doesn't notice when Misha jams his hands into his front pockets, which pull the already low waistband of his leather pants well below his hip points. Or at the play of muscles on the sharp V of his pelvic line as he pushes away from the wall and walks past her into the room.

"Okay. Good," he says, his voice curiously hollow and unenthusiastic. "Masha sends her regards. And she's right, you look... amazing. If any—"

"Where is she?" Evie says, looking past him.

"In our suite, watching an old Fred Astaire movie. She likes musicals." Misha tucks a lock of his artfully mussed hair behind his ear. "If this all goes south... she has to finish the job. But for now, she stays in reserve."

"Do you think the priests she saw are after you?" Evie carefully looks at a spot to the right of Misha.

He's just staring at her, head tilted, a look of concern on his face. It takes him a moment to realize he's been asked a question, and he shakes his head a little, hair coming loose again. "I doubt it," he murmurs. "I have... a lot of protocols in place. Ways to stay off their radar." He flashes Evie a wry smile. "Which, of course, I'm breaking with you. But it's almost time for me to leave New York anyway. So the risk is manageable."

He sighs and taps the toe of one boot against the carpet. "I think they're here for the book, like me. Eric Overstreet hasn't been as subtle as he thinks. In theory I could leave it to them, but..." He begins to pace, and says nothing for a whole minute. When he next speaks, his voice is rough with emotion. "Evie, I *have* to see this book burn. The last time I thought it destroyed, it had been in the possession of the priests. They said they burned it. *He* said—" Misha's mouth snaps shut and he backs away, palms up. When he speaks again, it's in a whisper. "I need to see it destroyed with my own eyes, this time."

He reaches out and grabs her, and his expression is so raw, so full of pain that Evie gasps, tensing. "And if I don't make it out of this, for whatever reason, I want you to bear witness that I tried to do the right thing. Can you do that for me?"

Evie nods, even as she tries to pull away from his grasp.

He lets go. But he doesn't back off. He stays there, in her space, looking down at her. "Last chance, Evie. You don't have to be a part of this. You can stay here in your room, have a nice vacation, maybe go for a swim in the pool. I won't think badly of you for it. In fact, it's the sensible thing to do."

She stares up into his strange, pale eyes, waiting for him to blink first. He doesn't. So Evie does. She turns away from him and marches out of the room, away from his gravitational pull. As she passes by the bed she lazily indicates the small mountain of new clothes on it, most still neatly wrapped in tissue. "Can't stay behind," she says. "Masha forgot to buy me a bathing suit."

She is halfway to the elevators before she hears the slam of her room door and the heavy tread of Misha's footsteps as he stalks after her.

Moments later, she feels his hand, hot and large, on her lower back. "We will talk about your foolhardy tendencies later," he growls.

She can handle this. Everything is fine.

The hall photographs of the endless horizons at sea, dark on the bottom and light on top, they're fine. The pale wood-paneled elevator with its screens advertising the hotel's restaurants and day spa, that's fine too. Bizarre, stalky flower arrangements in green and scarlet decorating the lobby, also fine.

All remains fine until they are ensconced in the car together. The road rumbling beneath them and the heat from Misha's body, the juniper-and-leather smell of him: it is all terrifyingly close to her and yet not close enough. Evie stares out the passenger window, twiddling her fingers nervously, worried that Misha is going to try to engage her in small talk. But he doesn't. He drives silently, solemnly, the entire half hour it takes to get to Atherton.

And now they sit in a valet line in the Overstreets' winding driveway. A line that is barely moving.

"God, look at all the people," Evie says, staring at the crowds bustling into the house, and the early birds already visible through the glass walls.

"Only seven hundred of his closest friends," Misha mutters.

"And the place still doesn't look full."

"Mm," he grunts. Then he shifts, restlessly. "Evie…"

"Hn?" She keeps her temple pressed against the cold window. She knows he's looking at her, maybe even leaning towards her.

"Evie, promise you'll listen until the end if I say something, without biting my head off?"

This was all the most terrible mistake, Evie thinks. Claudia was right, but not for the reasons she intended. The more time she spends around Misha, the more she sees the warm person that exists under that glossy, brittle surface, the harder she falls. Tonight is the hardest of all, because if she looks at him any more in that outfit, with the hair and the smudged eyeliner and the body, the words she'd been trying so hard to suppress are going to fly out of her mouth as soon as she opens it, like the evils of the world escaping from Pandora's box. And she never wants to see his face when it happens, when he realizes how pathetic she is, falling for him just like everybody else does.

"Why would I be angry?" she says, tonelessly. The valets are only six cars away now.

"Other than you being a little… off, all night?" Misha grumps.

"I'm nervous, okay?" Evie snaps back. Valets are five cars away. "I'm allowed to be scared. Humans get scared, it's a thing that happens. Just because you're not—"

"I'm scared too," Misha whispers. "I'm scared all the time."

"... What?" she says, and she looks at him, and it's all over. He's so fucking beautiful, he makes her bones ache.

"Evie, I shouldn't *exist*. And one day the universe is going to realize its mistake and wipe me out." Misha stares down at his lap. "And when it happens, I'm not even sure I'll fight."

The silence in the car has tangible weight, pressing down on her, keeping her from breathing. She shoves her hand under her leg, so she can stop it from reaching out to him, running her fingers along his arm, calming the nervous fidgeting of his hands. If she weren't such a mess, she could think of something funny to say. She could make his smile come back.

"You should fight," she says, quietly. "You're worth... you're amazing, Misha. Just... as a person. You are." She takes his hand, squeezing it gently in a way she hopes he takes as reassuring.

"I haven't been a person since 1916," he murmurs.

"What are you?" she asks. At this point it's almost a reflex. Evie thinks she knows, but part of her still rejects the idea. It's insane; far-fetched even in fiction, but to have it be real, and to have one sitting next to her...

Misha whimpers, a small, defeated sound. "I'm—"

"No. I know," Evie cuts him off. "I know what you are."

Misha's lush mouth pulls into a grimace and he tries to turn away, tries to pull his hand out of hers.

But Evie just holds on a little tighter. "You're my friend."

Misha looks at her, startled. He goes to say something, but the words desert him, and he closes his mouth. Instead, he turns her hand in his, and laces their fingers together. He squeezes back, gently.

The silence that blossoms is lighter now; warmer.

Misha relaxes into his seat, the tension releasing muscle by muscle. "As long as I can do this. As long as I can get rid of that fucking book... I'll have done one good thing."

"Okay, now you're just having a pity party," Evie says. "You've done about eight good things since I've met you."

Misha unlinks their fingers long enough to punch her in the shoulder, before dropping his hand over hers again. She looks at him out of the corners of her eyes and he's trying not to smile as he gazes out the windshield at the well-dressed revelers streaming in through the glass doors of the Overstreets' mansion.

"I'm worried about the crowds," he says. "What I'd started to say earlier... I can... make a link between us. So you'll always feel where I am, and I'll feel where you are. It's temporary. Only lasts about six hours. But I'd feel better if... It's a big house, filled with a lot of people..."

"Sounds reasonable," Evie says. "I mean, it sounds like it breaks several bedrock rules of physics but sure, why not."

"Okay." Misha blushes, his eyes dipping down to his lap again. "I have to tell you... the only way I know how to make the link is by kissing."

Evie isn't quite sure what her face is doing at this point but Misha takes it as refusal. He shifts in embarrassment. "I'm not being a creep, I swear. I didn't exactly get an instruction manual when..." He bites his lip again, and Evie really wishes he'd stop drawing attention to his mouth. A mouth that he was talking about using to kiss her. "I only found out how to do this by experimentation. I'm not even sure if the others can do it, or just me."

"So I have to kiss you," Evie reiterates, trying to sound blasé.

"Yes. On the lips."

Evie digs the fingers of her free hand into the thick leather handle of her bag, and wills her heart to stop thundering in her chest. "Fine," she sighs. "If that's the only way to do it."

Then Misha's hand is on her chin, gently guiding her face towards him. As he tilts his head to slot their mouths together, he whispers, "It doesn't hurt. And it doesn't... I don't take anything."

He touches his lips to hers, so soft, and she feels his tongue brush into her mouth. At first she isn't sure if the overwhelming, sparking current lighting her up is the magic, or just the act of kissing Misha. She grips the leather of her bag more tightly. She's not going to moan. She *isn't*.

He pulls back slightly, breaking the kiss, and she fights the urge to chase after him. His lips hover over hers, so close, but not touching, as he watches her.

As the sense of electricity fades, a tingle remains, like the feeling after eating a piece of ginger. The feeling moves down into her chest and sits near her heart like it belongs there. While she's thinking about that, wanting to touch the spot with her fingers, she realizes Misha has moved away.

"There," he says. "Not so bad?"

She's torn between sassing him and reassuring him and kissing him back and *oh my god*, she can *feel* him, she can close her eyes and know exactly where he is—

A loud knock on the driver's side window startles them both.

It's the valets. Misha pops the car's locks and the valets open the doors for them, one valet extending a hand to help Evie out of the low bucket seat.

Misha takes her arm as they walk up the path. As they approach the security team at the door, he pulls up an app on his phone and displays a code from it to the guards. It does something complicated, and then the guards' tablet flashes green, and the front door opens by itself. "Enjoy the party," one of the guards says.

And then there they are, inside a huge, triple-height main room that seems part atrium, part art gallery. The vast space contains several hundred of Silicon Valley's most important people, and the two of them. Misha snags a pair of champagne flutes from a passing waiter, and hands her one.

Evie narrows her eyes at the glass he still holds. "You going to drink that?" she asks.

"Of course not," says Misha. "When have you ever seen me eat or drink? I'm going to carry it around as a social prop until I eventually pour it into a plant pot." He clinks her glass and murmurs in her ear, and she can feel the grin on his face. "Bon courage, Evie."

Then he's off through the crowd, leaving ripples in his wake that range from admiring glances to outright staring. Tech bros are in no way hip or well dressed, and Misha stands out like a hawk among sparrows. Evie watches as some pale, round man in a *Star Wars* shirt points to Misha and says to his friends in disgust, "That dude is wearing *makeup*." She resolves to step on his foot the first chance she gets. When she looks up to find Misha again, he's vanished into the sea of schlubs in startup-logo hoodies and girls in polite little Banana Republic dresses.

Evie doesn't know anyone here. She's not big on parties at the best of times, and a party where she doesn't know a single other person is her own version of hell. She's still on edge from her last few minutes with Misha in the car (*we kissed, he kissed me*, her brain keeps whimpering) and she can't gather her social graces enough to approach strangers and make small talk. The people around her are all talking about dev timelines and VCs and APIs and their Series B and Evie knows *nothing* about this world.

She stares instead at the truly jaw-dropping modern art gracing the walls. A Rothko here, an Ed Ruscha there, a Cy Twombly between the pair of staircases curving up to the second floor. They arch around a massive Egyptian black-stone statue of Osiris, his nose long ago broken off by the petty worshippers of newer gods. Other rough, weathered statues of broken gods from a variety of ancient cultures stand in counterpoint to the abstract art: a Venus without her head. A crowned Buddha without his body. All have been muted down by the centuries from their original jaunty polychromes into the acceptable drab of the modernist interior.

Her champagne gone, she heads to a bar and grabs a refill from the bartender. He's black; there are only about five other black people in the whole gathering beyond the wait staff and the DJ. It's an overwhelmingly white crowd, with a smattering of South and East Asian.

Evie looks around for another wallflower to befriend. At one end of the bar is a South Asian girl in a pretty cornflower-blue dress. She is by herself, reading something on her phone. Evie heads towards her, getting her courage up to start a conversation, when the girl is moved in on by a trio of people who are clearly friends or work colleagues. She tucks her phone away and kisses them hello, and never notices Evie peeling away at the last minute to edge past them.

She decides to postpone making friends for the moment in favor of checking on Misha. She touches the spot over her heart and closes her eyes, waiting to feel which way it would tug her.

Misha is to her right, and above; he must be on the second floor. He feels content, through the link.

Evie climbs up, and sees him as she reaches the curve in the staircase. He's standing near the top of it, where the railing bends in close enough that she could reach out to the massive statue of Osiris and touch it, chatting to a group of people. She recognizes one of them as Selene Overstreet. The rest seem like hangers-on, all gazing up at Selene and Misha adoringly, looking for the right moment to impress. Selene wears asymmetric layers of beige/taupe over glossy beige leggings and gold heels, understated and incredibly expensive. Misha still looks like an off-duty rock star, but his outfit seems less out of place next to her than it did below, in the throng of brogrammers. The crowd is raucous, but Misha speaks softly, forcing Selene to lean in towards him, to move into his space. It's startlingly effective.

She watches, as if through glass, Misha's skill in working a conversation, his confidence with people. He knows he will be liked, whereas Evie hopes at best to be tolerated. She envies the ease with which he exists in his own skin, the way he wears his physical power so lightly, like it's nothing at all. Until the moment it is. Misha pairs his confidence with a surprising level of sensitivity, however: for all that sexuality was his weapon of choice, he was more respectful of her and of her consent than almost any other man she has ever met. Usually when men were as striking and as confident as Misha, they acted like they had a right to things. Not Misha; never him.

His eyes meet hers, and he trails off whatever he is saying to Selene. Evie can see the slight tension that goes through the older woman when she notices that Misha's attention has wandered away from her.

Evie turns and goes back down the stairs. When she looks back, Selene and Misha are arm in arm and laughing, disappearing further into the house. The sparrows who had surrounded them mill silently as they realize no more crumbs will be scattered for them and then, as one, they flock towards the nearest bar. They flow down past Evie, raucous in their comparison of this party, that retreat. Keeping pace with them, Evie learns that the near-billionaire founder of an e-commerce site bought an abandoned town in Montana and is paying people to come live there as his friends. But as his taste in drugs is as cheap as his appetite is large, they're all afraid he'll check out before the checks clear. "I'm going to do it anyway," a man in a green polo titters. "What if we become best friends and he leaves me everything?"

"I don't think he swings that way, Patrick," an expensively highlighted blonde woman rebukes him.

Patrick groans. "Ew, no homo, Cris," he whines, and then they're past Evie and she looks out across the crowd to get her bearings and instead gets a perfect view of Nicole Hamilton walking alone through the front doors. Even from this distance Evie can read her lips as she shows her phone screen and says "Press" to the security team.

The clear logic of it hits Evie like a blast of cold air: of course Nicole has fled New York's incestuous, gossipy magazine industry to insert herself into the more placid, sycophantic world of Silicon Valley tech journalism. She remembers at *Gotham* how the editors would mock their regular offers from Bay Area publications, all desperate to have a real New York editor on staff, as if anyone would fight their way up tooth and nail to the top of Manhattan magazine journalism, the toughest and best market in the world, just to leave it to go voluntarily to San Francisco. It's absurd. Only a *failure* would do that.

And so here Nicole is, in a short, ruched metallic-fuchsia dress that looks like a candy wrapper, her smile brittle and tight, her stilettos too high, everything perfect for striding through the lobby of the Standard at 10pm in the Meatpacking District but wrong, wrong, wrong here. She looks up and in the moment their eyes meet, Evie can see the exhaustion in her features. Nicole's gaze passes over her, expressionless, and Evie takes the coward's way out.

She ducks down into the crowd, for the first time regretting how tall her boots make her, and beelines for the open doors to the back gardens. Her heart goes rabbit-fast in her chest. Misha is upstairs with Selene now, but he will come down, and Nicole will recognize him. But for Evie being there, she'd probably think Misha was an idle cad who took her out a few times then ghosted her, par for the course in New York dating.

But now, if she's recognized Evie, she's going to be reminded of the feature Evie pitched to her, *The Break-Up Artist*. If she's looked through the folder Evie sent her, she'll have seen his photos with Stewart Pickford, heard his voice on the recording with Greg and Erin, read Octavia Mortimer's name in her notes as a Meserov client. And she'll know Misha as the person who destroyed her relationship with August Mortimer and, with it, her coveted editorial perch, sending all the scaffolding of her New York social status crashing down around her.

As the warm night air hits Evie and the sound of the party falls away behind her, she prays that Nicole has retained her old habits of never reading anything she was sent. She looks around. She's on a pathway through an immaculate lawn that falls into geometric terraces down a small hillside. Eucalyptus trees rustle at the edges of the grass, marking out the borders of the property. A pool lies off to Evie's right, its aqua glow somehow rich and comforting in the night, its surface pristine and as yet unmarred by drunken revelers. Another bar, at a terrace just above the pool. The air smells like fresh-cut grass and the more she walks away from the house, the songs of crickets begin to drown out the braying of the rich and the aural wallpaper of the DJ's mellow electronica.

Standing in the middle of this lush nocturne, alone among groups of happy, relaxed people, Evie pulls out her cloud storage app on her phone and stares at the research folder she shared with Nicole, a short week and a thousand years ago. Her finger hovers over it as she spares a moment of self-pity for the risks she took to collect all the information inside.

And then she deletes the whole thing.

Evie heads to the poolside bar, orders a whiskey, and grits her teeth against its burn. She resolves to talk to the next decent-looking person her age. What would Misha do? He'd be relaxed. He'd smile. She can do that, too. She turns and leans against the bar, posture open, and looks over the sparse poolside crowd.

Okay, there's a guy staring at her boots. White kid with bleached hair and a My Little Pony T-shirt. Well, at least it wasn't a tech company logo. Deep breath. "Hey," she smiles. Lifts her glass up.

"Oh my god. Are those Rick Owens?" he says, pointing at her boots.

"Yeah," she smiles.

"Oh thank Christ," he groans. "Finally someone at this party who can dress. If I see one more girl in a polo dress I'm going to cut someone." He puts on a falsetto and a big smile. "Hi, I'm Mimi and I'm a marketing manager at a tech startup! We just did our Series A and I'm so excited!" The smile bleeds away as he rakes his fingers through his spiky, bleached hair, rocking back and forth and growling, "Red. Rum."

They blink at each other, then the guy's eyes go wide. "I'm Andy and I was raised by bears so have no manners!" he chokes, sticking out his hand. Evie shakes it and introduces herself, and Andy gathers her into his group: two other bored-looking early-twentysomethings, their clothes and makeup noticeably trendier than the prevailing non-style of the rest of the partygoers. One Latina girl whose long brown hair fades to green at the ends is wearing pink leopard-print skinny jeans which, Evie has to admit, are pretty awesome.

Andy catches her assessing look over the group and stage-whispers, "We're the neighbors. They had to invite us."

"They had to invite *you*, Andy," says Leopard Jeans.

"And I had to invite you because otherwise, chances of sliding into homicidal mania at the next mention of venture capitalist?

ONE HUNDRED," Andy honks back at her. Then he swivels to Evie. His pupils are dilated and she doesn't know whether it's because of the low light or because they had all been pre-gaming with something a lot harder than alcohol. "Anyway. Why are you here?" he asks. "You look way too cool for this crowd. I mean," he says, gesturing over her outfit, "actual fashion."

"I'm a writer," Evie replies, swirling her whiskey glass and watching the ice cubes twist. "I live in New York. My friend and I got invited in some quota for non-tech people. I don't even know the Overstreets."

"Do you *want* to?" Andy asks. "Because I am in the mood to *spill* tonight." The little group decamp for the bar, then assemble themselves across several deck chairs near the pool. Andy rolls a joint, and waves it like a conductor's wand. "Now. Dearest Selene and Eric. Where shall I begin?"

"Aren't you worried she's going to write about this?" says the third person in the group, a skinny, short guy in corduroys with Ironic Eyeglasses and the biggest jewfro Evie's ever seen.

"Darling, I'm praying she does the full Truman Capote on us all," drawls Andy, sucking on the joint. He holds in the smoke, coughs, exhales in a long, contented sigh, and hands the joint to Jewfro. Then he blinks, and looks at Evie. "Oh, where's your friend? We haven't abandoned her, have we?"

"Him," Evie says. "And he's fine. He's much better at parties than I am." Then she touches over her heart, to make sure, and because she can. Misha is still on the second floor of the house, and she picks up that he's slightly more stressed than he was before. *I'm fine*, she thinks back, *I found people to hang out with. I'm by the pool. Watch out, Nicole Hamilton is here.* She doesn't know if any of that transmits. She has no clue how the link works, other than that it gives her a vague knowledge of where he is and that he's okay, but she figures it can't hurt to try. "I think he's already made friends with Selene Overstreet."

"Oh my god, abort, abort, she's so creepy," says Andy, aghast. "*Baby Jane* levels of creepy." He catches Evie's worried expression and leans forwards, patting her arm. "Okay so my dad works for Oracle, right? And we've lived here"—he gestures towards the bottom of the lawn, where Evie can see a French château-style grey stone house whose turrets just poke over the treeline—"pretty much my whole life. The Overstreets built this place about seven years ago and, god, I don't know. I can see their bedroom from my window and they do *not* pull the curtains. This place is a *fishbowl*." Andy makes a sour face, and reaches across to grab the joint.

"He's like the world's oldest goth," says Leopard Jeans. "Which? *Tragic*."

"Total germophobe," confirms Andy. "Even wears gloves when he has sex."

"You cannot know that!" squawks Leopard Jeans.

"Bitch I can," hisses Andy. "I see into his bedroom window from mine."

Telescope, coughs Jewfro into his fist, and Leopard Jeans cracks up. Andy flips them off and continues. "He buys weird statues and stuff. He never seemed that... interested in Selene? I mean, she seemed really sad when she moved in, quiet and kind of... lost. We assumed he was, like, secretly ace or something? But three years ago he started banging his PR girl and Selene, like, *transformed* herself."

Andy sighs and leans back, crossing his acid wash-denim clad legs. "She'd been *that girl*. The model who got the billionaire. Well, y'know, 'model'. Catalogue work or something." He doesn't do the air quotes, but Evie can hear them nonetheless. "No kids; too many bodily fluids involved for Eric, we thought. Also potential for hugging and actual affection. And nothing for her to really do, except play at charity and have status games with the other wives."

"This doesn't sound like *Baby Jane* to me," says Evie, refusing the joint.

Andy rolls his eyes and takes another hit. "Okay, so she clearly decides she's going to get off her ass and get her creepy man back. She drops like thirty pounds, starts putting some silicon in her valleys if you know what I mean, and hires a stylist to make her the best-dressed woman in tech, and you know what? He still didn't want her. It's kinda sad. I mean, she got what she wanted, the perfect life, and now she doesn't even have to have sex with Eric any more, but around here... people only talk to her because she's Eric's wife. If she stops being that..." Andy shrugs.

"Are you sure she isn't having an affair?" Evie asks, thinking of her laughing on Misha's arm. The thought of Misha doing his job, seducing Selene, fills her with a hot, molten sort of misery.

"Girl. *Girrrl*," laughs Andy. "Do you know how many little tech broettes come out here every year fresh out of college with the goal of using their boobs to get ahead, until they're either hitched to some shitty rich brogrammer, or get to spend a year or two reveling in being the only girl in the boys' clubhouse? Because she is so much cooler than the other girls, until of course another girl comes along who's willing to put up with more of the brogrammers' bullshit? Laugh off the drunken gropes, the casual sexism of 'boys being boys'? There's an inexhaustible supply of upwardly mobile twenty-three-year-old poontang in Silicon Valley, so why would anyone want her saggy forty-five-year-old butt? Like, she has *no* skills. Not even xml. Besides, here's the thing," Andy says, leaning close and adopting a faux-whisper. "Pretty girls have no game."

Evie thinks of Nicole. "Pretty blondes especially."

"*Right?!*" Andy exclaims. "They don't even need to be that pretty. They just need to be young, in a short skirt, and have long blonde hair. They contour, they highlight, they laser off their body hair, they stay a size 2. And that's all they have to do. Selene was a model. She always had guys after her. The only game she had to develop was about eight different polite variations of *no thank you* that would make guys she rejected go away and hopefully not try to kill her." Andy smiles, wry and sad. "Then one day nobody thought she was pretty any mo..." His mouth hangs open, fishlike, as his commentary tails off into a startled whine. He stares past Evie.

The link tingles in Evie's chest, so she isn't surprised when a too-warm hand comes to rest gently on her shoulder. "This is my friend from New York," she says, and Misha rubs her neck affectionately. "Misha, everyone. Everyone, Misha."

"Hi," Misha says. His voice is still down in the low, growly register he uses for flirting, and Evie hates how much she likes it. He squeezes her shoulder. "I'm sorry, I have to steal Evie away for a moment. Will you still be here in fifteen minutes?"

Andy has absolutely not recovered. He nods, mouth agape.

"Okay. We'll be back soon," Misha smiles. It's his polite smile, not his real one, but it's still devastating.

"It was great hanging out with you all. Thanks for rescuing me," Evie says as she gets up. And she means it; talking to Andy and his friends has been the best part of the party so far.

Andy whimpers a little bit. He's still staring at Misha. *I know*, Evie thinks.

They step off the pool terrace onto the flagstone path towards the house, Misha taking her arm in his. Out of the dark behind them comes a pained, high-pitched stage-whisper: "Oh my god, I want to ride that man like the Pony Express."

Misha stops and glances back to Andy, smirking. "Hard and fast and all night long?"

They're rewarded with the slow crashing sound of Andy falling over in his deck chair.

"You're very bad," Evie giggles.

"You have only just figured this out?" Misha hums. A drunk, laughing couple approach them, the girl's strappy, electric-blue heels sinking into the lawn and her friend steadying her. Once they pass, Misha's demeanor grows more serious. "I know which room the book is in. It feels muffled, as if it's in a case or something."

"What if it's in a safe?" Evie whispers. "I can't break into a safe."

Misha chews his lip. "Don't think it's in a safe. Not sure I could feel it through anything that reinforced."

Evie looks at him, aghast. Just how much is he winging this?

"Look," he hisses, exasperated. "I'm doing the best I can.

Which, for your information, is a hell of a lot better than most."

They step back into the house, noisy with guests. The DJ has upped the tempo of the music and, lubricated by alcohol, revelers are dancing in one corner of the ground floor near the staircases, while excited crowds ripple and sway across the rest of the room. Evie watches Misha change his gait, loosening it, getting drunker before her eyes. She knows it's an act, but he's good. Then Misha grabs her and turns, yanking her into him. She's pressed into his chest, their bodies touching and it's like a fuse has been lit—

Evie has no time to react before he whispers, "Hit me. Hard as you can. Then head back towards the bathrooms." Then his mouth is on hers, hard, inelegant, and messy.

She shoves at his chest and he staggers slightly, reaching for her again. She hauls off and smacks him right in his perfect cheekbones. Then she stomps off towards the ladies' room, and she doesn't have to fake the turmoil she's feeling at all. There's a smudge of gold on her palm.

She feels him behind her, pushing through the crowd, shouting for her. A few people look; she prays Nicole isn't one of them. Evie's lost sight of her and the last thing Misha's shoddy plan needs is another variable.

Misha grabs her arm and pulls her around a corner. There's a bleep of an access card, and then they're in a small service elevator.

Evie tries to calm her breathing as the doors slide closed.

Misha leans over her, resting on one arm, careful not to cage her in. "Sorry. There are cameras everywhere. I need a reason for you to leave alone." He hands her the valet parking ticket, and the access card. "Third floor, end of the hallway, door on the left," he says, reaching for the door open button.

"What—" Evie starts.

"You can drive stick, yes? Take the car and drive back to the hotel. Don't worry about me," he says.

Evie nods, but she doesn't like the look in his eye. It's determined; dangerous. "Misha, what are you—"

"I am going to cause a distraction," he says. "You get the book.

Then walk out. Slowly. Have another glass of champagne. Go take a selfie with your friends by the pool. They'll be checking the camera feeds later for people looking suspicious. *Walk*, Evie. Whatever you do, walk, don't run."

She stares at the buttons. B, 1, 2, 3. Pressing one of them will put her past the point of no return.

"I can't," she says, her voice small.

"Evie. Don't back out now."

"Why aren't *you* doing this?" Evie demands. "This was your idea. *You're* the criminal!" she whispers, furious. "I'm just supposed to witness you doing the right thing!"

"I *can't*," hisses Misha. He shoves his hands in his pockets and paces across the small space of the elevator, then leans his forehead against the opposite wall. "Please. You have to." It's the ragged edge in Misha's voice that makes Evie look up. He's pale, and just about shaking with nerves. His voice comes out a rough whisper. "It's not safe for me to be near it, around this many people. I thought I was over its hold on me but... I'm not." He squeezes his eyes shut. "I can feel it calling to me."

Evie gapes. She knows she should say something to reassure him, but she's too unsettled by the sight of Misha stripped raw, his usual self-assurance lost. It's like walking out and finding the sky to be a different color than blue. Errors of order, mistakes in the fabric of being.

Misha wipes a hand down his face, his eyes darting away. "I've lost control around the book before. I can't... I can't do it, Evie. It's not safe." He presses his fist against the brushed aluminum of the elevator. "*I'm* not safe," he finishes, barely audible.

Evie runs her thumb against the dull edge of the access card. Misha is watching her through his hair, a sort of desperation in his eyes. She sighs. "You're bailing me out of jail if this goes horribly wrong, yeah?"

Misha nods, and the very fact that he doesn't have a sassy comeback is disturbing enough. "Thank you," he murmurs, his fingers brushing the back of hers as he reaches to open the elevator doors. "I'll see you later."

And then Evie is alone in the elevator.

She takes a deep breath, and pushes the button for the third floor. Her hand only shakes a little bit.

The elevator takes her silently upwards on her short journey, and deposits her in a short hallway hung with more multimillion-dollar abstract art and topped with a high, peaked skylight that runs the length of the hall. She creeps forwards as silently as she can, under the judgmental eye of the night sky. She clasps her handbag in front of her stomach as she walks, as if it can protect her from harm, and she listens for any sounds at all. There's nothing; even her footsteps are inaudible over the distant buzz and hum of the party below.

She reaches the last door on the left and touches its knob, sure that it's going to zap her or set off an alarm. But it's just cold chrome, and she steps closer, grasping it and turning.

It's locked.

Evie panics for a moment, then tries holding the access card Misha gave her near the door. She's rewarded with the soft whir of a locking mechanism disengaging. Where had Misha gotten the card? She flips it over to see if there's a name or a photo on it.

Oh.

He pickpocketed it from Selene Overstreet.

She briefly wonders if all supernatural people are this shady, or just the one that bad luck delivered as her friend. She was going to have a long talk with Misha when this was all over.

But then she is inside the Overstreets' bedroom, a surprisingly Victorian affair with a black wood four-poster bed hung with silk canopies and a carved marble mantel around a crackling fireplace, the wall above it hung with early black and white erotic photographs.

The right-hand wall is one huge window. The left has double doors, presumably to a walk-in closet. But the rest of the wall space is lined with floor-to-ceiling bookcases, each and every one of them full of ancient-looking books.

Evie's heart sinks. How is she supposed to find Misha's Book of Hours in a room overflowing with them? All she remembers is a flaking reddish-brown leather binding, but that describes almost every tome on the shelves.

Evie is about to start yanking them down at random when a rustling sound nearly has her leaping out of her own skin. She bites down on her own fist so she doesn't yell, and takes a better look past the bed's heavy canopies.

There's a girl on the bed.

There is a girl on the bed and she's Evie's age. She's wearing a ball gag in her mouth and a blindfold and her wrists and ankles are tied with thick red ropes to the bedposts. She's a petite white girl, long silver-blonde hair, about a size 2. Her toes and fingernails are painted with a green metallic polish. The ball gag is bright red, with a black leather strap that's digging into the corners of the girl's mouth. Blindfolded as she is, she can't see Evie, and she hasn't yet seemed to realize there's another person in the room.

Evie can't do this.

She backs away, ready to flee, when she sees something else on the bed: a chased silver box, about the length and width of a sheet of paper, but about four inches deep.

A box large enough to contain a book.

Evie leans in and carefully opens the box. It's lined in faded electric-blue velvet, and inside is an old book with a flaking, cordovan-leather cover and gilded edges. She lifts it out, and the book comes easily into her hands.

It feels warm. The book is warm, like Misha is, and it settles into her hands like it belongs there.

The leather doesn't feel dry in her hands, despite what it looks like. It feels like the skin of a living being, soft and pliant, and the whole thing buzzes slightly, like a box of bees.

Evie knows it's the right book, but she wants to open it up, just to make sure. Just to see if it's really true that all the red letters spell out a sort of eldritch knowledge.

She picks a page at random; the beginning of Chapter 4. There's a little painting of a maiden and a unicorn, and the maiden has light brown skin like her and wears a crown, and there are flowers all around her. The illustration is beautiful. She'd been to the Morgan Library and seen illustrated manuscripts before, but never up close. This... this couldn't be the book Misha wanted to destroy. Why would he want to harm something so exquisite?

Unless it was because he himself was evil.

Evie begins to doubt Misha more and more as she flips through the book, the illuminated capitals and stylized red letters calling to her, but she keeps her eyes to the illustrations for now.

She'll take the book home and study it, and then decide if Misha should have it. Besides, if there was something more to the book, a secondary text in it, she should see what it was, if nothing else as a matter of investigative record.

Or...

Or she could sit down on the carpet and read it right here. Just a page or two.

There is the girl, but... that's an easy enough problem to solve. Not like she could fight back. Evie's eyes skate around the room, looking for something she could use to...

... To what?

She shakes her head. A chill passes through her, even though the fire and the heavy furnishings make the room far stuffier than the rest of the house. She needs to go. She should tuck the book in her handbag and leave. Enough time to read it at leisure, later.

She traces her fingers over the leather, and wonders if it's cow skin, or something else. She fights the almost unbearable urge to raise the cover to her nose and sniff it.

Which is when the door behind her clicks open, and a tall, cadaverously pale man in his mid-fifties walks in wearing a black silk dressing gown and black latex gloves. Evie recognizes him from the case research pictures.

It's their client.

It's Eric Overstreet.

She presses against one of the bedposts, hugging the book to her chest and hiding herself as best she can behind one of its heavy drapes. He walks around towards the other side of the bed, and maybe she can still get out if he takes a few more steps... then he notices the silver box lying open upon the bed, the book missing from it. His eyes travel upwards, unerringly, to where she's huddled.

He chokes out a startled shout of "Thief!" and lunges forwards.

The bed is between them, and they're both the same distance to the door. Evie squawks in terror and bolts as fast as she can for the door. She can hear the sharp bang of something falling over, maybe a bedside table, and thinks *good, maybe it'll slow him down*. Her hand reaches out for the doorknob—

—when she feels something in her hair, burning through it, a hot, searing thing.

She ducks instinctively, and only after she sees the hole the bullet makes in the door, where her head had just been, does she associate it with the banging sound.

A second bullet tears into the wood of the door frame and Evie freezes, hunkering down into herself to present as small a target as possible.

"Turn around," orders Eric Overstreet, in a surprisingly nasal voice, "and put the book down. I don't want to hurt it."

Out of the corner of her eye, Evie can see the pistol glinting in his hands.

CHAPTER TEN

THE ACRID ODOR of burnt hair hangs in the air of the bedroom. The blindfolded girl on the bed makes a small whimpering sound and writhes against her bonds, clearly uncomfortable with what she can hear.

"Give me my book," Eric says. He's naked under the robe, a protruding belly over a pigeon chest, all covered in sparse dark hair.

Evie turns towards him, hugging the book over her heart like a shield. "I'm sorry," she tries. "I was looking for the bathroom and I got lost?"

Eric snorts in derision and strides forwards. His gun never strays from where it is pointed, at the center of her forehead. His free hand reaches out for the book.

Evie shrinks away from his sallow, silk-robed figure, the grasping hand in the black latex glove. She backs up into something hard and for a moment assumes it's the door.

But doors aren't warm.

Then everything tips over beyond rational understanding.

Eric Overstreet's eyes look past her shoulder and widen and he begins firing the gun and the bullets should be hitting her but they're not, because she's been thrown to the side and there's someone in front of her and it's Misha and she watches him take three slugs to the chest and keep walking forwards and she knows she's not hallucinating because Eric sees it too and his eyes are *terrified* and he's backing up and firing again but his gun is going *click click click* and Eric is begging and the girl on the bed is screaming around the ball gag and Misha backhands Eric halfway across the room, right into a fucking awful porcelain lamp of the Rape of Persephone, and the gun bounces out of his hand onto the rug, *thud thunk*, and Evie decides it's time for her and the book to get the everliving fuck out of there but as she gets up to flee there's a hand on her upper arm like a band of iron and Misha turns her round to face him and his eyes are black, all black, like a Japanese horror movie, and he wrenches the book from her arms and even as she squeals, "No, don't hurt it," he shoves her towards the door and orders, "Walk out of here," and then he is ripping the book apart and throwing its pages in the fire and it's like voices in harmonic chorus are screaming in her brain.

She sees blood begin to drip from the book's torn spine, thick and dark.

She *runs*.

EVIE COMES TO herself outdoors, gazing at the shifting aqua-blue glow of the pool. She has a glass of champagne in her hand and no idea how she got it. All she knows is that the panic is receding, its cold steel claws extracting from her chest, the stifling pressure slipping back into the shadows. She's shaking, but it's from the increasing chill of the night air rather than nerves. The intrusive buzzing whispers of the book, its anguished screams, it's all gone from her head. All is silence now; even the crickets have gone quiet.

The valet parking ticket is still in her pocket, and she runs her fingers along its edges, flicking the corner with her thumb. It's soothing. Misha had told her to go say hello to Andy and his friends, but she thinks if she tries to open her mouth to speak to anyone, she'll throw up.

Her brain reels when it tries to parse the events of the past half hour. What it was like to hold the warm, living skin of the book in her hands, how it had entranced her, twisted her to the point where she was casually considering murder. How, under its thrall, she couldn't feel her link with Misha.

But most of all she sees the ebony nightmare of Misha's eyes, the bullets that didn't even slow him down as he walked inexorably towards Eric Overstreet. The way he had tossed Eric across the room, inhumanly strong and utterly without remorse or pity.

Finally she understands what Misha meant about a looking-glass world. About wanting to protect her. And she'd rushed in like an idiot, wanting to know everything.

She no longer wants to know.

It's done. New York, Chicago, Los Angeles, she doesn't care. As long as it's not here.

She'll go to the hotel and get a cab to the bus station. Misha's too upper-class to think about buses. She'll call her parents en route, say she's coming home for good.

Evie's mind spins in circles as she walks slowly back through the crowds in the house, holding the warm, flat champagne that she no longer has any urge to drink. She passes Nicole, surrounded by a group of laughing men, and she doesn't miss how Nicole's eyes follow her, but she can't bring herself to care any more.

She parks her glass on a table on the way out, and grips the leather of her bag so the valets won't notice her hands are shaking. There's nobody else leaving yet. A young valet grins as he dashes off with her ticket, thrilled to hit the sports car lottery.

She can feel Misha, strange and dark and different from how he was before, through the link that tingles just above her heart. He's still in the house, still up on the third floor. But he's moving.

The yellow sports car pulls up to the curb as the screaming starts.

Evie whirls around. There's a tremendous crashing sound, so loud and heavy that she can feel the foundation shake under her feet. Then there are people running, fleeing out of the house and all she can think about is Misha's whispered *I'm not safe* and then his soft, blue eyes eclipsed by black.

She's afraid to look back and see what he's done. She gets in the car and starts it up and as she slams the door shut she hears a woman telling the valets that the huge black Egyptian statue in the house had toppled over, breaking one of the staircases.

Not toppled over, Evie thinks, as she buckles her seatbelt. Not fallen, but pushed. By something that only looks like a man. And which may or may not be in control of itself.

Evie shifts into first gear. She fumbles the clutch and the car jerks forwards and stalls. One of the flood of party guests turns and sneers at her. *Little girl in a man's car*, his face says. Evie tenses her jaw and throws the car back into neutral, starting it again, and easing into first much more slowly. The car crawls forwards, the crowd assembling on the driveway resentfully making way for it. She wants to hit the accelerator hard and get out of there, but there are too many people around. Someone smacks the hood with their hand and she flinches, barely remembering to throw the car into neutral as she slams on the brakes. She waits for a group of revelers to stagger across the driveway in front of her and then shifts into gear again. All she wants is to be out of this house, away from the awful guests and the repulsive Overstreets and Misha, vicious Misha, who made a book bleed.

She realizes at the first stop sign that she has no idea how to get back to the hotel. It's dark and the streets are bland with the calculated anonymity of great wealth. Palm trees and green banks of shrubbery line the road, softening the iron fences that lie behind, hiding the houses that lie even further back from curious eyes. Evie rolls to a stop and frowns to herself as she reaches for her phone to pull up directions home. The stop sign is at the top of a pronounced incline, and she's really not sure of her ability to double-clutch without rolling the car backwards or stalling it.

Well, at least there isn't—

—a trio of police cars come screaming down the street towards her, lights flashing, sirens wailing.

Evie swears under her breath. The flashing lights of the cop cars send her heart beating into double-time again and she tries to pull away from the stop sign like someone who knows what she's doing, but the clutch doesn't catch and the car rolls backwards and then she stalls it.

She swears again and restarts the car. At least this time it doesn't roll backwards any further before she stalls it. She's on the edge of panic again, her heart thundering in her chest and her lungs too small and the car pressing in on her. She can feel Misha through the link, he's out in the night and coming in her direction, he must be driving another car because it's too fast—

The rearmost police car skews around in a U-turn pulls to a stop about a hundred feet behind her, the siren blipping off and the headlights flashing once.

She needs to leave. The fastest way out... the fastest way out may be the police.

Evie shifts in her seat uncomfortably and places both hands in clear view, on the top of the steering wheel. At best the policeman is going to be condescending. At worst he's going to assume she stole the car. He'll take her back to the station, a place of relative safety.

But then the passenger door opens and Misha throws himself into the car. "Thought you said you could drive stick," he growls, flinging his jacket into the back. "Move over." He pulls up the handbrake and starts climbing over her, pushing her out of the driver's seat. He has sunglasses pushed up into his hair, and his eyes are still all black. As he shoves himself past Evie, she can see the neat, burnt holes in the front of his shirt from the bullets.

She finds herself manhandled into the passenger seat and they're pulling off down the road at a sedate pace moments later. "How did you..." she starts, looking back at where Misha had... appeared from.

"Evie, I once outran a cheetah. Catching up to your appalling driving really wasn't very difficult." He looks at her, and there's something frayed, messy about him. Even the black pits where his eyes should be are expressive, which she wouldn't have thought possible. "I'm high as shit," he whispers. "I shouldn't be driving."

Evie glances behind. The cop car hasn't followed them. Maybe it hadn't been stopping for her in the first place. "You seriously stopped to get wasted after that?" she says.

Misha easily runs the car up through the gears and accelerates towards a freeway on-ramp. "No," he says, his fingers tapping silent polyrhythms on the steering wheel, drowned in the roar of the V-8 engine. "Apparently if you're magical and destroy something else old and magical, the power doesn't dissipate, some of it… feeds back into you. I feel… very strange."

He looks at her then. She can see reflected in the window how his black eyes widen as he notices how she's leaning away from him, huddled against the door. The car skews through several lanes of traffic, barely missing a pickup truck. The blare of the truck's horn snaps Misha's attention back to the road; he curses in, she guesses, Georgian as he settles back into the left lane and eases the speed down to eighty. "I'm sorry," he mumbles. "I did try to warn you."

"Yeah," Evie says. "Can you drop me at the airport tomorrow? I think I'm gonna…" She waves her hand in a small, ineffectual motion towards the window, the night sky.

"Okay," Misha says. "That's fine. Back to New York?"

"No." Evie shakes her head, a small motion against the window-glass as she watches the road go by. "Chicago. It's where I'm from. I want to go home for a bit."

"Oh." The tapping on the steering wheel stops. Evie can see out of the corners of her eyes that Misha is just staring out the windshield. He looks so tired. His broad shoulders sag. A few miles pass before he speaks again, yellow lines vanishing into darkness past the car.

"There used to be one of us in Chicago," he says, almost apologetically. His hands fidget on the wheel again. "The priests got her, or she moved on. I don't know. She's gone now. Evie, please be careful. Now that you've come into contact with something like me, it leaves a mark. Like a resonance. It means it's likely to happen again."

Evie lets herself sink into the bucket seat, and stare up at the black cloth of the car's roof. "The looking-glass world," she sighs. A world she now apparently can't escape. Where there are no answers, just the exchange of one enigma for another.

"Indeed," Misha says. "I'm sorry again," he whispers. "For scaring you. For everything. It was all very selfish of me."

He slides a hand off the steering wheel and touches it to his chest before moving it down to the gearshift.

His hand shakes. It's a little thing, but Misha has always seemed so assured, so in control, that any slip of that mask becomes profoundly disturbing. Before Evie can stop herself, she blurts out, "Are you okay?"

"Not really," Misha says. His hair has fallen forwards, shielding most of his face from Evie's view. What she can see of his expression is tense, trembling, as if he's trying to keep tears at bay.

Something twists in Evie's stomach. She is *terrified* of him. But at the same time, she aches to put her arms around him and reassure him. She knows it's weak of her. She knows she should ask him to pull over and she should get out and *run* and keep running. But instead, she digs around in the comforting, messy space of her handbag. "I've got tissues," she mutters.

"No point," he says, glancing over at her, his face a rictus of sadness and regret. "I can't cry, not any more." He rubs at the inner corners of his eyes, the black starting to fade away to the edges, like bruises. "My body doesn't make tears. Or blood."

"What *are* you made of?" Evie asks.

"I don't know," Misha chokes out, his voice cracked and rough and full of self-hatred. He hauls the car over to the breakdown lane and stops it. Then he just folds his hands on top of the steering wheel and buries his face in his forearms. "I don't know."

Evie has to tuck her hands into her armpits to keep from reaching out to him. She shivers, the car interior growing cold now that the engine is off. She listens to the intermittent whine and roar of other vehicles speeding past them. She's always been a little night-blind, and the blur of the taillights as they recede is strangely soothing.

There's a nudge against her shoulder. She looks up to find Misha holding his fancy designer jacket out to her with one hand. His head is still pillowed on the other arm, and he looks at her through a curtain of hair. "You're shivering," he says, pushing the jacket into her lap. He restarts the car. "It must be cold in here. Sorry. Temperature is another thing that's... gone, for me. I can feel it, but it doesn't matter."

Evie picks at the gold embroidery on the jacket as Misha pulls back out onto the freeway. "The book," she says. She draws the jacket over her shoulders. It's big for her, but she finds it comforting to be surrounded by something that smells of Misha, that perhaps some of his invulnerability might rub off on her. "It made me think things. Twisted me all up. I was halfway to believing the sky was red and casual murder was no big deal."

"Yah. It does that," Misha says. Then, a little tilt of the head. "It did that."

"Do you think—" Evie begins.

"No," Misha says, his tone sharp. He throws her a quick glare. "No, I can't blame the book for what I did. My choice was my own." He downshifts as they pull off towards their exit. "I was like you. Didn't believe. Thought it was all old wives' tales and the superstitions of the uneducated. But that's the problem. Doesn't matter in the end if you don't believe in the supernatural. All it has to do is believe in you."

They pull into the hotel's entranceway a few minutes later. Misha gets out and opens the door for her, but doesn't move to follow her inside. He flashes her a sad smile. "I'll pick you up tomorrow for the airport around nine, okay? Or you can arrange a car with the front desk. I'll pay for it, and the plane ticket."

"Where are you going?" Evie asks.

"Just... out." Misha fidgets, then rakes his hands through his hair. "I'm... I feel like I'm bursting out of my own skin. I need to go away, let some of this out. I can normally suppress it. I'm *good* at suppressing it... but with the transfer when I destroyed the book... I'm like a glass that's too full, and... Christ." He tilts his head back and looks up at the tall hotel building, at the lights in its high windows. Then he grins and looks down again, shaking his head. He rolls his right wrist, flexing his muscles from hand up to shoulder, but Evie has the uncomfortable feeling the strength he is testing is not a physical one at all. "I can't be here," he says, and the words come out as a thick, predatory growl.

"Okay," Evie says, backing away towards the hotel's glass doors. "Be careful."

"Evie," Misha whispers, an almost manic smirk tugging at his lips, "it is the night that should be careful of me."

Evie is only a few steps inside the lobby of the hotel when she hears the roar of the sports car and screech of its tires as Misha peels out of the driveway, off to Lord only knows where.

The posh quiet of the upscale hotel surrounds her as she walks deeper inside, the car's engine fading into memory. She waits for an elevator up to her room, trying to place the ambient instrumental tune playing softly in the lobby before realizing it's a lounge-music version of "No Diggity".

EVIE KICKS OFF her fancy clothes and wipes her makeup away. She doesn't even bother shoving the clothes pile off the bed before curling up under the covers and flicking off the lights. Not that sleep is likely to come. It's 2am and her brain is a formless, shifting whirlpool of increasingly paranoid and obsessive thought patterns.

She briefly debates knocking on Masha's door, to let her know her brother was... what? Out in the night; high on magic; not coming home. But she discards the idea, because she still doesn't know how much the twins share with each other, and the middle of the night isn't the time to find out. At best it would needlessly alarm Masha. At worst, Evie could be throwing herself right back into danger again. She snuggles down into the marshmallow-soft pillows and shuts her eyes. If Masha is worried, she'll text her brother like a grownup.

Evie feels above her heart. The link Misha had placed there is fading, going quiet, but she can still feel that he is somewhere nearby, in downtown Palo Alto, and he's okay. Odd, kind of sparkly-feeling through the link, but okay.

Evie sighs, and stares at the ceiling. Her thoughts turn to what it must have been like, to have gone through the transformation from human to... whatever Misha is. To be something incredible, perfect and terrifying, that can run down the wind, and then to be forced to suppress all that for fear of being hunted down and killed. Did he feel caged in, pretending to be a common human every waking moment? (Did he even sleep, or was that something else gone?) Did the physical power prowl within him, burning to be used? Did his other powers? All she had seen of his magic was the placing of the link, but he treated that like it was trivial, no more than a clever parlor trick he'd discovered on his own. What oceans raged inside him? When the spring tides rose within him, did his levees ever break? What did he do then?

What is he doing now?

Evie throws off the covers and pulls on a pair of jeans.

The link is dull, but still enough to follow.

IT'S A GIGANTIC nightclub inside an old movie theatre, where each of the three screening rooms has been made into a separate dance floor. Strobe lights and mirrored glass glint off baroque old plaster-work, California old, so maybe 1950. Evie gets in, with her blue jeans, only because it's late enough that there isn't any sort of line. It costs her $30.

The club is still surprisingly packed, and it smells like sweat and the dull aspirin tang of fog machines. Evie looks around, feeling lost, a sober stranger in a stoned land. The dark, gyrating shapes she passes are conspicuously happy, off some combination of alcohol or drugs or the euphoria of the dance. It's late enough that the hookups have started. Bodies grind against each other in darker corners. Mouths find solace pressed against other mouths.

And Evie is alone.

She pushes through crowds of college students and Guidos and young office workers and the bass beat is so heavy it's overwhelming the weakening link, until suddenly it's gone and she's left at the edge of the largest dance floor with nothing but an aching loneliness, made worse for being in a crowd. Several hundred strangers are halfway to going home with each other, halfway to just getting off in public, to the beat of EDM at brain-liquidizing volume. She hates it here.

A guy in his mid-forties, too tanned, too much cologne, jostles past her and then notices her, grinning. A gold chain around his wrist glints in the flashing magenta light as he leans forwards to shout something in her ear. He reeks of the sort of sweet, Technicolor shots they serve in places like this. Evie wrinkles her nose and backs away, moving next to a pillar so that her back is protected. The man mouths *bitch* and slips into the crowd.

Then there is a momentary shift in the tide of the dance floor, and Evie sees Misha. His golden-tinged skin glows against his thin black T-shirt, a v-neck that clings to every cut and curve of that turbocharged body. Those leather jeans that might as well be sprayed on. He's kissing a girl. As their position shifts, Evie can see that he has a thin scarf tied over his eyes. He's blindfolded. When he pushes his partner gently away, Evie can see his arousal through his jeans. A man slots in behind him and begins to grind against his ass, and Misha arches back, allowing the man's hands free rein to roam over his chest, down his stomach to palm at his erection.

Evie can't take her eyes off Misha, biting his lip and winding sensually to the music. He's so beautiful, the sight of him cracks her heart open. Evie had always understood that Misha was pretty, in a ridiculous solar-eclipse *it's fine as long as you don't look directly at it* way. Which is why she can only remember him in glimpses: the way his hands move when he talks, sure and elegant; the line of his jaw; how his dark hair slips out of its twist down the back of his neck; the points of his hip bones, framed by muscle, bare above his jeans. The slow blink he does just before he smiles at something.

But now she can look her fill.

She feels a buzzing in her, like she did when she held the Overstreets' book in her hands. But it can't be the book; she watched the book die, she saw it bleed and burn.

Misha is blindfolded.

She could go up to him on the dance floor and he would never be aware it's her. She could feel what it's like to have those perfect, lush lips on hers, those strong hands gripping her waist. He would never need to know.

It's the end, anyway, she tells herself. The last hurrah. Tomorrow morning she's getting on a plane to Chicago. No more supernatural. No more unexplained deaths or impossible boys who speak of 1916 like it was yesterday. No more being caught between her job and her dreams.

Her feet drag her forwards, into the mêlée of dancers, and she pushes her way through the writhing, ecstatic crowd towards the brilliant figure dancing at the center of them, the evening star around which they all revolve.

The handsome black man is still grinding against Misha's back, Misha leaning into it, running his hands down the man's thighs, lips parted breathlessly. Then the man turns Misha around and cups his face in his hands, smiling almost triumphantly. Misha places his hands over the man's ass, pulling him close, so that one of Misha's thick, muscular thighs goes between his legs. The man tips his head back in shuddering pleasure, then leans in and kisses Misha, hard and hungry.

Evie can only stand and watch, making a vague attempt to rock to the beat. She is wet and restless, violently turned on; she has been since she walked onto the dance floor and saw him.

Misha playfully puts a hand on his current partner's lips, then reconsiders, snatching one last kiss, and sends him back into the crowd. The girl next to Evie starts forwards, her eyes fixed on Misha with a fierce determination, but Evie mashes her heel down on the top of the woman's foot and neatly steps in front of her—

—into Misha's arms.

She feels electric, the heavy bass beat of the music travelling up into her crotch, the buzzing louder now, a throbbing hum of excitement rocketing through her.

He is everything she imagined.

He runs his hands up from her waist to frame her chest, so near her breasts that her nipples ache with the need for him to run his thumbs over them. She is insanely hot, her whole body a live wire; she thinks she'll come just from him kissing her, it's too much, and he's bending his face down, tilting it slightly in that way he does, and he sighs slightly as he opens his lips and moves towards hers. Just as their lips touch and the electric circuit completes, sending volts of pure ecstasy through her, she can't help it, she moans and whispers his name—

—and it's like she's pulled the pin on a grenade.

Misha's body tenses in horror and he yanks away from her, pulling off his blindfold. He grabs her and strides away towards the door, hauling her through the crowd after him, his hand like steel around her right arm. It *hurts*.

She tries to say, "Misha, let go," and pull back, but he turns around and hisses at her and his face is terrifying, wild eyes cold as pale crystal, edged in black.

Evie wants to curl up and die. There's being rejected, and then there's the look of horrified disgust Misha had given her when he pulled the blindfold off. She feels small and worthless and not even sure what had made her think that someone like Misha would look at her as anything other than what she was: a little mouse who made bad coffee and worse mistakes and was too weak in the end to hold on to her dreams.

They burst out of the front door into the cold night air of the city. Misha doesn't stop, keeps pulling her down the block until they reach the alley beside the club. He pulls her into the stinking darkness and shoves her against a wall opposite some dumpsters. She gasps as her shoulders smack against the cold bricks.

Misha presses his hands against those bricks, one thick forearm on either side of her head, and looms down over her, six feet of coiled fury. "Evie," he murmurs, low and vicious. "What were you thinking?"

What the hell *had* she been thinking? The buzzing euphoria of earlier, the feeling that she could get away with anything, it was... gone. There was just her, tired and dull and missing her bed, and Misha, furious. She suddenly has no idea why she stayed and watched him dance. Why she had made such a *fool* of herself, pushing through that crowd to try to kiss him like some corner-store Jezebel. "I, I was worried," Evie mumbles, "I wanted to make sure you were okay."

He leans down further, his lips near her ear. She can feel his warmth, smell the juniper-and-leather scent of him, and something else under it, something musky and feral, and it's still not okay that he's this close, it's not helping at all, and neither is the taut flex of his muscles as he leans down over her. "I was *feeding*," he hisses.

"Oh," Evie says. "Oh, shit." And it makes sense now, how he's practically glowing, the insane perfection of him gleaming like a blade in the moonlight.

"Yeah," Misha says, "*oh shit* indeed," and it's only a little bit mocking. "Evie. What I am. It's not cute. It's not a joke. I am a predator." His pale eyes bore into hers, and she's surprised by the desperation in them. "I could have killed you, idiot! If I had lost control, I could have taken your entire life for no reason, nothing more than I was enjoying myself too much to stop."

"But you... I can't imagine you losing control. You're always so... together," Evie says.

Then Misha runs a thumb over Evie's lower lip, and her world stops. "I could have lost control with you," he whispers, the words rough, as if they're torn out of a secret place within him.

The fight goes out of his body, and his broad shoulders slump as he leans his forehead against the wall. The ends of his hair tickle her cheek. "What you felt in there wasn't real," he breathes. "Whatever you think you felt... it was enchantment. What most things like me rely on to attract prey. I don't use it often, but tonight..." Misha sighs, weary and apologetic.

"Tonight, I did." He smiles at her, small and brittle. "Nobody is going to notice if a bunch of drunk people in a nightclub are a little hornier than usual. And I can let out some of this storm within me... safely."

Evie's mind is still lagging thirty seconds behind. What did he mean, *I could have lost control with you*? Her lip still tingles from his touch and he is still too damn close and everything is not okay and at this rate might never be okay again.

"Misha..." she starts. "It was... It is real. Please. I—"

Misha cuts her off with a sigh, and places a hand on her cheek, along her jaw. His touch is gentle, and warm, and she wants to press into it like a cat. But something's off. He's not looking at her. He's turned his head away, as if he doesn't want to witness what he's doing.

"I'll prove it," he says, despair edging into his voice.

She's about to say *Misha, no*, but though he hasn't moved, and their only point of contact is his feather-light touch on her cheek, Evie feels the heat of arousal sparking in her, fizzing through her bloodstream. Her mouth opens in an O of surprise, but all that comes out is a reedy whimper as her clit throbs and her back arches off the wall. It feels *amazing*.

"Continue," Misha says, his voice expressionless, his face still averted from hers. "Yes or no."

"I..." Evie gasps. "Uh." She swallows, and her cheeks flush hot with embarrassment. It's not... It's not what she really wants. But it may be all she ever gets.

"C-continue," she says, her voice small.

And then she melts as the fire unspools through her again. She's always taken a while to come off, and always best by herself. Almost never easily or well with a partner, although she's the first to admit that her choice in partners has been a trail of disasters. The tiny part of her brain that's still capable of rational thought can't believe that she's sparking up like a firecracker with all her clothes on, in a dirty alley next to a shitty EDM club. But she is. And it's *so much*, wave after wave of arousal building within her. She starts shaking, her knees buckling under her. Her foot slips and she slides down the rough brick wall.

Misha's arm slips around her waist, supporting her, pulling her off the rough, cold wall into the warmth of his chest. She is biting her lip, long past the ability to do anything other than let out little kitten moans and gasps as she shudders, her clit buzzing with phantom stimulation, her vagina wet and aching to be filled. Misha's hand lies gently on her back, over her clothes. Her head is tucked into the crook of his neck and her whole world is his warmth, his scent, and it's this, rather than his magic, that tips her over the edge.

She comes shatteringly hard and has to bite into the curve of his neck to keep from crying out. His other arm winds around her shoulders and rubs little circles on her back as she shakes through her release, her legs weak, her panties wet, her eyelids a tapestry of supernovas.

"See," he whispers, still holding her, and *God, never let me go*, she thinks. "It's a beautiful lie, but it's still a lie." Then those strong arms hug her a little tighter. "I didn't take. Just gave. Don't worry."

She feels like she's floating, at home in his arms, and still tingly and relaxed from her orgasm. "I trust you," she whispers back.

"You shouldn't," Misha says, his arms loosening, as he steps away from her. The cold night air hits all the places his warmth had been, outlines the space where he used to be. The sudden absence of his body against hers is a visceral ache.

He looks down at her with a sadness in his eyes that was old before she was born. "You made the right decision, to go back to Chicago. Your place isn't with monsters. Forget me. Keep trying to write your stories."

Evie nods. She can feel tears welling up in her eyes, threatening to spill down her face. Her college fantasies of being a top journalist feel as dead and dull to her now as the link Misha had placed in her. Writing up police brutality and bodega stick-ups, or even occult murders by San Francisco tech bosses, none of it holds any appeal for her. None of it has held anything for her for a long time, if she's being honest with herself. She's just been going through the motions of what she thought she should become. She looks up at Misha. "I don't think my dream is my dream any more," she says quietly.

Misha slumps, his back against the wall. "I'm sorry," he says quietly. "I'm very good at ruining things."

"No," Evie says, moving closer and bumping her shoulder against his. "Nothing to do with you. I just… I dunno. I think I've not wanted to admit it to myself for a while." And it's true: laying her journalistic hopes aside causes her no more regret than giving up an old, once-loved coat that she never wears any more. But it leaves an absence. When you've been telling yourself for years that happiness lies just over the next hill, the next achievement, what now? How do you find contentment, when you have no map for it?

Misha looks down at his nails. "You should still go back to Chicago. This is going to get worse before it gets better."

"The book's gone, though, right?" Evie says. "You destroyed it."

"Yes. But there's every possibility that Eric has read it, and will commit the ritual during the planetary alignment, next week."

"You're not going to let the priests just take care of that, are you," Evie states.

"No," Misha says, staring down at the filthy pavement. "Eric would sell me out to them in a second, for his freedom." He looks right at Evie. "That's another reason you have to leave town. I'm sure that at least some garbled description of us has been given to the police by now."

"Misha… what's your dream?" Evie asks.

He blinks at her, his lips parted. After a moment, he shrugs, the motion small and jerky, far from his usual grace. "I don't know. To atone for… for being a parasite, I suppose. It would be nice not to live in fear. To be able to have friends."

"You have me," Evie says.

"And you are leaving, for your own safety," Misha replies.

They both lean against the wall for several long, chilly minutes, quietly enjoying each other's company for the last time, listening to the shrill sound of revelers pouring out of the club in twos and threes.

"Are you, uh, done?" Evie asks, once the cold night air gets too much for her. She motions vaguely towards the club. "In there?"

"Done enough," Misha says, staring at his boots. He's shoved his hands in his jeans pockets, tugging them down even lower on his hips, and Evie's pretty sure he's not wearing any underwear. She blushes and jerks her gaze away, deliberately looking at the dumpster on the other side of the alley.

"Want to head home?" she says.

"Uh," he says, then he shakes his head. "I'm still... unsettled, under my skin. I need to walk for a while."

"Okay," Evie says. "I'm, um, I'm gonna get a cab, then."

"Need money?"

"Nah. I'm good." She smiles, a little weak. "G'night, Misha. Be careful."

He snorts in feigned disdain. Then his arm circles her and he pulls her in to him again, dropping a kiss onto the top of her head. "Be safe, Evie."

She gets a cab easily; despite the late hour there's still a fairly regular stream of taxis dropping people off at the club. As the car pulls away, she looks out the rear window at the pale eyes watching her from the alley, until she can't see the alley any more, until the lights of the club become blurry and indistinct in the distance.

EVIE WAKES TO a knock on her door. She groans, and when the knock comes again she grudgingly staggers out of bed. It's way too early.

Only, it's not: sunlight is pouring into the room.

She throws the door open to find Masha glaring at her, annoyed.

"I could have been someone to kill you," Masha says. "Next time you should at least see who it is before opening the door." She thrusts a large paper coffee cup at Evie.

Evie takes it and wraps her hands around the cup's life-giving warmth. She stares at the coffee in a daze as Masha pushes past into the room. Evie vaguely recognizes what she's wearing: Misha's striped shirt with the wide neck, and his trendy black sweatpants. "You're not ready to go to the airport," Masha says, looking pointedly at Evie's sleep shirt.

"I forgot to set my alarm," Evie says. "Uh, I thought Misha was taking me?"

"He's feeling emotional," Masha says as she flops down onto an armchair. "Sulking."

Evie perches on the edge of her bed, folding her legs underneath her and nursing the coffee. Hopefully its heat and bitterness will jump-start her brain into being able to cope with the exigencies of the day. Because there's something just out of reach that she needs to understand. Something's wrong. Going to Chicago is wrong, but she can't yet put her finger on why.

Masha isn't helping, sitting there in her brother's shirt giving Evie a reproachful look like she's personally responsible for his unhappiness—

Oh.

Evie knows where she's been happiest. What makes her happy. And he's right here.

She takes another sip of her coffee, this time for courage.

Then she returns Masha's stare.

"I've changed my mind. I'm not flying back to Chicago," Evie says. "I panicked a lot last night but now that I've had some time to calm down, I've realized that working with Misha is what I want to do. So I am not going."

"You could die. In fact, given what a disaster my brother is, you probably *will* die," Masha says.

"Everybody dies," Evie says.

Masha tilts her head and hums a sarcastic little note.

"Almost everybody dies," Evie amends.

Masha bows her head fractionally, in approval.

"But that's another thing. No more games. No more hiding," Evie says over the brim of her coffee cup. "He has to tell me everything. The truth. And so do you. I don't even know if you're… like him." She picks at the cardboard cuff on the coffee cup. "I don't even really know what he is."

"But you have an idea," Masha says. Her body posture is wary. She's pushed against one side of the armchair like she's ready to flee.

"Yeah, I do," Evie breathes. "And part of me is in denial that any of this—that you—can exist. Even then, it's going to take me a long time to be okay with it. But where I come from, you don't run away from your friends when they need you the most."

Masha looks at her for a long moment, stunned, waiting for Evie to change her mind. When it's clear she isn't going to do anything other than continue to sip her coffee, Masha rises slowly from the chair. She's still expecting to be stopped at any moment. "You're *sure*," Masha says. Her expression is wary, like she's half-convinced Evie's going to cut and run again, same as she did last night.

Well, that makes two of us, Evie thinks. "Yes, I'm sure. Please go get him."

Masha nods. She gets up without another word, walking slowly towards the hotel room door like she's on her way to deliver bad news. At the last minute, she ducks into the bathroom instead.

Evie waits, her confusion growing. She's just about to get up and see if Masha's okay when the bathroom door opens again.

And Misha steps out.

He sticks his hands in the pockets of his sweatpants and looks at her bashfully through his hair.

"So, uh, first," he mumbles, "there's this."

CHAPTER ELEVEN

MISHA APPROACHES HER carefully, as if he's expecting her to cry out, or run away.

But all Evie does is stare, as her brain works out likenesses and differences and a tiny part of her whispers *well, it's better than them being in some weird incestuous relationship* and another part of her brain squeaks back *there is no "them", they are the same person, omg, omg.* She feels completely unmoored from the world of a minute ago, and yet she is still sitting on the bed, still holding her paper cup of lukewarm coffee.

In among all her shock and confusion there's a hot flare of anger, because it was all a con. All those carefully arranged meetings with Masha. All the times she talked about her brother, like she was imparting a special confidence to Evie. It was just part of his cover. Their cover.

But when he slows a few feet in front of her, hands still in his pockets, shoulders hunched, she can't see a callous manipulator. All she sees is a scared boy, forced to live a life of hiding, afraid to lose what might be the only friend he's had in a very long time.

She could ask a thousand things, but when she opens her mouth what comes out is, "Does it hurt?"

Misha blinks at her, surprised. "Uh. No." He sits down on the bed, a respectful distance from her, and pulls his knees up to his chin. It's such a childish gesture; it makes him look so young all of a sudden. "It doesn't feel like anything at all, actually."

"Can you, uh, shapechange? Like, is that a thing you can do?" Evie asks.

Misha shakes his head. "No. Just me. Boy-me and girl-me." He glances over at Evie and guesses at the question in her eyes. "This is the original version," he says, indicating himself.

Evie's brain is still whirling, and after a moment she realizes she's probably been staring more than is polite. "So what pronouns should I use for you?" she stutters.

"He/him for this body, she/her for the other one," Misha says. "I... I'm glad there are so many words now for the ways people are. When I was figuring it out, the only words were insults, or unsayable in polite company. And perhaps it is a failure of courage on my part not to adopt they/them, but I have been as I am for a very long time now and change is hard, after a while." The hint of a smile plays at the corners of his mouth, as he traces a finger in lazy figure eights on the bedsheets.

Evie nods. "Okay. Cool. Haven't been misgendering you, that's good. Um. So. Why do you go out and bring me coffee, when you don't eat or drink like a human?"

"I'm trying to be *nice*, Evie." Misha frowns at her. "And, I like the smell." He presses his palms against his eyes and sprawls back on the bed. He's grinning, and it's like being bathed in sunshine. "Furthermore, you are the most confounding person I have ever met, and I would like you to know that." Long, elegant fingers reach out and poke Evie in the shoulder.

She squeaks in surprise as Misha nearly pushes her over, not hiding his strength as carefully as usual. Her coffee sloshes and a few drops stain her pajamas. "You do *not* get to call anyone confusing."

"Fair point," he says. But he's relaxed, and he's still smiling. Far better than the stiff, stressed person who'd walked out of the bathroom. Misha should be all ease and languid grace and anything else is just... wrong. She's happy at this little victory, proud to have caused the return of his good cheer.

She's suddenly, painfully aware that she's turned towards him like a sunflower seeking the light. That his smile has woken up in her the sort of fluttery feeling that she thought only existed in cheap books and fairy tales. That last night wasn't something she can blame on exhaustion, or magic. It was folly, pure and simple: she wants something that she cannot have.

She only realizes Misha had said something to her when he tilts his head and says a shy, "You don't have to, if you don't want to."

"What?" she says. "Sorry, I was..." She makes a vague, apologetic gesture with her free hand.

"I was trying to give you the explanation I promised you. The easiest way to begin is for you to put your head here," and he touches the scar on his chest, "and listen." Misha shifts slightly. "I'm not trying to be—"

"Misha, I got the picture last night," Evie replies. "If you wanted to be creepy, you would have already been creepy by now."

"Well, quite," he says, softly. "But I've been seducing people for a long time, and it's very easy to lead someone into believing they want something. I do it almost unconsciously, now. It's just habit." He flashes a quicksilver grin at her, lopsided and adorable. "So what I'm saying is, it's not you, it's me."

"Ugh, Misha, you're so full of shit," Evie says, putting down her coffee. "The Masha side of you is right. You really do overthink everything."

"Yet somehow I still end up at the wrong conclusions," he mumbles.

Evie rolls her eyes and moves closer to him on the bed. "Where?" she says.

Misha points at his heart.

She leans over and places her head against his striped shirt. Through the thin cotton, Misha's chest is ridiculously firm and warm and...

... Silent.

No breath.

No heartbeat.

She moves her head away and looks up at him, confused.

"I was born in 1892," Misha says. "At an estate outside Kutaisi. I was the youngest of several sons, so not much need for me. Mostly I ran free in the hills, a wild dog in a silk coat."

He shifts a bit and settles into a more comfortable position, cross-legged, tipping his head back against the headboard. "When I was twenty-three, because I was a naïve idiot who couldn't handle the entirely predictable end of an affair that had been doomed from its start, I cut out my own heart and gave it, still beating, to…" He runs a hand through his hair, and sighs. "… I'll call him the Devil, but it's not that simple. That, plus a few hundred souls of our family's serfs, for immortality, at the urging of a book which plucked at the raveled edges of my mind."

"Not… just immortality, though," Evie says, haltingly, leaning against the headboard near Misha. Near, but not touching. Still about a foot of space between them. Not that she's focusing on the distance, or the unnatural warmth he radiates. Or how much she'd like to put her head back on his chest.

"No," Misha breathes, staring up at the ceiling. "The rest was… a surprise." He shifts and sits forwards, suddenly earnest. "I wasn't tricked. I knew *precisely* what I was signing up to become: an incubus. A shoddy kind of demon who steals little fractions of human lives to sustain itself, and gives pleasure in return. But…" he rakes his hands through his hair and his voice drops to a rough whisper, "… but there were quite a few things never mentioned in the book." He sighs, restless. "I've spent considerable time exploring the boundaries of what I am and it's… I'm a monster, Evie."

His pale eyes flash up to meet Evie's green ones. "I went to see Pavel once I'd recovered from my transformation and got control of myself. I thought this meant we could be forever, he and I. One glance at me, and he knew exactly what I'd done. I will… never forget the look of disgust on his face. The things he said to me, I still hear them in my worst moments… I flew into a rage and destroyed part of the monastery. Knocked down stone pillars with my bare hands. The whole time he just watched me prove by my actions what a vile beast I had become. And I *was*, Evie. I knew I was. But I could not stop myself. I ran away, and I've been running ever since." His face is a mask of tightly controlled self-hatred, and when he speaks again, Evie has to strain to hear it. "The worst part of what Pavel said to me was that, while it may have been unnecessarily cruel, every single word was true, or became true."

Evie had seen hints of Misha's strength. Well, it had happened in front of her, within her field of vision, but her mind had refused to truly *see* it. As soon as she looked away, the images of a man who moved faster than a person should, hit harder, took a bullet like it was a bee-sting, they all dissipated like morning mist burned away by the calm light of rational possibility. She thinks back to the fight at the Met, how she must have seen Misha get shot. She even saw the bullet hole in his shirt, but because it wasn't possible that a man could be shot in the stomach and not bleed, she calmly accepted that it hadn't happened. Misha's continued existence rests on his ability to convince people that they didn't really see what they saw. How much, even in her terror after the Overstreets' party, had she underestimated what he could do? And what was Misha like when he didn't trying to hide himself? Had there ever been a time for that?

As if he can read her mind, Misha gazes distractedly down at his forearm, watching the play of muscles under his skin as he turns it back and forth. "Shortly afterwards my countries slid into thirty years of war. And I went with them, gladly. I was a soldier, and I told myself I was fighting for my motherland but really, no. I was fighting for nothing but my own anger. I've killed a lot of people. I can't say if any of them deserved it; they were just wearing the wrong uniform."

Evie picks at a small coffee stain on the duvet cover. "Who was he?" she asks, to change the subject. Misha's soft sorrow had dissolved on talk of war to a sort of focused intensity that makes her want to reach out and run a hand down his arm, make him aware by touch of how tightly wound he has become. Her traitorous body is already leaning towards him, betraying all common sense and likelihood of rejection. She shifts uncomfortably and re-crosses her legs, her clit humming with the memory of last night, outside the club. Of what he could do apparently as easy as breathing. Or not, seeing as he didn't actually need to breathe.

"Mm?" Misha says.

"Pavel? Who was he? The one for whom you…" Evie replies.

"Oh. My lover. The priest. He was immortal." The menace in his eyes melts away like early-morning mist as his lips begin to curl into a melancholy grin. "Hence my foolishness."

Evie smiles back. "I'm thinking of you running around on the battlefields of…" and then she blanks on the name of a single Russian or Georgian military battle. "Uh. Stalingrad?"

Misha shakes his head. "Never at Stalingrad. I was cavalry. A tank commander. Easier to hide my unnaturalness in a tank. If I were infantry," he frowns, "I probably wouldn't have lasted a week without being found out. They would have burned me. I was already under suspicion for being from an aristocratic background, and for being Georgian." He smiles at her, thin and sad. "There's a photo of me and my crew on our tank after Kursk. Not that you can recognize me under the goggles and the hat."

"That the reason there still is a picture?" Evie says.

"Yes. I learned another thing, though, fighting." He stares down at his fingers, restlessly interlacing them. "The book, and all our histories, say that the incubus feeds off sexual energy, but that's not the whole truth. It can be *any* emotional energy. Anger. Terror. Plenty of that on a battlefield. And what I feed off, I'm able to give in return. I'd ask you to imagine that, but please don't. I did it, and I don't even want to remember it." His next words are so quiet, so mumbled, Evie can barely hear them. "Their faces, when they'd die…" He rubs the back of his neck. "A few years after that, I attempted to kill myself. Went somewhere remote and tried to starve myself to death. Passed out; woke up fifty miles away in a room full of dead bodies. And all I could think as I got to my feet and staggered out of there was, at least they were smiling."

Evie looks around at the plain-fancy modern hotel room, and thinks of the thin, insubstantial secrets its walls would have heard before her: travelling businesspeople, unhappy with their partners, their lives; wealthy tourists, wondering if that's all there is. She shakes her head, slowly. "I have no idea how to process any of this."

"Yeah, me neither," says Misha. "You become numb after a while. Numb and... empty." He wipes a hand down his face. "I haven't even told you the really terrible stuff," he sighs.

"Maybe later?" Evie says, trying to keep her face blank as she gets off the bed and heads towards the bathroom. Because it's either that or she's going to hug the stuffing out of him, and this is not the time for her to lose what small semblance of chill she has left.

"Maybe later," Misha says, quiet, his eyes distant in memory.

Evie runs some cold water into a glass that still has smudges of toothpaste on the rim. She needs to let her brain catch up with proceedings before her libido drives her to do something pathetic and stupid. It was already refusing to hold onto the idea that the person sitting on the bed was a 120-year-old lust demon who could change gender at will and bench-press a pickup truck. There's a remoteness there, her mind holding the information at bay to keep her sanity intact. She tries to think back onto the times she's seen him use his freakish strength and speed, but the memories are smudged and indistinct, like ink that can't penetrate a glossy surface.

Evie leans on the bathroom counter and closes her eyes and tries not to think about how she could feel the slight indentation of Misha's scar when she had her cheek against his chest. About what it would be like to kiss her way down it.

She startles when she hears the clack of the hotel room's doorknob turning.

She abandons her glass of water and hurries out to where Misha is standing in the doorway. "Where are you going?" she says.

"Leaving. You clearly..." Misha bites his lip and looks away.

"Why?" Evie asks. She reaches out and grabs Misha's arm.

He stiffens under her grip, tense and wary. "I'm an *abomination*, Evie. It goes so far beyond just being an immortal parasite on humanity." Misha's voice is rough and sincere; his lips twisted into a scowl of self-hatred. "You don't have to pretend it's okay. I saw your face–"

Evie steps around him and gently closes the door. "You are terrible at reading people, sometimes," she says.

"Just you, actually," Misha responds, his voice small. "You mess up my... systems."

"Bed. Now," Evie says, mentally facepalming as soon as the words are out of her mouth. "Um, or chair."

She knows it's a testimony to just how off-balance Misha is that he shuffles quietly over to the bed without a sassy grin or innuendo-laden comeback.

Evie sits down next to him and leans into his shoulder. "I don't see a monster." Misha's body is taut. He's trembling; one wrong word and he'll bolt like a scared stag. "I see someone who tries to hurt others as little as possible," she continues. "Someone who could take whatever he wants, but chooses not to. Who tries to help, even if he has a tendency to be heavy-handed."

She turns to Misha. "I'm not a fan of you appointing yourself judge, jury and executioner with Greg Pickford, awful though he was. But I can understand where the feeling came from."

Misha sags, lying back down. Guilt and shame are written across his too-expressive features. "I fully admit that wasn't my finest moment. He made me so angry I... I lost control. He would have found someone else to abuse, after Stewart, but... I know I shouldn't have killed him. Shouldn't have taken so much. Once again, I couldn't stop, though."

They're silent for a while; Evie can hear a TV playing cartoons in a nearby room. A cleaning cart rattles down the hallway, the maids chattering in Spanish to each other. Misha just gazes up at the ceiling, flickers of emotion passing over his face like summer clouds as the tension slowly eases out of his body.

She flops down next to him, pretending a nonchalance she doesn't feel. "So, uh... do all incubi have two forms?"

"I don't know. I don't think so. But I was always..." Misha makes a vague hand motion, *not one thing or the other*. "I never had a very strong conception of myself as male. Some days I feel more female than others... and over time, I found I could transform into Masha. It started with me waking up one morning and thinking, *I don't want to be a boy today*."

"And people were okay with that?" Evie asks. "I mean, were you... out? Did they *have* out in the past?"

"Oh please, Evie," Misha grins, closing his eyes. He shoves her shoulder affectionately. "I was the eccentric youngest son of a powerful family. And I was in the cavalry, with a reputation as a duelist. If people weren't okay with it, they kept their mouths shut, or risked dying by my pistol." Misha snorts. "Besides, there was a lot of it about. *Especially* in the Hussars. I'll show you our uniforms, one day. Trust me, no officer who joins a regiment with trousers that tight and a jacket that ornate is entirely straight."

He reaches the arm thrown over his head up to grab a pillow, passing one to Evie before getting another for himself. They're still lying sideways across the bed like little kids, their feet on the floor. "I don't know about the other incubi, though. We keep away from each other, but... I think I'm very different from others of my kind. The others, I am told, use their power all the time, for the smallest of things. To me, it's always felt like cheating... but sometimes I have to use it. There's so *much* of it, Evie," he says, rubbing his hand over his sternum. "All of this inside me and no way to let it out without something horrible happening. Sometimes I have to use it, just to get rid of it. Like last night. If I don't, it becomes hard to control. It lets itself out anyway, if shoved aside for too long."

"I wish you didn't have to live like this," Evie says. "Constrained by all these rules."

"I am a minotaur in a labyrinth of my own design," he says. "The price of living in society. Don't feel bad for me. Every few decades, between cities, between lives, I go somewhere remote for a year or two and... let go." He smiles; expression blissful and distant. His voice softens into fondness. "I can run down the wind, you know."

Evie pictures Misha racing through a forest, wild and happy

and free, and even in her imagination it's such a beautiful sight it makes her stomach clench with desire. "I bet you can."

Those long, dark lashes flutter shut over his eyes. "You have no idea how good it feels to tell you these things. I'm terrified, but I feel so light, like I might float away. Like I've been holding my breath for a century, and I can finally exhale."

Evie puts her hand on his arm in a wordless show of support, and Misha smiles, placing his other hand over hers and lacing their fingers together. His eyes are still shut and he looks so peaceful, and so heartbreakingly perfect.

"Your hands are cold," he says softly.

"Yeah," Evie says. "It's San Francisco. I feel like I can't get warm here. At least in New York when it's cold, the buildings are overheated."

He reaches over and gathers up her other hand, pulling her gently towards him. "Come here. I'm very warm. Another fun side-effect."

Evie goes willingly, and briefly there's a moment where no hearts beat in the room as hers stutters, unable to believe this is really happening.

Misha swings his legs onto the bed, easing onto his side and moving her body with him. "Besides, the last forty-eight hours have been... a lot. I think we both need this." He arranges her so she's curled up with her back to his chest, the little spoon to his big one. Their fingers are still laced together, and her head is resting on his bicep. "Promise I won't be creepy," he whispers, his lips a fraction of an inch from her ear.

Evie has to use every bit of self-discipline she has not to push back into him. "Misha?" she whispers.

"Hm?"

"You can be creepy. Uh, if you like." She squeezes her eyes shut and inwardly kicks herself for her lack of eloquence. "What I mean is, I *want* you to be creepy."

She moves away from him, just enough so she can prop herself on an elbow and look at him. Now that she's let a few, halting, ill-chosen words out into the world, the rest come tumbling out in a giant avalanche of stupid. "I guess… I feel so dumb, I mean everyone falls in love with you, don't they? You're…" she disentangles her hand and darts a nervous touch to Misha's shoulder, "… you're the most beautiful person I've ever seen. And I wasn't going to be that girl who falls at your feet like everybody else but… *surprise*, apparently I am that girl."

Evie groans and plants her face into the pillow, because whatever look Misha is giving her, she doesn't want to see it. "Why did you also have to be funny and goofy and shy?" she says, her voice muffled by the pillowcase. She lifts her head up and narrows her eyes at Misha, who is looking at her with a strange intensity. "This would be so much easier if you were a little more of a jerk. And I—"

But she never finishes her sentence, because Misha surges forwards and shuts her up with a kiss.

She whines as he breaks it off, but he's still right there, staring into her eyes, his lips barely an inch from hers. "No, Evie," he murmurs. "People look and want, but all they care about is the surface. Nobody bothers to see *me*." And then his lips are on hers again, soft and strong and warm. "Nobody except you," he whispers into her mouth.

Evie opens her lips to respond and Misha licks into her mouth, tasting, pushing the kiss into more passionate territory. And she kisses back, hard, all the frustrated hunger of the past week exploding into heat within her. She ends up on her back, Misha above her, one of his large, strong hands curled around the back of her neck to support her head. Her hands find their way under his shirt to his bare waist, still unsure, still not believing she actually gets to touch.

As her hands wrap around the sleek expanse of muscle above his hips (his skin like satin velvet over steel), Misha moans and pushes away from her. He looks down at her, naked desire in his darkening eyes, and Evie wants nothing more than to see if she can make him moan like that again. She runs one hand up his side, dragging her nails gently over his skin, and is rewarded with a hiss and a push into her touch.

Then, just as she is about to run her fingers over one of his nipples, he captures her wrist and pushes her arm over her head. And that's… that is apparently a major turn-on for her because she arches her body upwards, trying to get closer.

"Evie," he says, and now there is darkness at the edges of his eyes too as he moves her other arm up over her head. "I want you. In a way that I haven't wanted anyone in a very long time. *But*," he breathes, leaning down, kissing and biting his way down the sensitive skin at the side of her neck, "I'll destroy you. I destroy everything I touch." Evie can barely think. Whatever Misha is doing to her neck, it's hotwired straight to her groin and she is panting and squirming, unable to control the sounds coming out of her mouth.

But then he's gone.

With what seems a superhuman effort of will, Misha releases her arms and sits back on his heels, looking at her like he is trying to memorize her in that moment, the flush on her cheeks, the way her lips are parted. "I don't want to pull you into my mess."

Evie feels her eyes grow hot and wet with tears. "Misha… I've been living so carefully for so long on the hope that tomorrow will be better, and it hasn't been. It's just shit after more shit. I haven't been living. I've been *existing*. Buried under the ashes of all my hopes and dreams and then you come in, flamboyant and crazy and infuriating, and blow all of that away and suddenly I remember what it's like to be on fire again." She wipes at her eyes with the back of a hand. "If the price of really living is dying, then I'll take it. *I'll take it*. I'm so tired of the other way."

She sits up and reaches around Misha to grab the hem of his shirt. "And I want you so much I can't breathe." She pulls Misha's shirt off, over his head, revealing acres of golden muscle and that one long, jagged scar, white-pink with age. She tosses the shirt somewhere onto the floor and, as he looks on in wonder, she presses her lips to the scar. "I've wanted to do this since I first saw it," she murmurs, kissing her way down the one imperfection on Misha's body, the thing that completes him.

He arches his body towards her and throws his head back. His hands come up, swift and sure, unbuttoning her top and pushing it down her shoulders. Then he hooks his fingers into the waistband of her pajama bottoms, easing them down over her hips. He pulls away from her, long enough to run his hands down her legs and take her panties off completely.

And then there she is, naked, with the most heartbreakingly gorgeous man she's ever seen looking up at her from between her ankles like she's the only thing he's ever wanted, like she's beautiful. She feels like she could come just from that look alone.

Misha prowls up slowly, painfully slowly, until her anticipation is so great it feels like a tangible weight in the air. He doesn't touch her, but he is so close she can feel the warmth of his body, sense the electricity between them.

Evie bites her lip as she shifts towards him and he moves slightly away, keeping the infinitesimal distance between them. She narrows her eyes at him and he tilts his head, a grin tugging at the sides of his mouth. Of *course* Misha would also be infuriating in bed.

He darts forwards and buries his tongue in her cunt. She just about screams, hands fisting around the bedclothes, as arousal slams through every muscle of her body. The sound chokes off into a ragged gasp as Misha sucks on her clit, and she can feel the bastard smiling against her. She can feel the low, predatory chuckle he makes in his throat (it feels amazing) as her thigh muscles begin to quiver. He is looking up at her through his lashes, his pale eyes measuring her every reaction.

But there's something... off.

As he looks down again, his fingers spreading her labia, Evie nudges a knee against his shoulder to push him away.

"What?" he says, concern written across his too-expressive face, his lips wet with her. "What's wrong?"

Evie is suddenly able to put her finger on what isn't right. "You're performing," she admonishes.

Misha blinks, confused. "This is... this is what I *do*, Evie." He leans forwards, resting his chin on her pubic bone. "The general impression is that I'm very good at it," he mumbles, a little petulant.

"Yeah, no shit, Misha," she says, and she can't resist the urge to reach down and rub her fingers through his hair, scratching his scalp like he was a cat. His eyes go half-lidded in bliss and he leans into her touch, turning his head so his cheek is against her belly. "But this shouldn't be something you do *to* me. You know?"

Misha hums, distant and evasive.

Evie's heart breaks a little. He doesn't know. "Look, you don't have to impress me. You don't have to perform, or try to make this unforgettable."

"But I *want* to," he grumbles, tracing a finger up her thigh.

Evie smiles. "And I don't want to feel like a client. Stop overthinking things, Misha. Just... be."

"Not sure I remember how to do that," he sighs.

"Yeah, I get the feeling you're a fast learner, though. Honestly, I'm sure you could just hold me all morning and it would still be the best time I ever had in bed." It's not a lie. Misha doesn't need to know how shitty most of her experiences have been, Evie thinks. Drunk sex. Sex where the boy finishes and that's it, leaving her sweaty and discontented. Sex where the boy did make an effort, but it was so boring that she faked orgasms just to get him to stop.

"Mm," Misha says, and a moment later he lets go, settling his full weight on her. They lie there for a while, Evie learning that being pinned to the bed by 200-odd pounds of boneless, relaxed incubus is surprisingly comfortable, especially when he reaches up and gently and lazily strokes his fingers down the side of her face.

"You're confusing," Misha grumbles at last.

Evie wraps a leg over his waist, tucking her ankle against the soft curve at the top of his ass. "Yeah, well, you're infuriating."

His lashes open and those searchlight-silver eyes are on her again, intent burning dark in them. "You *really* just want to cuddle?"

Evie snorts out a laugh. "Oh God. I forgot you're an actual lust demon."

Misha retaliates by nipping her belly, and it tickles, so she squirms, and suddenly he's moved up her body and they're chest to chest, her arms pinned over her head again. Misha is looking down at her, his expression playful. "One, I'm not a *lust demon*. Everything Wikipedia says about incubi is wildly incorrect. I know, because I wrote most of it. Two, I'll have you know I don't have any more of a sex drive than I did when I was human."

Evie rolls her eyes. "So you were always a little horndog."

Misha pulls back with a cartoonishly offended look on his face. "Little?" he snorts disdainfully. He takes one of her hands and places it on his abs, on the small trail of hair that leads southwards from there, and then quirks an eyebrow at her.

Evie looks into his eyes, those eyes that you could drown in, as she slides her hand downwards, over the waistband of his sweatpants and… Christ. He's rock-hard. She'd seen *that* photo of Misha, so she knew he was packing some pretty heavy artillery down there, but feeling the weight and breadth of him in her hand… hot desire slams into her like a rogue wave. And of course, being Misha, he's not wearing any underwear. She can feel everything…

… And so can he.

Misha's eyes unfocus and his mouth falls open as she runs her hand down his cock, down to the softness where his balls are, and then back up again. "Yeah," Evie says, her voice thick. "We're going to do a lot more than cuddle." There are so many things she wants to do to Misha, with him… she wants to see just how much of that monster cock she can get in her mouth. She wants to know what it takes to make him scream; to leave him so he can barely say his own name. But right now she just *wants*, as fast and hard as she can get it. The rest can happen later.

She slips her fingers under the waistband of Misha's sweatpants and eases them down over the lush swell of his ass. "What do you want?" she asks, breathless. "What do you like?"

Misha mutters something in Georgian then runs his teeth, ever so gently, along her jaw. "Nngh. So much. But right now I think I'm going to die if I don't fuck you. Is that okay?"

Evie nods, reaching up to grab his ass and pull herself against him.

Misha straight-up growls at her, shoving her down onto the bed and rolling his hips, grinding himself against her clit. Evie's brain is whiting out from desire and she's barely listening when he speaks next. "Do you need me to take it slow?" he murmurs, his voice already ragged around the edges from desire. "Because not everyone can..." He grinds his impressively thick cock against her again.

Never let it be said that Evie Cross backs down from a challenge.

She braces herself against his chest and pushes. Misha gets with the program pretty fast, rolling them both so he's on his back and she's above him. His sweatpants are still bunched down around his thighs and it's somehow sexier that he hasn't even bothered to get fully undressed. Evie takes a quick moment to appreciate the wide shoulders, narrow waist and cut physique of the man beneath her before she grabs the base of his cock, her hand barely able to go all the way around, and lowers herself down on it.

Evie cries out at the burn and the fullness and the waves of pleasure it's sending through her, and Misha is gripping her hips and looking at her like he is one moment away from losing it and fucking her through the mattress and *Jesus*, how big *is* he because she hasn't bottomed out yet, and the answer is *big enough to drag against her G-spot with every move*, and then finally he's all the way inside and it tears a moan and a shudder out of her.

Misha's hands come round to her ass. She looks down at him, and he's completely otherworldly, staring up at her in amazement and desire, like she was something he'd never expected to deserve. He shuts his eyes and bites his lip, tilting his head back and rolling his hips. His hands steady her, keep her immobile as he begins to move inside her. It's not a lot, just small, controlled movements, but there's so much of him that every little thrust sends waves of arousal slamming through her. She reaches her hands down and grabs Misha's forearms, probably digging her nails in too hard, as she arches her back and moans out a litany of curses.

Misha lifts her up a few inches, manipulating her as if she weighs nothing (and to him, she probably doesn't), and punches up into her. She cries out in a ragged gasp, already on the edge of coming, and Misha freezes.

"All... all right?" he says, sounding absolutely wrecked.

"Yeah. God. *Again*. More," she manages to respond, pulling at his arms.

He surges upwards, crushing her lips against his, groaning into her mouth. The kiss is everything their first one wasn't: rough, messy, almost punishingly deep, and between that and the way Misha is still rolling his hips, still moving inside her, she feels like she's about to come apart, to break up into splinters of light and float into the sky.

Misha's hands slide up her body to her breasts, finding her nipples and rolling them between his fingers until they're erect and almost painful. There's just too much stimulation; her body is a tangle of live wires. Evie doesn't know what is pushing her more towards the edge: his mouth, his hands, or his dick.

Then, with another low growl, he flips her onto her back and slings her ankles over his shoulders. One of his powerful forearms plants itself next to her head and then he pulls nearly all the way out of her before slamming back in one long thrust. She keens in ecstasy. Evie's legs tighten around him as she loses control of anything but holding on for the ride. The position Misha has her in maximizes the already-hard drag on her G-spot and it is taking her *apart*. She wants to reach out, run her hands all over his body, mark him, scratch her nails down his back, but every thrust Misha makes pitches her so close to the edge all she can do is wind her fists into the bedsheets.

He circles a hand behind her neck and lifts her head up, kissing her deep and filthy as he snaps his hips into her.

She's so close, and as his mouth moves down the tender skin of her neck and the kisses turn into bites, into marks, branding her as his, she falls over the edge into the bright abyss. She cries out, ragged and undone, as her body jerks like a live wire, clenching down on him as a thousand volts of pleasure spark off in her cunt and race up her spine, leaving her mouth in a rough moan of his name.

When she comes back to herself, still all floaty and full of sparks, Misha is letting her down onto the bed gently. He's still hard in her but he withdraws, giving her a chance to rest, knowing she'll be hypersensitive. She tries to press a kiss of thanks into the crook of his neck, but misses, and giggles to herself. She's still so much in the afterglow that it feels like the room is full of static electricity; an ionic charge heavy in the air around her that is causing the hairs on the back of her neck to stand up.

She has so many things she wants to say, ideas about what they can do next, but the words die in her throat as she looks up at Misha.

His eyes are completely black.

And she realizes he hasn't stopped because of her.

He's got his free hand gripping hard around the base of his cock and he is moving away from her, very slowly and carefully, like she is an unexploded bomb.

Or, more accurately, like he is.

Evie reaches out on instinct, to comfort him, to find out what's wrong, but Misha flinches away, an expression of absolute terror on his face.

That's when Evie's cellphone rings, cutting through the charged air between them like a falling knife.

CHAPTER TWELVE

EVIE SITS UP. "Misha, what's—"

"Don't touch me," Misha hisses, backing away from her across the bed. His eyes are still solid black, his expression tense. "Just, don't—"

Evie's ringtone saws through the air again, abrasive and insistent. She glances over at her cellphone as it vibrates on the bedside table. "Shit, it's Claudia. I have to get this. She'll call the cops if I don't."

Misha turns his head away, curled in on himself, and waves a hand at her. *It's fine. Do it.*

Evie grabs her phone and swipes at the screen a few times, swearing under her breath at the old model's refusal to do basic things like allow her to answer a call.

"Chica! I'm on break. What the hell is going on? I've texted you like a million times!" Claudia says, and Evie can hear the sound of glasses and plates clinking in the background. It's noontime in New York City on a Sunday, which means Claudia is probably setting up for a charity brunch.

"Look, Claudia. This isn't a good time," Evie begins.

"Are you okay? Because if that guy…"

That guy is currently leaning against the window, his back to her as he stares at the indifferent, cloudy sky, his sweatpants low on his hips. Evie shivers slightly, watching the play of muscles across his bare back, and her voice cracks slightly as she answers her roommate. "He's fine, Claudia. He's not a serial killer or anything, relax."

Misha snorts and turns, about to say something, but Evie glares at him and makes a shushing motion. He closes those freakish, ebony eyes and shakes his head at her.

"Mmhmm," Claudia says, disbelief thick in her voice.

"I'll call you later and fill you in, I promise, but I have to go," Evie says.

"Fine," Claudia sighs.

"Okay. Good luck at work today," Evie mutters, and hangs up the phone. She tosses it towards an empty corner of the bed, and groans her frustration as the phone slips across the sheets and thuds onto the carpet. Misha is watching her, something predatory in his dark eyes, and it makes Evie feel every bit of her nakedness. She reaches for her pajama shirt and slings her arms through it, hands tangling in inside-out sleeves.

"I'm sorry," comes the soft, rough whisper from across the room.

"What happened?" Evie asks, careful to keep her voice neutral.

Misha's lips twitch. "Control issues," he says. He slides his back down the window until he's sitting on the floor. "Apparently I can only have what I do not want. It's a clever curse. If I allow myself what I desire, it includes possible results such as killing you, or releasing enough energy to give every single person in this hotel the best orgasm of their life." There's a dull thud as he hits the back of his head against the window. "And that would bring priests."

Evie swings her legs over the side of the bed, and starts to button up her pajama top. "This happen often?"

"No," he says, staring down at his long fingers. His eyes are clearing, the black fading to a bruised ring around the blue. He makes a small, futile gesture with one hand. "When I get emotional…"

"Oh," Evie says. "I'm sorry."

"Don't be; it's…" Misha mumbles. "It's everything right now. You. The book. My past. The thought of someone as powerful as Eric Overstreet, someone who likes pain as much as he does, becoming… like me."

He pushes himself off the floor and comes and sits near her

on the bed. "I can handle it. Usually." Then the warm weight of his shoulder is against hers. "But if my eyes go dark, or I pull away suddenly, don't... don't be offended. Sometimes I need to have a moment to collect myself. For safety."

"I can touch you now?" Evie asks.

Misha nods.

She slides her arm around his waist, and it's magnetic, the way it feels like it belongs there.

"You don't have to go through this alone," she whispers, leaning into him, into all that warmth and muscle.

Evie feels Misha's arm curl around her waist as well, and the soft press of his lips to her temple as he squeezes her tightly in a wordless thank you.

Too tightly.

"Ow! Strong!" Evie says. "If you accidentally squish me you *will* have to go through this alone."

Misha bites her, because he is a shit. But Evie can feel that he's smiling again, which makes it all worthwhile. "My squishy human," he murmurs. She pinches his waist, and he giggles.

"Are you ticklish?" she says, delight dawning on her face.

"No!" he says, too fast.

Evie cackles and turns, both hands diving for Misha's waist. She knows he's fast enough to avoid her but at first he doesn't, falling back onto the bed and writhing to avoid her fingers. If he had lungs, the expression for his current state would be breathless with laughter. As he flails, he bumps her with a knee. She overbalances, falling on top of him.

"Hey," he says, his hands curling up her thighs to the base of her ass.

"Hi," Evie smiles.

Misha shifts slightly, so her legs slip between his. She can feel him against her thigh, thickening, hardening. "What's your opinion on trying again?" he says, his voice going husky.

"I'd, uh, I'd be up for that, if you think you, uh..."

Misha rolls his hips against her, his head falling back. "... I think I can manage. I want to."

"'Course you do, *incubus*," Evie snorts.

"We've been over that," Misha says, his grip tightening on her ass.

Evie grinds down on Misha, because two can play at that game. The way he reacts, moaning and burying his face into her neck, makes her have dangerous thoughts. She wants to push him again, chase him to the edge of that feral, almost-lost-control state, even though she knows it's a terrible idea. But the urge is overwhelming, to take apart the boy who takes everyone else apart with such ease.

And then he looks up at her, a hardness in the set of his lips. His eyes are nearly black again. He shakes his head, a tight, frustrated motion, and sits up, effortlessly maneuvering her so she's sitting too, both of them on the edge of the bed, legs dangling off like awkward teenagers. Misha bows his head, his hair falling forwards to cover his face. His hands grip the edge of the mattress, and Evie can see the tension that runs up his arms and into his shoulders, every muscle standing out, the mattress creaking in protest. She watches him from the corners of her eyes.

"I think," he says, after his hands slowly unclench, "that it might be best if I... if I play a role." He looks up at her then, and the rawness in his beautiful face is heartbreaking. He smiles, small and hesitant. "I want to be myself, more than anything." Those long eyelashes flutter closed over eyes that are still an eerie mix of ice-blue and black, no white to be seen. "But perhaps for now there should be a layer between myself and... everything."

Evie sighs and leans against him, against his shoulder. "You don't have to. We don't have to—"

"I *want* to," Misha snarls, twisting, and holy shit, Evie can feel the rage roll off him, running through her and igniting all the anger she's tried to bury along the course of her life, setting it smoldering again like peat fires, deep down under the dirt where her foundations lie. "I *want* something, for the first time in nearly a century."

Evie knows his fury isn't directed at her, it's inward, towards the bargain he made and the powers he can't always control. But it's still there, filling everything with its red heat.

She breathes, grinding her teeth, trying not to scream, not to break something. Misha is watching her, lips twisted in a horrified self-hatred. "Great," he whispers, edging away from her. "That's just... well done me."

He stands up and paces, arms out wide in a mix of supplication and frustration. When he reaches the farthest point in the room from her, he rakes his hands through his hair, staring down at the floor. "Are you okay?" he mutters.

"Yeah. That was. Um." Evie swallows, trying to process the sharp spike of fury she'd felt. "It all seems so harmless when it's just about pleasure," she says.

Misha chuckles, and it's a low, nasty sound. "Welcome to the full measure of the monster."

Evie's eyes slide off him towards a safer view. She stares at one of her fancy boots, fallen over onto the floor. What can she say to him? That she's beginning to think the priests are right? That his kind shouldn't exist? That glimpsing even the tiniest hint of his powers, not to mention what he could do at full stretch, was terrifying?

And there he is, the monster, digging his bare toes into the carpet, twisting his fingers. Trying so hard to be a person, and hating himself for every little failure, every time he puts others at risk. Unable to return to the boy he was before, because that person—impetuous, passionate, with emotions running as fast and strong under his skin as a spring flood—that person, as an incubus, would be the death of anyone he loved. The most heartbreaking thing of all was that Evie could still see the faint outline of that reckless boy who sold his heart to the Devil in the taut, bitterly disciplined man before her, like a nuclear shadow, like scorch marks on a wall marking where a life had been obliterated.

Misha rolls his shoulders and stretches his neck. "I'm going to take a shower," he says quietly, to nobody in particular. "Get the stink of pheromones off my skin."

Evie nods.

She can barely hear his soft footsteps towards the bathroom, and only knows he's reached it by a slight creak of the door's hinges. But then she hears heavy strides approaching her, and his arms circle her from behind. She flinches. It takes two breaths for a normal human to walk from the bathroom to the bed, and Misha had done it in less than one. He tightens his arms around her, and buries his face in the side of her neck. She feels more than hears him as he whispers, "I'm sorry."

His arms relax, and as she turns to look at him he shifts away, avoiding her eyes. Evie reaches out, running a hand up the too-warm, solid breath of his shoulder, burying her fingers in the soft baby hair at the back of his neck. When he looks at her in confusion, she presses her lips to his cheek, tender, chaste. "You're doing okay, Misha. I won't lie and say I'm not scared of you, but you're okay."

Misha makes a little disbelieving huff into her neck, but snuggles in closer, some of the tension bleeding out of his body. They sit like that for a while, like shipwreck victims, leaning into each other, scared that the land they can see on the horizon is just another trick of the light.

Finally Misha shifts them so they're both lying down on their sides, facing each other. "You should get some sleep," he murmurs, stroking down her arm with two fingers. Then as his fingers draw back up her arm, she can feel a few little golden sparks curling through her, down towards her groin. Her eyes dart up to Misha's, now ice-blue again, and he's raising an eyebrow at her.

"Yeah," Evie says, and realizes in that moment that she's happy. Everything is on fire and has ceased to make sense and she's in bed with an actual demon and she's happier than she's been in years. "Yeah, Misha. Do the thing."

A smile spreads over his face like sunshine. His fingers run along her shoulder and over her collarbone. He wrinkles his nose and it's strangely adorable. "I like doing this. I like that you know what I'm doing."

Evie just bites her lip and wriggles closer to him, because it feels *really* good.

"So," he says, dragging his fingers slowly and softly between her breasts, then spreading his hand down over her stomach, "I was thinking."

Evie doesn't manage more than a soft, questioning moan, somewhat wishing he'd shut up so she could focus on the warm tide of arousal washing over her, the building pressure in her loins. Her brain goes a bit sideways, thinking about how much she wants to fuck him, again.

He traces two fingers down her stomach, over her mons, and then stops, right at the beginning of her labia. Evie makes a hurt little sound, which gets an amused snicker from Misha. He's propped up on one elbow, relaxed and radiating contentment. And also sex. Because Evie still remembers the first time he'd done this to her, and it had been one of the best orgasms of her life with him only touching the side of her face. Now with his fingers barely a half-inch from her clit, the feeling is staggering.

Her leg starts to shake and she arches up, trying to get his fingers a little lower. She knows she's making the most ridiculous noises right now but she doesn't care. She presses her eyes shut and concentrates on the feeling building inside her, how wet she knows she is already, how much the muscles of her walls are already starting to flutter.

"I was thinking that when we try to fuck again, because we *are* going to try again, that it might be fun if I was your sub," Misha murmurs.

Evie opens her eyes to look at him, and he smiles softly at her, touching his tongue to his bottom lip. He lowers his chin and looks up at her through his lashes. This man is absolutely going to be the death of her, in an infinite number of ways. And then he says, "You could put a collar on me, and I would do whatever you asked."

"Gluh," Evie says, and from the angle of Misha's head it's easy to imagine him kneeling between her legs, looking up at her, waiting for her command. She knows it's deliberate; the arch-seducer's masterclass, now in session.

His fingers finally move lower, further in, and she sucks in a hiss as he carefully circles around her clit, never touching it, over the lips of her cunt, fat as they are with arousal. He leans forwards and presses a gentle kiss to her mouth as he thrusts three fingers inside her. At the same time, he rubs her clit with his thumb and she arches up and screams his name into his mouth.

The thing he does is overwhelming enough when he's just touching her face. But when he's managing to hit her G-spot and her clit at the same time and *that's* where all his magic is going into her body, it's way beyond too much. Her brain dissolves into a cascade of light; her body spasms in bliss and somehow he's moving with her, staying on target, and his power is still flowing into her through those fingers and she has a second orgasm straight after the first, wetness streaming out of her, eyes rolled back in her head, completely giving herself over to the waves of pleasure rocking through her.

Evie comes back to herself slowly, and Misha is still with her, his eyes clear and fond. "You okay?" he says, brushing an errant curl out of her face.

"Mm," she says, snuggling closer, her body so relaxed she feels halfway to jelly. "I got off a bunch of times and you didn't, though."

"It's not a contest," Misha replies. "I also didn't kill you or seriously fuck up everyone in the hotel, and it was touch and go for a while, so I'm fine with how everything turned out."

"Still, though," Evie says, and lazily traces her hand down Misha's chest, and she's still not over those abs, no sir, not by a long shot. She runs her hand over that sharp hip bone peeking above the low waist of his sweatpants, and chases the line of muscle down from it towards his cock. He's half-hard, and as she pulls his sweatpants down over the curve of his perfect ass, she establishes that, no, her memory was not exaggerating about the size of him. She makes a happy, sleepy little hum as she gets a hand around him and begins to stroke him; she's more pleased than she'd like to admit by the way he bites his lip and hisses as her thumb passes over the bundle of nerves underneath the head of his cock.

"I think I'm gonna need two hands. Maybe my mouth too," she mumbles, wriggling her way down the bed. "Lemme know if you need me to stop."

"I really hope that won't be—*hnnh*—necessary," Misha gasps, as she runs her tongue up the slit at the head of his cock, gently licking under his uncut foreskin.

Evie hums as she takes as much of him as she can in her mouth, which is, to be fair, not a lot, and the feeling of him moving to full hardness while in her mouth is pretty amazing. Aside from the whole ridiculously handsome thing he has going on, he's completely shaved, and the only thing she tastes on him is herself.

She pulls off him and carries on stroking him with her hands. "I know you have mixed feelings about the choices you made," she says softly, pausing to run her lips and tongue over his balls, loving how responsive he is, how his cock twitches in her hands and beads with precome, "and I know I'm biased," another lick up the length of his shaft, a kiss to the tip with a little thrust of her tongue to dip under his foreskin, and that gets her a hand around the back of her neck, "but I never would have met you if you hadn't become an incubus." Another kiss, and she sucks him down quickly into her mouth again before coming off to an audible groan from him, "and I'm pretty sure you're the best thing that's ever happened to me."

Misha snorts disbelievingly, but the fingers on the back of her head skritch gently at the nape of her neck.

She pops off one more time, grinning. "Still infuriating, though." And yeah, the view up that chest to that face, that's not something she's going to tire of, possibly ever.

That face is currently managing to give her a look that balances desire and exasperation almost perfectly. But his eyes are still clear and blue as he growls, "Evangeline Cross, I have been on the edge of coming for about two hours now and if you don't stop talking and get on with it, I might *die*."

"Drama queen," she mumbles, as she kisses her way down

past his balls. She lifts one of his muscular thighs onto her shoulder and keeps heading south with little kitten licks, until she reaches the tight furl of his ass. When she tongues Misha there, he twists and arches, letting out the most sinful, erotic moan she thinks she's ever heard. She's still fisting his cock, but admittedly she's slowed her pace as she navigates southwards. So she's not surprised when a large, strong hand wraps over hers, gripping harder and speeding up the tempo.

Evie tries to match the thrusts of her tongue to the rhythm Misha has set around her hand, as they both stroke his cock, and judging from the way that Misha has completely failed to speak English for the past few minutes, she's doing something right. As his strokes get harder and messier on his dick, the rhythm completely gone, she thrusts her tongue in as far as it can go. She takes her free hand and runs it between her legs; they don't have lube but she's still wet enough for them both, and so she adds a finger in him next to her tongue.

Misha positively keens as he arches, and he barks out something that sounds like a command and might be in Russian or Georgian but Evie ignores it in favor of seeing if she can make him cry out again. But he says the thing again, low and rough and apparently hot guys growling in fluent sex-wrecked Eastern European languages is a kink that she very much has and didn't know about until this exact moment.

The command is accompanied this time by a hand gently tugging in her hair so she reluctantly gives Misha's ass a kiss goodbye, and then his balls, and then the top of his cock, and then she has to stop because he hauls her up over him, lifting her easily with one arm, and that also hasn't stopped being amazingly hot.

Misha is shining, his eyes crystalline-bright, his face angelic as he looks at her. Their joined hands are still thrusting over his cock, and she realizes he's done that to show her what he likes, what works best for him. One edge of his mouth quirks up in a smile and he stutters a few sentences in what she's guessing is Georgian.

Evie shakes her head. "Baby, I don't understand, speak English," she says.

He blinks at her, then his brain seems to switch on a bit more and he rumbles, "You're going to come again when I come. It will happen. Be prepared." He bites his lip as a shudder of pleasure goes through his body, his head tipping back. "And kiss me," he breathes.

Evie's lips brush his and at first it's gentle, controlled, their lips barely touching each other and the sensation so much more for being so little. Then Misha moans, and he's coming, she can feel the tautness in his body, the hot wet spurt of his release on her stomach. And out of nowhere, she's coming too, her orgasm pounding through her already oversensitive, exhausted body. Evie makes a startled noise and their kiss turns messy, animalistic, teeth clacking against each other, lips catching and bruising. Neither of them are really there, too wrapped up in their own pleasure to coordinate their mouths. And the fact that Misha is so messed up he can't even kiss straight is, Evie thinks, possibly the hottest part of the whole morning.

Misha makes a low, contented sound in his throat, and Evie looks up at him, heavy-lidded and satisfied. His eyes have started to go dark again, but not all the way; just the white of the sclera fading to a dark grey, leaving the ice-blue irises and lust-blown black pupils.

Their hands have stilled on his cock, but Evie is reluctant to take hers away, enjoying the feeling of it as it softens. Misha's torso is officially the wet patch, but he's warm and she's exhausted from more orgasms than she's ever had on a Sunday morning (or any other morning) so she just makes herself at home and curls up on that broad chest.

"You going to let go of my dick?" Misha whispers, and she can feel the smile in his voice even if she's too wrecked to actually look up and see it.

"Nah," she says. "I like holding it."

Misha wraps his arms around her in a lazy hug. "Believe me,

I'm not going to stop you from spending as much time with my dick as you want."

"Good," Evie mumbles. "S' a nice dick." She gives it a little pat.

He starts to stroke her hair, humming a soothing little tune. Evie's losing the battle to stay awake, and as her eyelids grow heavier she feels Misha shift beneath her. "Go to sleep, *chemo sikharulo*. Meet me for dinner later." He presses a kiss to her forehead and murmurs into her hair, "Make sure you shower. Smelling like an aroused incubus is…" he huffs out a quiet laugh, "… well, you'll attract a lot of attention."

He gently detaches himself from her grip and rises gracefully and silently to his feet. Evie whines and flails out an arm, her hand ending up on the plush curve of his ass. "Stay," she mumbles.

"Can't," he says. "The Tweedles will have sent me about a dozen emails demanding updates by now."

"Why?" Evie groans. "It's Sunday."

"Yes," Misha says. "Saturday was the Sabbath. On Sunday they both jump back on electronic devices like starving men at a banquet. I must go write up a semi-fictional report to get them off my back. After I have my own shower." He grasps Evie's hand where it's been rubbing idle circles against his right ass cheek, and bows down to her, pressing a courtly kiss to her fingers. He gazes through his eyelashes over her hand to her, and murmurs, "Much as I'd rather stay in bed."

Evie giggles sleepily. "How many girls have you gotten using that look?"

Misha snorts, goofy and awkward. "So many. Boys too." He smirks and shifts his stance, something a little less louche, a little more military. He bows to her hand again, but doesn't kiss it. Instead he presses his thumb down onto her knuckles, and does something with his fingers on her palm that wakes up parts of her she thought would be down for the count for the rest of the day. At the same time he licks his lips—not ostentatiously, just enough to be noticeable—and then he says, his voice husky, "I remain, sir, your obedient servant." There's a little faked catch of breath before he says *obedient*, which comes out as a low purr.

He raises an eyebrow, silently asking for her opinion, his face halfway between wry and serious.

"Ten out of ten. The tongue over your lips and the fingernails on the palm at the same time, that's effective," Evie says. Her tone turns thoughtful as she adds, "I'd always figured seduction was something bad, but with you it's just… fun."

Misha grins, pleased. "Of course. It's making people feel good about themselves. Best game in the world." He squeezes her hand one more time before letting go. "I'd like to say it was all art, but I was young, easy, and looked great in cavalry breeches. I didn't have to put nearly as much effort in as I thought I did."

Evie yawns and plumps the pillow around her. "If mankind ever builds a time machine, I bet the first thing the scientist does, instead of killing Hitler or something, is to go back and tell their eighteen-year-old self to worry less and shake their ass more."

"Quite," Misha says. But then he falls silent, so she glances up. He's biting his lower lip and looking down at her, his eyes soft and fond. He reaches down and gently boops her nose. "Sleep well, little one. Call me when you get hungry."

EVIE ROLLS OUT of bed around 4pm, still somewhat dazed. She staggers to the bathroom and parks herself under the hot spray of its huge shower-head. Her and Claudia's little apartment has pretty good water temperature (if you get the mixer tap exactly right) but the volume is nowhere near the forceful cascade of the hotel's modern water system assaulting her shoulders and back. She thinks she might stay under here forever. She's sore, but not badly so. Just a pleasant morning-after feeling, a little floaty, a little bow-legged.

Her eyes close and, as she begins to soap herself, she thinks of Misha. She has to stop and lean against the tiled wall as a sharp twist of feeling goes through her, fluttery and warm, as she remembers his lips on hers, of the way the muscles in his shoulders moved when he was over her.

She shifts the water to a cooler temperature. She's barely known Misha two weeks and in that time he's turned her world upside down, made her admit things she'd been desperately ignoring about herself, about her own dreams and desires, and she's... she's gone and fallen for him, hard.

She's sure it's not love, not yet. More an infatuation, brought on by an easy wit, an incredible body and, seriously, the best sex of her life. But, she thinks, as she looks forward to the affair's inevitable end, *this one's going to bruise.*

Evie finishes showering, throws on a long T-shirt, and pads over to the armchair by the floor-to-ceiling window. She curls up in it and looks out over the Palo Alto skyline, flat and green and spread out in a way New York never is. And she thinks back to the Evie Cross of a mere four days ago in Manhattan, hopelessly naïve and grasping in all the wrong places for answers. Cross-referencing slow poisons and Russian assassination-by-radiation techniques and worrying that Misha was a serial-killing sociopath. If only the answers had been that simple. Stripped of context, of course, the answers were the same: he had killed Greg Pickford; he'd admitted to killing others. It's different, though, knowing what he is, that he can't survive without a measure of harm to others.

She knows she should feel more disturbed about Misha having to feed on people to exist, but he genuinely seems to try to hurt others as little as possible: a few days, a week off a stranger's life, time that they'd never miss or even realize were being taken, and would probably waste anyway. She thinks of all the hours she'd pissed away playing video games and reading fanfic and doing literally anything other than working on her own stories. She'd give all that up, to keep Misha around. She'd give up a lot more.

She knows it's her crush talking, because her rationalizations still ring hollow, even to her. As much as she wants to let go of her concerns about what he is, she can't. He feeds on people, and it seems okay because you can't see the wounds. But he still takes pieces of their lives. And if he takes too much, too fast, like he did with Greg Pickford, their hearts give out.

She watches a red-tailed hawk spiral in the middle distance as it idly scans for prey, and she wonders what to do. They have to finish this thing with the Overstreets, stop Eric from becoming an incubus like Misha, and then... then everything will revert to some measure of normal. They'll go back to the office in Manhattan. Gemma will hopefully blossom further, now that she's in an environment of peace and safety. Claudia will achieve recognition, Beatriz will get her happily ever after, and Evie will find her purpose. She'll have time, after all this mess in Palo Alto is over, to get used to what Misha is, to what they're doing. And, once the first flush of infatuation fades, to figure out whether this is where she really belongs.

She calls Claudia next. Her roommate is at home, exhausted from a high-society charity lunch, and watching Sunday-night reality TV while downing a nice bottle of Sancerre left over from work. Evie can hear women yelling at each other in the background as Claudia says, "So why couldn't you talk earlier?"

Evie exhales. She figures truth is the best option; Claudia will worm it out of her sooner or later anyway. "I was sleeping with Misha."

"He can still be crazy even if he sticks his dick in you, babe, and not gonna lie but you have form with that," Claudia says, as the TV in the background grows quieter.

"There's a bunch of things I can't tell you, but, uh..." Evie says, curling up in her armchair as if to dissuade eavesdroppers in the empty room, "... he's actually pretty amazing. And I'm happy." She is; even as she says it Evie can feel the warmth in her chest, the smile spreading across her face. "For the first time in a really long while, I feel like I'm on the right path, even if it wasn't the one I planned for myself."

"Wow," Claudia deadpans. "That must be some USDA prime dick."

Evie giggles. "Yeah. It kinda is."

Claudia groans in frustration. Evie can hear the sofa cushions squeak as she shifts her weight. "Evie," she says, drawing out her name over several long seconds, like she was talking to a particularly inattentive little cousin. "Felicitations on sleeping with your hot boss, I'm sure that totally won't end in disaster. But listen to your gut, not your pussy. Your gut said he was scary. And he's a lot bigger than you. I get... I get a bad feeling from him, okay?"

Evie just sighs into the phone. She can't think of anything to say that's not either an outright lie, or something that will cause Claudia to become even more concerned.

"Okay."

"Call me every day, Evie, or so help me I will call the cops and report you as abducted."

"That's not—" Evie begins. "Claudia, I *have* a mom. I don't need another mom. Misha would never hurt me."

"But he's hurt other people in front of you?" Claudia says. "Look, I watched this play out with my aunt and uncle. I sat at the kitchen table while Mom iced her broken cheekbone and listened to her say that it was her fault because the dinner was cold. Don't try to pretend everything's okay when it's not."

"Fine, Claudia, you win!" Evie all but shouts. "Everything is not okay, but it's not okay in a way that I cannot explain to you right now, and I am in no danger from Misha." In her mind's eye, she pictures Misha in hunting mode, aggressive and brutally graceful as he takes down the two bodyguards Greg Pickford had sent to retrieve his husband. "We're mixed up in something dangerous on this investigation, but Misha is probably the safest person in the world for me to be with right now."

"I don't know why I bother," Claudia whispers. "You don't listen. You don't listen!"

"You bother because you're my *friend*," Evie replies. "Besides, I always tell you to ask for a raise and you don't listen to me."

There's an uncomfortable pause at the other end of the line, and it gets quiet enough for Evie to hear the TV in the background even at lowest volume, the women still yelling at each other, something crashing to the ground.

"I asked, though," Claudia says, her voice small.

"What?" Evie squawks. She sits up so fast her head spins.

"They said no, some bullshit about a review next season, blah blah blah." Claudia snorts. "So fuck them, I'm applying to other catering companies. And a couple hotels."

"I'm sorry, Claudia. They're jerks."

"Yeah. I know," Claudia says, tired. "I worked so hard for them, I thought they had to have noticed."

"We're here only a couple more days, I think," Evie says. "I promise I'll call you every day, and when we get back we'll go out and drink lots of margaritas. I have a job now, it'll be my treat."

"Okay," Claudia sniffs. "Evie, be careful."

"I will," Evie says. She hangs up and tosses her phone on the bed.

She pulls on some of the clothes they'd bought on Saturday morning, a flattering pair of jeans and a pretty embroidered tunic, and texts Misha about dinner.

He texts back and says he'll be down in ten, so Evie takes one look at her hair, gives up, and wraps the hot mess of curls in a scarf. She's just finished slipping on her sneakers when she hears a tap at the door.

It's Masha, in the same simple day dress she'd worn on Saturday. She smirks, and says, "I thought it might be better if I stay in girl mode tonight. In case there's anyone who recognizes boy-me from the party."

Part of Evie's mind is still freaking out over how Misha can just... be a girl when he wants to be. And is arguably better— no, scratch that—*definitely* better at the whole performative femininity thing than Evie is. The other part, the part that's basically ceded control to her lower half, sees that smirk and drives straight off the road and into the nearest gutter.

Before she can overthink it, she steps forwards and kisses Masha. It's not the same as kissing Misha. Her lips are softer, fuller. There's still a lot of chest in the way, but it feels of lace and yielding fullness, not Misha's velvet and steel. Her hand finds its way to Masha's hip, and that's also different, how much her waist curves inwards. How there's a perfect place for her fingers to rest.

The kiss isn't lengthy, or overly passionate; it's just a hello kiss. But it's nice, and Evie's a little surprised by how much she likes it.

Masha's surprised too, judging by the look on her face as Evie steps away.

"I like both of you," Evie stutters in explanation. "All of you?"

Masha grins and reels Evie in for another kiss, this one a little dirtier. Her nails run down Evie's back, and curve over her ass possessively. "Both of me is fine," she says.

"I'm having confusing thoughts about gender," Evie says when they come up for air, a little dazed.

Masha shrugs. "It's a confusing subject. Especially with me. And it's all right if you prefer one version of me more than the other." She links her hand into Evie's and pulls her into the hallway.

"No," Evie says, as Masha links arms with her and they walk towards the elevators. "I always wanted to, with another girl, but... I'd never met the right one."

Masha raises an eyebrow and shoots her an amused look.

Evie laughs, and blushes at the same time. "I didn't want to be that girl, you know, the one that's curious but can't go through? My roommate's a hundred percent gay and she's had some bad experiences with girls who weren't as bi as they thought they were."

"Well," Masha says, as she presses the elevator button, "whatever happens, happens. And if you find out you prefer your fantasies to stay fantasies?" She bites her lip and shoots Evie a suggestive look under her lashes. "I know a boy."

Evie rolls her eyes and leans into Masha. She's comfortable, and fits against her in a different but equally pleasurable way as Misha. "Are his lines as bad as yours?" she sighs.

"I have it on good authority they're worse," Masha hums, throwing her arm around Evie and leaning into her in return.

"The Kieselsteins happy for now?" Evie asks.

"The Kieselsteins are never happy. But they have been temporarily pacified," Masha says. "I've told them they have to go through Gemma for anything during the working week." Then she grins. "And Gemma only has your cell, not mine."

"Ugh," Evie groans. "You are the *worst* boss."

THEY TAKE A taxi to a Japanese place in downtown Palo Alto. Real sushi is one of Evie's favorite things, but she hasn't been able to afford it for a while. Even the bodega $9.99 takeout Salmon Lovers' Special has been out of her budget.

Masha worms this information out of her the same way Misha did when they first met: ask a question, and then leave so much silence that the person answering feels compelled to fill the space. Evie had started off with "Anything, whatever you want," before doing an actual facepalm in the back of the taxi. Masha had snorted in amusement, then grabbed Evie's hand and laced their fingers together.

The place is small, plain, pleasantly dark, and full of Japanese people. The guy at the sushi counter is about a hundred years old and looks like he misses the days when you could smoke in restaurants. When he's not slicing fish, he's watching a baseball game on the TV that's hung over the corner of the bar. Evie's feeling pretty good about the likelihood of excellent sushi in her very near future.

Masha bats her eyelashes at Evie as she pushes the menu towards her. "Remember, yesterday I bought myself a fourteen thousand dollar jacket because it made me sentimental about my old cavalry uniform. Order anything you want." Then she hooks her ankle around Evie's, under the table, and it's lovely, the casual, tactile way Masha is with her, how easy and pleasant it is to have contact with that too-warm skin. It's grounding, a simple *you're here, I've got you* that Evie hadn't realized how badly she needed until she was given it.

Evie orders a mixed plate of sushi, and a seaweed salad, and a couple à la carte pieces. Their waitress assumes it's for both of them, and neither woman corrects her. Masha orders Evie a carafe of warm sake and, as the first sip burns down Evie's throat, she acknowledges what a good idea it is.

Her miso soup has arrived, as had a small plate of uni and another of salmon roe, when the baseball game on the TV gives way to local news. Evie glances over her shoulder and notes a very blonde newscaster in a bright-red suit droning on about air quality warnings. She goes back to her sushi in time to see Masha go completely still.

Evie turns, slowly, a cold dread clutching at her stomach.

The red suit has adopted a tone of great seriousness, while keeping her expression as unmoving as possible so as not to mess up her heavy TV studio makeup. *Silicon Valley is reeling from the news of StarTech founder Eric Overstreet's death on Saturday night, during a summer party at his Palo Alto mansion. Initial reports state that Mr Overstreet surprised a burglary attempt and his neck was broken in the resulting scuffle. Our thoughts and prayers are with his wife Selene at this difficult time—*

Masha's eyes are wide with terror.

"Anything else I can get you?" their waitress chirps as she puts down the big wooden board of sushi Evie had ordered.

"Uh, no, we're fine," Evie manages to say, and the girl finally leaves. Evie looks over all the food, the colorful, expensive little bundles, that she no longer has appetite for.

Masha has withdrawn into herself, staring down at her hands. She looks guilty.

"Masha, what did you do after I left?" Evie whispers.

Masha doesn't answer for a long moment. "Not that," she breathes. "I didn't... at least, I don't think I did."

Evie glares at her. "You don't *think* you did?"

Masha makes a helpless little gesture, and her beautiful face, that too-expressive mouth, begins to tremble. "I was..." she gestures to her eyes, "... on the edge of control. Maybe over, for a few moments. I don't..." she puts her hands over her face, "... I don't remember. I didn't intend to hurt him that badly, but he... he tried to kill you, and then he shot me." She sighs. "I may have thrown him too hard."

Evie leans back in her chair and pushes the raw fish away from her, sick to her stomach. "And you didn't mention this to me because...?"

"I was hoping for the best," Masha says, from behind the mask of her fingers.

Evie thinks back to how radiant Misha had looked. "Did you feed on him?" she whispers.

"No!" Masha hisses. "I know I didn't do that. There was no need. The book. I was so full of the book... I don't think I killed him either. I threw him hard, but..."

"... but it would be easy for you, wouldn't it," Evie says softly. "Accidentally. You wouldn't even have to exert yourself. Hell, you'd barely notice. How strong *are* you? Like, lift a car strong?"

Masha looks at her then, raw and scared, her eyes shining with betrayal. "Please believe me, that I had no intention of—"

Evie closes her eyes. "Just don't." She waves a hand, cutting Masha off.

They sit there in silence, the chirpy sounds of J-Pop and the soft *klak* of chopsticks and plates swirling around them. Masha folds her hands over the paper placemat, and says finally, "There was the girl. On the bed."

"Yeah, the blindfolded girl," Evie says. "Not exactly something they're going to mention on the news when giving the obituary of a 'beloved Silicon Valley entrepreneur'."

Masha's eyes roam the room. Everywhere but on Evie's face. When she speaks, it's so quiet Evie can barely hear. "I'll bet you anything that she's dead, too."

"If she's alive...?" Evie says.

Masha shrugs helplessly. "Then... then it was probably me who killed Eric."

*　　*　　*

THEY BOX UP Evie's untouched dinner and taxi back to the hotel in awkward silence.

Masha hovers in the doorway, not touching, hands tucked under her own arms, as Evie shoves the sushi box into her room's mini-fridge.

Seeing her body language reflected in the mirror above the dresser, Evie wonders how much Masha needs touch, too. Evie had assumed it was something Masha did for Evie's sake, part of her whole uncanny ability to read other people's physical needs. But now, she realizes, maybe Masha craves it just as badly. Needs simple affection, unencumbered by expectation or transaction.

Masha tucks a stray lock of hair behind her ear, staring at the ground, and she's so far away.

That inconvenient feeling in Evie's chest twists again, that sparkling warmth that Masha-Misha causes in her by their simple proximity.

She wants to stay mad. She wants to just have a moment, a goddamn moment, where she can deal with the fact that Misha might have lost his shit and snapped Eric Overstreet's neck while in full black-eyed demon mode.

But instead she takes four strides over to the door and throws her arms around Masha.

Masha stiffens for a moment, like she's going to flinch away, like she thinks she doesn't deserve this. Then she absolutely melts into Evie's arms. "Th-thank you," she whispers. And then, "I'm sorry." She steps away from Evie slowly, reluctantly, and reaches out and rests her thumb under Evie's chin. "See you tomorrow?"

"If Eric is dead, are we done here?" Evie says.

Masha presses her lips together. "I have a date with Selene Overstreet on Tuesday night. Taking her to the ballet."

"Surely she'll cancel?" Evie says.

"She hasn't texted me to do so," Masha says. "I find that curious. I find a number of things about this entire situation curious." She shakes her head. "I want to find that girl, too. Make sure she's okay." Then she refocuses on Evie, her expression honest and open. From Masha, a creature of labyrinthine secrets, it feels like the rarest of blessings. "You don't have to stay."

"I'd like to," Evie says.

Masha nods, then runs a hand up Evie's neck into her hair, pulling her close for a chaste kiss on her forehead. "Until tomorrow, then, little one."

EVIE IS WOKEN up a little after 6am by her phone, trilling its way off the bedside table.

It's Gemma, back in New York. "Evie," she says, her normally self-assured voice rough and panicky, "have you seen the article?"

"What article?" Evie asks, even though terror clenches at her gut, because there can only be one article, and it could only have come from one place.

"It's about us. About the agency," Gemma says. "On Medium. It's called—"

"—*The Break-Up Artist*," Evie finishes.

"Oh thank God, you have seen it. Has Misha? He needs to call the Kieselsteins, they're *furious*," Gemma says. "And I'm getting calls from other journalists, I don't know how they got the number, and there's a woman who wants Misha to kill her husband."

"Fuck," Evie says. Her heart is pounding; she wants to vomit even though there's nothing in her stomach. "Is there anything about our current case, here in San Francisco?"

"First paragraph," Gemma says. "It straight-up accuses Misha of killing Eric Overstreet."

"*Fuck*," Evie groans. The sob that comes out of her throat surprises her, but then she's crying, hot tears coming down her cheeks. "Oh fuck, Gemma, we're so screwed." She almost confesses to Gemma that it's all her fault, but at the last moment she chokes it back, holding her guilt inside herself like a poison. "Don't answer any call where you don't recognize the number. Just let them ring out. No voicemail, no nothing. And lock the door. Any answer will be taken as encouragement for more investigation."

"Good. That's what I've been doing. I answered the first couple only because I didn't know—"

"Gemma, you did fine. You're the most competent person I know. Nobody's mad at you," Evie says. "I'll speak to the Kieselsteins. If any of the freelancers call, tell them not to talk to anyone, and that Misha's handling it."

"Is he?" Gemma asks.

"I'm going to see him right now," Evie says. "He'll have to."

BUT SHE DOESN'T go see Misha immediately. He knows; the Kieselsteins would have already called him directly. First, she needs to understand how much damage has been done.

She makes some of the watery coffee from the hotel machine and looks up the article. The byline positively smirks at her, *by Nicole Hamilton*, a serious, black and white photo of Nicole next to it. The article is nothing but Evie's notes, reordered and strung together with some innuendo-laden connecting prose. Nicole always was a lazy editor.

However, Evie is a very good investigator, and every shred of evidence, every stolen photo of Misha and Stewart Pickford, even the audio recording of Misha and Greg and Erin, it's all there. The names of the other six suspicious deaths among the Meyer, Luchins & Black divorce clients. There's no question where these things could have come from. Only Evie was present that afternoon with Greg and Erin; only Evie saw those photos of Misha and Stewart. Misha will know it was her.

Nicole has managed to contribute a low-resolution, overly enlarged cellphone picture of Misha and Selene from the Overstreets' party that she must have snapped herself. There's a few more blurry cellphone images of the aftermath: police outside the house; the fallen, broken statue of Osiris; panicking crowds.

The article doesn't come to any meaningful conclusions. Evie had stopped writing before she learned that her facts didn't fit any rational hypothesis because the truth was utterly irrational. But Nicole's not writing out of journalistic integrity. It's a hit piece, pure and simple. She even takes a swipe at Octavia Mortimer, shaming her as a wife who kept having to hire Misha to chase off the nubile young subjects of her husband's serial philandering. There's no final "gotcha", only spite, and rampant speculation disguised as fact. But as far as Misha is concerned, the damage is irreparable. His name, his photo in the press, tied to unusual deaths. The scar where his heart no longer is, white and clear in the lurid photos of him and Stewart Pickford.

Near the end, Nicole mentions the book.

Evie curls up and presses the heels of her hands against her eyes until they hurt, like she can press the vision of the article out of her head, go back to a time before it existed.

In an act of almost unfathomable courage, Misha had placed his secrets, guarded so long and so fiercely, into her hands. And within a day, they'd run through her fingers like so much water, spilling all over the internet for everyone to see.

Pandora has opened the box, and her sins have flown out into the world.

And they can never, ever be put back.

CHAPTER THIRTEEN

Evie calls Misha. She has no idea what to say to him. How do you span a betrayal that vast, that complete? All she knows is that she needs to speak to him as soon as she can, and she prays that the right words will come.

But it's already too late.

After a few heart-stopping rings, there's just a click, then three trilling notes and a robotic voice stating *this number is not in service.*

She's already pulling on jeans and a shirt, her phone still wedged against her ear, when she realizes she doesn't even know what Misha's room number is. He'd always come to her room. Even in trust, he was secretive.

Evie runs downstairs, hoping to catch him there, to see the flash of that ugly yellow sports car pulled up in front of the hotel doors. But there's nothing, just the sepulchral emptiness of a grand lobby at an in-between hour. She drags herself to the front desk to ask after him, and what little hope she had is quickly crushed. The receptionist has never heard of Misha Meserov. No guest by that name, so sorry. And no, they can't give out guest names or information based on descriptions. Evie leans against the counter, dizzy with how rapidly and completely everything has collapsed.

She digs out her keycard and hands it to the sleek black woman working the reception counter. "I'm in room 532," Evie says. "Can you tell me the name my room is booked under? Who's paying the bill?"

The woman helping her gives her a look which, while not unfriendly, manages to communicate a certain level of amazement that Evie wouldn't know who booked the room, but her fingers clack across her keyboard for a minute, and then she says, "It's booked under Evangeline Cross, and the bill is a corporate Amex registered to a… Meyer, Luchins & Black?"

Evie sags. "I have a colleague who would have booked under the same card. Can you just tell me if he's checked out?"

The woman's nails, glistening with a bronze metallic polish, tap across the keyboard again. "Yes. Checked out first thing this morning. I can—" the woman starts, but she's cut off by the ringtone of Evie's phone.

Evie's heart nearly leaps out of her chest as she glances down at the screen. Her sense of blossoming hope fades almost instantly at the unrecognizable number: a New York area code, the old 212. She answers, tentative, afraid it's going to be a journalist.

It's worse. It's Abigail.

"Evie, what the blazes is going on?" Abigail says immediately. No hello, no nothing. "Misha left me a message this morning that he's going away indefinitely. And now there are priests demanding to be let into Misha's office."

"I'm sorry, I have to take this, thanks for your help," Evie mumbles to the reception woman, as she backs away towards one of the lobby's squishy red armchairs. She breathes as she walks, hunched over, trying to make herself as small as possible. She can feel the panic attack coming on, heart rate ratcheting up and her chest constricting like a steel vice. "Abi, d-don't let them have anything. Don't let the priests see the pictures of him. Did you see…"

"… the article?" Abi finishes. She sighs. "Yes. It's made the rounds. The Kieselsteins are furious, Evie. They're talking about suing you and Gemma for breach of your NDAs. They know it must have been one of you who got that recording."

Evie collapses onto the chair. "It was me," she whispers. She's about to start crying, the corners of her eyes pregnant with tears. None of this is any more than she deserves. "Not

Gemma. Not for a moment. She's... she's a really good person and probably the best secretary I've ever met. Please tell them not to sue her. It was all me."

"We'll talk when you get back to New York," Abi says, stern. "Meanwhile I'm going to lock up Misha's office and Gemma can answer any calls from home. We're still very much dealing with the fallout." Abi exhales, short and harsh. "I could really use being able to get in touch with Misha."

"Yeah, me too," says Evie, pressing the heel of her hand to her cheekbone to try to keep the tears from falling. "But he's gone." Her voice breaks halfway through the sentence, like a lovesick teenager.

"Okay. Well. Tell him I need to talk to him, if you do see him," Abigail says. "Do you know when you're coming back?"

"Today, I guess," Evie says. Their job is done: the book destroyed, the husband killed, the divorce from Selene now a moot point. Her breathing has calmed down, and now she just feels sad, like a heavy weight is pressing down on every part of her. "I gotta go pack up my stuff. I'll see you soon, Abi."

"I'll send you a meeting invite for a week from today. Don't come in until then," Abi says. "Meyer, Luchins & Black as a company will have a better idea where it stands on this by then, and then we can talk about what happens to you. Don't run, or fail to show up. It'll just make things worse."

"Okay," Evie says. "Thank you. Don't worry. I'll be there." This, she knows: there will be no escaping to her parents in Chicago, no short break to figure things out. That luxury is gone. She has to go back to New York and fix what she broke. And then, presumably, say goodbye to the city.

There's no way she can get back up after this one.

Evie goes up to her room, wanting nothing more than to crash back into her bed and pretend the last twelve hours never happened. Back into the nest of messy white sheets that still smell of him, of juniper and lime and old leather.

But as she comes down the hall, she sees her door is open. Fear clutches at her for a moment, until a bored-looking hotel maid wanders out and shoots her a barely concealed look of annoyance. "Five minutes," the woman mumbles, throwing Evie's sheets and towels into her cart's laundry hamper. "You check out today, yes?"

Evie nods. She walks back to the elevator area; there's a window that looks out over Palo Alto and a big vase of ugly, angular greens and vivid orange flowers on a side table. She perches on the windowsill and pulls out her phone. She stares at her message app, jiggling the phone so that the bright Northern California sunshine dances white across the screen. The hallway is quiet but never silent, surrounding her with a lullaby of humming electrics and the low rumble of the air conditioning. Distantly, she hears the maid's cart pass down the hallway; supplies rattling, a wheel squeaking. She tells herself when it stops, she'll type the message she's been composing from the shrapnel in her head. She doesn't want it to stop.

It stops.

Knock, knock. *Housekeeping*. The beep and click of a door opening.

The blank shine of sunlight across a screen, interrupted.

I'm sorry. I know nothing can make up for what I did. I was pursuing something I thought I loved, even though it was foolish and hurtful. I stopped; the night we went to the Overstreets. I deleted all those files. But it was too late, apparently. I hope you're well and I never meant to hurt you. You're the best person I know.

She doesn't look to see if it's delivered.

Instead, she goes to pack. She stands in the wreckage of her room, between the freshly made bed with its taut, bleach-scented sheets, and the chair with all her beautiful new clothes thrown over it. Evie crams her lovely things into as few carrier bags as possible, crumpled silks and denim and cashmere, tags tangling together. She tries not to dwell on how fast a whole new world had opened up to her, and how it had snapped shut even faster. She does not succeed.

Evie Cross, unemployed again, turns in her keycard, checks her credit-card balance to see if she can afford a flight home, and boards the bus to the airport. She texts Claudia on the way, nothing more than a banal *I'll be home later today or tomorrow :)*.

She huddles in Arrivals, in a bright area overlooking the runways as families and lovers reunite behind her, searching discount travel sites for the cheapest possible flight home. There are plenty, a few even affordable, but something keeps Evie from just buying a ticket and going. She finds herself staring out at the gleaming planes taxiing to and from their gates, her eyes unfocused in the early-June sunshine.

And she thinks of his skin, and how it tastes. The many moods of his pale eyes, and his too-large, ridiculous smile. Of strange, sad Misha, so strong and so wounded at the same time. Who does not believe in love, but cannot help being kind. And who she has put into the most terrible danger.

Evie shudders as she thinks of the hunter-priests seeing Nicole's article, looking at the photos of him and Stewart that she had copied, the photos that show his scar, that make it crystal clear to a knowing eye exactly what he is.

Her phone beeps. She glances down at it and sighs. StarTech wants to install a firmware update, and she's about to hit *Accept* on the terms and conditions when she realizes she'll likely face half an hour without service while her cell reboots itself, and what if Misha texts her back. She hits *Remind Me Later* and goes back to the important task of tapping the phone against the palm of her hand and staring regretfully off into space.

Her phone does ring a couple minutes later, but it's only Claudia. "So what's that bullshit text message about?" Claudia says. "You only use emojis when you're lying, or drunk. Please don't be still drunk."

"It's over, Claudia. I'm coming home," Evie says.

"Lemme guess. You got fired, dumped, or both?" Claudia asks.

"Mmmhmm," Evie says, slumping further down in her ugly airport-modern orange chair.

"You wanna talk about it?" Claudia asks. A door slams, and Evie can hear Claudia's feet padding down steps, and the noise of the New York streets rising around her.

"No, I..." She swallows. "I really, really don't want to talk about it for a while." She knows she should tell Claudia about the article, about Nicole, but when she thinks of how angry Claudia will be on her behalf she feels her throat tighten. She can't deal with anyone's pity right now. She doesn't deserve it.

Claudia is talking, and Evie forces herself to listen to her friend's words. "... maybe this was a blessing, Evie. I still think he was bad news."

"'Kay, thanks, Claudia," Evie whispers. She can feel the tears bottling up, hot and insistent, behind her eyes, and she's not going to cry in the airport, not here, in this strange, overlit, liminal corridor.

"Also wish me luck," Claudia replies, her voice teasing. "I have an interview at Soho House right now."

"Ohmigod!" Evie says, sitting up. "Good luck!"

And then a flash of black and scarlet catches at the corner of her eye.

CLAUDIA'S VOICE FADES away as Evie drops the phone from her ear. Three men in priests' robes walk down the Arrivals hallway, their eyes wary, their hands clutching the sort of long aluminum hardcases that could contain anything from fishing equipment to semiautomatic weaponry. The fourth, their leader, is a strikingly handsome black man, the rich darkness of his skin set off by the scarlet trim on his fitted black suit.

She recognizes two of them from her afternoon in the shopping plaza with Masha: the smaller, Mediterranean-looking priest and the smiling Asian-American one. The Asian-American priest is now serious, talking in an urgent undertone to a tall, scarred, Nordic blond with a severe expression and a few days' growth of beard, who nods curtly at his words.

Evie is out of her seat and on a collision course with the priests at the same time as her brain races to figure out a plan. She may not be able to fix what she broke, but perhaps she can stop it becoming fatal. Because, Evie remembers, it's

Monday morning, and Misha has a date with Selene Overstreet on Tuesday night. She knows where he will be. And, more importantly, the priests might know too.

But if they don't... this could all backfire terribly.

"Hi!" Evie chirps, a little too loud, as she skids to a stop directly in front of the black priest in the suit, the obvious leader. Her shopping bags clatter against her leg; she is dimly aware that she couldn't be making a worse first impression if she tried.

He stops, one eyebrow rising slightly, his aristocratic expression clearly bidding her to talk now or get out of his way. The other three priests subtly move around her and their leader, protecting him. This close, she can see the strange eye-and-pyramid symbol embroidered on their left shoulders.

"I know why you're here," Evie says, softening her voice to barely above a whisper. The leader's eyebrows rise higher. "I have solid information on the incubus you're looking for. I was there when he destroyed the book."

Off to her side, she hears a sharp inhale. It's from the blond; she can feel him looming next to her. His colleagues are looking at her with varying degrees of suspicion, but the leader, she can't read him at all. He is examining her, his brown eyes pinning her in place like a butterfly to a board.

Something shifts, then. A decision is made. The man extends a hand, his palm pale against the darkness of the rest of his skin. His grip is warm and strong as he folds Evie's hand within his, and his eyes manage to be both friendly and full of concern. His voice, when he speaks, is rich with a soft Nigerian accent. "I am Cardinal Adonis of the Vatican's Shadow Secretariat. May we speak to you in private, Miss...?"

"Cross, Evie Cross," she says.

And the Cardinal's hand lets go of hers and touches her shoulder, gently but firmly propelling her along with them, out the door, and into the back of one of two big, black luxury SUVs waiting at the curb for them. Evie has just enough time to think that she's spent more time in nice cars in the past week than she has in the rest of her life combined, and then they're off.

She shares the back seat of the SUV with the Korean-American priest, who introduces himself as Kevin. Evie picks up on hints of a Midwestern accent in his voice, and manages to get out of him that he's from Indiana originally but is now based in the Bay Area, before the Mediterranean priest in the front passenger seat turns around and hisses at them. "Don't mind George," Kevin says, teasing. "It's his first time in the US. He's very good at what he does, but we don't normally let him talk to people because of all the growling and the biting."

"Or perhaps it is you who should come back to the Citadel and relearn some discipline," George mutters.

"So what do you do?" Evie asks him.

"Same as my namesake. I hunt monsters," comes the surly reply from the front seat.

They drive, not to a hotel as Evie expects, but through downtown San Francisco, ending up at a magnificent old Telegraph Hill mansion, all the more impressive for being a little ragged around the edges. It gives an impression of age, and of persistence in the face of change. The door is opened by a fierce-looking older Italian woman in black lace, who merely nods at the priests as they walk past her. The blond one smiles at her, muttering a "Looking well, Daniela," as he passes, earning him an eye roll and a halfhearted swat on the shoulder from the caretaker.

The caretaker clucks at Evie, gesturing to be handed all her bags. Evie freezes up, her hands curling tighter around the rope handles with the instinctive city-girl fear of letting her things out of her sight. Daniela seems to take this as a personal affront. The woman points to the floor next to a fancy Chinese blue and white porcelain umbrella stand. "Bags go here," she says, in a raspy, forty-a-day voice. "Then you go in there, and don't look like a refugee."

Daniela has a valid point. Evie surrenders her gifted finery in its shiny, boxy bags and then goes where the caretaker indicates.

The entranceway opens into a formal sitting room, all antiques and dark colors, the tall windows curtained in heavy silk. The Cardinal indicates an uncomfortable-looking wing chair, all green brocade and clawed wooden feet. "Miss Cross," he says, as the rest of the priests settle down on the other sofas and chairs. "I have several questions for you. The first being, of course, how you know who we are—"

"Don't kill him," Evie blurts out, as she drops down onto the chair's lumpy horsehair cushion.

"Do you... truly believe you are friends with this creature?" Cardinal Adonis admonishes, shifting his weight forwards in the same way one of her favorite professors did when he wanted to emphasize just how hare-brained her investigative conclusions were.

"Yes," Evie says, leaning forwards too, mirroring his body posture. "And I did something terrible and fucked-up and now you're here because of me, but he is a good person."

Adonis opens his mouth to disagree. Kevin is shaking his head in amused disbelief, George is watching her with the impassive, hooded eyes of a hunter, and the blond guy... his face is in shadow. She can't read him.

Evie pushes on. "Look. If you know about him, you have to know about the book." She glares directly at George now. "I know you've been snooping around after it. I saw you taking selfies in Palo Alto."

Kevin coughs something into his fist that sounds suspiciously like *busted*.

She turns her attention to Adonis and the still-shadowed face of the blond, who is standing, leaning against a bookshelf. "I'm guessing you two are the big guns. When did you get called in? When the book vanished? Or when that article came out with his picture in it? What are you here for, to retrieve the book or to kill an incubus? Because that incubus did your job for you."

Adonis sits back, his eyes widening in shock.

"He destroyed it," Evie grits out. "I watched it burn. I watched it *bleed*. He took it from me after it had half-convinced me to try to murder someone. And he told me that the last time he had seen it, a hundred years ago, a priest had told him it would be destroyed. So why didn't you?"

Out of the corner of her eye she can see the scarred blond stiffen, start to speak. Adonis makes a small gesture, and the man falls silent.

"What do you know about incubi, Miss Cross?" Adonis asks, his tone carefully neutral. "Because we know quite a lot. We have seen... dozens of them. The old ones that come to us, begging for a mercy killing, unable to handle the empty evil of their long lives. The young ones, drunk on power, revenging themselves on anyone who ever slighted them."

George speaks up, then, his tone condescending. "Whatever this one did to enchant you, you need to know that it is a trick. Incubi are not attractive creatures. They use their powers instead. The greatest lie that the Devil sells them is that the ritual will make them young and beautiful. It doesn't change your appearance. You stay as you were, as if in amber, from the moment the bargain is struck. The same face that you've always hated. The same body that was never good enough. Forever. All the ritual does is give you the power to charm people into thinking you are beautiful. The incubus does not care about you. You only believe that it does. The compulsion will pass in a few months, and you will see."

"You're wrong," Evie says. "You're absolutely wrong. He took three bullets in the chest for me. If you knew what he did, how hard he tries to live in a way that doesn't harm people..." She sighs, exhausted. "How scared he is all the time." She points at George. "And you're wrong in particular, because Misha's so beautiful it will take your breath away."

George shakes his head, a low, mocking laugh escaping his lips. They don't believe her. Evie's glance travelling over them only confirms that: George's disdain, Kevin's cool blankness, and, worst of all, Cardinal Adonis's pity. The three of them are looking at her like she's the sort of poor mixed-up girl who's too dumb to recognize that she's a victim. She's going to lose this. She's going to fail to convince them that Misha deserves to live, because they refuse to see anything differently than the way they've always seen it. Her last, impulsive, all-in bet is just as much a bust as everything else she's done.

Still, she tries one last time, because she won't go down easy. "What is a life worth?" she whispers, staring down at her hands. "Is it measured only by its tally of mistakes? Or do you consider the good, too? This person you condemn as a monster, without knowing him, without ever having spoken to him, would it surprise you to know of all the people he's helped? Of his friends, who would feel his loss desperately? Gemma and Beatriz, Stewart and Abigail. Me. Will you look at all of us and call us deluded, when we know the man, and you know only a crusade?"

Her words hang in the air of the old, dark room, like dust motes. Nobody moves. The only sound is the distant ticking of a grandfather clock. And then the subtle susurration of fabric, as Cardinal Adonis crosses his legs.

"He is not a man," says the Shadow Cardinal, his voice low and certain. "He is a parasite upon humanity, by his own choosing."

All is lost.

Evie presses her palms against her cheeks because she will not break down in front of these priests, she will not give them that victory. She sucks in a ragged breath and tries to raise her chin up.

There is movement: the blond priest, who had kept himself disinterestedly apart, steps out of the shadows to whisper something into the Cardinal's ear. The lamplight illuminates his green eyes, wet with unshed tears, and his white knuckles as he digs his nails into his palm.

As the man meets her gaze, a name rises to Evie's lips.

"Pavel," she whispers. "You're Pavel."

EVIE KNOWS SHE'S hit a nerve when the blond priest spins with the sort of fluid, deadly grace she's only ever seen before with Misha, and strides over to the unlit fireplace, turning his back on all of them and resting his head against the cool brick of the chimney.

The other priests are looking between Pavel and her in confusion.

"Paul," says Kevin, his tone surprisingly wry. "Paul Ahasuerus, you sly dog. What on earth is going on?"

"Oh!" Evie says, clutching the arms of the uncomfortable wing chair that had felt like a penance, and now feels like her throne. She addresses her words to the broad planes of Pavel's back. "You haven't told them." She turns to the other three priests. "About a hundred years ago, your friend and freakily immortal co-worker here—"

"Did you know that as recently as a decade ago, explorers discovered a previously unknown species of parrot, deep in the Amazon?" Paul, or Pavel, says, as he straightens and turns towards them. There's a high blush in his cheeks, and Evie thinks she can see other scars on his face, ancient, but never fully faded. His lips twitch, as if he doesn't know whether to laugh or scream. "They had the most unusual vocalizations that zoologists had ever heard, until one of the scientists put a video of them on YouTube and found out, in fact, that the parrots were swearing. In Georgian."

"Brother," says the Cardinal, "I do not give a shit about parrots."

"I'd like to speak with Miss Cross," Pavel says. "Alone." He's leaning against the fireplace, his arms crossed. Evie looks at him, *really* looks, and he's thicker than Misha, especially through the waist and thighs; all power, to Misha's dancer's grace.

"I think we came here for a mission—*two* missions—and we shouldn't get distracted from them," George says.

"I think there's a really good story here and you are going to have to bodily throw me out of this room to keep me from hearing it," grins Kevin.

"Whatever you have to discuss, you can do it in front of us," the Cardinal declares, in a tone that doesn't invite discussion.

A rough imperiousness colors Pavel's voice when he next speaks. "I work with the Secretariat as a *favor*, Adonis. I warned you when you were appointed Shadow Cardinal that there may be things I cannot or will not explain to you—"

"That's okay, I'm happy to explain," Evie says. "He's a shitbag who dumped his boyfriend a hundred years ago after said boyfriend made the world's most epic sacrifice for him."

"That's not…" begins Pavel.

"This is the greatest day of my life," Kevin breathes.

"Tell them, Pavel," Evie says. "Tell them you really believe they should hunt down and kill Misha, especially when he's out here doing your job for you, since you promised to destroy the book a hundred years ago when you had it, and you obviously didn't. Also, was that book bound in human skin? Because I think it might have been, and I'm retroactively super grossed out thinking about that."

George fixes Pavel with an accusing look. "I'm now understanding why the file on this particular incubus was so… scant."

"I didn't know it was him, Brother George," Pavel insists, his hands balled into fists. "I *swear* to you, I didn't know."

The Cardinal uncrosses his legs, sitting up straighter. "Please do explain, Pavel."

Evie wants to say more, but she remembers how effective Misha's tactic was, of opening a silence and waiting for the other person to fall into it like a trap. She remains quiet.

Pavel sighs, and sits down on a plain bench near the fireplace. He almost begins to speak several times, but he stops himself before words escape him. Eventually, he says, "I spent the early part of the last century in Russia, at a seminary outside the Imperial capital of St Petersburg. Russia is vast, and terrible things were hiding there. It was my duty to attend to them." His voice drops away to nothing as his lips move around the next name, as if, after carrying it secretly and silently inside him for so long, he has lost the courage to speak it aloud. "Misha…"

Pavel swallows, and his voice quavers as it returns to its usual rough tenor. "Misha was the youngest son of an old Georgian princely family. He had three or four older brothers and an older sister, so succession was not a concern. An heir and a spare, as they would say. Misha—he wasn't called Meserov then, he had a different name—he was mostly ignored, allowed to run wild on the family estate, tearing around the mountains on his pony... until his misbehavior became so bad, his father sent him to join the army. Not just any part of the army, of course. A socially prestigious Hussar regiment, stationed in the capital. The idea was to install some discipline, or at least for him to form useful connections in the Palace."

"One of Misha's middle brothers, Irakli, had entered my seminary a couple of years previously. It was standard in those days: the oldest learned to look after the estates; a middle one went to the priesthood, the youngest to the army. I was travelling frequently then, but Irakli was a favorite among his teachers: quiet and perceptive, and dedicated to his studies. I remember how cheered he was when Misha moved to St Petersburg, to have a family member so close, and how much everyone enjoyed the anecdotes Irakli would tell at dinner of his younger brother's adventures.

"I had found the book." Pavel runs a hand over his face. "Evie, we destroy it every time we find it. You have to understand, though: it keeps reappearing. I have watched it burn countless times, and then ten, twenty, fifty years later, there it is again. This time, I took it back with me and locked it in a lead box in my chambers, determined to find a way to get rid of it once and for all. I would like to blame its influence for what happened next, but I am afraid I cannot."

He shuts his eyes. Whether it's to avoid the judgment on the faces of his colleagues or to better remember the past, Evie can't say. "Irakli becomes increasingly concerned for his brother; his fellow seminarians beg him for stories, but there are none. He gets leave to go into the city a couple of times to see Misha, and returns even quieter than usual. He comes to me for advice, as I had a reputation for worldliness due to my travel. Misha was... not as sophisticated as he thought he was. A childhood running free in provincial Georgia was no primer for the delicate machinations of the Imperial Russian court. He quickly became entrapped, the plaything of someone very powerful. They threatened to ruin him if he left." Pavel sighs. "I had no wisdom for Irakli. I was preoccupied by the book, and I had been a common soldier, never a courtier.

"A few weeks later, shortly before matins, one of the apprentices comes to me to say that there is a drunk cavalry officer passed out in the hayloft above our stables," he continues. "There was little doubt who it could be. I strode out, still only in my night-robe, to the stables fully intending to give him a verbal lashing that would leave him feeling on a par with the martyred St Bartholomew."

Pavel smiles, lost in his memories. "In those days, the Hussar uniforms were tailored to within an inch of their lives. Sometimes I wondered how some of them could breathe. And there was Misha, asleep, half in and half out of his dress uniform. I was very old even by then, and I have seen many things, but Misha sprawled like the young lord he was in the hay, the pre-dawn light on him, his hair across his face... I will always remember that moment. I shake him and I'm about to yell at him when he turns his head and I see the black eye, the split lip he was trying to hide. He flinches, and says, *please, I have nowhere to go. I have been ruined.*"

There's a sharp intake of breath, and Evie looks over to see Kevin with his hand over his mouth, rapt. George seems revolted, and the Cardinal is impassive, an obsidian rock around which the emotions of the room wash like a restless sea.

"I let him stay. We gave him a room, and space to recover. He accompanied Irakli on his studies, for something to do. He was brilliant and blasphemous and funny, and he developed an attachment to me. It was nothing, I thought; he was merely overreacting to the first person in a long time to show him kindness without expectation of return. It would pass, and I could..." Pavel swallows, "... ignore how he made me feel until then."

He smiles, thin and bitter in memory. "It did not pass. We had an affair," he continues. "It was ridiculous for me to love a mortal. I did not tell him my secret, but he knew I was uneasy. We would fight, and call it off, half a dozen times, and then halfway through a furious argument we'd end up in a closet, practically tearing each other's clothes off.

"I finally told him. Not everything; just that I was immortal. I needed him to understand why it was doomed, but Misha was too impetuous and romantic to see reason. Maybe if I had also told him…" Pavel gestures, banishing the thought. "I had to leave for a few months. There were rumors of a great old evil resurfacing in London and I was called to investigate it. While I was gone, Misha picked the lock to my chambers and spent the first month in my library, reading all of the esoteric texts that he found there, including…" Pavel pauses, "… the book that I was still figuring out how to destroy permanently. Then he vanished. Irakli wrote to me in desperation, asking if Misha had come to find me in London. He hadn't gone back home to the Caucasus.

"One spring day he reappears at my door. I can tell immediately that something is wrong. He is too still. Misha was never still. Always in motion, foot tapping to a beat only he could hear… but there he is, completely still. Not breathing. And he says, *Pavel, I have solved our problem.*

"He unbuttoned his shirt to show me the scar. I'm afraid the horror, the sheer physical revulsion at what he had done showed on my face. Because while I revealed to him more than I have to any mortal, I never told him that my purpose on this earth was to kill things like that which he had become. Perhaps…" Pavel shakes his head. "We argued. Terrible things were said by both of us. I regret my words, bitterly. But I said them.

"He returned to his regiment and I to my cloisters. I burned the book that evening in a fit of fury; his former abuser died mysteriously a few days later. I think we might have come back to each other, in time, but just as that door opened, everything fell apart. There was the war, and the revolution… our monastery was burned; Irakli was killed. Misha abandoned his regiment and fled back to Georgia, to fight for its independence. Which they won, and lost, and then fought for again in 1924. They lost again. Misha, his entire family, and over ten thousand others were executed after their uprising was put down by the Soviets.

Shot and thrown into mass graves on the orders of Lavrenty Beria and Joseph Stalin who were both, by the way, Georgian. As far as history is concerned, that was the last of him."

Pavel opens his eyes then, and they shimmer with emotion in the dim light of the room as he looks directly at Evie. "Of course, you and I both know that shooting an incubus does nothing but make it angry.

"I believe he spent the next few years tracking down those directly responsible for the massacres in Georgia and exacting his own retribution. An incubus can give pleasure, but it can also give the opposite. Kisses like daggers in the night. Bodies dead from no visible wound, their faces rictuses of pain and terror. We received reports... cries for help. Which I ignored.

"And then I lost track of him. He changed his identity a couple of times, burying his very identifiably Georgian name with his family. There were rumors of him during the next war, first in Berlin, and then back in Russia. But every lead I tried to chase down disappeared through my fingers like so much smoke. I was worried about him. The wars and the August Uprising were... dark times for him. It's very easy for that sort of power to change someone, turn them cruel. It has been my nightmare for a hundred years that someday he would surface again, twisted and foul, and I, knowing that I made him thus, would have to kill him."

Those green eyes flecked with gold are intense enough to freeze Evie like a rabbit in the hunter's crosshairs. "The man you describe to me, Evie... he has changed so little. Maybe a little wiser. That is all. I can't tell you how relieved I am that he is still himself."

"If you all promise not to kill him, I know where he'll be tomorrow night," Evie breathes.

"And why do you think telling us all this helps him?" the Cardinal asks.

"I want him to stop having to be afraid," Evie says, the words out of her mouth before she can stop them. "And I don't think this is over."

Off the Cardinal's questioning glance, Evie continues. She explains the strange death of Eric Overstreet; the disappearance of the bound girl on the bed. The fact that Selene Overstreet hadn't cancelled her date with Misha. And, finally, she explains her accidental betrayal of Misha's trust.

"The demon has to be half a continent away at least by now," says George. "Why would he stay? A very public murder, his identity and location blown on the internet…"

"Because he's not finished here," Pavel says, quietly.

"I don't think he killed Eric Overstreet, either," Evie says. "The Overstreets had the book for several months. They practiced the ritual. If you track where they've been, and John Doe murders with missing internal organs, it's either the world's biggest coincidence or, as Misha said, someone's already read to the end."

"The wife," says the Cardinal.

"Yeah," Evie says. "Eric had what he wanted: a pretty, younger girlfriend, and a plot to cheat Selene out of her share of their company in the divorce. He didn't need this."

"Do you think Misha's in danger?" Pavel asks.

"I think Misha is careless with himself," Evie says. "And Selene Overstreet is very rich and very powerful."

The Cardinal nods. "Leave us, Miss Cross, and wait in the foyer. We must confer."

Evie goes back out into the entryway. They close heavy, carved-wood double doors behind her, cutting off the sitting room and its conversation from her.

She paces, at first, flinching at the muffled, indistinct sound of raised voices from the other room. Then she gives up and perches on a plain wooden hall chair next to an ornate lamp whose base, of all things, is a ceramic flock of parrots. Daniela comes in soon after, asking if she wants coffee.

Evie realizes then that she never had breakfast, so she nods, and soon a tiny cup of espresso is brought to her. It's somehow exactly what she needs, its bitter warmth spreading through her stomach like the first faint whispers of hope she's had all day.

That hope gains butterfly wings when Pavel steps out through the sitting-room doors. Evie holds her breath, waiting for his verdict.

"He'll run, won't he, if he's confronted by the four of us?" Pavel asks, crossing his arms and leaning against the door frame.

"Yes," Evie says.

"What if it's just me?" he says, his voice going quieter.

"Maybe," she replies. "He blames himself, you know."

Pavel looks down, then. "Of course he does. Can you find him? Tell him I want to see him?"

"I can try," Evie says. Then a smile spreads over her face. "How hard can it be? It's Misha; he doesn't understand the concept of slumming it."

Pavel laughs then, and Evie can see in him the ghost of a younger man, one who was once very much in love. "No. He really doesn't." He fishes out his phone. "Tell him... tell him I'm sorry, and I miss him. I don't forgive him because there was nothing to forgive."

"Okay," Evie says. "Can I take a picture of you?" At Pavel's sharp intake of breath, she adds, "Because he might not believe me." Then her brow furrows. "Hey, wait. You breathe."

"There's more than one kind of immortal," Pavel says.

"But you all hate being photographed."

Pavel nods, a short, unhappy jerk of his head. "But for this, I'll allow it."

Evie snaps a quick selfie of her and Pavel. It's awful; she looks like a half-dead chipmunk with four chins and she got a particularly unflattering angle on him too, but she's absolutely sure Pavel would not last through the usual *ten selfie attempts for one keeper* ratio of modern life.

And then before she knows it she's back out in the midday sunlight, with Pavel's phone number and a promise.

She calls up a car service and starts googling listings of luxury hotels in Palo Alto.

*　　*　　*

SHE STRIKES OUT at the Four Seasons. At the Ritz-Carlton, there are a couple of cars in the parking lot that are flashy enough for Misha (she assumes he's ditched the yellow sports car), but her carefully constructed sob story to the hotel manager about Misha being her drug-addicted best friend who is an overdose risk brings up nothing.

By then, both the sun and her bank balance are getting low, so she requests a rideshare on her car service app to go to the next hotel, a boutique/design place that's about a half-mile walk from a motel where she can afford to stay for the night if she doesn't find Misha. She prays to whoever up there might be listening and well disposed to her that Misha hasn't discovered Airbnb.

The hotel doorman calls her name, shaking her out of her thoughts, and lets her know her car has arrived. It's a black SUV with two people already in it other than the driver. They're all white men.

Something about it makes her uncomfortable.

Evie breathes in shakily, and contemplates just telling the driver she's changed her mind, paying whatever penalty fee and getting another car.

But she's got less than $100 left in her account and very little time.

"Miss Cross?" the driver says, with a friendly smile. "Going to the Rosewood?"

The passenger in the front seat checks the time on his phone and sighs ostentatiously, giving Evie an unimpressed look.

It's such a normal gesture that it quells the needling paranoia at the base of her neck. She crosses her fingers, slips her handbag strap more firmly over her shoulder, and gets in the car.

She's in the back seat, on the passenger side. The man next to her is skinny, nervous, and keeps glancing over at her out of the corner of his eye as they pull back onto the freeway. She doesn't feel like making conversation, so she deliberately turns away from him and stares out the window, pretending deep interest in some of the blandest vistas Northern California has to offer.

Which is how she notices they blow straight past the Sand Hill Road exit and get off onto 84 instead.

"Um," she says. "I think we just passed my stop?"

The driver glances back at her in the rear view mirror and indicates the impatient guy staring at his cellphone in the front passenger seat. "Don't worry, Miss, we just have to make one other stop before yours."

Evie sighs and sinks back into her seat. The sun's already going down, the sky fading to pink and orange at the horizon, and deepening into cobalt above them. If she does have to walk half a mile to the motel, she sure as hell would have preferred to do it in daylight.

And then Evie starts recognizing the neighborhood.

Her unease grows into panic as they pull down the quiet Atherton street of walled mansions, so different in daylight. She'd almost say it looks friendlier now, but she knows she has no friends here.

Evie lunges for the car door as the iron gates of the Overstreet mansion swing open to admit them. All she manages to do is break a nail against the door handle. The car doors are locked tight, and so are the windows.

Then she feels a blunt piece of metal pressing into her side, below her ribs. She looks down, slowly, carefully.

It's a gun.

"Miss Overstreet wants a word with you, Evie Cross," smiles the driver.

"How," Evie breathes.

The guy in the front passenger seat snorts as he looks up from his own phone. He flashes its screen at her as they pull up to the mansion's front door, showing her the map that has tracked her every movement since Friday night. "Don't carry a StarTech phone, if you don't want the Overstreets to know your business."

CHAPTER FOURTEEN

THE BLINDS ARE drawn. Evie hadn't even realized the mansion had blinds, but now the vast expanses of glass are rendered sightless, transforming the house from a fishbowl into an oubliette. The broken statues of yesterday's gods in the huge atrium look up at her with something close to kinship in their blank stone eyes as she's frogmarched up the stairs: *we became inconvenient, too.*

Evie is taken to a large, bare room on the third floor, which looks like it was once used for nothing but yoga. With the blinds up, it must have a magnificent view. There's a small dresser in the corner, with a fancy, fat candle burning in a glass jar, but the scent it emits in no way covers up the sharp odor of piss and shit coming from the figure tied to one of the two chairs. A pale curtain of hair covers the figure's face, and Evie thinks at first the ropes binding her are soaked through with blood, but then she realizes they're just an incongruous dark red color. And then the girl looks up, and Evie sucks in a shocked breath as she recognizes first the ball gag, and, second, the face.

The bound girl from Friday night is alive. Even if it looks like she's been tied to that chair since the party.

The other chair is full of Selene Overstreet, casually elegant in a honey-colored cashmere jumpsuit.

"It was always you," Evie says.

Selene rises. She's wearing little gold ballet flats, and they scuff softly across the wooden floor as she walks around behind the bound, shaking form of Eric Overstreet's lover. The girl flinches away, as best she can within her ties, as Selene's fingers briefly caress the back of her head. "Yes," Selene smiles. "I'm afraid it always was. But you and your... *friend*, you were instrumental in my final decision to do this. I hope you realize that."

The two men holding Evie's upper arms—the original passengers from the fake Uber—shove her into the chair that Selene has vacated, while Selene slinks towards the dresser in the corner.

She returns with a coiled length of sky-blue rope. "So ironic that Eric, in order to get rid of me, hired the very proof of concept of what I was thinking of becoming." Evie can feel the smugness radiating from Selene as the men yank her arms behind the chair. The rope, softer than she expected, tightens around her wrists a moment later. "He was magnificent; better than I could have expected. Won't he be surprised when he sees me tomorrow night."

Evie stiffens, struggling against her captors. One of the men backhands her across the temple, casually, violence as easy as breathing. Her head snaps to the side and, once the pain and dizziness recede, she feels a warm trickle of blood at her hairline. "You're doing this tonight?" Evie says.

"Mm," Selene hums. "And you and Eric's little slut from PR will be my hostess gifts. Can't meet the Devil empty-handed."

"You're not going to end up like Misha," Evie hisses.

"No, I'm going to end up much better than your friend. I have more souls," Selene says, her mouth tight and smug.

The rope winds around Evie's waist and chest, and one of the men squats down to tie her ankles. She suppresses the urge to kick him in the face, knowing it would only be an invitation for him to beat her up.

"I mean, it won't make you beautiful," Evie says. "And, uh, I only see two souls here. Jury's still out on whether you actually have one."

The smack comes out of nowhere, Selene's hand stinging across her cheek. "You're as bad as the rest of them," Selene seethes. "Assuming I'm stupid, because I married a rich man.

That I'm somehow not a person who can exist independently of her husband." Selene's fingers tighten around Evie's jaw and tilt her head up. "Misha may have burned the book, but I'd already memorized it. I have a photographic memory. A PhD in applied psychology and computer science." Her smile widens. One of her front canines is slightly crooked, stained along the gum line. It clashes with the rose-gold shine of her lipstick. "And I have fifty million souls on the servers in the basement."

"What?" Evie says. Misha had alluded to the need to bring souls to the bargain, as well as your own heart, but she hadn't asked, so delicate was the task of getting Misha to speak about his past at all.

"Oh, so you *haven't* read the book," Selene purrs, walking away.

"Fifty... million?!" Evie says.

Selene flicks her highlighted hair and glances back as she and the two men head towards the door. "People really should read the terms and conditions of their firmware updates." She mimes prodding at the screen of her phone. "Accept," she chirps. Then she flicks a hand at one of her heavies. "Oh, Rick, gag her, would you?"

Rick, the thin man who had sat in the back seat with her, comes back and pulls a dirty red bandanna out of his pocket. He steps around behind Evie and the big guy from the passenger seat stands in front of her. There's a stain on his tie; it looks like ketchup. Evie tries to turn her neck to see what's happening behind her, but the guy in front of her reaches out and grabs the corners of her jaw, digging in hard with rough fingers. Her mouth drops open in an attempt to lessen the pain, and suddenly there's the taste of filthy cotton in her mouth. She tries to pull away but the force on her jaw is inexorable.

The unmistakable sound of ripping duct tape comes from behind her, then she can taste it, smell it, the strange chemical-plastic stink of the tape, as it's wound around her entire head, keeping the bandanna filling her mouth.

Selene glances at her phone and huffs, impatient. "I have

to get ready," she says, walking towards the door. Her ballet flats make almost no sound on the floor. "You can lock them in here and go have dinner," she adds, with a dismissive wave of her hand to the two heavies. "There are plates for you in the kitchen. I'll need you back at 11pm."

"Yes, Mrs Overstreet," says the thin one.

Selene pauses in the doorway, and smiles. "It's Miss McCracken now, Rick. Didn't you hear? My husband passed away."

They all leave. The thin one, Rick, automatically reaches for the switch next to the doorway as he goes out, flicking the lights off. There's the hollow click of the door closing, a second click as it's locked. And then there's nothing but the dim greyness of the approaching dusk filtered through the blinds, and the ragged breathing of the girl in the ball gag.

They took Evie's phone, of course. Not that Evie could have done anything on it without Selene knowing, she realizes now.

That sends a spike of sheer terror down through her guts, as she thinks about everyone she called since the party. Abigail. Claudia. Her parents. Would Selene go after them? Were they, in fact, loose ends she'd need to tie up, permanently?

Evie wriggles in her chair, testing the limits of the ropes that bind her. From her time at the strip club, she knows they're shibari ropes, made for BDSM. Made to comfortably restrain people for a long time, and almost impossible to break free from.

The ropes don't give, but her chair creaks.

Evie begins to wonder how soundproof the room is. If this is where Eric Overstreet kept his bondage ropes... she curses herself that she was too distracted to look up when she was hauled into the room. If there are hooks or rings on the ceiling, she'd be willing to wager that the room was built to conceal the sounds of Eric's sex life from his wife, and from the servants.

Evie's also smart enough to know that, even if she does manage to untie herself, there's nowhere for her to go. Windows in real life don't break nearly as easily as they do in the movies, and she's three stories up—though, she thinks with a morbid hilarity, she will have plenty of rope. The incongruousness makes her smile, despite the sick pressure of the wadded-up bandanna in her mouth.

She needs help.

But there's no cavalry she can call. The only phone numbers she knows from memory are Claudia's and her parents'. The plan had been for her to find Misha, not to confront Selene. Pavel and his team wouldn't be looking for her here, if they're surveilling the mansion at all yet. There was nobody watching over Evie any more.

Watching...

Evie gasps, immediately choking on the fetid stink of duct tape. Suddenly, vividly, she remembers a conversation from the party on Friday night, one that had seemed trivial at the time.

And she knows exactly where Misha is.

He's with Andy, bleached-hair Andy with his acid-washed drop-crotch skinny jeans and his Fluttershy T-shirt. Andy whose bedroom looks right onto the Overstreets'.

Andy who just about swallowed his own tongue when Misha flirted with him.

It would be so easy. All Misha would have to do is track Andy to a bar or coffee shop, and smile at him. *Hey, don't I remember you from the Overstreets' party? Yeah, wasn't that a crazy night...*

Evie shakes her head. Part of her immediately dismisses the image of Misha and Andy as ridiculous, a complete stretch, the conjecture of her desperate mind. But the greater part of her is so sure, because in her heart, she knows Misha isn't done here.

If he is done, she's dead. It's that simple.

And she's not ready to give up yet. She prays that he isn't, either.

She begins to rock the chair back and forth. It's wooden, and older, with some give in its joints. Evie can feel more than she can see the girl in the ball gag staring at her. But the rationality of daylight has long gone away, leaving only the night, and the wild thoughts that take root in the darkness.

They've bound her legs to the chair legs, her arms and chest to the chair back. One problem at a time.

Evie kicks out hard, once, twice, three times, and enjoys a brief moment of victory as the front legs crack off their joints, before gravity exerts its inevitable due and she crashes backwards. There's a sharp pain as her head hits the floor and the darkness vignettes around her.

She blinks awake.

She's on her back.

Her legs are free.

It's awkward, but after flopping around Evie manages to struggle to her feet, hunched over and shouldering the chair she is bound to like a turtle shell. She staggers over towards the dresser in the corner and turns around, trying to get the ropes binding her arms and chest over the small flame of the scented candle. But the sheer awkwardness of her position means she can't get the ropes close enough to the flickering light deep inside the little glass jar.

The candle's burned down too far.

Evie groans around the gag and backs up to the dresser, reaching out for the candle jar. Her fingers feel ungainly, low on circulation. Even though the room is dark, she closes her eyes, to help her concentration. She leans a little further back. Her fingertips brush the jar's warm surface.

She mumbles something distinctly unladylike and pushes herself a little bit more. If she can just grab the jar—

—her clumsy fingers knock it over.

A faint odor of smoke sours the air and this time, Evie shouts her curses. The warm, small light of the candle flickers, and gutters out as the jar clacks against the top of the dresser before rolling off it, onto the ground.

The tears come fast, tears of exhaustion and frustration and self-hatred. Evie keens through the gag, the ugly sorrow of someone who knows she has nobody to blame but herself for the situation she's in.

She leans against the dresser, with no earthly idea what to do next. Her mind keeps spinning, from the fear and the adrenalin, but every path it heads down is a dead end.

She glares down at the candle, its glass jar glinting dimly in the darkness, and resists the urge to punt it across the room. That's just childish.

Then it comes to her so fast she wants to bang her head against the wall for her own stupidity. There's a candle. There must be something to light it with.

Evie wiggles down, her thighs complaining about the stress, and fumbles about behind herself for the top drawer of the dresser. She yanks it open and waddles forwards, pulling the drawer out enough so all its contents tumble towards the front with an assortment of clacks and clunks.

Her fingers touch more jars first—spare candles, waiting for their turn. Evie imagines the housekeeper who has to check on this room every morning, sweep it and clean it and light a new scented candle, and wonders where she is, if she's safe. If she's already vanished, another victim of Selene Overstreet's "practice".

She bends back and shoves her hands further in the drawer and feels around, throwing the extra candles out on the ground. At first, there's nothing but the wooden bottom of the dresser against her fingers.

But, finally, Evie's knuckles brush the small, rectangular form of a disposable lighter.

She grabs it, and lights it. The heat from the lighter's metal top begins to burn into her fingers almost immediately. The pain becomes sharp, and her fingers twitch, longing to drop the lighter, end the agony. But she bites down on the gag in her mouth and shoves the top of the lighter up until it's as close as possible to the ropes binding her to the chair. She can't even tell if the lighter is still lit, just that the heat on her fingers and wrists is burning her alive and maybe, maybe there's enough flame to make the ropes catch.

It's not the rapid escape to freedom she'd pictured in her head. It's long minutes of trying to ignore the blistering agony in her fingers, trying to stop her hands from shaking and breathing long breaths around the pain.

Evie begins to lose hope. For all she knows, she's holding a guttering lighter and doing nothing more than burning herself, like a particularly inept Joan of Arc. She'd been so sure she could get out of this, somehow. That this wasn't the end.

It can't be the end. She still hasn't made things right with Misha. She'd befriended a miracle, once, and by god, she will prove herself worthy of his friendship. She will fix this.

... Somehow.

Evie sucks in a breath around the disgusting rag in her mouth as the lighter becomes almost hotter than she can stand.

Then there's a smell like burnt hair, and the ropes around her chest creak and give, just a little.

Evie fumbles the lighter and nearly drops it. She slowly, carefully works it back into position again and tries to relight the flame. Flick, press. Flick, press. Nothing.

Then, finally, it catches. The heat blossoms forth again, searing the already raw skin of her fingers. The pain fades into irrelevance as she clutches her little plastic salvation as hard as she can, as each tiny pop signals another strand of rope burning away. It still takes another five minutes to get to the point where, with a creak and a sigh, the ropes finally slacken. She lets the lighter go, listening to it clatter onto the floor as she waits for the tingling pain in her fingers to die down.

Evie quickly frees her hands and the broken chair drops away from her onto the ground. She yanks the tape and gag from her mouth, then winces as she grabs her hair in one hand and rips the tape from there, too.

Then Evie walks up behind the girl in the ball gag. She squats down next to her and speaks quietly in her ear. "I'm sorry I didn't do this on Friday night," she says, unbuckling the gag. "I'm sorry I left you there. Things got... a little crazy."

The gag comes off easily and the girl doesn't say anything, just moves her jaw around a little, then closes her mouth and swallows. Her breath stinks.

Evie gets busy untying the ropes. They come easily, and the girl slumps down, sliding off the chair onto the ground. She lies on her side, just... breathing. In the darkness, Evie can make out that her eyes are open, but not much else.

"Are you okay?" Evie asks gently. "Can I..."

"I, I'm sorry," the girl whispers.

"What?"

The girl curls up and speaks so softly, Evie can barely hear it over the distant hum of the house's climate control system. "I... soiled myself."

Evie can't think of anything to say in response, so after a long moment she just strokes the girl's shoulder, as if she were a frightened animal. "It's okay," Evie mumbles. "It's okay, you didn't mean to, you wouldn't have..." Then she swallows. Up close, the smell of the girl is awful. "Look," Evie says. "Selene and Eric's bedroom... I have to get in there."

The girl starts shaking her head in terror, a rapid back and forth, almost like she's having a seizure.

Evie switches tack, fast. "No, just me, not you. You, you're free, go wherever you want—"

The girl makes a sound that's half laugh, half despair. She's still shaking uncontrollably.

"I just, I don't have the access card for the bedroom. Is there a code or something? Trust me, getting into that room is the only way I can get help," Evie says, glossing over the unavoidable fact that she might just be completely wrong. That Misha is not even in San Francisco any more.

Evie realizes the girl is muttering something, and leans in closer.

It's numbers. The girl is saying "Five, three, five, four" over and over again.

"Is that the code?" Evie says, as quietly and soothingly as she can.

The girl nods. "Ch-chinese, it's, it's a joke," she says. "Sounds like the words for *not alive, not dead*."

Evie snorts. "At this point I can't even tell whose joke that is," she says. "Selene's, or Eric's."

"Eric," the girl whispers.

"Are you going to be okay?" Evie asks. "If I go? Can you get out?"

The girl just lies there.

Something twists in Evie's guts at leaving her, but she knows that trying to bring her along is a non-starter: the girl looks like she can barely walk, and Evie needs to move fast. Plus, she thinks selfishly, if the girl does try to flee, it might cause enough distraction that Evie can get to the bedroom and stay there unnoticed for long enough that Misha, if he's watching, can see her.

She pats the girl's shoulder one last time, says, "Good luck," and heads to the door.

Which, like nearly all domestic doors, locks from the inside.

Evie unlatches it and cautiously opens it a sliver, squinting against the bright, clinical light of the hallway. She tries to orient herself based on the frantic events on Friday night. Third floor, down the hall, last door on the left.

She waits. There's nobody in the hall. The house is silent, but for the hum of air and electrics.

Evie darts across the hall to the bedroom door. She doesn't give herself time to think about what will happen if Selene is actually in the master suite, but some instinct tells her that Selene isn't the sort of woman to return to the scene of the crime. The marital bed and all its memories are dead to her.

Evie punches in the code and nearly falls to her knees in gratitude and relief as the door unlocks. She slips inside and flicks on the lights.

The room is a scene of devastation, a far cry from the heavy luxury it exuded when Evie was last there a few days ago.

The luxurious four-poster that dominated the space looks like it's had acid poured on it, the center of the mattress charred and melted. Everything is smashed, the Rape of Persephone bedside lamp broken across the floor: a torso here, an arm there.

Evie forces herself to walk towards the blinds, which, like in the rest of the house, are pulled down tight. It gives her time to think about what could happen if Selene ends up with Misha's power, but without his compassion, his strange guilt and gentleness. A woman whose rage was so great that murder wasn't enough, she had to do violence to the very bed she'd shared with her husband. Who had to torture the girl her husband had found comfort in.

Evie remembers the terror she'd felt when Misha had shown her a tiny fragment of his own anger.

She throws the blinds up and prays, for the first time in her life, that a man she loves is in someone else's bedroom.

And she worries if he is, whether it will be enough.

She tosses the place, frantically pulling open drawers and looking in cabinets—it's not like it could get any more wrecked than it is already—and in the en suite bathroom vanity she finds what she's looking for.

She rushes back to the bank of windows next to the bed, the ones from which she can see, past the swimming pool and through a line of eucalyptus trees, the lit window of a faux-château turret bedroom.

And in big, boxy letters, she writes *RITUAL* in Selene's brick-red lipstick.

Evie's halfway through writing *MIDNIGHT* when the clack of the doorknob opening sends ice water through her veins.

When she turns, it's the skinny one, Rick. He doesn't even look angry. He just looks tired, as he points his gun at Evie. "Found the other one," he says into a Bluetooth headpiece, and then he listens for a moment, and nods.

A moment later, the larger guy comes in, too. He's carrying an industrial-strength cable tie as he strides towards Evie. "Look," the guy says, "this can go two ways. I can tie your wrists, or you can fight. If you fight, I break your nose and tie your wrists anyway."

Evie drops the lipstick and extends her wrists in front of her. They're zip-tied together, tight enough for the plastic to dig into her skin, and then the guy grabs her by the back of the neck and propels her towards the door.

"She says it's time to start," Rick mutters as Evie is shoved past him, and the other guy grunts in response. They guide her to a small staircase, considerably less grand than the main one, that leads up one flight to a doorway. She's shoved up the steps and through the door, which clicks shut ominously behind her at the same time as the soft night breeze tugs at her thin clothes.

Once Evie regains her balance she finds she is on top of the mansion, on the largest of its several flat roofs.

Evie has a New Yorker's appreciation for roofs, and this one, like everything the Overstreets owned, is modern, objectively beautiful, and utterly soulless. Fancy lowlights illuminate a wooden deck, with raised benches and carefully manicured conifers framing the centerpiece: a Japanese rock garden, complete with large stepping-stones so one could admire its immaculately raked pebbles from up close without destroying their symmetry. In the center is a square stone dais, at one end of which sits the decapitated stone head of a crowned Buddha, mounted on a stick.

At the other end of it stands Selene Overstreet, in bare feet and a simple, loose black silk jumpsuit, cut low in front. She holds a silver dagger in one hand, its strange, wavy blade gleaming in the moonlight as it lies across her other palm.

Selene smiles as she sees them, fingering the blade as if unable to wait for its bite, then nods sharply at Rick.

He shoves Evie off the edge of the deck, onto the perfect rock waves of the Japanese garden. Without her hands to catch her fall, she lands awkwardly, the pebbles biting into her knees as her impact scatters them. Before she can recover, hands grab her ankles and there's the plastic hiss of another cable tie being tightened around them.

Nearby, in the eddy of pebbles on the other side of the flagstone path, she notices a pool of shadow rocking and whimpering. It's the girl. She hadn't gotten very far, if she had left the room at all.

Armed men stand on the deck, one at each of the four corners of the garden. Evie recognizes the three from her car, and another, who'd been one of the doormen at the party three nights and a lifetime ago.

And, as a distant church bell tolls the midnight hour, Selene opens her mouth and begins to chant.

*   *   *

THE WORDS COME out of Selene's mouth low and fast. Evie can't understand them, or even tell what language they're in. Latin, maybe, Aramaic or Greek or Hebrew or another ancient language. Or perhaps it's just plain English; maybe the book and its ritual appear to readers in their own language. The path to hell, as they say, is as smooth and easy as the Devil can make it.

Evie is suddenly aware that she's cold, whereas before it had seemed temperate up on the roof, and that clouds had crept silently across the sky, hiding the faces of the stars. There would be no celestial witnesses tonight.

Selene is chanting louder now, the words still flowing into each other like mercury, heavy and poisonous, as the shadows flourish in the moon's absence.

She stops, with a sharp, barked fricative, and her eyes search the roof garden. The knife gleams dully in her hand. "Show yourself," she commands. The sudden English crashes loud against the hard surfaces of the rocks, the only sound for miles.

Then Selene's eyes fix on a point behind Evie.

Evie turns, as best she can, and... there's nothing there. No, that's not right.

There is *a nothingness* there.

It's as if part of the sky has been removed, leaving an utter and complete void, in the shape of a man.

The air feels ionized, pregnant with a furious storm. But there's no lightning, nothing flashy, just a figure from which no light emerges or reflects. Wisps of darkness waft off its body, poisoning the air around it to a dull, warped grey. Longer tendrils steam off its head, like antlers, clawing at the shadowed sky.

Selene is staring right at it, her eyes bright with the sort of madness that the nearness of desire brings.

"I have fifty million souls in my power," Selene says, her voice soft now, and sugary, the voice of a pretty girl used to asking for favors, used to getting them. Then she indicates Evie and the girl with a sweep of that strange, wavy knife. "And the living blood of these two to spill for you, plus my own heart. Will you accept my sacrifice?"

Evie glances around. Selene's four goons are staring down at the rocks below their feet, obeying orders, just letting this evil happen.

And then the Devil, this monster of negation, nods. Its antlers thicken and writhe, as if it is drinking the air in triumph.

Selene marches slowly towards this manifestation of evil, chin up, face radiant, in the manner of a bride savoring every step she takes down the aisle to her beloved.

But then she steps off the path, her bare feet crunching bright among the dull grey pebbles of the garden. She's walking towards the girl, her knife raised, hand outstretched.

The girl shrinks away, whimpering in terror.

Selene grabs her neck and forces her backwards onto her heels. Evie can barely make out Selene's face for the shadows, but she swears the woman's mouth twists into a smile as the knife comes down in a hard stab into the flesh of the girl's stomach, over her hip.

The girl cries out then, sharp in the night, but the cry breaks off into great ragged gasps of pain as Selene yanks the knife across the girl's stomach, slicing it open.

The blood, when it comes, is dark, like the darkness of the thing that watches them all with something akin to amusement. The stench of hot iron fills the air, and the girl's cries have tailed off to a distant, high whimper, the terror of a rabbit.

When Selene lets go of the girl's neck, she crumples to the side, folding over the terrible wound in her stomach. Evie keeps staring at the girl, even as Selene's feet kick a path through the pebbles towards her, even as she knows that she's next.

She sees the wet tubes of the girl's intestines slip out of the gash in her stomach, heavy and embarrassed. She watches the pebbles around the girl darken as the pool of her lifeblood expands, surrounding her in shadow.

The knife leaves a trail of dark droplets in its wake.

And still Misha has not come.

Evie shuts her eyes as Selene's feet scuff softly over the flagstones that separate her side of the garden from the dying girl's. She's going to die because she wanted too much. Love and independence and to be recognized as good at something, really good. She thinks of all the girls who will be alive tomorrow, who let their day jobs become jobs, who gave up their dreams and settled, and she's near tears all of a sudden, full of regret for a life that seems now, as it approaches its end, to be nothing but the blind, blundering efforts of a fool.

When she departs the earth, Evie will leave nothing behind. The world will be no different for her having lived in it. Sad parents, a Facebook memorial page, that's all. She closes her eyes. How she'd wasted it all.

Selene's hand is small and dry and strong on the back of her neck, and strangely cool. She sinks her manicured nails into Evie's hair and yanks her back onto her heels.

"You can still stop this, you know," Evie whispers.

"No I can't," Selene says, and brings the knife down.

The pain is unbelievable, ice-cold and dizzying in its vastness. A roaring fills her ears and she thinks dully, *oh, this is what Death sounds like, coming for me*, but then Selene flinches, stilling the knife buried in Evie's guts, and Evie realizes that Selene hears it too.

Selene pulls the knife out, the full cut unfinished, and wipes the blade against the leg of her jumpsuit.

As Evie tries to fight against the darkness closing in on her, she hears the roaring sound change frequency, and grow louder. And she knows what it is.

It's a sports car.

It's not her own death she hears howling up the road and crashing through the gate.

It's Selene's.

But as the pain pulls Evie into the welcoming, blissful embrace of unconsciousness, as Selene begins to cut out her own heart, all Evie can think is: *he's too late.*

CHAPTER FIFTEEN

Evie is jolted back awake when the edge of her forehead smacks against the cold pebbles. Everything is dark and blurry, filtered through the pain of the four-inch-long gash in her stomach. Someone, somewhere, is screaming, and she's not sure if it's her. She can taste her own blood in her mouth, coming up her throat. More blood trickles between the pebbles in front of her, gradually covering them, the slow, inexorable progress of her demise.

There's a palpable feeling of rage in the air. The four guards at the corners of the garden are nervous. Their hands twitch towards weapons in shoulder holsters and their eyes never leave the access door to the roof. The closest one pulls out his pistol and walks towards it, cautiously, gun raised and ready to fire at whatever might come through.

And meanwhile, Selene reaches into the jagged wound in her own chest and pulls out her heart. It pulses dully in her hand, glistening in the night.

Evie dimly wonders just how many horse tranquillizers this woman has taken, to be able to stay so calm. She feels oddly tranquil now, too. The pain is distant, something happening to another Evie, far away. It's cold, and she's tired, and she'll sleep soon.

The Nothing, the man-shaped hole in reality, flows towards Selene to consume her heart. It opens its mouth, and there's a sound like the death rattle of a dying world, of a million desperate souls crying in torment. Selene's face blossoms into a smile of ecstasy and—

—the access door flies off its hinges.

There's the rapid staccato clap of gunfire and a flurry of motion as the guard by the door goes down, his gun twisted out of his hands and used to drop the other three guards. Then silence, and Evie smiles as she glimpses a blur of pale skin and dark hair rushing with a panther's deadly grace towards Selene.

Misha is here.

It's too late for her, she knows it is, and when she tries to take her next breath she begins to choke on her own blood. It bubbles up into her mouth, hot and thick.

She lives long enough to see Misha crash into Selene, his eyes black with rage, and rip her whole arm off. "No sacrifice," he growls. "No deal." He takes Selene's heart and tears it to pieces with his bare hands.

Her eyesight begins to fade as Selene sinks to the ground, clutching at the blood pulsing from the ragged mess of her shoulder, her face a rictus of terror and fury. When Misha reaches down to snap Selene's neck, it is merely a dim tournament of shadows, and then it is nothing at all.

She lives long enough to hear the Devil laugh.

And then death comes for Evie Cross.

EVIE WAKES UP to being hugged to Misha's chest. She feels odd. Light. All her pain has stopped. Even the little everyday aches of inconvenience that she has learned to ignore are suddenly, startlingly noticeable by their absence. The cable ties binding her wrists and ankles are gone, and even though they'd bitten into her flesh, there's no remaining discomfort. She wonders if she's a ghost now. She wonders if ghosts exist.

She can feel the stickiness of the drying blood in the corner of her mouth, the way it catches against Misha's shirt. The heat of him, and the solid muscle.

She glances up. Misha isn't looking at her, for all he's clutching her to him like he's the only thing keeping her anchored to this life. His eyes are black, and he's shouting at the Devil, "Take it back! Take it back, I don't want it!"

The Devil reaches out and caresses Misha's head, like a proud father would. Misha jerks away hard, his lip curling into a snarl. He's rewarded by a loud peal of laughter from the Devil, like the tolling of rusty bells, and then, in a change of pressure so pronounced it makes Evie's ears pop, reality rushes back in like a tide to fill the hole in the world that the Devil made.

The Nothingness vanishes. Evie and Misha are left, the only living things on the roof.

Misha presses his face into her hair and rocks them both gently, still holding her for all he's worth. "I'm sorry," he says into the crook of her neck, "I'm so sorry, Evie, please forgive me—"

Evie can't do anything but blink at him. She has at once nothing to say and a thousand things to say: *I'm sorry*, and *you came back*, and *I don't understand why I'm alive again*. And if she is alive, if this isn't the last fevered spiral of her dying mind, should her first words be something lucky? Her grandma always said *rabbit, rabbit* on the turning of the new year; if that was first out of her lips, would it change the poor fortunes of her life?

She looks at Misha to figure out what to do next and he's hiding his face from her, shame coloring his perfect cheeks. His eyes are the solid black of the Devil, and he's vibrating with energy, shaking apart with it, a thousand times worse than in the aftermath of the book-burning. "Misha, look at me," she says, putting her thumb on the dimple in his chin, and turning his face to meet hers. "Misha... Shit. Come on. You have to hold it together. Everything's going to be okay, just try to calm down."

"No, it's not," Misha says, his voice shaking. "Everything's gone wrong. It's all wrong, Evie, I've fucked up so bad, but I just... I couldn't let you die. So I brought you back. And now..." He shivers again, jaw tight with furious despair.

And Evie's just opening her mouth to ask him what exactly he means by *brought her back* when her words are drowned out by the dull thump of feet running up the stairs.

Misha laces one hand into Evie's and uses that to push her behind him as four black and scarlet silhouettes step out onto the roof. Each one is armed with a shotgun, and a short, roman-style sword. Somehow Evie knows: the shotgun to slow the incubus down; the sword to chop off its head.

"Come no closer," Misha commands, and his voice comes out strange, chased by its own echo, as if there are two voices inside him. Evie gasps as she notices that from Misha's raised arm, wispy tendrils of darkness are emerging like smoke, as if he's absorbed so much of the Devil's energy that it's trying to get out of him by any means possible.

Her mind reels. Misha interrupted the ceremony mid-sacrifice and killed Selene. Evie assumed that meant the power Selene sought was never given, but after another glance at Misha she wonders if it had been given after all, just not to the person who had asked for it. Perhaps it was grabbed, desperately, by someone who needed to save a life.

Perhaps that is why the Devil laughed.

The smallest silhouette steps forwards, raising his shotgun. "Let the human girl go, monster." Evie recognizes the voice: George, of course. The hardliner.

Evie feels more than she sees the moment Misha's body tenses, ready to attack. "I'm not his prisoner! Please, get back," she calls out. "Don't push him." Her voice cracks. "Please."

Nobody moves. There's no sound but the crickets in the grass far below, and the rustle of the priests' robes in the night wind.

"You are the incubus Misha Meserov, born Mikheil Mkheidze in 1892," comes the rich bass voice of the Shadow Cardinal. "We have questions for you. At this time, we intend you no harm."

Misha's eyes burn with a cold, savage fury. Fine tremors run through the tense muscles of his back and his hand grips Evie's harder than should be comfortable. He indicates George's shotgun, which is still aimed directly at Misha's chest. "And here I thought we were going to dance," he says through gritted teeth.

Off to the right, Kevin snorts into his sleeve, hiding a laugh.

George raises the gun, to point it at Misha's head. "It's still a possibility, abomination."

Cardinal Adonis flicks a hand at George, motioning for him to lower the gun. Pavel hasn't moved, hasn't spoken. He's staying in the darkness by the doorway, his face hidden in shadow, but Evie can feel his eyes on them. Well, not on her. He looks only at Misha.

Misha snarls. "That's more like it. You've never *just talked* to one of us in your lives. There's no talking. Only killing."

"And you doubt us?" the Shadow Cardinal replies, his voice rigorously calm. "When you yourself know, in the black space where your heart used to be, that your kind should not live." He gestures at the dead bodies littered around Misha: the guards; the girl. Selene. "When you murder them yourself without a shred of feeling."

Misha laughs then, a cracked and painful sound. "Without feeling," he rasps. "That's rich." He shakes his head. "You have no idea what I feel. How *much* I feel. You know what it's like to be me?" His voice rises, loud across the hard surfaces of the roof, and Evie shivers. Everything's falling apart and she has no idea how to stop it.

"*This* is what I feel," Misha roars, and the darkness flows out of him, tendrils becoming torrents. Evie is knocked aside by the force of it, letting go of Misha's hand. It's like being hit by a riptide of self-hatred and misery, and she can barely breathe from the weight of it dragging her under, fast and deadly.

George is firing, the cough of his shotgun the only sound, and presumably the shot is hitting Misha but he doesn't even flinch, it's like throwing pebbles at a lion. The gun runs out of shells, and George drops it, sagging as the despair gets to him, too. Evie can't explain it. It's as if that little voice that whispers at the corners of her mind *you're no good, you're just a faker, just trash* is shouting now, drowning everything else, all rational thought beyond *end it, kill yourself, do the world a favor.*

She watches as George clutches his head, crumpling into sobs. As the Shadow Cardinal sees something none of them can, over their heads, his gaze a thousand miles away, tears coursing down his dark cheeks. As Kevin hugs himself, rocking back and forth at the nightmares behind his eyes.

"Stop it, Misha, you're killing them!" Evie yells.

"I'm not taking anything," Misha growls. His eyes are still solid black. "I'm just helping them to get to know their prey."

Evie looks over at their last hope: Pavel. Of all of them, he knows Misha best, yet he has stayed silent this whole time. Perhaps he thought that getting involved would simply provoke Misha more. Which is fair enough, but at this point things couldn't get much worse.

"Say something!" she yells at him. "Talk to him! Tell him what you told me." She grits her teeth and tries one last time, desperate, fighting against the leaden press of inertia telling her *give up, it's no use, nothing you've ever done was any damn use at all*. But she has a pretty good idea what Pavel's mind is spiraling on right now, with Misha throwing industrial levels of guilt and despair at them. "Tell him what you should have told him then!"

Pavel drops his weapons and steps hesitantly to the edge of the rock garden, where the lights are bright enough to illuminate him.

And Evie has a front-row seat to Misha seeing his old lover's face for the first time in a hundred years.

In other circumstances, it would tear her apart with jealousy. Right now, it might be the only thing that can save them.

The shock of seeing Pavel knocks the fight out of Misha for a moment. Evie can feel it: suddenly the suffocating blanket of despair evaporates, and she can breathe again.

Pavel drops to his knees slowly, breathing Misha's name like a prayer into the night. His face is reverent, and Evie wonders if Pavel had ever truly understood that he still carried a heavy burden of love for Misha, or if the sweet and deadly weight of it had only rushed back into his heart in that moment, when he looked into Misha's eyes again.

"I want to ask your forgiveness," Pavel says, "for all the terrible things I said. I... I've missed you so much, Misha."

Pavel reaches out towards Misha, who is standing still, frozen in shock like a beast of the forest caught unexpectedly in man's light. His hair blows across his face, his black eyes. Evie can see the lost boy in him then, free of his first, difficult loves, but still afraid they were right about him.

"I'm so glad you're alive. You have no idea." Pavel runs two fingers down Misha's cheek, slow and gentle, trying not to spook him. Pavel's eyes are wet, and his face holds the overflow of a century of love. "Somehow… You haven't changed a bit, you know?"

Misha lurches back as if burned.

Pavel immediately puts his hands up, *no harm*, and stutters, "Misha, please, I—"

Misha shakes his head, terror in his dark eyes. "I'm not—" he begins. "I can't—"

And then he vanishes.

THE SILENCE AFTER Misha disappears is total. It's finally broken by the distant sound of sirens, and the clatter and rasp of Kevin picking up his sword and sheathing it.

Pavel is still on his knees, inconsolable, his eyes both distant and, at the same time, burning with singular focus into the empty space where Misha was, as if staring at it could make the air itself throw forth an answer.

"Well, that's new," Kevin says, his attempts at an easy, conversational tone scuppered by the quaver in his voice. "Pavel, can they do that? Because, uh…"

Pavel finally looks away from the spot Misha vacated, and shakes his head. "No. I've never seen it." He looks up then, at Evie, his eyes red with sorrow.

Evie shrugs. "I have no idea what's going on."

"I find that hard to believe," drawls Cardinal Adonis.

"Where is he? The incubus?" George says, whirling around, as if Misha were the Bogeyman, about to jump out of the shadows at him.

"Long gone," Pavel whispers. "Off to the jungles of Borneo, perhaps, to teach the orangutans rude gestures." He rakes a hand through his hair. "Misha is spectacularly good at many things, but he's best by far at running away. We'll not find him, should we comb the entire world looking." His smile of apology for the news he delivers is nothing but pain. Evie reaches out and squeezes Pavel's hand. It's ridiculous, they share nothing, other than an overwhelming fondness for Misha.

"So there's no point in waiting here for him to reappear," the Shadow Cardinal says. He glances off to the right, where red and blue lights flash on the horizon. "Kevin, call the clean-up crew, and go down and claim jurisdiction—"

"—from the cops. Got it," Kevin says. Evie's about to raise all sorts of church and state questions when Kevin hands off his sword and gun to George, and unbuttons his cassock, revealing a black dress shirt beneath.

Kevin flashes a smile at her, and an FBI badge. "This ain't our first rodeo, Evie," he says, then heads down the stairs to meet the police.

"You'll be coming with us, Miss Cross," the Shadow Cardinal says. "We have questions."

"About Misha?" Evie says. "Because I can tell you now, I don't have answers."

The Shadow Cardinal arches an eyebrow. "Also about you. Such as, how you are alive." He points at the dead girl, collapsed in a drying pool of her own blood. Then he points to a matching pool on the other side of the path. "Two trails of blood. Yet only one dead girl." He turns back to Evie. "Where were you wounded? Show me."

"Uh," Evie says.

"Evie, none of us has answers," Pavel says, his voice unbelievably tired and sad. "We only have theories. And we're trying to help."

Evie presses her lips together and lifts her shirt. She doesn't want to see what's there, because she, too, has theories.

There's a jagged pink scar, four inches across, on her stomach.

It looks weeks old, the yellow of fading bruising surrounding it like a halo. "Okay," she breathes, and shoves her shirt back down over the scar.

While she's distracted, straightening her shirt, Pavel lunges forwards, grabbing her shoulder with one hand and pressing two fingers forcefully under her jaw with the other. "What the—" Evie begins, but the hard look in Pavel's eyes softens almost immediately, and he releases her.

"She has a pulse," Pavel says to the Shadow Cardinal. Over the man's whispered *thank god*, he turns to Evie. "Sorry. We had to know."

"No, it's okay," Evie says. "I had my doubts for a minute there, too." She looks at the three priests left on the roof, all of whom are watching her. "What would have happened if I didn't?"

"Please come back to the safehouse with us," Pavel says, changing the subject. "We have people coming to deal with this. They'll handle the bodies, make up a story to tell the relatives."

"Any news getting out of ritual sacrifices is… bad," George adds. "It makes people think there must be something to it."

"They get curious; start looking for books," the Shadow Cardinal sighs. "And we have not yet found a way to make that cursed tome stop reappearing."

Evie nods. She's not even tired, although she wishes she were. It feels wrong not to be tired after this.

She looks back at the blonde girl crumpled over the pebbles of the Japanese garden, spoiling their perfect patterns. "She was innocent," Evie says. "The girl. She had an affair with Eric Overstreet, that's all. Selene tortured her."

The Shadow Cardinal bows his head, acknowledging Evie's comments as he takes her elbow gently in his hand. "I'm sorry for her. But listen to me, Evie Cross. We've done unimaginably well to stop Selene at the cost of only one innocent life. Sometimes we only find them after they've murdered hundreds."

"But you didn't stop Selene," Evie says, withdrawing her arm from the Shadow Cardinal's grip. "Misha did."

Pavel sighs behind them. "Evie, I give you my word. Our

intentions are peaceful." He touches her shoulder, feather-light. "You saw it, didn't you? The Nothingness?"

Evie freezes, and nods, remembering all too clearly a person-shaped, antlered hole in reality, laughing at them.

"Our mission is, and has always been, to stop *that*. To keep it from twisting more monstrosities out of misguided humans," Pavel says. He smiles then, a sad smile born of knowing too well the ways of darkness. "And if you'd seen what we've seen, you'd know why we shoot first."

Evie keeps her mouth shut, thinking of Misha shivering in shame at the things he had done, and of Selene, who reveled in casual cruelty.

"Ours is an ancient order, founded to protect pilgrims and the innocent," says the Shadow Cardinal. "We had hoped to bring the monsters we hunt back to a state of grace, through Christ or the sword."

"It has overwhelmingly been the sword," Pavel adds.

"Quite," replies the Shadow Cardinal. "In this manner, we have failed. And perhaps this is why we exist in a perpetual stalemate, keeping the number of creatures down but never eliminating them, or their source."

"Come on," George snaps. "Name one that we could have left alive."

"This is my point," Cardinal Adonis smiles, his teeth brilliant white in the darkness. "You have to understand how unusual Misha is, and by extension you are, Evie." He holds the roof door for her, gesturing for her to descend. "Your help would be invaluable."

Their small group descends the stairs from the roof and crosses through the house, its cold, silent spaces now more than ever a mausoleum, rather than a home. Outside, the flashing lights of police cars bounce off hard walls and vast windows; Kevin is leaning against one of the cars, chatting animatedly to a knot of cops. One of them laughs. Off to one side, a yellow sports car has left deep gouges in the lawn where it skewed to a stop, its front a heap of twisted metal. The priests' familiar black SUVs are little more than dark shapes, parked in the shadows next to the mansion's shattered gates.

Evie slows, unsure where to go. She's exhausted and wants to throw up, and she's sure the whole universe has come to an end, because how could it not have, except the cops are still over there laughing at Kevin's dumb joke, and a nosy couple are walking their golden retriever slowly past the Overstreets' open gate, and somewhere in the distance a car radio is playing Jay-Z.

"Come with us," Pavel says, gently. "It's late. You can decide what you want to do in the morning."

And she does, because she has nowhere else to go.

Two hours later, they're sitting in the dining room of the house in Telegraph Hill, having demolished a pan of Daniela's lasagne. Kevin is still off handling the clean-up, but he calls in to say that everything's going well. It's the only interruption in the silent room, other than the small, domestic chatter of forks and plates against each other.

Daniela brings a tray of espresso and amaretti and Evie wonders if it would be impolite to just put her head on the table and fall asleep there. She takes one of the little cups, though, and lets the bitter liquid burn down her throat.

She watches Pavel out of the corner of her eye as his hand hesitates over the tray. He grabs a couple amaretti and a coffee, and a smile tugs at his lips as he brings the cup to them.

There's the clank of spoon against china; George is stirring a coffee which must be half sugar by weight. It's followed by a slight clatter as Cardinal Adonis picks up his cup off the saucer. The room is stifling, a blaze roaring in the fireplace, its light dancing over the heavy brocades and dark carved wood.

Or maybe it's just Evie that's too warm. Everybody else seems to be fine.

"So, uh," she starts.

They're not obvious about it, but the three priests shift

slightly, turning their attention to her. The Shadow Cardinal first glances at Daniela, who bows slightly and leaves the room.

"What happens to me now?" Evie says. "Can I just... go?" She almost adds *if I promise not to tell*, but decides against it. It's best they not dig into her shaky history with secrets.

"I find it interesting, Miss Cross, that you open with what *will* happen to you, rather than what *has* happened to you," the Shadow Cardinal says. "Perhaps you tell us what occurred on the roof before we arrived."

Evie sighs, and sets her empty coffee cup down. She had hoped to avoid this conversation, but it's pretty clear Cardinal Adonis had gotten where he was by being the smartest person in the room, in any room. Evasion won't get her anywhere. "I'm not sure I'm ready to talk about the whole dying thing," she breathes.

Cardinal Adonis just looks at her, calmly. And then tilts his head slightly.

She glances over at Pavel, hoping he'll throw her a line. But the blond bastard just shrugs and grins. "I skipped the dying part, if the truth be known."

Evie rolls her eyes at him. She can understand what Misha saw in Pavel, besides his obvious, rugged good looks. She misses Misha furiously in that moment. He'd look completely at home in this room, slouching in an overstuffed chair with his leg slung over one of its arms, a lock of hair falling loose across his face, taking great delight in verbally sparring with the Shadow Cardinal.

"I mean... I died, or I came very close to it," Evie says, her voice quiet. "And then I woke up, and Misha was there, holding me. But I was out for... a couple minutes. I know he did something. I just don't know what it was."

"What happened during the sacrifice?" Pavel says, leaning forwards, his forearms resting on his knees. "Selene's heart... what specifically happened to that?"

Evie barks out a laugh, despite herself. "Misha took it from her and tore it up. He was, uh... pretty brutal about it."

"He tore off her arm," George says. "Brutal is an understatement."

"George, be quiet," Cardinal Adonis says.

"No, George is right," Evie says. "Look, don't fool yourselves about trying to win my loyalty, because it's always going to be with Misha, but he can be absolutely terrifying when he lets go." She shifts in the chair, and pulls her legs up under her. "Misha said *no deal*, and I thought he was talking to Selene, but maybe… he was talking to… was that the Devil?"

Pavel opens his mouth to say something, then closes it. "It's complicated," he says, finally. "But what we know of the Beast is, it's a stickler for details. A sacrifice was in fact made, and the…" Pavel sighs, a certain sarcasm tugging at his features, "… the *gift* it bought must find a recipient. It didn't go to Selene. Incubi burn when they're killed. She died a human."

"The power that would be Selene's went to Misha, which is the last thing he wanted," Evie replies. "He couldn't have refused it?"

Pavel indicates her and smiles. It's one of his vast repertoire of stoic, sad expressions. "Unlikely, after he used some of it for you," Pavel says. "Once you take the tags off, there are no refunds, no exchanges."

"But he didn't make me like him," Evie mutters. "I'm just…" Her hand goes up to her chest, where her unsacrificed heart still beats.

"It doesn't make sense," George says.

"Doesn't it? They kill; why can't they heal?" Pavel replies.

"He has already found all sorts of unexpected uses for his powers," Evie says. "If anyone could find a way to do something good with the Devil's gifts, it's Misha."

Cardinal Adonis makes an amused huff. "Your friend seems to break every rule we know."

"If it's any consolation," Pavel mutters, "he's been doing that since at least 1912."

"It's only a consolation if he reappears, and we can convince him to help us," Cardinal Adonis retorts, then looks pointedly at Evie.

Pavel reaches out and squeezes her wrist. "We should discuss this in the morning. Enough has happened tonight for a hundred days."

"It has indeed," the Shadow Cardinal says, rubbing his hands over his face in exhaustion. "It has indeed."

OF ALL PEOPLE, it is George who pulls Evie aside the next morning.

Kevin arrives during breakfast, grinning through his exhaustion and holding Evie's handbag aloft like a triumphant spoil of war. Showered, fed, and reunited with her ID, Evie realizes there is nothing keeping her in San Francisco. She gets up from the table and thanks everyone and says she'll be leaving in the afternoon. Cardinal Adonis nods, and they all make awkward promises to contact each other if any trace is found of Misha.

She is curled up on the Chesterfield in the living room, composing an email to Claudia and surfing cheap-travel websites, when she becomes aware of a presence nearby. It's George, standing a good six feet away, hand tentatively resting on the back of the same wing armchair Evie had first sat in, as if waiting for permission to approach.

Unprompted, he says, "You should be careful about running back to your normal life too quickly."

"Excuse me?" Evie replies.

"You need time to mourn," George continues. He won't look her in the eye; he's gazing down at the faded, threadbare Oriental on the floor, at its muted hues of navy and burgundy and dusky orange. "To process the trauma that happened. Don't bury it. It comes back worse, if you do."

"Okay," Evie says.

"Okay," George echoes, and gives her a curt nod. Then he turns to go. He pauses when he gets to the doorway, hand trailing nervously along the frame. "I'm sure they'd let you stay here as long as you need. They're very kind like that," he says.

He finally looks at her, a hesitant expression in his usually fierce brown eyes. "After all, they let me stay."

He leaves Evie to her phone screen, to price lists and timetables of flights back to New York. She sighs. There's nothing she needs to go back for, not immediately. She has her meeting with Abigail in six days where she's going to be fired and/or sued. But before that, her life is her own.

She checks her bank balance, and has a moment of disorientation and surprise when she discovers her first paycheck from Misha has cleared. It's weird to see actual money in her account. Four whole figures, for the first time in forever. And the last.

Evie stays.

George and Pavel leave on Wednesday morning to start the long series of flights that will take them back to Rome. Pavel hugs her so hard he lifts her off the ground, and makes her promise to keep in touch via text, whether or not Misha reappears. George shakes her hand, stiffly, and says, "Courage."

The Shadow Cardinal leaves the following afternoon for Las Vegas, the first of several stops in North America. Evie teases him about it at breakfast, and receives an unexpected lecture on the distribution of evil in America, and how, contrary to gothic fiction's promises, it's the newest cities, with the most transient populations, where a person is most likely to fall victim to the supernatural.

"What about very old cities?" Evie asks.

Cardinal Adonis puts down his fork and sighs. "Old cities mean old evil. I would take a hundred trips to Las Vegas over a single call to Paris, or to Beijing. When I speak to God I pray for only one thing, Miss Cross: that I may never see another catacomb again." The corners of the Shadow Cardinal's lips twitch, and Evie bitterly regrets his leaving, because she would hear the catacomb stories, if she could.

Kevin and Daniela remain. It turns out Kevin is an FBI agent of sorts, the West Coast liaison between the Vatican's Shadow Secretariat and American law enforcement. It's his job to sift through reports of untimely deaths, strange occurrences, and random disappearances to see if any of them might be worth bringing to the Secretariat's attention. But, as part of it, he also has to listen to every nervous parishioner in the surrounding diocese with a suspicion too weird for the parish priest to handle.

Which is how Evie finds herself accompanying him to an exorcism on a wet Friday morning out in the Napa Valley, despite Kevin's confession that "ghosts aren't a thing". It's anticlimactic: no flying furniture or rotating heads, just a barn that the new owners swear has "bad vibes, man". An orange cat licks its polydactyl paws with bored disdain as Kevin lifts a crucifix and calls, "*Ecce crucem Domini, fugite partes adversae.*" It disappears, nose wrinkled, when he lights a thick bundle of sage.

After the rite they stomp back through a rain-soaked vineyard to the SUV, Kevin carrying a crate of Zinfandel under his arm. It seems like a giant waste of time, and she tells Kevin that, but he just shrugs as he puts the wine in the wayback. He doesn't mind wasting his time. "We saw the Napa Valley, got some free booze, and nothing tried to kill us. My kind of day," he says, as the SUV bounces down the winery's gravel drive. "Some of us aren't actually looking for more excitement in our lives, ya know."

Mostly that rootless week in San Francisco, Evie wanders the streets. She goes to City Lights and Fisherman's Wharf, Alcatraz and the Aquarium, watching normal people go about their business. Out of place, out of time, she haunts the city, feeling like there's a thick, invisible buffer between her and everyone else. Even the tourists have somewhere to be, but not her. She sleeps badly and flinches often, and finds in restaurants she can no longer sit with her back to the room.

News headlines roll over her, and she finds she's too numb to care. Selene Overstreet's death is reported as a murder-suicide, and the press blames her for her husband's death, too. The general response is a collective shrug and a vaguely disinterested *they never seemed right*. They weren't public enough, or pretty enough, for anyone to care.

Nicole's article disappears off Medium, but to Evie it's a hollow gesture. The damage is already done.

The big scandal of the week turns out to be Ron Freedman, the tanned, fit Aesthetica Moderne CEO, caught on a store security camera cheating on his long-term partner with an employee. Evie reads his lawyers' arctic statement: *The woman in question is no longer an Aesthetica Moderne employee; we wish her the best in her future endeavors.* The woman in question is, of course, Beatriz. Misha was right: she won't be getting her happy ending after all. It doesn't seem like any of them will.

She texts both Gemma and Claudia, checking in on them. Claudia got her job at Soho House and is busy and happy in it, and—in true Claudia fashion—is already nursing a massive crush on one of her co-workers. Gemma says things aren't as bad as expected with the agency, and she'll tell Evie more once Evie gets back to New York.

Evie takes a red-eye home on Saturday night, exchanging not sleeping on the safehouse's too-soft mattresses for not sleeping in a too-small airline seat. When she finally trudges up the steps to her and Claudia's top-floor walk-up, it's almost 11am on Sunday and Evie wants to drop dead from exhaustion.

She dumps her bags on the floor and collapses onto the sofa to catch her breath. It's weird to be back in the tiny apartment after her recent forays into mansions both old and modern. To have Claudia's bag spilling out over half the two-seater sofa, to be able to reach out from where she's sitting and touch the rail with all her clothes on it that's shoved against the wall. She knows that at night they'll hear sirens from ambulances heading to the hospital up the block, and in the morning she'll catch a cockroach making a break for it in the kitchen when she flicks on the light. No matter how much they scrub the tiles in the shower, the grout will still be stained black, and no matter how cold it gets in the winter, the radiators will make the bedrooms too stuffy for comfort.

Claudia emerges blearily from her bedroom in an oversize T-shirt and a pair of boxer shorts. She shambles towards Evie like a particularly affectionate zombie and flops half on top of her in a sloppy hug. "Missed you," Claudia mumbles.

"So the job's still good?" Evie asks.

Claudia nods, and Evie can feel the motion against her hair more than she can see it. "Almost double the pay, running all of special events catering."

"Got any open shifts?" Evie says. "I'm looking."

Claudia lazily pats Evie's shoulder. "I can put you on tonight."

"Okay, thanks, Claudia. I'm really proud of you, you know." The sentiment doesn't come out as impressively as it did in Evie's head, because halfway through, her voice cracks in a yawn. "I'm just gonna go…" She gestures towards her bedroom, yawning again.

Claudia gives her a thumbs-up and, as soon as Evie relinquishes the sofa, stretches out over the rest of it.

Evie faceplants on her bed and sleeps for the rest of the day, and then works barback for Claudia at a post-film-premiere party full of attractive people who seem vaguely offended she doesn't recognize them. They don't get the last revelers out until 2am and then the staff all roll down the street to a dark little bar with sticky floors and a late license where they can yell and swear and only smile if they feel like it. Evie goes too, because she has nothing left to be good for. Who cares if she goes to her meeting on Monday with a hangover? She's only going to get chewed out and then fired. But after an hour of watching Claudia moon over and then fail to talk to Annabelle, the front-of-house manager she's crushing on, Evie ducks out. She tells herself it's because the smell of stale beer and warm shots finally gets to her, but it's not. She takes a late, almost-empty train home to Bed-Stuy by herself and curls up in bed again, just as the sun begins to lighten the horizon.

Monday morning comes with regrets, but not too many, and Evie (aided by coffee) is mostly on time to her meeting at Meyer, Luchins & Black. She gets an odd feeling of déjà vu as she hustles across Eighth Avenue and through the rotating gold-and-glass doors of the building, but it's distant, spring's keen desperation fading to summer's ennui. They send her up to the twenty-ninth floor, and once there, Evie's escorted to one of the bigger conference rooms. Don and Dee Kieselstein, Abi, Bobbi Huang from Corporate, and a couple other senior partners whose names Evie doesn't remember are all seated on one side of the long table. Gemma sits alone on the other side, her hands clasped on the table like a penitent saint.

Evie slides into the seat next to her.

Abi clears her throat. "Well. I suppose we should begin."

But they don't. There's the rustle of paper and the tapping of fingers on touchscreens and Don Kieselstein is clearly in a mood, but nobody wants to go first.

"Is the law firm in trouble because of this?" Evie asks, to break the silence.

"We don't believe so at this time," Dee says, leaning back in her chair. "All Meserov has ever done for our firm is standard private investigative work, for which he is licenced. It's all above board." Her small, sharp eyes bore into Evie. "We were of course shocked to learn of his, shall we say, *side activities*, but consenting adults are consenting adults."

"Well, if it's any consolation, I don't think he's coming back for a while," Evie says.

"I am interested in the information you supplied to Nicole Hamilton," interrupts Bobbi Huang. "It was you, am I correct? The recording? The photographs?"

"Yes, it was absolutely me. Gemma had nothing to do with it. Whatever bad thing is going to happen, it's my fault, so blame me, not her," Evie babbles. "And, not that it matters, but I shared a research folder with Nicole when we were contemplating working on an article together. Then I decided I didn't want to publish it any more and I deleted the information. I didn't give her permission to publish any of that."

"Is there any more of your research that she didn't publish in the article?" Bobbi continues.

"What do you mean?" Evie asks.

Bobbi consults her laptop. "The article is… decent, from a

legal point of view. Everything is either directly sourced, with proof in the article, or is couched in enough *allegedlys* to make defamation difficult to prove. I mean," she continues, as she scrolls down the screen in front of her, "I'm laying aside the whole matter of her arguably stealing this information from you and releasing it without your consent, because I assume you have no desire to be involved in a lawsuit against Nicole?"

"I have fourteen hundred dollars in my bank account and no other assets," Evie says.

"I'll take that as a no," Bobbi replies. "But there is one part of the article that is vulnerable." She peers over her glasses at Evie. "Did you provide Nicole any confidential information regarding Octavia or August Mortimer?"

Evie sits back and thinks. Had she? No; she was concentrating on the whole Pickford drama. She had listed Octavia Mortimer as a client of Misha's, but that was all: a name. As soon as she'd discovered the Mortimers' connection to Nicole, she hadn't written another word about them.

"No," Evie says. "There was nothing in my notes about the Mortimers. I'm sure of it."

Bobbi smiles then, sharp and wolfish. "That's wonderful news, Evie. I'm very glad."

"What am I missing?" Evie says.

The young male lawyer next to Bobbi speaks up. "August Mortimer has engaged our firm to sue both Nicole Hamilton and the site that posted her article for libel. I'm afraid that's all we can say at this time."

"Will I need to testify?"

"More than likely," says the lawyer. "I presume you're staying in New York?"

"Uh," Evie mumbles, looking down at her hands. "I'm probably going back to Chicago, actually."

"Wait, what about the agency?" Dee says, her voice sharp.

"What about it?" Evie asks. She's at a loss. She'd assumed the Kieselsteins would want the agency shut down, swept under the carpet, never to be spoken of again.

"We've had over three hundred calls in the past week," Gemma says, a little smile playing on her lips. "Of which maybe thirty are valid clients, but still."

"We have also had an... unexpected surge of interest in our Family Law practice," Dee comments, drily.

"But you're forgetting, we don't have Meserov," interjects Don. "Without that—"

"*Don*," Dee says, a hard finality in her voice.

"—you really expect these two *little girls* to manage what *he* did?" Don finishes, his voice going high with disbelief, as he makes a choppy, dismissive gesture at Evie and Gemma.

Evie's about to tell Don where he can shove his sexism, when Gemma quietly, calmly looks him in the eye and says, "In going over our records, while Misha took the most delicate, high-profile cases, the majority of casework at Meserov & Co has been done by a small group of loyal freelancers under his direction. I have contacted those freelancers to let them know about Misha's... sabbatical, and they are all willing to continue working for us."

"There you go," Dee says, giving her cousin a triumphant look. "Apparently there is an overwhelming demand out there to break up relationships." She switches her attention to Evie and Gemma. "And you are in a place to meet that. Beyond that, our firm still needs an investigative consultancy for Family Law, and we'd prefer to stick to people we know. You'll need to become licenced, but I'm told the private investigators' exam isn't hard."

"Uh," Evie says. She glances at Gemma, who looks back, nervous and hopeful. Then, to Dee, she says, "We need to talk, to make sure we can do this. Can we get back to you?"

"Of course," Dee says, standing. "But hurry. I have a new client who thinks her ex-husband is physically abusing their kids. If she can prove it, she gets sole custody. We don't need a seducer for that. We need someone who can pass for a nanny." Her colleagues get up too, and begin to file out of the conference room. "Keep the room for as long as you like. And Evie, once you've come to a decision, you know where my office is?"

"Yeah," Evie says.

The glass door swings shut and then it's just her and Gemma in the big conference room with its view over Midtown rooftops, the green of Central Park just visible in the middle distance.

"I'm sorry to spring all that on you," Gemma says. "I was nervous about doing it by phone."

"It's okay, I get it," Evie says. She puts her head in her hands. "It's still a lot, though. And Dee is absolutely manipulating us."

"Mmhmm," Gemma says.

"*Only you can save the abused children*," Evie intones, in a passable approximation of Dee's heavy Brooklyn accent.

"Yep," Gemma says. "That was definitely low."

"Ugh," Evie says into her hands.

"I agree."

Evie peeks at Gemma from between her fingers. "We'd be idiots to walk away from this, wouldn't we?"

"What if... we didn't work for other people any more," Gemma says softly, teasingly.

Evie sits up. "You're not scared of messing this up? At all? Because we're going to mess this up. I, *specifically*, am going to mess this up."

"Evie, I'm *terrified*," Gemma breathes.

"Yeah, me too," Evie says. She glances at the door, at the lawyers' offices beyond. "So are we doing this?"

EPILOGUE

THE FIRST SNOWFALL of the year in New York City falls almost exactly six months after Evie and Gemma restart Heartbreak Incorporated. Beatriz joins them as their third, and while she's not Misha, she's soaked up a lot of his methods over five years of working with him. Gemma organizes, Evie researches, Beatriz strategizes.

It's Gemma who takes their first assignment, going undercover as the nanny in the NoHo home of an urbane, expatriate-British actor for three months. Her recordings are crucial in proving the man's emotional and physical abuse; he loses custody. The Kieselsteins are thrilled, and for the first time Evie thinks they might really make a go of this. Afterwards, Evie and Beatriz will occasionally catch Gemma with a faraway look in her eye, scrolling through old WhatsApp messages from the kids. Beatriz hugs her and says, "I know."

Gemma goes back to organizing them all, and doesn't take any more cases.

Not everything goes well; there are a few blunders, but nothing goes apocalyptically badly either, and Dee tells them that even Misha didn't deliver on a hundred percent of cases. Don mostly just scowls at them.

Evie texts Pavel about a conversation she overhears on the subway, a nursing assistant talking about patients at her Bronx care home dying with smiles on their faces. The Shadow Secretariat looks into it and catches an old, cautious incubus masquerading as the nursing home's janitor, quietly killing off people who were already close to death. When it's all finished, Pavel and George come down to Manhattan and take her out. They all get very drunk, the men strung up on fear and adrenalin, and Evie from the sheer relief of being with people who *understand*, who were there too, who know she's not crazy. Sometimes she thinks she should tell Gemma and Beatriz; sometimes she thinks they might already know. But she's spilled enough of Misha's secrets without his permission. Instead she goes out drinking with Pavel and George and listens to their war stories, giving to them the same gift of understanding that they give to her.

One sweaty August night at 3am, Claudia drunkenly slurs *you're hot and I think I love you* at her work crush, Annabelle. Then she blushes and runs out of the bar, but Annabelle chases her and kisses her right there under a streetlight outside their crappy after-hours place, and they only stop when a passing taxi driver honks at them. They move in together in October. They're blissfully happy, besottedly planning matching tattoos while touching each other like they're something precious. Evie lasts two whole weeks before the sheer *tenderness* of them sends her looking desperately for somewhere else to live. She finds a little studio in Chelsea just before Halloween.

And then, a week shy of Christmas when it gets dark at 4pm, New York has its first true snowfall of winter. The news says the city should expect fourteen inches of snow overnight. The Department of Education cancels the next day's schools; the power company sends out storm warnings. The year is winding down, and Evie, Gemma, and Beatriz decide, *fuck it*, they'll leave early, before all the transport shuts down.

But at a quarter to five, Evie feels the air shift in the office. She looks up to see an achingly familiar silhouette in the doorway, dusting off snow, bedraggled and desperate and still so, so beautiful. Misha's hair is a wild, wet tangle, down to his shoulders, and he's wrapped in a frayed blue greatcoat over little more than a T-shirt and tattered jeans. His half-laced boots leave puddles on the floor. He's hugging himself, trying to seem smaller, no longer sure where he fits in.

Evie tries to think of something to say, something warm and witty to put him at ease, but that's never been her strong point, and anyway her brain is busy just *glitching*, so she stands there and gapes while she tries to reboot higher functions.

It's Beatriz who saves them. She looks up from the laptop she was about to shut down and says, "Oh, hey, we have a target we can't figure out. Can you come look at this for a sec?"

Misha shakes himself slightly and walks over to her, a little dazed. He stands behind her, peering over her shoulder at the screen as she scrolls through files. "We've tried Mikki, Spike, *and* Christine, and nada." Finally, Beatriz turns in her chair and frowns up at him, gesturing at the screen. "But his wife's convinced."

Misha squints and leans closer, tapping at the laptop to page through files. "My guess is it's not about attraction," he mutters, in a voice rough with disuse. "It's about shame. He's doing something he wants to keep secret. Likely fetish-based." He looks around them, then, taking in the three desks that now occupy what used to be his private office, at the clean surfaces that became the norm after Gemma gleefully digitized them and set them up with a case-tracking database that, frankly, kicks ass. "He do any large cash withdrawals on regular intervals? Might mean he goes to a specific club night, or has a standing appointment with a specialist sex worker."

"We can check," says Evie.

Misha nods, his expression still a little distant, a little absent. "I hate cases like this, because most of the time, they don't need to get divorced," he says. "They just need to talk to each other openly about sex. But occasionally..." he runs a hand through his tangled hair, "... it's something really bad. Call-the-FBI bad." His eyes cut over to Evie as he adds, "Not San Francisco bad."

Beatriz nods, and then nobody knows what to say. Fat snowflakes are falling outside the window and they all stand there, half caught between coming and going, and shift awkwardly as they try to figure out what to do next.

"Are you, uh, coming in tomorrow?" Gemma asks him. "Only, if so, we should order another desk…"

"I can work on the sofa," Evie shrugs. "I've done it before."

"We need a bigger office," Beatriz says.

Misha looks around again, at the little art-filled sanctuary he's built, the business he's created to try to do some good with his existence, at the people he's befriended. Evie's suddenly afraid he's memorizing it, and them, one last time before he goes.

But then he nods, and says, "We do."

Evie wants to hug him, but she's not sure where they stand now. She chokes off a slightly too high *great*, and then tells the other girls that they can go, she'll close up because she lives closest, she only has to walk home.

Beatriz does hug Misha on her way out, and Misha pats her back and smiles, and returns Gemma's little wave, and then it's just him and Evie. There's a million things she needs to say to him, a logjam of words tumbling against each other to get out, and she hasn't the faintest idea where to begin. She starts with the least messy. "The priests aren't hunting you," she says.

"I know," Misha says. He's staring off to one side of her, hands in the pockets of his coat, like something is happening in another dimension that only he can see. "I'm not worried about them any more."

"Pavel asked me to let him know if you came back. Is that okay?" Evie says.

That gets Misha to focus on her. "Are you friends now?" he asks, emphasizing *friends* with the mild and dawning horror of a man realizing that his current paramour is in contact with his messiest ex. It was so normal, like the three of them were just college students, and not two immortal beings and someone who'd, technically, died and come back to life.

Evie shrugs, and can't stop the grin that comes over her face. "We text." She doesn't mention anything beyond that. She's proud of her restraint, especially as Misha's disdainful side-eye makes his opinion clear on the whole subject of Pavel and Evie being in communication.

"I don't want to see him. Or text him," Misha says. He says it gently, his gaze slipping again to somewhere off to one side of Evie. It's clearly a situation he's thought about, often even, frequently enough over the years that there is neither anger nor longing left in his words. Only the resigned desire to keep his hard-won distance from the traumas of his past. He lifts his chin. "There are some things that are very difficult to forgive."

"Okay," Evie says. She slips on her winter coat. "They want to talk to you, though. The Shadow Cardinal, I get the feeling he's setting his sights higher than the books, or the... creatures it makes."

"The word you're looking for is monsters," Misha says, distractedly. "So it is to be a recruitment talk. That should go swimmingly. I do hope they try to speak to me about Jesus. Sure, schedule us for lunch in two weeks. The Russian Tea Room." His voice drips with sarcasm.

Evie sighs. She has no idea how to navigate around this new, jagged, distant Misha, full of strange storms and ship-swallowing moods. "I'm sorry," she says. "I shouldn't have brought it up."

"Oh no, believe me, Evie, I will never forget the Devil laughing at me on that roof," Misha says, low and vicious. "And one day I will laugh back at it. But not as the priests' pet abomination."

"I'm glad you returned," Evie grits out, yanking on her ugly-but-warm woolly hat with its pompom a little more forcefully than necessary and grabbing her handbag. "I missed you. I apparently even miss you when you're being an insufferable jerk, but it's fine, I get it, I kinda deserve it after what I did."

"I wasn't going to come back," Misha snipes. He's turned away from her, facing the RUN DOG RUN painting.

Evie stops. "Why did you?"

"Someone taught me I didn't have to be alone," he replies. "Got me rather addicted to being happy." His gaze drops, to his wet boots, and the carpet beyond. "I'm tired of running, Evie. But I'm also very bad at standing still." He turns to look at her, hands still jammed in his pockets, and it feels like an apology. "How have you been doing, really?"

"I'm good," she smiles, and she finds it's the truth. "I wanted to investigate things, after all. And now I get to do that." She leans against the door frame to what used to be his office. "You built something good here. And we've kept it alive."

"I'm glad," he says. "I'm sorry. This was all supposed to be a lot more suave."

"Well," Evie says, "I did lead with your ex."

"You did." Misha tries to fight the smile that's tugging at his lips and then gives up, grinning wild and happy and free. "You're so terrible at this. I can't believe my poor agency is still in business."

"Well, you better stick around, make sure it stays in business," Evie says.

"Mm." Misha looks around the little office one more time, then shuts off the lights and pulls the double doors closed. "That is the plan."

Evie sets the alarm in the reception area and locks the front door and then there they are, outside in the hallway, a place of partings. "Uh, I live in Chelsea now. I was going to walk home?"

Misha offers her his arm. "And I shall escort you." He glances at her, the corners of his eyes wrinkling in amusement, as he stage-whispers, "For there are monsters out there."

Misha walks with her down Eighth Avenue through silent flurries that alight on the dirty city like blessings, like the promise of a new beginning. He kisses her on the corner of 43rd Street, with the blizzard having emptied Times Square of everything but its cacophony of advertising screens, here rendered indistinct and magical by the snow. And as they walk through the snow-filled streets south towards Evie's home, New York feels to her like a place of boundless opportunity, a city of a million stories, a thousand second chances, where each and every street corner has its own miracle if you look sharp enough.

Evie should know. The rarest, most magical one of all is holding her hand.

FIN

ACKNOWLEDGEMENTS

For me, books are born in bars and coffeeshops, and find their form across dinner tables and park benches and sleepless, thrilling nights of discovery. I am therefore incredibly grateful to the friends that smiled upon me kindly when I went off into long, no doubt boring tangents about aspects of *Heartbreak Incorporated* and its characters. Tea Berry-Blue and Jay Edidin were there in the beginning, as they so often are, but so was Shay Brog, and I wrote the whole back half of this sitting across from Darryl Braithwaite in our favourite Soho coffee shop. Abe Reisman, who has the nonfiction career that Evie coveted, coached me on all the bits about New York magazine journalism and commissioning that I got right, and had nothing to do with the bits I got wrong. My agent Nephele Tempest shepherded this book gracefully at the 11th hour into the hands of Kate Coe, and I couldn't have asked for a better, more welcoming editor. And of course my copy editor Tamsin Shelton, who gently bumps me back onto the path of clarity when I stagger too far from it. Last of all, to my daughter, for whom I do all of this.

ABOUT THE AUTHOR

ALEX DE CAMPI HAS A magpie heart, which is a polite way of saying she could never pick a lane and stay in it. She writes graphic novels (the Eisner-nominated noir *Bad Girls*; the critically acclaimed pulp horror *Dracula, Motherf**ker!*, so many more), prose novels (medieval thriller *The Scottish Boy*; paranormal thriller *Heartbreak Incorporated*), film and TV (*Blade Runner: Black Lotus*), and sometimes poetry. Recently she and director Duncan Jones collaborated on the sci-fi thriller *Madi: Once Upon A Time in the Future*, and she and writer-editor Khai Krumbhaar produced *True War Stories*, an anthology of soldiers' deployment tales.

She once snuck across the Russian border, and later she explored the mountains of North Vietnam in a jeep armed only with a cassette tape of Boney M's greatest hits. She had also sailed across the South China Sea a few times. She has lived in Hong Kong, London, Manila, briefly in Mexico, and one or two more places in between, but at present she resides in Manhattan with her daughter, a pair of elderly pit bulls, and a cat.

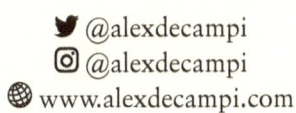

 @alexdecampi
 @alexdecampi
 www.alexdecampi.com

FIND US ONLINE!

www.rebellionpublishing.com

/solarisbooks   /solarisbks   /solarisbooks

SIGN UP TO OUR NEWSLETTER!

rebellionpublishing.com/newsletter

YOUR REVIEWS MATTER!

Enjoy this book? Got something to say?

Leave a review on Amazon, GoodReads or with your
favourite bookseller and let the world know!